Underwater Wonders

In the clear depths of the pool a silvery fish
darted. One of the reclining gray figures stirred;
raised a long, algae-slimed arm; extended a bony
hand from which the tatters of skin streamed like
carnival ribbons; made a languid grab for the fish.
The terrified fish flashed out of reach. The cadaver-
creature seemed to watch it go, slowly turning its
head on a neck whose naked vertebrae shone white.
Then the corpse looked up, lifting the remains of its
face toward the humans standing beside the pool.
For a long moment it sat staring up at them with its
eyeless sockets. Both arms slowly rose, floating skyward in supplication. The fingers flexed and swayed.

And then the other cadaver-creatures began to
wake, to move, to watch . . .

Ace books by Paula Volsky

THE LUCK OF RELIAN KRU
THE SORCERER'S LADY
THE SORCERER'S HEIR
THE SORCERER'S CURSE

THE SORCERER'S CURSE

PAULA VOLSKY

ACE BOOKS, NEW YORK

This book is an Ace original edition,
and has never been previously published.

THE SORCERER'S CURSE

An Ace Book/published by arrangement with
the author

PRINTING HISTORY
Ace edition/July 1989

ISBN: 0-441-44458-X

Ace Books are published by The Berkley Publishing Group,
200 Madison Avenue, New York, New York 10016.
The name "ACE" and the "A" logo
are trademarks belonging to Charter Communications, Inc.

PRINTED IN THE UNITED STATES OF AMERICA

10 9 8 7 6 5 4 3 2 1

Prologue

In the caves far below the surface of Dalyon, the luminous Vardrul clans gathered upon the shore of the Grizhni death-pool. Beside the water, the lightless corpse of Grizhni Nine lay awaiting final submersion. The slim little body was youthful, the still face almost childlike. She had embraced the Ancestors at an uncommonly early age, but such accelerated joining was characteristic of her clan.

Despite the fierce energy of some individual members, Clan Grizhni as a whole traditionally lacked vitality. It seemed as if Nature, outfaced and enraged by the Cognitively engineered human/Vardrul union upon which the line was founded, had vindictively elected to withhold an essential spark of commonplace vigor. Thus, Grizhni lives were marked by brilliance and brevity. Offspring were few, and the mortality rate among the infants cruelly high. Over the course of the Great Vens the line had sickened upon the concentrated excess of its own eccentricity, dwindling at last to its present sad remnant. Of the family once renowned for its genius and disharmony, but two members remained to celebrate this latest Ancestral joining. One was the elderly, learned Grizhni Inrl; the other was Grizhni T'rzh, Patriarch of his clan and brother/consort to the deceased.

The Grizhni stood upon the flat Speaker's Stone. Deprived of this artificial elevation, he would still have towered above his companions, for he was unusually tall by Vardrul or human standards. His long white frame was extremely spare, even emaciated; yet the breadth of shoulders and tautness of muscle suggested considerable strength. His features were strong, commanding, and very angular, the facial bones thinly covered. His dark eyes, aflame with power and intellect, were far larger and more brilliant than those of a man; but their midnight coloration, suggestive of humanity, was atypical among the Vardruls. His hands, too, recalled mankind. A throwback to his forebears, The Grizhni possessed human phalanges, increasing strength at the expense of flexibility. His carriage was erect and somewhat rigid,

1

his aspect simultaneously less graceful and more forceful than that of his compatriots. He lacked the true Vardrul fluidity of movement and gesture; for all that, his lithe coordination would have been accounted noteworthy among Men.

The Grizhni's hiir, or personal luminosity, was very low, as might be expected. Although the ultimate Ancestral union of a kinsman was in theory cause for rejoicing, harmony so perfect and selfless was in reality not always attainable. The Patriarch's grief at the loss of an adored sister/consort—who, like so many of the Grizhni kinsmen, had died childless—was dissonant but only natural. The Grizhni might choose a new consort from another clan at some time in the future, but she would not be a true sister/consort—with the death of Grizhni Nine, that avenue was closed forever.

The Grizhni began to speak, his voice unusually low and resonant in comparison to the fluting tones of his companions. His face was unrevealing, the expressive ridges of muscle that ringed his great eyes relaxed to the point of invisibility; yet his listeners read his sorrow clearly in the unremitting dullness of his flesh. The Patriarch's address was short and simple, in keeping with Vardrul custom. Its contents would have proved largely incomprehensible to a human audience, even had literal translation been provided. No human could have grasped the references to the Balance of Hdsjri, or to the Knowledge of Ancestors. Nor could any human have hoped to understand the full power and significance of the ceremony that was to follow. The Patriarch delivered his remarks with a certain alien impassivity characteristic of Clan Grizhni. His companions might almost have imagined him indifferent to the loss, save for the state of his hiir.

Eulogy concluding, The Grizhni stepped from the Speaker's Stone, and his place was taken by Grizhni Inrl, who spoke briefly but with deep emotion, for Inrl owned none of his Patriarch's remoteness. Others from outside the clan followed. The Grizhni listened expressionlessly, black eyes fixed upon the corpse of his sister/consort. Despite the exceptional beauty of his voice, he did not join in as the Vardrul harmonies rose to celebrate the final Ancestral joining of Grizhni Nine. The death-pool received the body, which sank to take its place among the kinsmen. The visitors exited, leaving the last two Grizhni kinsmen alone.

Inrl extended a glowing hand, which the Patriarch clasped. Classic Vardrul tentacles met atavistic boned digits. At the moment of contact, each of the Vardruls experienced the powerful surge of warmth, understanding and affection that only the touch of a kinsman carried. The Patriarch sensed the other's devotion, sorrow, and one thing more. He realized that Inrl was dangerously ill. His old teacher's own Ancestral joining could not be far distant. Presently the Grizhni Patriarch would find himself alone, the last of all his family. And the Grizhni's hiir, which had risen slightly as the clan-warmth flooded his veins, plunged to new depths.

Inrl's own light dimmed in sympathy, but he offered no verbal condolence, for words were wholly inadequate. The pressure of his hand, the expansion of his ocular ridges and the rapid, erratic flickering of his flesh conveyed far more than words. Aloud he inquired merely, "You will come away, beloved pupil/Patriarch?"

"I will stay for a time," replied The Grizhni. "I will know the Ancestors, and perhaps in knowing them encounter the lost Grizhni Nine."

Inrl rippled his fingers in assent, and his hiir sank. He was saddened but not surprised. Prolonged and intense communion with departed Ancestors often proved dangerously attractive to the newly bereaved. If carried to extremes, the attachment sometimes drew the living insensibly into a premature Ancestral joining. It was best to limit such contact, but the raw grief of Grizhni T'rzh was not to be denied.

"Convey my affection to the Ancestors," Inrl requested. "And to Grizhni Nine, should you meet her."

"Beloved kinsman/teacher, I will do so."

In dull-fleshed silence Grizhni Inrl departed the death-pool chamber.

The Grizhni scarcely heeded his kinsman's withdrawal. His eyes were fixed upon the glowing water beneath which his sister/consort reposed. Beside her lay the others of the clan, all those others he had lost throughout the Great Vens of a singularly dissonant life. One by one his kinsmen had left him, and now for the first time he knew an urge to join them. They would welcome him gladly, no doubt, despite his alien jointed fingers and his humanoid turbulence of nature. For all of that he was one of them, and perhaps he would find harmony in their embrace. His hiir rose at the thought, his white flesh glowed faintly, and he sensed himself fit to know the Ancestors.

It was not easy. In recent Great Vens the Ancestors had withdrawn themselves, and Knowledge was no longer easy of access. Extreme effort and a protracted period of rigorous concentration were required before The Grizhni felt himself moving backward in time along the internal path of inherited memory that led to Knowledge. Slowly at first, very slowly; and he focused his will, reaching in, deep in, far back, deeper and deeper, backward and deeper, until at last his hiir leaped, his flesh shone brilliant, the warmth rushed through him and the Ancestors were with him.

He met the nearest, most familiar ones first. His parents were there—he could feel the power of his father's mind, his mother's serenity. His grandparents were near, and a troupe of the siblings he had lost and mourned. Grizhni Nine did not seem to be among them—he did not feel her gently playful presence. This he missed, but if she would not or could not manifest herself, it was useless to search, for such meetings were not altogether subject to voluntary control. She would come to him another time. In the meantime, the oneness of those who had been so close to him in life surrounded and filled him, and he began to heal. Perhaps they could have made him whole had he remained among them, but this he could not do. Too soon the tide of Knowledge swept him from their embrace to bear him back in time, backward through the generations, further and much deeper, to an earlier age in the history of his people; an age of determined, forceful Ancestors filled with energy and resolve. Their motives, intentions and desires were exotic. Yet they were kinsmen all, blood of his blood, and their affection called out to him across the Great Vens.

Further and deeper. The Grizhni voices were changing now, the Ancestors increasingly foreign. It was not difficult to fathom the cause. He was approaching that fateful union—so many generations removed—wherein human and Vardrul blood had mingled to found Clan Grizhni. As he approached that point of convergence, humanity clamored harshly in the hearts of the Ancestors. The voices were dissonant, the impulses wild, violent, and incomprehensible to a true Vardrul.

Or were they?

To The Grizhni, those fierce human desires possessed a familiarity at once seductive and disturbing. Their intensity awakened his own profoundly disharmonious responses, and he desired the intimacy of those Ancestors almost as much as he feared it. Because of that fear, he had always held back in his communions, turning aside at the last moment to evade Knowledge of his most human forebears. So much control over his own mind and impulses he had always been able to maintain—until now. This time, the current was too strong. Something had changed; a force unknown and inimical was at work, bearing him back against his will, pulling him down, deeper than he had ever before ventured, down into a black vortex of human emotion.

They were with him now, those distant dissonant Grizhni kinsmen. They filled him, flooding him with their passion and

4

violence. Their obscure rage possessed him, and in the midst of his revulsion he was conscious of familiarity and recognition.

Knowledge did not end there. Backward, further and deeper. The Grizhni no longer struggled, for the force that gripped him was irresistible. Further and deeper, beyond understanding to a time when his kinsmen were strangers. And there the Grizhni Patriarch met and first knew the Fal Grizhni Terrs, son of humans, self-taught savant whose human Cognition had lent him Vardrul form, resulting in creation of the Vardrul Clan Grizhni. Not even Cognition, however, could transform Terrs's mind and heart. The voice of the Fal Grizhni Terrs remained invincibly human. It was a strong, insistent voice, whose owner had never known true peace. There was bitterness there, hostility, vindictiveness; all of it directed against humanity. The Grizhni Patriarch felt his Ancestor's anger and shared in it. Hot, vicious impulses throbbed in his blood. In the midst of his rage, his inner, most essential self experienced astonishment. Extraordinary, almost incredible, that the Ancestors—hitherto unfailing source of comfort and oneness—should now incite their kinsman to dissonance. In this tacit sanction of all that he had always striven to suppress within himself was ugliness and something of perverse pleasure.

The Fal Grizhni Terrs's hostility was immediate, concentrated and purposeful. But not until he had passed beyond Terrs did the Grizhni Patriarch discover the nature of that purpose.

Backward, further and deeper, further than he would have believed possible, much deeper than he wanted to go. And still that resistless force dragged him down through the blood-warm dark, down through the levels of ancient consciousness where hurricane blasts of forgotten emotion buffeted his mind, down at last through something that seemed a wall of invisible flame. The term "wall" best expressed the Patriarch's sense of passage through or across a barrier, the transition from one domain to another. And then he was through, beyond the fire, traversing the unimaginable realm of pure, undiluted humanity wherein he beheld a succession of madly distorted self-images, Ancestors all. Alarm, confusion and excitement warred within The Grizhni. The Ancestors' voices were discordant, and all the innate disharmony within him answered. The Vardrul side of his nature still resisted, but this resistance ceased as he felt himself drawn back to the source of hatred and discordancy.

Further and deeper, down to the very wellspring of cruelty and strength, beyond the Fal Grizhni Terrs to the First Grizhni, legendary savant-patriarch of Surface.

And there in that place, in the presence of that vast and pitiless will, the universe darkened. There died peace and oneness, serenity and harmony. The mind of the First Grizhni touched the mind of his Vardrul descendant, and wholly human sensations possessed the Grizhni Patriarch. Deeply and truly he knew his most terrible Ancestor. No words were exchanged, and none were needed.

Conquest. Vengeance. Blood.

The Grizhni Patriarch burned with his Ancestor's desires.

Reclamation of the Surface territories stolen from the Vardrul clans. Justice for the murdered Ancestors.

Destruction. Death. War. The time has come.

Vengeance. Darkness. Darkness.

Now.

So cataclysmic was the violence of his sensations that The Grizhni, appalled, found the strength to break free of Ancestral Knowledge. The divorce was abrupt as an amputation. For a time his shocked mind ceased to function. The turn of Purple Coloration had arrived before he regained awareness of his surroundings. He stood alone beside the water in the death-pool chamber of his clan. His ocular ridges were writhing spasmodically, and his hiir fluctuated wildly. He noted the alternating brilliance and dullness of his own flesh with wonder. At last, drained and thoroughly shaken, he made his way from the room.

In the corridor outside waited the F'tryll'jnr Lesser Matriarch, together with Dfjnr'l Gallr, and the R'jnrllsch Lesser Patriarch. Mindful of custom, they had not presumed to intrude upon The Grizhni's solitary grief. That they had news of happy significance to relate, however, was evident by the state of their collective hiir.

In response to The Grizhni's perfunctory inquiry, The F'tryll'jnr announced discovery of a puzzling phenomenon. Directly above the chambers of the K'fr'llsch Excavation, in the region marking the center of the great island of Dalyon, the atmosphere had turned black. Something or someone had vanquished the sun, and the darkness never lifted, not even during the Colorations ordinarily given over to eye-searing Surface daylight. The shadow itself was reputedly delightful—warm, fragrant and invigorating. Those kinsmen who had ventured Surface to explore returned bright-fleshed and exhilarated. The origin and nature of this atmospheric transformation were unknown, but one happy fact was plain—the darkness was expanding. Steadily it was spreading over the land.

The Grizhni listened with close attention, and at the conclusion of the narrative remarked simply, "We must see for ourselves." The fingers of his companions undulated, and something uncontrollable impelled him to add, "Perhaps our time has come at last."

They gazed at him with their huge pale eyes, and the hiir of the F'tryll'jnr Matriarch leapt. No one missed his meaning, for the prophecies of the Ancestors lived on in the mind of all.

Vardrul emergence into a world made ready to receive them. Reclamation of the long-lost Surface. So much had been prophesied, and who would question the wisdom of the Ancestors?

One thing more had been promised—a great leader. And who should that leader be if not Grizhni T'rzh, remote and unfathomable like all his clan, yet possessed of force and brilliance far beyond that of other Vardruls? His innate dissonance armed him for war, and his human intensity equipped him to battle humans. Perhaps he had been born for it.

Their thoughts and emotions were easy to read. The Grizhni regarded his glowing companions, and felt his own hiir rise. Excitement brightened his flesh, but could not banish an underlying sense of unutterable discord.

The time has come. Vengeance. Darkness.

The First Grizhni's hatred lived on.

Darkness indeed.

Chapter One

❧❧❧

"STOP, THIEF! YOU DETESTABLE LITTLE GUTTERSNIPE, GIVE THAT BACK!"

The speaker, a bespectacled ancient clothed in dilapidated livery of black and rust, screamed and gesticulated. The accused, a sugar-faced urchin, cast one glance back over his shoulder and increased his flying pace. Clutched tightly to the urchin's chest was a leather satchel recently torn from the old man's grasp.

"I ORDER YOU TO STOP! IN THE NAME OF THE LAW, YOU RUNNY-NOSED VERMIN! DO YOU HEAR ME?"

The urchin did not comply.

"STOP HIM! FRIENDS, COMRADES, CITIZENS OF LANTHI UME! STOP THE THIEF!"

Many citizens on the docks paused to stare, but none lifted a finger to help. Inactivity might have been the result of simple incomprehension. The white-haired hysteric was yelling in Szarish, and few of his Lanthian listeners understood the language. The old man turned to his companion—a very youthful gentleman, no more than eighteen years of age, personable despite his shabby attire and undernourished pallor. "MASTER DEVRAS—HE'S GOT THE DOCUMENTS! CATCH HIM, KILL HIM, GET 'EM BACK AT ANY COST!"

"I'll try, Grono." Despite his assurances, Master Devras seemed unsuited to homicidal endeavor. Average in height, natural slimness emphasized by mild malnutrition, with shaggy brown locks, dreaming gray eyes and pale, finely cut features, Devras hardly appeared a man of action. Cerebral air notwithstanding, his hesitation was minimal, and the next instant he was sprinting across the docks in pursuit of the stolen satchel.

The urchin, evidently well versed in the arts of evasion, dodged and wove nimbly among the crates and bales that cluttered the wharf. From time to time he managed to overturn a box or basket in the path of his pursuer. Devras successfully circumvented all obstacles until a great wicker hamper of Strellian soapfruit crashed to the dock at his feet. The hamper split, the

8

soapfruit spilled out, and the big, overripe yellow globes went rolling in all directions. As they struck the planking they burst, and the golden lather for which they had been named came foaming exuberantly forth. The stuff was sticky and damnably slippery. A bubbling swamp swiftly overspread the dock. Devras set his foot in the fragrant muck and felt himself begin to slide. A soapfruit exploded beneath his heel, and the slide became an uncontrollable skid. Amidst the cheers of the populace, he headed straight for the edge of the wharf. A grunting collision with one of the pilings was all that preserved the young man from a plunge in cold sea water.

Devras clung briefly to the piling, then turned to spy his quarry disappearing into the narrow passage that ran between the two old warehouses looming at the far end of the dock. He followed and found himself in a maze of twisting back alleyways. The larcenous urchin was nowhere to be seen. Devras investigated several passages in quick succession, but was soon forced to admit defeat. Thief and satchel were gone. With heavy heart and dragging footsteps he returned to his starting point, where he found his valet guarding the meager remainder of their belongings. The two small, battered trunks and the big crate of books still lay where they had been unloaded from the Szarish vessel *Archduke Jalonzal*.

Grono was sitting on the books. Now he rose to inquire, "No luck, Master Devras?"

Devras shook his head mutely.

Grono whitened. His hand clenched upon the knob of his walking stick. His voice shook as he observed, "We are ruined. Ruined. Utterly ruined."

"Grono, it's not as bad as all that."

"It could hardly be worse! I tell you, we are ruined! Destroyed! Finished! Undone! Master Devras, that satchel contained all our money!"

"Not quite all." The young man dug in the pocket of his threadbare jacket to extract five copper Szarish dumies and a Lanthian dakkle. "There. I was keeping them for an emergency. We're poor, but we're not destitute."

Grono regarded the small coins without optimism. "Master Devras, you do not understand the world. That is *chicken feed!* It will keep us—poorly—for at most a couple of days. And after that, what is left to us? We will starve, we will freeze! I will beg from door to door for your Lordship, and these Lanthian decadents will set their dogs on me—oh, I see the face of the future, and it is foul!"

"No such thing." Devras spoke equably. "We're not altogether helpless, you know. We'll just have to earn our bread, that's all."

"Earn it! *Earn* it? How, sir? Are we menials, are we tradesmen?"

"No, and for one good reason—we are both wholly unqualified. What employment are we fit for, I wonder?" Devras thought about it and soon hit upon an answer. "Translation. Both of us are perfectly fluent in Lanthian as well as Szarish. There must be a use for that. Moreover, I know High Strellian, Travornish, Old Umish, Neraunci and even Vipponese. There's any number of classics that I might translate from the original. Only consider the collected works of the Venerable Disitch—"

"Pox on the Venerable Disitch, sir! This trifling, petty clerkdom you describe is far beneath the dignity of the new lord of Har Fennahar! My Lord Har Fennahar has a position to maintain in the eyes of the world!"

"'Lord' Har Fennahar," Devras mused. "It has a foreign sound. I can hardly think of myself as a lord, especially a lord of Lanthi Ume—a place I've never seen before. I wonder if I'll ever get used to it?"

"Your Lordship *shall* grow used to it!" the old valet asserted majestically. "It is your Lordship's duty and privilege. You are the very last of the Har Fennahars, sir. By virtue of that fact, you inherit the title. You are master of Fennahar House—one of the greatest of mansions, I am told—and you are rightful heir to all the vast Fennahar fortune. Even were you not the last of all your line, there is reason to suspect that the title is rightfully yours, for a close study of Prenn's *Peerage* indicates that your noble progenitor Rillif Har Fennahar was the true Lord Har Fennahar at the time of his emigration to Szar."

"I don't know whether he was a lord or not, but he certainly wrote splendid accounts of his explorations. I've always been quite fond of Great Great—how many greats are there again?— Grandfather Rillif."

"He was the Lord Fennahar," Grono insisted. "I do not know why he chose to abandon his home and his rank, but he was indeed the rightful lord. And you, his direct descendant, are likewise lord. And when we have proven the truth of this, the name of Har Fennahar will shine brightly again as in days of yore! When we have proven—" The valet broke off abruptly as unpleasant reality intruded upon his consciousness. "But how are we to prove it, Master Devras? The documents, the letters, genealogical charts, the references, and the certificate signed by the Archduke Zargal himself—all of them in the stolen satchel!

10

All of them gone forever! Without them, how shall we prove my young master's identity? We never shall! We are lost, we are ruined!"

"Calm down, Grono," Devras advised. "We'll manage something, somehow. In the meantime, take heart. Men have overcome misfortunes far greater than ours. Think of the moral triumph of the blinded Venerable Disitch, who discovered all the world within the confines of his dungeon. Think of the philosopher Omee Nofid, who overcame infirmity, poverty and prejudice to produce his *Refutations*. Think of Heselicus, who wrote, 'Adversity owns three faces. It is the assassin of the weak, the bedfellow of the indifferent, and the preceptor of the courageous.'"

"Permit me to say, sir, that this Heselicus person did not own the fine sensibilities of a gentleman."

"Perhaps not, but he was rather clever. Furthermore, he amuses me."

"Amuses, sir? Amuses? Disaster strikes, and your Lordship professes amusement? An attitude of negligent superiority, of almost insolent indifference in the face of catastrophe, is not unsuited to the dignity of a great aristocrat, but your Lordship's response borders on frivolity. It is downright unnatural, sir."

"Not really. If you'll recall Chapter Four of Zebbefore's *Seeds of Civilization*, it's argued that the basic nature of Mankind comprises six—"

"There is your problem, Master Devras!" Grono cut the other off mercilessly. "There is your great weakness! Always with you it must be the old books, the ancient philosophers, obscure histories, and similar inessentials! Where is the value in that? Always you must dwell in the land of dreams and imagination!"

"It's not an unpleasant land, Grono."

"Visions, fancies, illusions! You lose sight of the real world, sir!"

"Not altogether a bad thing, at times."

"Bah! You are far too young for such weary fancies. It is to be hoped that advancing age will increase your store of worldly wisdom. In the meantime, fortunately for all concerned, Grono is here to safeguard your Lordship's interests. I shall protect them with my life, sir! I now repent my momentary despondency, for it is clear that you stand desperately in need of my knowledge and experience. They are at your Lordship's service! Already I have marshalled my resources to produce a plan of immediate action."

"You have my full attention."

"We go immediately to the moneylenders," Grono decreed. "Your Lordship will accept a sizable loan. With this loan you will set yourself up in a style suitable to the dignity and consequence of the new Lord Har Fennahar. You will purchase garments, lodgings, conveyances and equipages of appropriate magnificence. Thus arrayed, you will present yourself to his Grace the Duke Bofus Dil Shonnet, and you will claim your rightful place in society. Once invested with the title and fortune of Lord Har Fennahar, you will repay the original loan, and the sun will shine upon your head forever more. And there you have it, sir. Simplicity itself, and we are freed of the necessity of mean employments!"

"That's a very interesting scheme, but I foresee an obstacle. We are both hungry, ragged, penniless strangers. Foreigners, with no connections and no one to vouch for us. Who will trust us? Who will lend us so much as a dakkle?"

"To the discerning eye, the natural brilliance of true merit inevitably reveals itself—"

"If you were a moneylender, would *you* trust two pauperized Szarish strangers?"

Grono was silent.

"I've an alternative plan," Devras suggested. "Time wears on, and it will soon be dark. Let's find lodgings for the night. We'll dine as best we may. In the morning I'll seek employment as a scribe, amanuensis or translator. While I do so, you'll roam the city, nailing up the broadsides that I pen, offering reward for the return of my stolen papers—no questions asked. They're of no use to anyone other than myself, so it's not impossible that they'll turn up. In the meantime, I write home to Szar requesting duplicate documents. We wait a little for reply—say, a couple of months or so—and at the end of that time, whatever the results of our efforts, we go to the Lanthian Duke to plead our case. What do you say to that?"

"Your scheme is not unreasonable, but I am not altogether content with it," the valet fretted. "I would prefer a more active manifestation of warlike virtue."

"'The virtues of war represent the triumph of fear over self-preservation.'"

"Heselicus again?"

"Who else?"

"A base-minded churl if ever there was one. Master Devras, I am greatly troubled. It is beneath the dignity of the Lord Har Fennahar to drudge for his living like a peasant, and I cannot in all conscience allow it. I will find a way to keep us fed, but your Lordship must not lift a hand to sordid labor."

"Labor isn't sordid, Grono. If you've ever read Fu Kruneleef

12

—but no, this isn't the time to argue the point. See how long the shadows are—the daylight will soon be gone. We'd better seek lodgings for the night."

"Very well." Stifling his objections with obvious effort, the valet lifted his eyes to the glittering towers of Lanthi Ume. Above the towers shone a red point of light, far too large and bright for an ordinary star, and clearly visible during the daylight hours. "We do not know this place. Where shall we find decent shelter that we can afford? And how shall we transport our belongings? We cannot carry two trunks and a crate of old books. We must abandon something, preferably the books."

"The books come with us!" Devras replied with unwonted vehemence. "Even if we must hire a porter. As for our lodgings, I've an idea. Veeb's *Strolling Through Lanthi Ume* contains an account of an ancient neighborhood—quaint, atmospheric, colorful, original, and above all, inexpensive. We'll try our luck there."

"Ah, that sounds promising, sir! And what is the name of this sweet refuge?"

"It is called the Destula."

In a quiet glade directly above the K'fr'llsch Excavation a small group of Vardruls had assembled. The last two members of Clan Grizhni were there. With them stood the F'tryll'jnr Lesser Matriarch, the R'jnrllsch Lesser Patriarch, Dfjnr'l Gallr, and at least one representative of each clan. The kinsmen's voices were muted and their ocular ridges rigid with wonder, for never before in all the inherited recollection of the race had Surface extended so cordial a welcome. The atmosphere was magnificent. Intensely black, thick, warmly moist and richly fragrant, its caress rivaled the touch of a kinsman's hand. There was something indescribably heartening in that pitchy air, something that fostered courage, hope and harmony. The hiir of the kinsmen rose in response. Their bodies shone like beacons in the night, while the blood sang in their veins. Even the Grizhni kinsmen were affected. Grizhni Inrl, aged and ailing though he was, brightened noticeably, and for a moment the vigor of youth seemed to return to him. The Grizhni Patriarch took a deep breath and his flesh ignited, glowing with a concentrated brilliance ordinarily reserved for Knowledge of Ancestors alone.

His companions could not guess it, but something like Knowledge quickened the pulses of the Patriarch. The will of his forebears pressed upon his mind and he shared their fierce compulsions. The black air served as a tonic. A sense of inevitability possessed him, and it was not disharmonious. His course was clear.

If The Grizhni's hiir expressed his inner state, his words did not. Aloud he remarked only, "It is true. Transformed Surface welcomes us."

"As the Ancestors promised." The F'tryll'jnr Lesser Matriarch shone only a little less brilliant than The Grizhni himself. Likewise shone the various clanmembers, all of them drunk on the superb black air.

They had noted his elevated hiir, his air of certainty, and they gravitated to him instinctively.

"Do the Ancestors speak, Patriarch?" inquired Dfjnr'l Gallr.

"All of Surface speaks," returned The Grizhni.

"Has the time come indeed, and do you lead us? Will you be Greater Patriarch of all the clans?"

Fierce exaltation seized The Grizhni, and his hiir leapt impossibly higher. All doubts temporarily banished, he rippled his fingers in assent, despite the handicap of his alien bones.

Chapter Two

❧❧❧❧❧

"Great news, your Lordship! Great news!" Grono entered in high excitement, banging the door shut behind him. A platoon of cockroaches scattered at the sound. "Destiny smiles upon us!"

Devras Har Fennahar lifted his eyes from his work. He sat in a dank, hideous chamber nearly devoid of furnishings. Situated below canal level, the room was windowless, and therefore a smoky oil lamp provided the sole illumination at midday. Feeble yellow light played on oozing, mineral-crusted walls; a low ceiling from which the cold moisture dripped continually; and a damp stone floor alive with roaches. The fireplace was empty and the air was frigid. Devras sat on the wretched pallet that served as both bed and desk. Spread out around him were books, folios, writing implements, and sheets of paper. The pages were covered with close, neat handwriting, suggesting good progress on the latest Vipponese translation. The translation throve and flourished, but the same could not be said of its author. Even in the dim, uncertain light, the young man's unhealthy pallor was obvious. He had swathed himself in a rag of a blanket to ward off the chill, but the folds of moth-eaten wool could not disguise the painful emaciation of his form. Privation notwithstanding, Devras had lost none of his indolent, almost dreamy good humor. Smiling a little at the valet's indestructible grandiosity, he laid his quill aside and inquired encouragingly, "What's up?"

"Opportunity arises, sir! Our luck has changed at last!" In response to his master's look of mute inquiry, Grono explained, "I have learned that his Grace the Duke Bofus holds his famous annual soiree tomorrow, a fete in honor of all Lanthian nobility. Beyond doubt, that includes the Lord Har Fennahar. Your Lordship will shine among the great! Come, sir, what have you to say?"

"A party?" Devras displayed little interest. "I see no point."

"No point? No point?" Grono drew himself up, the light of battle flaming in his eyes. His wattles quivered in disapproval, the sure sign of an imminent tirade.

Noting the ominous symptoms, Devras silently armored himself in pleasant imperturbability.

"May I ask you, sir, what you are about?" the valet demanded. "Can it be that you fail to recognize the opportunity afforded by this gathering of the wealthy and the powerful? Do you not see that this soiree could prove the means by which your Lordship may prefer yourself to the notice of the great, deriving untold benefit thereby? To a man of good judgment, sir, such opportunities are as commands from the gods. *This* command, your Lordship, issues not from the lips of any god, but rather those of a goddess—the Goddess Fortune."

"Goddess Fortune. That's very neat, Grono. I like that. 'Goddess Fortune' is good."

"It well becomes your Lordship to scoff and sneer at my advice! My weight of years deserves scant courtesy, my wisdom merits no respect—"

"You know perfectly well I respect you—"

"Then prove it by following my counsel! You cannot rot forever in this dungeon, squandering youth and health upon these miserable clerkly scribblings. How long have we spent in this dreadful place?"

"About seven weeks, I believe."

"Seven weeks! Oh, that the last surviving member of the noble House of Har Fennahar should come to this! Is this the way your Lordship strives to repair the fortunes of your House?"

"Until the restoration of my lost documents of identity, there's little I can do—other than labor to stave off starvation," Devras observed. "And if I don't get back to that translation I'm working on—"

"Translations—Bah! Miserable, beggarly, scholarly drudgery. Your Lordship demonstrates a lamentable lack of ambition."

"In your opinion it's better to attend a party, curry cringing favor with all who might prove useful, than to spend that same period of time studying the classics in an effort to expand my mind? Eh, Grono?"

"Oh, you've a wrong-headed way of putting things, sir." Grono grimaced, impatient as always with his young lord's seemingly incurable perversity. "Education is all very well, I grant you. An educated mind is indeed a seemly ornament to a noble name. It is not so important as mastery of horsemanship, but it has its uses, I suppose. However—the world offers benefits of far greater worth than dry, dead kernels of history, philosophy and literature."

"Name them."

16

"The lord upholding the dignity of his House is surely the happiest of mortals, for he fulfills his highest and truest purpose in life," Grono admonished, magisterial tone belied by his battered livery and shrunken, hungry figure. "Such a lord must live much in the light of the world. He is a great courtier, a great soldier and statesman, admired, respected and feared. Above all, he lives in the splendor that befits his rank, and he carries himself always as an aristocrat, a man set apart from the common herd. A man's character and worth are commonly valued according to the prosperity of his external appearance—alas for the degenerate times in which we live!"

"I suspect that's been equally true at all times, Grono. Heselicus writes—"

"But we digress," the valet cut his master off ruthlessly, resuming with renewed enthusiasm. "The members of your noble House were once renowned for their careless extravagance and magnificence. I have it on no less authority than Prenn's *Peerage* itself that your ancestor Giniver Har Fennahar once held a feast that lasted for seven days and seven nights. Fifty-three thousand woodland game birds were consumed, the guests ate off plates of solid silver studded with sapphires, five hundred slaves and prisoners of war were slain by way of entertainment, and black pearls were flung to the Lanthian populace. Now *there* was a lord!"

"Picturesque," Devras conceded. "But you must understand that the world has changed—the excesses of our ancestors would be judged ludicrous in our present age of perfect reason. No longer do we indulge in gross displays of extravagant gluttony, and our modern executions are performed with discretion. And as for me, I don't think I could ever be comfortable with aristocratic magnificence, since I wasn't brought up with it. We've always lived quietly and simply—"

"And in dire poverty." Grono concluded the other's thought with a sigh. "I know, Master Devras. It is a great misfortune. Your poor father, noble gentleman though he was, possessed no knowledge of the world. His blind faith in the myth of the Aaldri Panacea led to his financial ruin and early death."

"Had the Panacea been discovered, all humanity would have benefited." For the first time since the conversation began, Devras's air of detached amusement faded. His recollections of his mother and father were few. He had been a small child when both parents died, but the loss of all family and kinsmen had left him with a sense of isolation, an aching void that even the care of the devoted Grono could not entirely fill.

"Very true, but the universal Panacea never existed—a fact

17

that your poor father could not bring himself to accept, and therein lay his undoing. High-minded and idealistic he was, but impractical, unrealistic, naive despite all his wit—characteristics that your Lordship has clearly inherited."

"Am I very like him, then?"

"Very like, both in appearance and in character. Rest assured you will not share his unhappy fate, however, for Grono is here to prevent such calamity. Now harken well, Master Devras. As last surviving descendant of all his illustrious line, it is the sacred duty of the present Lord Har Fennahar to restore his family to the position and glories formerly enjoyed, that the name of Har Fennahar may shine brightly again as in bygone days! And therefore," Grono concluded in triumph, "it is your Lordship's solemn obligation to make every effort, to take advantage of every opportunity—and hence, to attend the Duke's soiree tomorrow night!"

Devras, who had endured the foregoing without comment and without enthusiasm, thought a moment, then brightened as a loophole presented itself. "Can't do it," he replied.

"You *must* do it, else shirk your familial responsibility. When shall another such opportunity arise? Consider, sir—even the greatest of the Select will be present. The Lord Vaxalt Gless Vallage, Preeminent of the Select and intimate of the Duke, is expected to attend. If you could but win the favor of the Lord Gless Vallage—"

"Can't do it," Devras repeated.

"The quality of the Ducal kitchens is legendary. Go to the soiree, and for the first time in many weeks your Lordship will enjoy a meal of superlative substantiality," Grono suggested craftily.

"Tempting. But impossible."

"I will not hear your Lordship! No obstacle is insurmountable!"

"Think again. I've no invitation," Devras reminded his valet. "It's all very well to call me 'Lord' Har Fennahar, but the fact remains, one doesn't enter the Ducal Palace without an invitation."

"If you had such an invitation, would you go?"

"I suppose so, yes. However—"

"Then your Lordship may rejoice. Your troubles are at an end. Behold!" From the depths of his pocket Grono drew forth a square of fine white pasteboard, embossed with the elaborate arms of the Lanthian Duke. It was an invitation requesting the

18

presence of his Lordship Devras Har Fennahar at the Ducal Palace the following evening.

"Grono, where did you get this?"

The valet was silent.

"Oh, this is promising! It can only mean one thing. The Duke's read my letters, and he recognizes the justice of my claim—" Devras broke off as he took a closer look at the invitation. "What's this clinging to the surface? Something's flaking off—"

"Don't touch that, Master Devras! Just leave it alone!"

"What—?" Devras inspected the card closely, running his finger across the slick surface. "White paint to hide the original name, with my name inked in on top. This thing is a fake!"

"No, sir! It is a perfectly genuine invitation, no more than three or four years old, or so I am assured by the vendor of curiosities from whom I acquired it. Only the date and name have been altered to promote the interests of the innocent."

"Your work?"

The valet inclined his head modestly.

"Grono, what are you thinking of? This is illegal. You want to see me fined, imprisoned, deported? Is that it?"

"Not so, sir! I desire to see your Lordship happy, secure, honored, revered, and gloriously wealthy."

"And you imagine that forging an invitation to a party is the way to achieve that?"

"Perhaps. It is at least a chance, and you must venture it. Duty, sir. Duty. Also, remember your promise. If given an invitation, you would go. Your Lordship's solemn word."

The jaws of the trap had snapped shut, yet Devras still struggled feebly. "There's another problem," he offered lamely. "I've pawned my clothes, everything but for the rags on my back. The money went for the food we've been eating for the past three days. All functions at the Duke's palace require formal dress, and I can hardly appear as I am." Grono opened his mouth to reply and Devras held up one hand. "Moreover, we cannot hope to redeem my clothing. We've no money and nothing left to pawn." He reflected. "Except the bracelet. I suppose I could sell that. I may as well; it'll have to go one day in any case." Upon his left wrist he wore a massive, very old silver bracelet inscribed with symbols belonging to the Select of Lanthi Ume. It had been in the Szarish branch of the Har Fennahar family for generations.

"That bracelet is a family treasure! It was carried from Lanthi Ume by your noble ancestor Rillif Har Fennahar, and you have no right to sell it!" exclaimed Grono. "How much might your Lordship get for all these old books?"

"Not the books!" returned Devras, shaken. "The bracelet goes before they do!"

"Never while I live! Never, sir! Happily, your Lordship need not contemplate such drastic measures." Grono crossed to the trunks sitting on the floor in the corner, opened one and withdrew a cloth bundle, which he presented to his master with a flourish. Devras opened the bundle to discover his one good suit of clothes, clean and intact.

"Grono! How did you get these back? Where did the money come from?"

"Simplicity itself, your Lordship. I merely sold a measure of my blood to the Marvelous Weevulp, to nourish his famous Vampire Fishes."

"Grono, you *sold your own blood*! I'd never have allowed it if I'd known! Oh, this is monstrous!"

"It was nothing, sir. A trifling sacrifice that I account as nothing, in view of your Lordship's resulting gain."

"But my dear friend, to sell your very blood—! I'll never forgive myself!"

"Ah, do not distress yourself, sir. I tell you I am happy. The pain and weakness I have suffered are trifles undertaken gladly for your Lordship's sake. The opportunity thus afforded your Lordship renders such misery tolerable, even pleasurable."

"Grono, what can I say?"

"Say nothing, sir. At times the heart is too full for speech. As my devotion to your Lordship's welfare is literally written in my heart's blood, it is enough for me to know that I have effectively safeguarded your Lordship's interests. That is all I ask."

"Grono, I'll make it up to you!"

The valet lowered his eyes meekly, the better to disguise the flame of triumph. Lord Devras Har Fennahar would attend the Duke's soiree after all. There was no way he could get out of it now.

Chapter Three

With his valet's admonitions still hammering in his ears, Devras Har Fennahar sought the Ducal Palace at a fashionably late hour. Grono's notions of gentility demanded the use of a respectable conveyance and therefore Devras traveled by public dombulis, expense notwithstanding. The valet's act of flamboyant self-sacrifice surely deserved his master's reciprocal consideration. Twenty-four hours' worth of sober reflection, however, had clarified Devras's views upon this matter.

What he did to get my clothes back places me in his debt, and of course he uses that. Grono almost perfectly fits Heselicus's definition of the Morally Manipulative Man. It's an enviable talent. The clothes themselves hardly seemed worthy of major sacrifice. Devras wore an aging suit of charcoal silk; dove-gray waistcoat flowered in silver; decent lace at throat and wrists; white stockings, his only pair devoid of holes; silver-buckled shoes; and a tricorne hat. His appearance, if not festive, was respectable enough, and excessive simplicity could be ascribed to the Szarish taste for asceticism. The actual Szarish mode in the reign of the vastly popular Archduke Zargal ran to jeweled cravats and feathered gauntlets, but there was no reason to inform the Lanthian quality of this fact.

Embarking from the Destula Pier, Devras was carried along the old Straightwater Canal, soon passing beyond the boundaries of the festering slum in which he had spent the last seven wretched weeks. Around him glittered the fabled palaces of Lanthi Ume, nearly as remarkable in reality as in legend. What legend failed to convey, however, was the sense of degeneracy and decline that permeated all the city. Legend overlooked the decay and disintegration of the great public edifices; the filth of the canals; the indescribable squalor of the spreading slums and the desperation of the inhabitants. Unnoticed and unsung were the legions of homeless beggars; the roving bands of adolescent bully-boys; and the dreaded fleets of pirate sendilli that terrorized the waterways by night. Equally obscure was the Shonnet Asylum, a ghastly cageful of lunatics, idiots and demonstrably dangerous misfits. Few outside the Nine Isles knew of the Bankrupt Gangs composed of debtors consigned to hard labor in the streets and shipyards. And fewer yet had heard of Hungry Alley, discovery site of several childish corpses, the victims of starvation. Such things were common knowledge in Lanthi Ume, but news of their existence had not yet traveled far.

Onward glided the dombulis, past the Shonnet Gardens; past Old Market Square; and past the crystal image of the savant Jun, which had spoken aloud three times in history, at moments of extreme civic peril, to offer friendly but ill-informed advice. On it went along the Sandivell, heading for the wealthier section of town, where the fashionable strolled the lamplit canal paths. As he traveled Devras observed the changing composition of the crowd, noting with some disapproval the presence of military men of three different varieties; Ducal Guardsmen in their familiar uniforms of green and gold; officers in black, with golden double-headed dragon insignia marking them as Selectic Guards, a corps of relatively recent formation; and maroon-clad soldiers of Gard Lammis. A native Lanthian with any sense of civic identity would have detested the ubiquitous presence of the Lammish men, familiarly known as "Chamberpots" in honor of their distinctively shaped headgear. The Lammish troops occupying the Vayno Fortification, ostensibly to ensure, as the present Keldhar of Gard Lammis put it, the "preservation of our beloved sistercity's happy state of golden tranquility," constituted a nearly insupportable affront to civic autonomy. But Devras, having lived all his days in the foreign city-state of Szar, viewed the scene with equanimity.

Another ten minutes of travel brought him to the junction of the Sandivell and Lureis canals, where a moss-covered tumble of ancient ruins supposedly marked the site of vanished Grizhni Palace, once lair of that grim local bugbear, the demon-savant Terrs Fal Grizhni. He did not heed the ruins, nor did he heed the red light that burned in the sky directly above the unhallowed spot. The light—no ordinary star—was clearly visible during the daylight hours, and had been for some weeks past. Presumably the phenomenon presaged some great good or ill, but Devras did not speculate. His attention was fixed upon a certain mansion—venerable, imposing, graced with four slim blue spires—one of the most noteworthy of the many extraordinary palaces that ringed the Lureis Canal. This was Fennahar House, ancestral home of the Har Fennahar family and his own rightful property, if only he could prove it. Empty now save for the caretaker and a couple of

22

underlings, Fennahar House awaited the arrival of its lord. In the absence of a legitimate heir, the entire estate would revert to the Lanthian Duke. Despite all his innate trust in human nature, Devras found it impossible to suppress all suspicion of the Duke's self-interest in the affair, inasmuch as his own five increasingly urgent written requests for a personal audience had gone unacknowledged and ignored by his Grace Bofus Dil Shonnet.

The Lureis Canal was still a marvel by night, her palaces painted with light, her venerises riding at anchor like miniature floating mansions. Straight ahead loomed the Ducal Palace—vast, ponderous, lit with the glow of countless candles. The graceless old heap of gold still made a brave show by moonlight. Time had damped the harsh glitter of gold leaf and stained glass, tamed the heedless architectural exuberance of an earlier age. The palace, in all its oppressive ostentation, had assumed the spurious beauty of antiquity. At the foot of the building clustered a sizable fleet of small private vessels. It was clear that this annual crush of the Duke's, open to all nobility of the city, was heavily attended.

The dombulis touched the Ducal moorings. Devras paid his reckoning and stepped to the wharf. The boat departed, leaving him stranded upon a gilded shore. The moorings were crowded with late-arriving guests, gorgeous in their jewels, furs and brocades. Their mutual greetings resounded with careless confidence, and Devras felt invisible in their midst. With some reluctance he trailed the glittering mob through the great open portal and into a disturbingly proportioned entrance hall with a ceiling four stories high; up a stairway of rose-veined marble to an ornate landing, and thence to the overwhelming reception chamber. There he waited at the entrance while the arrivals were announced one by one. He heard the great names that figured so prominently in Lanthian history—Dule Parnis, Kor Malifon, Wate Basef, Rion Vassarion, and the others. The line inched forward and his nervous tension mounted. The hand that clutched the counterfeit invitation was clammy. If he weren't careful, his sweat would smear the ink, destroying all of Grono's beautiful work, among other things.

He caught a glimpse of the room ahead, a flash of brilliance, a swirl of color and movement. Now for it. With apparent nonchalance he handed the spurious invitation to a green-and-gold lackey, who accepted it without demur. The pasteboard was passed on to the chamberlain, and then his own name rang out:

"The Lord Devras Har Fennahar."

Devras walked into an enormous room crammed with the illustrious, and almost instantly longed for his former sense of invisibility. They were looking at him. They were all watching, either openly or, worse, covertly. And he remembered that the famous name of Har Fennahar was thought by all to be extinct, that his own claim to the title had hitherto gone worse than opposed—it had been completely ignored. Well, from this night on Lanthian society would note his existence, but probably label him an imposter or else an earnest crank. Even those willing to consider the legitimacy of his claim would be on the alert for signs of fakery. They would inspect him with care, weigh his every utterance, sift through his story for inconsistencies. They would analyze his appearance, his bearing and manner. The affair would provide the bored courtiers with endless food for gossip, and it was beginning already. Following an instant's startled silence, a fervent hum of conversation arose.

Devras's face heated, and his pulses jumped. Would they eject him at the very outset? Almost he could feel the hand of the footman under his elbow, hear the laughter as he was hurried to the exit. But it was not the time to display the slightest uncertainty, and he cast about for the words to bolster his slipping confidence. What was it that Ees Wulleroy had written? "The man whose heart seems made of lead must sculpt himself a face of marble." Good advice. Squaring his shoulders, Devras advanced upon the receiving line with a firm step. His expression was consciously tranquil as he received the nonplussed greeting of the Duke's designees. Along the length of the line he met with the coolest reserve, but no one chose to challenge him openly as yet. Collective surprise and confusion worked in his favor. A moment later and it was done—he was through the line, a more or less accepted guest.

Now what to do? Enjoy the festivities, revel in Lanthian opulence? Scarcely. He was not here for pleasure. He had come to advance his own fortunes, a task for which he owned little natural aptitude. He must recommend himself to the notice of the great, preferably of the Duke himself; win the Duke's ear, insinuate himself into his Grace's graces, somehow secure recognition of his perfectly valid claim to the Fennahar title and fortunes. An unappetizing prospect, all this courtly jockeying, but necessary. He might as well get on with it. He could begin by tracking down the Duke.

Devras cast a searching glance about the room. He saw clean-shaven men in knee breeches and brocade coats, lacy cravats spraying, jeweled swords and buckles winking; women in sweeping gowns of pastel silk, bound in by stays that nipped the waist

24

and pushed the bosom high to create spectacular décolletage; dowagers in their antiquated gear; marriageable daughters flaunting fashionably immodest, semitransparent draperies; here and there, a few grave figures garbed in the time-honored dark robes and double-headed dragon insignia of the Select. Conversation among the polychrome clusters was animated, and many were the curious stares directed at the stranger standing solitary and silent upon the sidelines.

As Devras completed a methodical circuit of the receiving chamber, the whispers and pointed commentary arose in his wake, increasing his already acute discomfort. He did not spy the Duke, and it was with a sense of relief that he finally passed through the great gilded doors, along a short gallery and into the enormous ballroom, where couples pranced to the strains of the new Linniana. Unacquainted with the Linniana, Devras could not join in. The Duke was not present, and there was no reason to linger. But the music was sprightly, it was many weeks since he had heard anything better than the piping of buskers, and now he paused to listen. As he listened he watched the dancers, noting despite all present futility that several of the aristocratic daughters, in their flirtatiously revealing draperies, were extraordinarily pretty. The couples glided and chasséd expertly; and it suddenly struck Devras that a number of them were probably related to him by blood. His Har Fennahar forebears had been Lanthian for countless generations. They would have intermarried with other noble Houses of the city, and traces of Fennahar blood surely flowed in the veins of many present. He had relatives here—the remnants of a family—but they wore the masks of alien names and titles. He was a stranger to them, likely to remain so, and he felt more alone than ever.

For a moment longer he watched the dancers, then wheeled abruptly and left the ballroom. His search continued through the suite of the gamesters and gamblers; then through a quiet salon where clouds of colored smoke rose from the braziers to delight the devotees of the brain-soothing Rainbow Serenity essence. A dozen or so such devotees reclined upon silken cushions, their glazed eyes fixed upon the shifting clouds. Duke Bofus was not among them, and the atmosphere made Devras's head spin. Quickly he hurried away, passing through chambers and galleries of gaudy, disconcerting immensity until he came to the crowded banqueting hall, where the table was set up for buffet dining.

Here at last was something he could appreciate. The buffet—a vision of Paradise to the undernourished heir of Har Fennahar—offered every variety of delicacy. There were great roasts garlanded with parsley and bay leaves; ducks, chickens and game birds baked in puff pastry; fragrant ragouts in golden chafing dishes; cold pink and silver fish in a pool of aspic dotted with water lilies; a bed of assorted exotic mollusks; vegetables carved to resemble flowers and beasts; fruits lush as summertime; and a lapidary display of glazed confections. Devras loaded a plate, found a chair, sat and began to eat. As Grono had predicted, it was the most substantial meal he'd enjoyed in weeks, and beyond doubt the most luxurious he'd ever tasted. For a time he gorged, wholly preoccupied with the alleviation of chronic hunger. When the pangs had subsided, the pace of his chewing slowed and his eyes lifted from plate to table.

Any chance of smuggling some of that back to Grono?

Stealing? came the internal query, and the response was immediate: *Hungry.*

He set his empty plate aside, rose and sauntered back to the buffet. Grabbing a fresh plate, he quickly heaped up slices of meat, fowl, and cheese. When the plate was piled high he looked up from his work to find a number of fellow guests contemplating him with an avidity customarily reserved for the foie gras alone. Impossible to wrap Grono's provisions unobserved, and he couldn't afford to be seen. Then he pictured the old man's emaciation and resolved that Grono *would* have his dinner, no matter what.

Devras draped a napkin over the plate. Assuming an air of vague abstraction, he turned and drifted toward the exit. He carried his burden openly and many guests eyed him askance as he passed by, apparently unaware of public scrutiny.

The corridor outside the banqueting hall was crowded with guests. In search of solitude, Devras ascended a curving staircase that led to a relatively quiet gallery on the third story. Even here, he was not alone. A jeweled knot of courtiers chattered and giggled a few yards down the corridor. Reluctant to approach them, he turned aside and slipped through an unlocked door into a chamber blessedly silent and empty. Setting his plate down on the nearest table, he rapidly transferred food to napkin, bundled the linen and dropped the parcel into his coat pocket, which now bulged unobtrusively. Only then did he pause to take stock of his surroundings, and his mood lightened at once.

He had found his way, as if by instinct, to the Duke's library. Here the oppressive glitter did not weary his eye. The soft patina of aged wood, leather and parchment soothed his sight and mended his spirits. All around him towered the shelves of books —thousands of volumes, the accumulation of a dozen lifetimes.

The dukes of the Dil Shonnet line were not renowned for their literacy, but they were indefatigable collectors. Let it be known that a scholar's work was rare, extraordinary, nearly unobtainable—and a copy would inevitably find its way to the Shonnet Archives. It was a marvel of a library, and the urge to explore the contents was almost irresistible. It was not here that the Ducal quarry would be flushed, and yet, a few minutes of self-indulgence couldn't hurt—a very few minutes—

He soon stumbled upon an obscure treasure: *History of the Select*, by the unjustly neglected Lanthian savant Rev Beddef. Devras drew the volume gently from the shelf. Never before had he held a hand-lettered copy of poor old Beddef, who had been so brilliant and so unlucky—murdered by an angry city mob. He needed to examine it at leisure.

There was furniture enough for comfort, but the table and chair in the middle of the room were anomalous. The chair was relentlessly luxurious, plushy and cushioned, fringed and tasseled in gold. The table, a solid block of marble heavily carved in bas relief, had a deep, square well cut into the center. Neither chair nor table seemed to belong in a library. Devras eyed them dubiously for a moment, approached and stooped to peer down into the table-well. He could see nothing. The hole was dead black, impossibly black. Frowning, he sank into the too-soft chair. At once an insinuating voice inquired conspiratorially, "What is your will, Great One? How may I serve you?"

"Who's there?" Devras glanced around him. The room was empty.

"What is your desire, Radiance? How may I assist?"

The voice came from the well in the table. Devras leaned forward to peer into nothingness. "Is someone down there?"

"What work may I present for your pleasure, Magnificence?" asked the table, its voice smooth and oily.

"What work—you mean, a book?"

"Any book your Supremacy might deign to honor. Although," the table added suggestively, "I offer other treasures, delights more delicious than books, and perhaps more worthy of your notice, Perfection." Soft, voluptuous music undulated out of the well. The scent of frangipani filled the air.

"What do you mean?"

"Bend down, bend down," whispered the table. "Gaze deep into my well, and you shall see for yourself, to your everlasting joy."

"What shall I see?"

"Mere words cannot convey it. Have faith. Bend down, bend

down, bend down . . ." The voice trailed off swooningly.

"Are you still there?" Devras demanded.

Silence from the well.

"Is anyone down there?" Still no answer, and he bent to squint into the hole. Instantly his face was bathed in heavy, sweet-smelling vapor. His vision swam and his pulses throbbed. Devras sank back into the chair's fat embrace, his breath coming in gasps. For a moment he lay there, stunned. Then, as his eyes cleared, the room around him took on a new aspect. He suddenly perceived its beauty and significance. The forms were exquisite, the colors unutterably glorious. Each figure, each flower, each animal carved into the base of the marble table before him possessed a life of its own. Surely he spied motion there? And Devras knew that the veil that had obscured his true vision since the day he was born had been ripped away at last.

"Is your Supremacy content?" inquired the table.

"Yes," sighed Devras. "Oh, yes. Yes."

"What might enhance your Grandeur's pleasure? Your humble servant longs to provide it."

"I came for—something. To see a—book," Devras recalled with difficulty. "Book."

"I yearn to make myself your Effulgence's slave. What book do you desire?"

"It was—" Devras struggled to remember, ignoring Rev Bed-def's treatise, still clasped loosely in one hand. "There are so many—"

"You are uncertain? Let me be of service," the table begged. "Bend down, Coruscation, bend down. Gaze deep into my well. Bend down . . . bend down . . ."

Devras dazedly complied. Fresh tendrils of vapor stroked his face, kissed his lips, insinuated themselves into his mouth, his nostrils, his lungs. Once more he sank back in the chair, his breathing labored, his vision all but extinct. He strove to speak, and could not.

"Your will, Transcendence? Your desire?"

Devras gasped for breath.

"I understand. Your Elevation desires counsel," the table observed with unmistakable satisfaction. "Your will in all things, Omnipotence, but may your humble servant make a suggestion?"

Devras gestured aimlessly.

"I will present for your delight a rare edition of Veemefer's *Distillation of Ecstasy*—a marvelous work, remarkable for its inventiveness, ingenuity, and vividly detailed descriptions. The particular edition I aspire to present to your Erudition is enriched with a series of the artist Nardin's Animated Engravings. Hand-colored, Notability. Although the engravings lack the extreme subtlety of Nardin's mature work, they nonetheless reveal the hand of the master in their perfection of anatomical detail, their eloquence of facial expression, and their exploration of the nearly limitless flexibility of the human body. Exaltation, allow me."

To the accompaniment of soft music, a great folio volume rose slowly from the well and tilted itself to the angle most convenient for Devras's viewing. As the young man watched with clouded eyes, the book opened itself to Chapter One of the *Distillation of Ecstasy*. On the right-hand page was the printed text. On the left, Nardin's beautifully executed figures cavorted. Devras goggled in glazed fascination as the tiny forms writhed and jerked. He became aware of a muted, unctuous voice. The table was reading the words aloud, presumably to spare him the drudgery of reading them himself. As it came to the end of the text on each page, the page automatically turned.

Devras's intellect was blanketed over with sludge. His tongue was semi-petrified. It was with the greatest difficulty that he tore his eyes from the busy engravings and muttered a single command. "Stop."

"I rejoice in the privilege of obedience, Stateliness. Is my pace too swift for your pleasure? Are there passages that you desire repeated?"

"This—isn't—what—I—wanted—"

The book promptly descended.

"There are many others," the table offered. "You have only to choose. Your humble servant will make it easy and pleasant. Your Solemnity need only bend down, gaze into my well, bend down, bend down..." The music caressed him. The vapors rose.

"But—" Devras inquired with extreme effort, "don't you have anything by the Venerable Disitch?"

A burst of laughter greeted this question, and Devras turned to discover a stranger at his side. Candlelight glinted on a shining bald dome of a skull, ringed with a wiry brown fringe; on a pair of bright, sardonic, very vital brown eyes surrounded by the wrinkles of early middle age. The newcomer possessed a crinkled, streaky beard and moustache, indifferently trimmed; strong nose with a bumpy bridge; and white teeth bared in a smile of sunny sarcasm. His figure was a shade below middle height, paunchy, and clothed in a fine dark robe that didn't hang well. The double-headed dragon of the Select glared from his shoulder as if it felt uneasy there. Devras perceived it all as if through a luminous magnifying lens. A thread hanging from the dark robe. A stain of yellow on a front tooth.

"Forgive me, but you are in error, sir," the savant observed in a dry, conversational tone. "The Venerable Disitch is not likely to enhance your enjoyment. May I suggest a more suitable work—Veemefer's *Distillation of Ecstasy*, perhaps. Or even the *Red Darkness* of Master Partherald. But not the Venerable Disitch."

Devras was not too far gone to recognize obvious mockery. "I know my own mind," he mumbled resentfully, and passed a hand across his eyes, the pupils of which were vastly dilated.

"So it would appear." The other's smile widened, and he cackled with laughter.

"You doubt my knowledge of the—the—the classics, sir?"

"To classics of which variety do you refer, sir?" The paunchy Cognizance was clearly enjoying himself.

Devras, suffused with slow, dull annoyance, marshalled his faculties as best he could. When he spoke, his voice was slurred and halting but careful, and the words were tolerably intelligible. "I know the classics. I love the classics. I have read Disitch. I have read Heselicus. Lapivoe. Omee Nofid. Wulleroy. Zebbefore. Fu Krun—"

The list would have continued interminably, had not the other interrupted in some surprise, "You've read Omee Nofid?"

"Yes. I have been told it is a waste of time, but that does not deter me."

"You are a scholar?"

Devras nodded slowly, as if his head moved through glue.

"Then why are you fooling with that slimy old pander of a table?"

Devras thought about it. He concentrated hard and finally managed to inquire, "Is it not a library?"

"Oh, certainly, and a good one. But that table—the thing was designed in the past century by the Select for the pleasure and demoralization of the Dukes of Lanthi Ume. Our Duke Bofus hasn't much use for it, but it's still a favorite among the courtiers. Didn't you know that?"

Devras shook his head dully. "No. I thank you, Master—?"

"Raith Wate Basef," replied the stranger. The name was naggingly familiar. "And you are—?"

"Devras Har Fennahar."

"Har Fennahar—ah!" The savant seemed unaccountably struck by the name. "Extraordinary, if true. I'd thought that line extinct."

"Only in a financial sense," responded Devras, sublimely unconscious of indiscretion.

Wate Basef suppressed a derisive cackle, and observed, "Even a dazed and incoherent Har Fennahar is a rare find indeed. Eventually this specimen will regain its power of speech, and then we may hope for great things. Come on, lad—" Above the grieving protests of the table, he hauled Devras out of the chair. "You need some fresh air. Lean on me." Pursued by the table's entreaties, he led the heir of Har Fennahar from the library, through countless corridors and galleries and eventually out onto a balcony where the stars shone overhead and moist breezes blew off the Lureis.

Devras grew passionately absorbed in the play of lights on the surface of the canal, the swirls and eddies in the water, the curve of an orange peel floating directly below. His companion watched him closely. As he stood drinking the cool night air, a phrase from the earlier conversation rose to the surface of his mind to float there as the orange peel floated on the Lureis.

"You say," asked Devras carefully, "that the library was designed by the Select for the demoralization of the Dukes of Lanthi Ume?"

"Correct. Generally in hopes of securing Ducal favor."

Devras mulled this over for a time, until his mind went wandering and he found himself counting the number of golden threads in the embroidered dragon on Raith Wate Basef's shoulder. With an effort, he turned his eyes away. "But—" It dawned on him slowly. "You yourself are a member of the Select?"

"It's impossible to keep secrets these days."

"You slight your own Order?"

"Given the nature of the powers that presently govern the Select, disloyalty may be accounted a virtue."

Devras regarded his companion with mild interest. Had he been more himself, he would have boiled over with questions. As it was, he knew only a shadowy uneasiness. Surely it couldn't be wise or even altogether safe to criticize the powerful Select so freely? The mists lifted a little from his mind then, and he recalled that he had heard this man's name somewhere or other, perhaps on the lips of the gossipy used-book seller in Old Market Square. The ancient and noble Wate Basef family had a reputation for inconstancy and instability. And this latest lord of Castle Io Wesha, this Raith Wate Basef—didn't he have the shakiest reputation of the lot? He was known far and wide as a brilliant savant of the Select. Even his enemies—of which he had many —couldn't fault his Cognitive talent. His gifts, however, had not won him advancement within his Order, for all that ability was offset by qualities of willfulness, exaggerated individualism and contentiousness. He was a troublemaker, a gadfly, a smiling rebel in the ranks of the Select—imprudent, insubordinate, ruinously articulate. In short, a famous and a dangerous character.

Wate Basef had been speaking steadily while Devras's thoughts drifted. What was the man saying now? The other's voice crashed in on his mind.

"—And so there can be no denying," Wate Basef insisted, "that their suppression of information—reports concerning the remarkable level of Cognitive activity inland, the rumors of a spreading shadow—directly violates the principles on which the Order of the Select was originally founded. True, we've always guarded our secrets. I have no quarrel with that. But information of such concern to the general public has never been withheld before, and should not be so now."

Devras's empty-eyed silence proclaimed incomprehension.

Smiling the sarcastic smile that nearly buried his eyes in his face, Wate Basef observed, "No matter, the effects of the vapors will wear off. In the meantime, as the nature of the Select seems to intrigue you, perhaps you would like to see his Preeminence Vaxalt Gless Vallage, who tonight regales us with his charm, wit, and unconscionable lies. I don't think I'll be able to hold my peace."

Too muddled to request an explanation, Devras merely inquired, "Where?"

"In the Duke's theatre. I'll show you the way. Don't worry, I've no intention of losing sight of you."

Devras vaguely wondered why. But there was little time to ponder the question as he felt himself steered back into the florid labyrinth.

Chapter Four

❧❧❧❧❧

Devras shuffled through the brilliant crowd, passive as a marionette upon its strings. The puppeteer, Raith Wate Basef, moved him neatly along the mirrored corridors until they came to the so-called Shonnet Whimsy, a small private theatre, site of the masques and pageants to which the Dukes of Lanthi Ume were traditionally partial. Wate Basef secured them good seats, not far from the apron of the raised stage. Devras sank gratefully into the velvet chair. For all his euphoria, he was confused and dizzy. Now he could rest. His companion offered a steady stream of explanation and observation, all potentially useful, but nearly all beyond Devras's present scope of understanding. Two bits of information, however, managed to penetrate the fog.

"That's his Grace of Lanthi Ume," remarked Wate Basef, pointing discreetly. "The Duke Bofus Dil Shonnet."

Devras's eyes followed the pointing finger to a short, tubby, roan-haired gentleman, splendidly attired in white-and-gold brocade. There he sat, in the flesh—master of the queen of city-states, descendant of a hundred princes, arbiter of the Fennahar fates.

He didn't look it. The Duke had pudgy soft hands, a receding chin with an abortive goatee, and slack carriage. The cast of his features was soft and cherubic, the smiling lips sweetly formed. His large, long-lashed eyes of clear sky blue beamed vacant amiability upon the crowd.

Try as he would, Devras could see nothing particularly impressive about Bofus Dil Shonnet. *Wasn't I supposed to talk to him about something or other? Oh, well.* The object of his scrutiny sucked contentedly upon a sweetmeat.

"A giant among men," Raith Wate Basef observed with a quiet cackle. He pointed again. "The Duke's daughter and heir presumptive—her Ladyship Karavise Dil Shonnet."

A daughter more unlike her father could hardly be imagined. Lady Karavise was twenty-six years old and, to the consternation of her future subjects, still unmarried. Her figure was tall, too

33

slim, and she held herself erect as a Guardsman on parade. Her face was intellectual and patrician, but she could not, strictly speaking, be called beautiful. Where were the soft pink cheeks, pouting lips and languishing eyes that beauty demanded? Karavise's face was fair and clear, but the bones were too pronounced —the cheekbones too high and prominent, the chiseled jawline too strong, the brow too high. The lips were finely modeled, but too decisive. Her eyes, large and sky blue beneath high-flying black brows, might well have been considered very beautiful, but for their expression. A young woman's eyes should be meltingly soft, perhaps sparked with a tinge of mischief. Lady Karavise's were cool, penetrating and, according to her detractors, calculating. She was crowned with chestnut hair drawn back from a tall brow, and clothed in a silk gown whose flowing lines softened her attenuated figure.

Devras concentrated, and a thought formed slowly. "The Lady Karavise isn't dressed as an unmarried daughter."

"The Lady Karavise has a mind of her own," Wate Basef returned with unwonted respect.

Devras did not pursue the issue. Allowing his eyes to wander over the audience, he grew enthralled with the play of color, the flash of jewels, the delirious extravagance of plumes and laces. He could have watched for hours, his drugged mind happily empty, had he been left in peace. But someone had him by the arm; someone was shaking him.

"Wake up, lad! Attention!" Wate Basef commanded. "Gless Vallage is before us. The comedy commences."

The Shonnet Whimsy was now full, with hundreds of courtiers packed into its limited space. All watched attentively as Vaxalt Gless Vallage, Preeminent of the Select, mounted the stage. In his wake trailed a brace of satin-clad flunkeys, bearing the Midnight Lens—a delicately complex conglomerate of screens, prisms, crystals and lenses supporting a great iridescent bubble of the thinnest glass. The entire contraption stood almost as high as a man. At sight of the mysterious device, Devras strove mightily to restore mental order, and was in part successful. He saw that Raith Wate Basef, seated beside him, was watching Gless Vallage wih an elaborately cynical smirk. Quickly surveying his fellow spectators, he noted that the Duke's daughter Karavise eyed his Preeminence with frozen hostility.

If Preeminence Vaxalt Gless Vallage marked the cynicism or dislike projected in his direction, he showed no sign of it. Tall, distinguished, and imposing in his dark robes of office, he carried himself with confidence and ease. The square-jawed face was serene beneath a luxuriant thatch of perfectly groomed silver hair. An experienced public speaker, his voice was resonant and authoritative, his manner gracefully assured. Dismissing his attendants with a gesture, Vallage launched into a brief preamble in which explanation of his purpose was liberally interspersed with compliments to the Duke Bofus. Judging by the childlike smile that lighted his Grace's countenance, Bofus relished the flattery. Her Ladyship Karavise did not. Karavise's expression of open disgust intensified as she listened.

"And thus we come by degrees," Gless Vallage completed his introductory remarks, "from the lights of our city gathered here this evening, to those far dimmer, distant lights that illumine the heavens."

"Hypocrite," Wate Basef remarked.

Gless Vallage took no notice, if indeed he had heard at all. "The stars, fair friends," he continued smoothly, "are more than celestial ornaments. Their influence is with us always; they guide and shape our lives from birth unto the very moment of death. In remote indifference they rule our destinies. And yet, distant though they are, they deign to speak to us. The heavens are an open volume which those among us who possess the knowledge may peruse at leisure."

"Don't you just love the way he speaks?" one rouged matron in Devras's vicinity inquired of another.

The other woman nodded. "Such a voice! Such eyes!"

The smirk on Wate Basef's face deepened. Devras was finding it easier to pay attention.

"Not many of us can read the stars," admitted Gless Vallage, with a humorously rueful shake of his handsome head. "To those who have not passed long years in study, their language is as incomprehensible as High Strellian would be to me."

A ripple of appreciative laughter greeted this sally. Duke Bofus giggled with the rest. His daughter's face remained stony.

"Therefore I am delighted at this opportunity to present to you, with the compliments of your friends among the Select, the Midnight Lens, which may be regarded as a universal translator. Tonight, with the aid of the Lens, we shall unravel the mysteries of the stellar messages."

"'Universal translator'—launch that on the canal and sink it!" Wate Basef suggested. "It's a glorified viewing device, nothing more."

Many heard him, and there was a nervous rustling in his section of the audience. Lady Karavise turned a brief glance back over her shoulder; then her eyes returned to Gless Vallage.

"It has come to our attention"—a note of grave concern crept into his Preeminence's mellifluous voice—"that some have been taken aback at a recent phenomenon—the appearance of a star shining at midday in the skies over Lanthi Ume. There have been many expressions among the citizens of confusion, uncertainty, and even apprehension regarding the unnatural character of this star."

"I'll swear it's pretty," observed Duke Bofus.

Wate Basef snickered.

"But not all men own your Grace's noble courage." Gless Vallage bowed to the Duke. "We of the Select have received many requests for intelligence concerning this star. With the aid of the Midnight Lens, I now propose to offer an explanation that will set your minds at rest. I wish to make it clear to all of you from the very outset that there is nothing to fear—nothing whatever. You may regard this singular star as a new jewel in the crown of our city's beauty. And now—attend me, if you please —I activate the Midnight Lens." Gless Vallage spoke a few words, wove a couple of practiced gestures. The crystals and prisms at the base of the Lens glowed with sudden color. As the prisms began to revolve, a murmur of admiration arose from the audience. The great glass bubble darkened, then cleared to reveal an image of the Lureis Canal as it had appeared hours earlier, with the afternoon sun blazing in a blue sky above the palaces and boats. The new star—a bright point of red light—was clearly visible. Spontaneous applause broke forth, and Gless Vallage smiled graciously. "Behold the star of Lanthi Ume," he invited. "Surely Nature's loveliest tribute to our city! A heavenly compliment indeed!"

"Oh, Vallage, you ought to be hanged for the liar you are." This time Raith Wate Basef's voice was bitterly low.

"We shall examine the star more closely." In response to Gless Vallage's commands, the view reflected in the Midnight Lens shifted skyward to center on the star. His Preeminence spoke again and the blue sky deepened to purple, then to black, while the constellations came out of hiding and shone in their accustomed positions. The new star blazed with a brilliance that surpassed them all by far. Once again the audience applauded.

"And now"—Vallage paused an impressive moment—"the stars will reveal their secrets. Your Grace, lords and ladies, you will observe the crystals and prisms that support the celestial sphere. They glow with varied colors, as you see. Those colors are spectral manifestations of the stellar emanations, each shade carrying a precise and particular meaning."

Wate Basef released his breath in a low hiss. "Charlatan!" he muttered between his teeth. "Mountebank! You and that expensive pile of glass garbage!"

"As many complex phenomena influence the emanations, exact interpretation demands no less of art than of science—"

"Lies, Vallage, lies!"

"—And it is to be hoped that my abilities may prove equal to the task. My noble friends, you will note that the prisms of the Midnight Lens reflect a preponderance of blue and green. These two colors, so favorable in themselves, are particularly joyous in combination. Their conjunction promises a period of dazzling prosperity for Lanthi Ume and all her inhabitants. The flickering indigo shade at the base of the lowest prism symbolizes the sea waves over which our merchant vessels will sail home from foreign shores, laden with treasure to enrich our vaults." Vallage's voice was rich and warmly reassuring, seductive as a practiced courtesan's.

Duke Bofus and most of his guests seemed entranced with these glowing predictions. Not so Raith Wate Basef. *"You aren't going to get away with this!"* he promised and then, apparently no longer able to contain himself, raised his voice to a pitch clearly audible throughout the theatre. "Preeminence—before you proceed, one question, if I may."

"Who asks?" Gless Vallage quickly located the inquisitor. Hostility glittered in his eyes, then vanished. "Ah, Cognizance Wate Basef, you honor us. I will ask you to postpone all questions until the conclusion of my presentation. My noble friends," he resumed, "you will observe the streaks of orange—"

"I would prefer to ask now," broke in Wate Basef, his tones crystalline. "I am sure you will indulge me."

Gless Vallage paused unwillingly.

Murmurs of surprise among the spectators.

"Why has he stopped?" Duke Bofus demanded plaintively of his daughter. She patted his arm and said nothing.

Gless Vallage hesitated, as if weighing possible responses. He settled upon tolerant good humor. "Raith, Raith, I should have reckoned on that famous curiosity of yours." Vallage's amused chuckle contrived to underscore his own good breeding in the face of the other's discourtesy. "Ask, then. Is there something you do not understand?"

"I understood him well enough," Duke Bofus remarked to his daughter. "I thought that Basef fellow was supposed to be clever."

"Ssssshhh!" she admonished. He stared at her, hurt, then shrugged and sneaked another sweetmeat.

"Indeed I do not understand," conceded Wate Basef, smiling with all his teeth. "I do not understand how your Preeminence can commence a discussion of the diurnal star without explanation of the ancient prophecies foretelling its appearance."

"Our time here is limited." The muscles in Vallage's jaw tightened almost invisibly. Other than that, his genial expression remained intact. "I do not wish to weary my noble listeners with superfluous detail. They desire a concise statement of the essential facts."

"Thank you, Lord Vallage. 'A concise statement of the essential facts,' eh? Just so. How then does your Preeminence justify suppression of the most vital facts in this matter—facts that affect the safety of every Lanthian, indeed of every human upon the entire island of Dalyon?"

"My colleague Wate Basef has always been impetuous," Vallage addressed himself to the spectators as if he shared a private joke with them. His smile was a masterpiece of amused forbearance. "Judge him gently. Rest assured, friend Raith, our noble audience need not fear—"

"Need not fear the direst curses of the Lord Terrs Fal Grizhni?"

With that, Wate Basef arrested the attention of the entire assemblage, for the long passage of time had not expunged the dark memory of Fal Grizhni from the Lanthian consciousness—far from it. Down through the years a wealth of legends had attached themselves to the fallen savant's name. Mighty demon-sorcerer, nightmare son of Ert, Grizhni was the strangely compelling villain of a score of popular folk tales. Deeds of unimaginable infamy were attributed to him, and in some quarters it was believed that he, undying and malevolent, would return one day to smite the city that had offended him.

The Duke's guests studied Wate Basef in rapt curiosity. Bofus himself pulled his goatee and asked Lady Karavise hopefully, "Is he going to tell a Fal Grizhni story?"

Gless Vallage could no longer maintain his expression of good humor. His eyes were narrow as he faced Wate Basef. "I have said that we are not interested in these old wives' tales. They are out of place here. You understand me, Cognizance?"

"I understand you very well, Preeminence, perhaps too well for your ease, but that is scarcely the point in question. I ask you again, for we all have a right to know—why do you attempt to disguise the fact that this new star presages disaster?"

The audience buzzed in excitement, while Devras struggled, with his impaired intellect, to judge the sanity of his new acquaintance.

"Cognizance, you forget yourself." Gless Vallage's face was stiff with anger. "You babble of legends, dreams and fables. I cannot permit a savant of the Select to parade his folly in public. For your own benefit, I order you to cease."

"Order? *Order?*" Wate Basef laughed annoyingly. "By what authority do you presume to *order* me, Vallage?"

"By my authority as your superior in the Select. Do you forget that? If you do, then the Council of the Select will surely remind you."

"You harbor delusions." Wate Basef evidently employed his assured smile as a weapon. "Or perhaps you are simply ignorant. In order to prevent you from making a greater fool of yourself, I must remind you that your power as Preeminence is limited by statute. You have no jurisdiction over the personal lives of senior savants."

"But I have full power to deal with insubordination on the part of any member, seniority notwithstanding. When the words and actions of a savant reflect public discredit upon our entire Order, I am forced to exercise that power. I do so now." Gless Vallage's self-control did him credit. His eyes were ablaze, but his voice remained steady and cool.

"My words reflect no discredit upon the Select as a whole. But even if it were so, I would be justified in speaking, for it is clearly stated in the original Selectic Charter that the interests of the Select are invariably superseded by the interests of the city of Lanthi Ume. Page twenty-six, paragraph two, sub-paragraph e, if you care to investigate."

"I am not interested in splitting legal hairs." Gless Vallage exuded contempt. "Your behavior is a public embarrassment tonight, as it has so often been in the past. You try the patience of this entire company with your mad freaks. I order you to retire."

Judging by his facial expression, Wate Basef's reply might have proved enlightening. But his sentiments were lost to posterity, for at that moment the voice of the Duke's chamberlain boomed from the rear of the theatre. "A Rider from Fenz requests an emergency audience of his Grace. An urgent message for his Grace!"

Down the central aisle came a group of the Duke's retainers, leading the Rider from Fenz, an exhausted and filthy man clad in the plain garments of an inland pioneer. The Rider—bloodstained, death-white under his tan—was held upright by a couple

39

of footmen, who guided him past the staring courtiers to face the seated Duke. When they released him, the Rider tottered, but managed to stay on his feet.

The Duke's blue eyes widened. "Are you sure you should be up and about?" he inquired kindly.

"Your Grace," rasped the stranger in a voice that was pitiful to hear, "I bring news of a massacre. Fenz has been destroyed!"

"Where's Fenz?" asked Duke Bofus.

"Explain," commanded Lady Karavise.

The messenger took a deep breath, gathered his strength and replied clearly. "First, there was the darkness. We'd been hearing about it for weeks from the river traders, but no one believed them. They were right, though. It came, just like they said. We saw it on the horizon one morning, sitting up on top of Dambar Ridge. Three days later, it reached Fenz."

"What reached Fenz? Where's Fenz?"

"The darkness came, your Grace," explained the Rider. "Like nothing the world has ever seen. It was Cognition, must have been."

"Describe it," Karavise directed.

The courtiers were rising from their seats, hurrying forward to congregate about the Rider. Devras found himself moving down the aisle, propelled by Raith Wate Basef. Somehow, he could not have said how, he ended up at the foot of the stage in the front rank of the crowd gathered about the stranger.

"Black. Blacker than anything you can think of. Torches and lanterns don't light it up. You don't know. . ." The Rider's voice trailed off briefly. "It was hot with a kind of dampness that made you feel dirty all over. And there was a stink about it like a rotting swamp. After it had been like that for a few days, people started feeling queerly, then sickened. They couldn't hold their food down, and they couldn't work."

"Then the settlers died of a pestilence?" asked Karavise.

"No." The Rider shook his head. "Let me tell you. After a few more days of this, we were very bad off. Half our folk were laid up, and none of us felt right. We were all heartsick of stumbling around in the dark, and it never lifted, not for a single hour. Then, when we were good and beaten down, they came."

"Who did?" inquired Bofus, much taken with the tale.

"I don't know, your Grace. They were like men, but they weren't human. They were white all over, and they had a sort of glow about them that you could see even in that darkness. They walked on two legs like men, and they carried weapons like men, but their faces—they've got these giant eyes—" The Rider shuddered. "Whatever they were, the darkness didn't trouble them the way it troubled us. And they knew how to fight. They attacked Fenz like a trained army. We didn't even know they were coming until they were on us, and then they just tore us apart. They slaughtered everyone. Children—women—everyone. Their leader personally killed at least six men. Whatever he is—man, beast or demon—he aims to destroy us all." The Rider's strength was failing. His head drooped and he swayed dizzily.

"Do you know where these beings came from?" Karavise leaned forward in her chair. "Why did they attack your settlement, and what did they want?"

"Destruction. They wanted complete destruction."

"Did they loot?" she asked.

"No. They only killed."

"But why?" Duke Bofus was amazed. "Why?"

"Who knows, your Grace?" the Rider murmured faintly. "Perhaps it's their nature. There's danger approaching your city, Duke. Be warned. Send forth your armies to crush it now, before it's too late." His strength failed altogether, and his knees buckled. The chamberlain and a footman caught him before he fell.

Duke Bofus regarded the exhausted man with bewildered sympathy. The courtiers whirred and hummed like glee-flies.

Vaxalt Gless Vallage had stepped to the edge of the stage, the better to hear the Rider's message. Now Raith Wate Basef glared up into his Preeminence's eyes to exclaim hotly, "Is this what you wanted, Vallage? You see it's begun. Shall we tell them the truth while there may still be time, or aren't you convinced yet?"

Vallage leaned down to reply in the deadliest of whispers, "You will not breathe another word of this matter in public. You will not mention the name of Grizhni in a public place. As your Preeminence, I issue a direct order. If you disobey it, I will break you once and for all. You will live out your life as an Expulsion." The two men locked eyes.

Duke Bofus gazed worriedly at the semiconscious Rider. After a moment he thought to order, "Somebody deal with this!"

At a command from Lady Karavise, servants bore the messenger from the theatre, to entrust him to the care of his Grace's own physician.

Wate Basef turned to the Duke. "May I ask if your Grace intends to dispatch troops to the Fenz area?"

"Dispatch so many men on the unsupported word of one messenger?" Bofus fidgeted. "At the moment, I don't know. This requires much deliberation."

"A small patrol, then," Wate Basef pressed him. "Send at least

41

a small patrol to investigate the Rider's report. I suggest you do it quickly."

"I promise to consult with various ministers at the earliest opportunity. The very earliest." Bofus glanced at his daughter as if seeking aid. "There are many questions to be considered. We should speak to that Rider again, don't you think?"

Urgency sharpened Wate Basef's voice. "You can't afford to wait. Don't you see—"

"You have been answered, Cognizance," Gless Vallage noted crisply. "His Grace has stated his intentions, and you need no longer concern yourself with the matter. In due course, his Grace's subjects—and you along with them—will be apprised of their ruler's decision."

Wate Basef hesitated only a moment, then spoke in a voice that carried through the theatre. "Ladies and gentlemen, there are certain facts touching upon the appearance of the new star—as well as the Cognitive darkness and the attack upon Fenz—that I may not reveal in public. However, there is no prohibition of which I am aware that legitimately prevents me from discussing them in private." His aggressive smile made its reappearance as he saw Gless Vallage go rigid with surprise and anger. "Those of you who desire additional information—in short, those who desire the truth—are invited to attend me at my lodgings in the Mauranyza Dome tomorrow morning upon the stroke of nine. All are welcome."

Gless Vallage was speechless. So too were most of the courtiers. Lady Karavise was first to break the silence. "I will hear you, sir," she said levelly. Her father gazed at her in blue-eyed wonder.

And Devras Har Fennahar was struck with inspiration. What better means than this to prefer himself to the notice of the great? A wide golden path to wealth, acceptance and knowledge opened before him. The world was bathed in magical radiance, and the mists that fogged his glazed eyes were roseate. As if from a vast distance he heard his own voice proclaim with ringing enthusiasm, "I'll be there!"

Chapter Five

"How did your Lordship come to accept this invitation?"

"To tell you the truth, Grono, I'm not quite sure. Last night is a blur—I only remember bits and pieces. I don't regret it, though. What are you looking so glum about, anyway? You're the one who wanted me to go out and meet people. Well, I'm doing it."

"Very good, but I question the wisdom of your Lordship's choice. This Wate Basef person is a man of uncertain reputation. It is said that his contentiousness has cost him the favor of his superiors, prevented his advancement in the Select, even blunted the force of his Cognition. I have all this upon excellent authority."

"What authority?"

"Ixi Meep, the fishmonger in Old Market Square, a man of sound judgment and excellent character."

"Ah, a sage."

"More so than your precious Heselicus, sir. Master Devras, your association with this Wate Basef person will damage your standing in the eyes of the world, and that you cannot afford."

"Oh, nonsense. You worry too much. You're probably peeved that I'm dragging you up all these stairs."

Devras and Grono were climbing the stairway that hugged the inner curve of the Mauranyza Dome. Raith Wate Basef's lodgings occupied the entire top story of the structure, and it was a long way up. The morning sun shone muted through the heavy red glass of the Dome, washing the stairwell with strange red light. Devras could look straight through the wall to behold Lanthi Ume spread out below him, her palaces unnaturally incarnadined, her canals apparently brimming with wine.

Ka Nebbinon Bell was tolling the last stroke of nine when they reached Wate Basef's door. The savant, rumpled and haggard with sleeplessness, admitted them at once.

Wate Basef's lodgings consisted of a single gigantic chamber shaped like an inverted red bowl. Great panes of colorless glass

43

set into the walls and ceiling admitted natural light. The furnishing included an unmade bed, a few sagging armchairs, battered cabinets, bookcases, and a huge circular work table. Every horizontal surface was buried beneath a clutter of papers, books, tools, soiled clothing, discarded bed linens and dirty dishes. Grono's wattles quivered at the sight, and his lips took on a lemon-sucking pucker. With obvious effort, he maintained silence.

In the least disreputable of the chairs sat the Lady Karavise Dil Shonnet, beautifully straight-spined and very smartly turned out in gray-green velvet morning attire. As the newcomers entered, she favored them with a cool, appraising stare. Wate Basef made the appropriate introductions, and Grono's scowl was instantly transformed. Turning a beatific countenance upon the Duke's daughter, the valet exclaimed, "Truly Fortune favors my noble young master! Your Ladyship's providential presence is as the sunlight banishing the dark night of Injustice!"

Karavise's brows rose.

"Yes, Madam!" Grono continued unabashed. "It is to you in your sweet womanly compassion that my young master may turn in his hour of trial. Your Ladyship, my master is the rightful Lord Har Fennahar, heir to the title and all the Fennahar estates. Hitherto his claim has gone unrecognized by the Duke Bofus, and yet I have no doubt that your intercession—"

"Grono!" Devras gritted in an agony of embarrassment.

"Pardon me, my lord, but I must speak. Your Ladyship, my master has written to his Grace your father no less than five times," the valet charged on. "His requests for an audience have been ignored, his correspondence has gone unacknowledged. Madam, my young master's cause is just, and yet he must live in misery—"

"*Grono!* Enough!" Devras pleaded, red-faced. "This is not the time or place!"

"I beg to differ, Master Devras! If you will not speak on your own behalf, then I—"

"I apologize for my valet," Devras broke in desperately. "He presumes greatly upon your good nature—"

"Is his statement accurate?" Karavise inquired gravely, large eyes glinting with amusement.

"Yes, but I wouldn't have chosen this moment—"

"Then we must direct your claim to his Grace's attention." She turned to the valet. "Grono, if Master Har Fennahar's claim is legitimate, then I will assist him. However, as your master has rightly observed, it is neither the time nor place to address the

44

issue. We have come here today to confer with the Cognizant Wate Basef. Cognizance, I believe you've certain information to impart?"

"I do, Madam, but I'd expected more people present to receive it. Can they be so indifferent?" asked Wate Basef.

"Less indifferent than skeptical. Following your departure last night, Preeminence Gless Vallage addressed the courtiers. He assured them that the danger is imaginary, and went on to explain that you have been in heavy spirits of late, due to your failure to win advancement within the ranks of the Select. In brief, he cast doubt upon the soundness of your reason," Karavise concluded dryly.

"Most present seemed to believe him, to the best of my recollection," Devras added. "And that included the Duke."

"His Grace *will* trust in Vallage," Karavise conceded, low voice curiously metallic.

"He might as well trust in a patch of quicksand," observed Wate Basef.

Karavise smiled, but Grono did not. "Intolerable, sir!" the valet protested. "I cannot hold my peace in the face of slander! Preeminence Gless Vallage, scion of an ancient House, deserves credit for his accomplishments no less than reverence for his nobility. Surely he is admired and respected by all!"

"Not quite all," Wate Basef replied with a cackle.

"And who are you to malign him, sir? You, after all, are his subordinate in rank and his inferior in the Select."

"That finishes it, Grono!" Devras exclaimed, humiliated beyond endurance. "You may return to our lodgings and wait for me there." The valet gaped at him, astounded.

"Oh, don't send him away for speaking the truth, lad," Wate Basef advised. "Perhaps when he knows the facts, friend Grono will come around to my way of thinking. Let us put it to the test. To begin with, are you two from Szar familiar with the name of the Lanthian savant Terrs Fal Grizhni?"

"Certainly," replied Devras, who knew history as few men knew it. "As the story goes, Fal Grizhni was Preeminent of the Select during the reign of the Duke Povon Dil Shonnet. He was a great savant and a wicked one—said to be a King of Demons, hated by one and all. In his malevolence and lust for power, he plotted to murder the good Duke. His treason was discovered, his palace was razed, and Grizhni himself was slain by Ducal Guardsmen. It's said that he filled the cellar in which he was finally cornered with black fire, and summoned black demons to fight in his defense. The virtue of the Guardsmen triumphed,

45

however, and Fal Grizhni died cursing all of humanity. I'd judge that most of this tale is apocryphal, but there's probably a kernel of truth in it."

"Correct." Wate Basef nodded. "And the kernel with which we need concern ourselves comprises those maledictions of his, which, as it happens, were rather specific. Evidently resorting to the highest possible Cognition, Fal Grizhni—perhaps the greatest savant of all time—inflicted a curse of darkness upon the island of Dalyon. This malignant shadow, inhabited by creatures hostile to mankind, is destined to appear, so Grizhni prophesied, when a star shines at noon and a lion gives birth to a dragon."

"How do you know this?" Karavise asked.

"I discovered a document in the Selectic Archives," Wate Basef told her. "It was a record of the inquest held following the destruction of Grizhni Palace, and it was written in the hand of Preeminence Jinzin Farni, who was Terrs Fal Grizhni's immediate successor. Several of the Guardsmen taking part in the attack testified at the inquest, and thus we have a presumably reliable account of Fal Grizhni's last moments, his threats and final prophecies."

"What did you do with the information?" Devras asked.

"In accordance with regulations I turned the transcript over to my superior in the Select, Preeminence Gless Vallage, who simply let the matter drop. To be fair to Vallage, there was virtually nothing he *could* do with it, for as matters now stand, I confess we're nearly helpless. Only if we had some knowledge of Grizhni's technique could we hope to undo his work, and even then it would take a savant of unusual ability to accomplish the task. At any rate," Wate Basef continued, "the months passed without incident, and my misgivings subsided. There seemed no immediate cause for alarm and perhaps the danger would never materialize, or so I told myself. This sense of false security was shaken when the diurnal star appeared several weeks ago. Very shortly thereafter, the Select became aware of Cognitive activity —inexplicable, intensely powerful activity—far inland. When I attempted to raise this issue at a Congress of the Select, Vallage refused to open the floor to discussion, thus preventing me from addressing the Council. Convinced at this point that I needed fresh ammunition, I returned to search the Selectic Archives, and that's when I struck gold."

From the welter atop the work table, Wate Basef plucked an ancient, yellowing sheet of parchment. "I found this letter addressed to Preeminence Jinzin Farni. The seals were still unbroken. After I opened the letter, noted the date, and checked it against Selectic records, the reason became obvious—Preeminence Farni died several days before the communication reached him, and thus it had lain among his papers, untouched and unread for all these years. The letter came from the city-state of Szar, and it was written by one Rillif Har Fennahar."

"My Great-to-the-nth-power Grandfather Rillif?" exclaimed Devras, much amazed. "The explorer?"

"The same, lad, and I've high hopes that you as his descendant may be able to augment our store of information. No doubt all three of you will want to examine the letter, but to save time I'll summarize the contents. It would seem that Devras's ancestor Rillif Har Fennahar was nephew to Preeminence Jinzin Farni. Preeminence Farni—evidently no fool—shared my apprehension concerning Fal Grizhni's malediction. Like me, he was helpless to address the problem without some understanding of his predecessor's Cognitive methods. Unlike me, he had an idea where such knowledge might be found. On the basis of some sort of evidence or information that has not come down to us, Farni guessed that Fal Grizhni's records and workbooks were hidden away in the caverns of the Nazara Sin. I don't know how Farni reached that conclusion, but the old boy was perfectly correct. He dispatched his nephew Rillif to the caverns to search for the records. And according to this letter, Rillif found them."

"In that case," concluded Karavise, who had followed the narrative closely, "we may assume that Rillif Har Fennahar carried Fal Grizhni's records back to Lanthi Ume and presented them to Preeminence Jinzin Farni's successor."

"Unfortunately not. Rillif found the records—in this letter he describes the notebook, scroll, golden plaque and so forth—but he wasn't able to carry them from the caverns. The inhabitants stopped him."

"Inhabitants?" inquired Devras, entranced. "Cave Men?"

"Not Men," Wate Basef explained. "The caves that underlie so much of this island are inhabited by the Vardruls—shy, intelligent, humanoid creatures known to the ignorant as the 'White Demons of the Caverns.' In an earlier age, certain members of the Select undertook to cultivate the friendship of these beings. Obviously Fal Grizhni must have been one of them, since he entrusted his life's work to their care. At some point, however, catastrophe occurred. There seems to have been strife or upheaval of some kind, and the tenuous contact between Man and Vardrul was broken. Sealing the known entrances to their caverns, the Vardruls sequestered themselves, and down through the years they have carefully shunned humanity. It was these Vardruls who foiled the efforts of Rillif Har Fennahar. Following his expulsion from the caverns, Rillif did not return to Lanthi Ume, but seems to have proceeded directly to Szar, from whence he wrote to his Preeminent uncle."

"That is peculiar. Why didn't he come home?" asked Karavise.

"I don't know, and the letter doesn't explain it. In fact, it would almost appear that Rillif wrote under some sort of constraint—as if, perhaps, he feared that his correspondence might fall into the wrong hands. He said—let me see—" Wate Basef scanned the parchment swiftly. "He wrote:

> 'For reasons that you surely understand very well, I must not return to Lanthi Ume. The title of Lord Har Fennahar may pass to my younger brother Frev, who is far more fit than I to carry it. Do not concern yourself over this, Uncle Jin, for I do not regret it in the least. What I have gained is worth more to me than ten thousand such titles.' "

"The proof—the proof! Rillif Har Fennahar was indeed the rightful lord, and his title descends directly to my young Master Devras!" Grono exulted. "I knew it, I knew it was so! Oh, I knew it!"

"Probably true, but let us speak of it another time," Wate Basef suggested. "To conclude the matter of the letter, Rillif writes of his marriage to some woman referred to only as 'Verran,' expresses his great joy and all that nonsense, then returns to issues of import near the end. He finishes off:

> 'Fal Grizhni's records remain in the caverns—quite safe, but inaccessible. Rest assured that the Vardruls will not relinquish them. For the present, I am powerless to act further on your behalf. Thus it is to be hoped that you will enlist the aid of all the Select, whose collective ingenuity combined with High Cognition may succeed where I have failed in securing the means to avert the danger that threatens all of Dalyon. If willing energy and hardihood may serve to advance this endeavor, know that you may rely on the active assistance of
>
> Your Affectionate Nephew,
> Rillif Har Fennahar'

"Of course," Wate Basef remarked, "Farni didn't live to follow his nephew's sensible advice. Quite likely, Rillif never knew that—overseas correspondence in his day was nearly impossible, and he had no Cognition to aid him. He never would have known that his letter went unread—until now."

"And now?" asked Karavise. "You'll inform the Select?"

"Easier said than done," Wate Basef told her. "When I discovered Rillif Har Fennahar's letter, I appropriated the original and delivered a copy to Gless Vallage, as I judged this prudent. Rather than referring the matter to the Council of the Select, Vallage cited his authority as Preeminence to command my silence and to demand the original of the letter. I've refused to give it to him, and there the matter rests."

His listeners stared.

At last Devras observed, "That makes no sense at all."

"Muckraking! Mudslinging!" Grono muttered.

And Karavise inquired coolly, "Why would his Preeminence wish to suppress information? What could he gain by it?"

"I don't know," Wate Basef admitted. "He's ambitious, and perhaps fears the affair reflects discredit upon the Select and their leader, or something of the sort. I haven't the time or inclination to plumb the sewer of Vallage's mind. All I care about now is finding Fal Grizhni's records, for our time is running out quickly. The prophecies have been fulfilled. A star shines at noon. I don't know anything about the lion and dragon, but they must be somewhere, for the poisonous darkness has appeared, and it's spreading outward toward the sea. If we don't succeed in arresting its progress, then we may as well start planning our flight from Dalyon right now, for the entire island will soon be lost. I need whatever help I can find. May I expect your support?"

The silence that greeted this query was broken by the sound of a knock on the chamber door.

"Reinforcements. Excellent." Wate Basef opened the door to find a group of armed Selectic Guardsmen waiting upon his threshold. With them stood a short, slight woman of indeterminate age, clothed in masculine garments of gray merino. Her yellow, almost phosphorescent cat's eyes were set incongruously in a pointed murine face. Upon her shoulder twitched and chittered a flesh-colored rodentlike creature with great, hypertrophic ears.

"Well, Snarp," Wate Basef addressed the woman uneasily.

"Well, Basef," replied Snarp, her voice a flat monotone.

The tall commander of the Guards snapped a sharp salute. "The Cognizant Raith Wate Basef?" he inquired courteously.

Wate Basef nodded.

"Nerrel, Captain of Selectic Guardsmen. I regret to inform you, sir, that his Preeminence Gless Vallage has ordered your confinement. You are not to leave your apartment."

"That's ridiculous," replied Wate Basef, after a brief, stunned pause. "What does that two-faced politicking prestidigitator think he's doing?"

"You are confined to your quarters, sir, until such time as you are brought before the Council of the Select on charges."

"Before the Council! On what charges, might I ask?"

"The primary charge against you is disclosure of secret information, contrary to the interests of the Select. Secondary charges include extreme insubordination; public behavior reflecting discreditably upon the Select; and sundry minor infractions of the Code of the Select."

"Ha! Those charges will never stick."

"I sincerely hope not, sir," Nerrel returned, not unsympathetically.

"Look, Captain," Wate Basef attempted, "are you aware that Gless Vallage has no legal authority whatever to order my confinement? He can drag me before the Council if he's fool enough to think it will do him any good, but he doesn't have the right to lock me up."

"I don't know anything about that, sir."

"Snarp, tell him," Wate Basef requested.

Snarp was mute.

"Believe it, Captain," the savant urged. "If the Council judges me guilty, then I can be fined, suspended or expelled from the Select. Upon expulsion I can, if the situation warrants, be turned over to Ducal authorities for prosecution. But Vallage himself can't arrest me."

"He's right," Lady Karavise agreed. "His Preeminence usurps Ducal authority. And," she added in glacial anger, "he'll answer for it. Captain, you will return to Gless Vallage and inform him that his actions are illegal."

"I'd like to tell him that myself." Wate Basef made a move toward the door.

"I'm sorry sir, but you can't leave." Nerrel neatly blocked him.

"Captain, do you know who I am?" asked Karavise.

"Yes, Ma'am," Nerrel replied respectfully.

"I have instructed you to release the Cognizant Wate Basef. Do you not acknowledge my authority to issue such orders?"

"To be honest, Ma'am, I'm not sure about that."

50

"Snarp, tell him," Wate Basef prompted.

In silence Snarp lifted a skinny hand to caress the creature jittering upon her shoulder.

"I see." Karavise's eyes narrowed. "In that case, would you honor the authority of a release order in writing, signed by the Duke? Would that satisfy your scruples, Captain?"

"Completely satisfy them, Ma'am."

"Then I will bring one. Cognizance Wate Basef, be assured you'll have your freedom shortly. Master Har Fennahar, and Grono, I trust we'll meet again. And as for Preeminence Gless Vallage, he'll hear more of this." Turning to the Guardsmen, Karavise commanded, "Stand aside."

The men were swift to obey. For a moment Snarp pondered and then reluctantly stepped back. Lady Karavise swept from the room like a cold velvet breeze, and the Guards closed ranks behind her.

"She has done the right thing," Grono informed his master sotto voce. "And you should follow her Ladyship's example. Sir, my initial fears were well founded! This Wate Basef person is an unsavory character, and you will be tainted by association if you remain in his company! For the sake of the Har Fennahar name and reputation, I must urge your Lordship to come away at once!"

"Might be easier said than done, Grono," Devras replied with a bemused shrug. He turned to Nerrel. "Captain, are my valet and I free to go?"

Nerrel hesitated.

And Snarp said, "No."

The private dombulis carrying Lady Karavise sped swiftly along the bright arteries of Lanthi Ume. Leaning back on a pile of cushions, the young woman folded her arms tightly. Her lips were compressed, her eyes filled with frank worry as she gazed up at the red star smoldering in the blue sky overhead. The worry intensified as her regard shifted from sky to embankment, and she studied the composition of the crowds upon the shore, noting the prevalence of wretched beggars and the arrogant presence of Lammish soldiers. At length she was borne to the Ducal moorings, where the dombulman assisted her to land.

"Wait here," she commanded, and entered the palace in search of her father. She discovered Duke Bofus in his office, where he sat building a castle of cards.

"Father!" exclaimed Karavise, advancing into the room. "I need your help."

51

The Duke laid his cards aside at once. "Why certainly, my dear," he replied, paternal concern darkening his features. "What's the matter?"

"Raith Wate Basef has been arrested."

"He has? Really? What's he done now?"

"Nothing, Father. Nothing at all. He must be released."

"Why surely, my dear, if that's what will make you happy. How do we release him?"

"You need only sign an order. I'll write it out and you sign it. And while I'm about it, I'd better write one for Devras Har Fennahar, just in case."

"Who?"

"Devras Har Fennahar. Isn't that name familiar to you? He's a very young man—only eighteen or so—recently arrived from Szar, and he claims to be the last of his family, the rightful Lord Har Fennahar. I've no idea whether it's true or not. His manner very much predisposes one in his favor, but of course, that's no way to judge. Anyway, he claims to have written you requesting an audience five times within the last two months."

"Five times! Has he? Has he really? Gad, he must be industrious!"

"You never heard from him? I can't understand—" As she spoke, Karavise whipped efficiently through the correspondence overspilling the basket atop the Duke's desk. Presently she discovered a letter, its unbroken seal bearing the famous Har Fennahar crest. Shortly thereafter she exhumed another, and then another. "Father, these letters are weeks old! You've never even read them?"

Duke Bofus stirred uncomfortably. "Now, Kara, you're not going to scold?" he inquired. "There are so many letters, and they're all from people wanting things from me, and if I kept up with them, I'd be reading letters all day long. Is that what life is all about? Don't worry, my dear. I'll get to young what's-his-name's letters, I promise. In fact, if it will please you, I'll even look at them now—"

"Father, it would please me most to see Raith Wate Basef and young Har Fennahar restored to freedom. You'll do it?" Quill in hand, Karavise was scribbling a release order.

"Of course. But it's very puzzling," the Duke mused. "I'll take my oath *I* never ordered them arrested."

"I know you didn't. Gless Vallage ordered it, and he doesn't have the right. Gless Vallage is going to regret it."

"Gless Vallage had Wate Basef and what's-his-name locked up? Well"—the Duke took a thoughtful sip of his sweetened posset—"maybe we'd better not be hasty about this. If Gless Vallage did it, he must have his reasons. He's a mighty clever man, dear."

"Oh, that he is—I'm very well aware of it. Father, you're missing the point! Gless Vallage can't order the arrest of any citizen—that's your prerogative. He's usurping your authority, don't you see that? Beyond that, Wate Basef happens to be innocent of any crime. You have to free him, Father."

"Well, I'd certainly like to do that, dear, but I don't know. I just don't know. I think I'd better ask Gless Vallage about it first. It's too bad I didn't know about this an hour ago. I could have talked to him about it while he was here."

"Vallage was here an hour ago? What did that gray snake want?"

The Duke regarded his daughter in pained astonishment. "Kara, dear, I don't like to hear you speak that way," he remonstrated mildly. "It's not very nice. Gless Vallage is a mighty fine man. Why don't you like him?"

"He's a liar, a toady, a hypocrite, and it makes my skin crawl to be in the same room with him, but those are only minor details. Far more to the point—I think he's politically dangerous. He's got all the resources of the Select at his disposal, and that's too much power for any subject as ambitious as Vallage to own. He's treacherous, and I suspect he'd sell you to your enemies in half a second, or sink a knife in your back himself, if he thought he stood to gain by it. He wants too much when he's already got too much. Does that answer you, Father?"

Duke Bofus smiled. "Now, Kara, my dear, you mustn't fret. You're my clever girl, but this time you're wrong, quite wrong! Gless Vallage is our friend. I know this, for he has shown his kindness in a thousand ways. And you shouldn't dislike our friend, dear, because he thinks very highly of you. He's always saying nice things about you. Between the two of us, I think he's fond of you. You know, Kara—I want you to have a happy life. That's more important to me than anything." The Duke's eyes—so like his daughter's eyes in shape and color, so utterly unlike in expression—misted over. "A young woman needs someone to look after her, and I—well, I won't be here forever. Now, Gless Vallage's wife died last year—"

"Fell down the stairs, didn't she?" interjected Karavise absently. "Or was she pushed?"

"He's a mighty eligible man, dear, and I've often wished that you and he—"

"Oh, no. No. No!" Karavise's entire body stiffened. "I won't discuss it!"

"Now, darling—"

"In any case, if you want to betroth me to someone, the Duke of Hurba would be a much better choice. An alliance with Hurba would be most advantageous at this time. With the Hurbanese military strength to back us, we'd finally be in a position to boot those Lammish troops out of the Vayno and out of Lanthi Ume. You realize that the Lammish garrison exerts a stranglehold upon—"

"Kara, darling, you cannot marry the Duke of Hurba! You would then be obliged to reside in Hurba, and it is so far away! As for the Duke, he beats his servants and he stinks of garlic. He is not a gentleman, and I fear you wouldn't be happy as his wife."

"I wouldn't become his wife—there's no need to go to such extremes as that. A simple betrothal would suit our present purposes. And once the Lammish are out of our city, we'd find a way to rid ourselves of Hurba, or to put him off indefinitely, whichever seems preferable."

"Oh, my Kara, you cannot know how cold that sounds—how heartless. After all, the Duke of Hurba is a man, and it cannot be right to trifle with his feelings—"

"It's right if the interests of Lanthi Ume demand it. Our city's plight grows desperate. As for the Duke of Hurba, rest assured he has no more affection for me than I for him, and his feelings, if he has any, will scarcely be wounded—"

"You cannot know that, my dear, and it is wrong to use other human beings, for any purpose, ever. I should be distressed if I believed you spoke in earnest."

Karavise sighed.

"No," the Duke continued, "my darling girl would do well to marry a Lanthian gentleman, and then she will remain here in her own city, near her loving father. Now, Gless Vallage—"

"Yes, you said he visited you today. What did he want?"

"He brought word of another attack upon an inland settlement, similar to the incident at Fenz, wherever that is." The Duke did not note his daughter's sudden intense stillness. "Another village was destroyed in the dark. Gless Vallage was kind enough to bring the news himself, for he didn't wish me misled by distorted rumors and unreliable reports. Vallage informed me that the Select will deal with the matter. In fact, he himself will direct the investigation, which will be conducted in all discretion, to avoid

54

arousing public alarm. He was most considerate, most reassuring."

"He was, was he?" Karavise's voice was grim. She let fall the quill and came to stand before her father. "Pay attention to this. Those attacks are important. We cannot afford to ignore them."

"Oh, my dear, they are so very far away. And those inland settlements are constantly beset with danger—that is nothing new, alas!"

"Lanthi Ume is in danger. All of Dalyon is in danger. It all confirms what Wate Basef has told me—"

"We're back to Wate Basef again?"

"Yes. You must release him, Father! And you must hear what he has to say, preferably today. And patrols must be dispatched inland—"

"Now, darling, I can't do all of that," replied Duke Bofus peaceably.

"Can't? What do you mean, 'can't'? Why not?"

"Because I promised Gless Vallage that I won't take action in this matter without consulting him. In view of his friendship and devotion to my interests, I felt it was the least I could do."

"But Father—*you're* the ruler here!"

"I've given my word, dear. You wouldn't wish to see me break it?"

"Just speak to Wate Basef. Hear what he has to say."

"I can't very well do that, can I, if he's been arrested? But I shall discuss the case with Gless Vallage at the earliest opportunity. If Vallage has acted wrongly, he will see the error of his ways, and Basef will surely be released. You see, Kara, I know that everything will turn out for the best in the end, even if it doesn't seem so now. Whatever happens was *meant* to happen."

Karavise ground her teeth in frustration. "But Father—" she protested.

"Now I want you to stop worrying, my dear, because it will upset your digestion. All's well, you'll see." The Duke picked up his drink and took a swallow. "This posset is delicious. Would you like some?"

"But *Father*—" Karavise's normally pale face was flushed with wrath. "Won't you even—"

"Don't scowl, dear, it grieves me. I know what will cheer my lovely girl. I'll buy you a new necklace. Would you like that? Gless Vallage will dine with us this evening, and I want you to look pretty for him."

"*Damn* Gless Vallage!" Karavise exploded.

The Duke looked on in bewilderment as his daughter stormed out of the room, slamming the door behind her.

Silence reigned beneath the red glass bowl at the summit of the Mauranyza Dome. Around the circular work table idled Raith Wate Basef, Devras Har Fennahar and Grono. Between these three and the exit stood Captain Nerrel and his Selectic Guards. Off to one side, apart from the others, Mistress Snarp lingered like a patch of fog.

The prisoners were playing at Antislez with a deck of Obranese cards. Sunlight streaming through the windows gleamed on Wate Basef's bald skull, glinted on Grono's spectacles, struck sparks off the silver Har Fennahar bracelet on Devras's wrist. The three men sipped beakers of tea and frowned over their cards.

At last Devras addressed his host in a low voice that did not escape the attention of the Guards. "She's been gone for three hours now."

"Patience," Wate Basef advised, without lifting his eyes from his cards. "King takes your Prince. Down two in the oubliette. Discard, Grono."

Grono grudgingly relinquished a card. As his host left the table to replenish the teapot, the valet addressed his master in an urgent whisper. "May I suggest to your Lordship that this misunderstanding between Cognizance Wate Basef and Preeminence Gless Vallage is none of your Lordship's concern?"

"Looks like we're in it now, Grono," Devras answered equably. "King plays Ten. No discard."

"Not so, Master Devras! Your Lordship need only dispatch a brief message of explanation and contrition to Preeminence Gless Vallage. In view of your Lordship's youth, inexperience, and the regrettable influence of the bad company into which your Lordship has inadvertently fallen, I'm certain his Preeminence will consent to pardon—"

"I don't think I'll do that. I want to find out more about all this. After all, how could I in good conscience seek the privileges of Lanthian nobility without assuming its obligations? As Zebbefore so rightly noted, 'Man's greatest debts are paid in coin worth more than gold, and such payment paradoxically enriches the debtor.'"

"That pen-pushing pig Zebbefore has poisoned your Lordship's mind!" Grono's reply, half-stifled with passion, was nonetheless overheard by Wate Basef, who cackled aloud. The valet turned on him indignantly. "Make sport, sir, make sport! I dismiss your hyena-laughter with the contempt it deserves!"

"I assure you, friend Grono, I don't find our present situation comical." Wate Basef returned to the table, poured fresh tea and picked up his cards. "Executioner over King, Queen, Prince and Envoy. Oubliette harrowed in red."

The game was cut short by the return of Lady Karavise, who entered the chamber composed as usual, but tense about the eyes and nostrils.

"Did the Duke sign?" Wate Basef inquired without preamble.

"No. I couldn't get him to do it." She appeared astonished at her parent's unwonted intractability. "He says he won't make a move without consulting Gless Vallage. I'm not sure how long it will take me to change his mind."

"I can't understand Preeminence Vallage," Devras mused. "Surely he doesn't want Lanthi Ume destroyed?"

"No. He wouldn't wish harm upon the city he so earnestly desires to rule," Karavise agreed thoughtfully. "Self-interest dictates his loyalty, and therefore his behavior mystifies me."

"Let us forget his Preeminence for now," Wate Basef suggested. "We've matters of greater significance to consider. Will the three of you come with me? There's something I must show you." Without awaiting reply, he rose and repaired to the far side of the room, where he began clearing the floor of clutter. After a moment the others followed, to join in removing the last of the dishes and linens, thus uncovering a great hexagonal slab of black glass. Beneath the polished surface, thousands of golden flecks glittered like a galaxy, seeming by some trick of design to extend an immeasurable distance.

Wate Basef answered the unspoken question. "It's called an *ophelu*—that is, an old Krunian glass of enlightenment. Who stands on the glass and performs an invocation to Krun is vouchsafed visions. It's my hope we may witness the destruction of Fenz, which could tell us much. Are you willing?"

Confused affirmative mumbles.

"Step onto the glass, then. All of you. You too, Grono. Come on." When all four stood upon the ophelu, Wate Basef produced a tiny jar full of white crystalline matter, depositing small heaps of the stuff at the vertices of the hexagon.

"What's that?" demanded Grono uneasily.

"Yes, what is it, sir?" inquired Captain Nerrel, who had drawn near and now watched closely.

"Only incense, Captain. Part of our invocation, and quite harmless," Wate Basef explained.

"Stop him," Snarp commanded.

"Better let me see that, sir," suggested the Captain.

"Certainly." Basef dropped a pinch of powder into the out-stretched palm of Nerrel, who examined the substance in puzzlement.

"Stop him," Snarp repeated.

Wate Basef bowed his head and spoke. As the rhythmic syllables flew from his lips, the six powdery mounds ignited. Flames leapt and circled the ophelu. Thick white vapors arose.

Devras watched in admiration as Raith Wate Basef, whose greatest enemies had to acknowledge his Cognitive force, stood chanting the ancient invocation to Krun. In vain, however, he awaited the promised vision of Fenz. The vapors thickened and changed, whitened and whirled in crazy spirals. Through the roiling mists, the red glass chamber and all its furnishings seemed to dance a Linniana. He caught a flashing glimpse of Guardsmen racing across the room. Nerrel stood near, blade in hand, mouth wide open and yelling, but the Captain's words were inaudible. And then all of it—glass dome, furniture, guards, weapons, Snarp's pointed face and all—retreated, faded away and vanished in a rush of snow-white wind. Devras felt himself snatched up and flung violently through blind white space, hurtling over and over helplessly as if caught in a breaking wave. His eyes snapped shut, his single cry of alarm was lost in the roar of a Cognitive hurricane, and then it was over and he was set down brusquely in a wholly unfamiliar place.

Chapter Six

Devras cautiously opened his eyes. He stood on a hexagonal slab of black glass set into the floor of a quiet stone chamber. A cold, fresh breeze blowing in through the open window carried the scent of open spaces. Close beside him stood Raith Wate Basef, head bowed. Lady Karavise clutched her plumed hat firmly to her head. Grono still leaned on his cane.

Grono was first to recover the power of speech. Eyes glaring wildly, he turned on Wate Basef. *"What have you done to us? Explain yourself, sir! Where are we? Answer! WHAT HAVE YOU DONE?"*

"I've taken the liberty of removing you people from Mauranyza Dome," the savant replied, stepping from the glass. "We stand in my workroom at Castle Io Wesha, a few leagues outside of Lanthi Ume. Gentleman and Madam, I bid you welcome to my house."

The courtesy of the greeting did not mollify Grono. "How dare you, sir?" the valet demanded, white hair almost bristling. "How *dare* you pick us up and shift us about as if we were so many sacks of turnips? You have carried us off against our will —you have kidnapped us, sir! Yes, you have kidnapped us, but we know how to defend ourselves. We do not fear your cursed sorceries!"

"I apologize for the lack of ceremony," Wate Basef conceded, straight-faced. "In my own defense, I can only point out that no other method would have served so well. However, I assure you there is nothing to fear—"

"I do not fear, sir. I am outraged! You have in your mad folly kidnapped a noble lady, the future Duchess of Lanthi Ume. Beyond that, you work the ruination of my young Master Devras —a most virtuous and promising lord, but lamentably ignorant of the world and a fit victim to your blandishments! You have angered the Select, their hand is raised against you, and now you seek to involve my master in your sordid affairs. But I say to you, it shall not be! You shall not drag him down with you, for

59

I'll prevent it! The Lord Har Fennahar will not share in your disgrace! I demand that you return us to Lanthi Ume at once!" Lifting his heavy stick, Grono menaced the astounded savant.

"That's enough, Grono!" Devras's uncharacteristically angry tone halted the valet in mid-gesture. "You don't know what you're doing. Cognizance Wate Basef was both right and resourceful in bringing us here. I'm now convinced that his concerns are legitimate, and I'm willing to help him if I can. Keep that in mind, and govern your behavior accordingly."

Grono stared at him, stricken. "Master Devras, I cannot stand idly by while you destroy your own life and hopes, through youthful naiveté! Sir, am I to watch you totter upon the verge of a precipice, without attempting to draw you from the brink?"

"Your intentions are noble, my dear friend, but it is time I made my own decisions."

"Your Lordship, do but consider. Even now, it is not too late. I'm sure that a direct appeal to his Preeminence Gless Vallage— and a promise of good behavior—"

"Grono. You must accept it. I want to be here."

The valet turned imploringly to Karavise. "Madam, you possess knowledge of the world. Will you not school my poor young master by your wise example? Command this kidnapper to restore us to the city. He will not dare to disobey *you*."

"I suspect he would dare," Karavise replied with a slight smile. "But we shall not put it to the test. Like your master, I'm increasingly inclined to trust in Cognizance Wate Basef's judgment and to share in his fears. At the very least the matter demands further investigation, and I do not wish to return to Lanthi Ume at this time. I am sorry, Grono."

His last hope dashed, the valet eyed his master in grief and frustration. Noting the genuinely pained expression, Wate Basef's habitual smirk faded, and he observed not unkindly, "Grono, if I am a kidnapper, at least I'm no gaoler. I won't hold you here against your will. You've but to say the word, and I'll send you back to the Mauranyza Dome. The Guardsmen will question you, but they won't hurt you. Do you want to go?"

Grono straightened and turned to face his foe. "No, Cognizance," he replied with dignity. "I will stay here. If my Lord Har Fennahar is set upon this reckless course, he shall not pursue it without benefit of my counsel. I do not approve. But I remain with his Lordship."

"Excellent. And now," suggested Wate Basef, disregarding the valet's accusatory stare, "we can finish our conversation in peace." Leading his guests out of the workroom and down a flight of granite stairs, he brought them to his own chambers, one of which contained a table and chairs, with a fire already laid upon the grate. Wate Basef summoned a servant, ordered the fire lit and a meal prepared. He was swiftly obeyed. The household retainers, well accustomed to their master's sudden comings and goings, maintained Io Wesha in a state of perpetual readiness. Within minutes the room was warm, the table was set, and dishes of cold mutton, bread and fruit appeared thereon. The guests had barely begun to eat before their host informed them, "We've little time to plan or prepare. They're sure to find us here, perhaps before tomorrow morning."

Silence greeted this announcement.

"It won't take the Selectic Guardsmen long to guess where we've gone, once they examine that ophelu," Wate Basef explained. "Snarp is certain to know what it is."

"Who is that Snarp woman?" Karavise inquired with a hint of disdain.

"Mistress Snarp is the designated Enforcer of the Select, whose task it is to effect the judgments and penalties of the Council, or in many unacknowledged instances, the personal vendettas of his Preeminence. She possesses the qualities requisite to her position—dedication, ruthlessness, fanatical devotion to duty. She's known as an expert in the arts of detection and pursuit, she understands all weaponry, and she is unquestionably a mistress of murder. She has a keen mind and some small competence in the use of Cognitive artifacts, as Vallage has unfortunately seen fit to instruct her. She has no human ties or affections. If she possesses any weakness at all, it is for her pet quibbid—the ratlike thing with the ears that sits on her shoulder. Some benighted folk claim that the quibbid is Snarp's own child, the result of an incestuous union with her own father, a demon of Ert—which is such a pretty fancy that I wish I could believe it. Alas, Snarp's antecedents include no demons. Actually, I doubt that she possesses antecedents of any persuasion."

"What do you mean?" asked Devras.

"It's my belief that Snarp is a Cognitive creation, designed to serve the ends of Gless Vallage. Mind you, I can't prove this, but there are certain signs—anyway, I believe that Vallage constructed her in his workroom."

"Are you saying that woman isn't *alive*?"

"I'm saying she isn't quite human. All of you, beware of her."

"She would hardly presume to trouble *me*." Karavise's chin lifted haughtily.

"Perhaps not, but frankly I wouldn't care to risk it. Let's hope the question doesn't arise. Now—" Wate Basef pushed his half-eaten lunch aside. "Let us address the main issue. There's no further need for recapitulation, and thus the question becomes—how best to deal with the situation that now confronts us? To my mind, there's but one conclusion. We require the Cognitive writings of Terrs Fal Grizhni. Evidence suggests that these records may yet exist, hidden away in the caverns of the Vardruls. Hence it becomes necessary to retrace the footsteps of Devras's ancestor Rillif Har Fennahar. We must penetrate the caverns and succeed where Rillif failed in securing those records."

"Retrace Great-Grandfather Rillif's footsteps!" Devras's eyes were filled with light. "Prodigious. But how should we find our way to these caves? Didn't you tell us that the inhabitants have sealed the entrances?"

"You may be certain they didn't seal all the entrances," replied Wate Basef. "And I've maps that should help us."

"The inhabitants, these Vardruls," observed Karavise, "evidently have no love for mankind. We may expect no cooperation from them. Rillif certainly received none."

"Rillif had no Cognition to aid him. We are not similarly deprived."

"Perhaps Great-Grandfather wasn't altogether deprived. According to family tradition, his silver bracelet possessed unusual properties. Here it is." Devras slid the ornament from his wrist. "Sometimes it seems to heat, for no apparent reason. Other than that, I've never noticed anything extraordinary about it."

Wate Basef took the bracelet, examining the incised runes with interest. "Nice piece of work," he opined. "Select-crafted beyond doubt, and very old. That inscription in the early Selectic Code tells us that the bracelet warms in proximity to Cognitive articles. It would obviously have proved invaluable to Rillif Har Fennahar in his search through the caverns for the records and Cognitive aids of Fal Grizhni. It will serve us equally well." He returned the bracelet to its owner. "Did your ancestor leave anything more in terms of writings, maps, artifacts or the like?"

"Only the accounts of the explorations he undertook subsequent to his emigration. Apparently he had an active, long and full life. It's said he was fortunate in his marriage. His wife—a woman named Verran, described in the old family chronicles only as 'a fair Lanthian widow, who loved the sunlight'—bore him several children, whose names I can't recall offhand. And that's about all I know of Grandfather Rillif."

Wate Basef was disappointed. "I'd hoped there might be more information."

"No doubt you have need of it, sir," Grono observed. "Let us suppose that we humor your fancies—that we follow you to the caverns—that in the face of all difficulties we locate the writings you seek. What then? You have informed us that Terrs Fal Grizhni was the greatest savant ever to draw a breath. Are *you* his equal, sir? Are you equipped by nature or by Cognition to undo the master's work?"

Devras awaited an answering flood of smiling sarcasm. None was forthcoming, and he glanced at his host in surprise. Wate Basef's face was unwontedly expressionless. After a brief pause the savant replied, "I can't be certain. There's a fair chance I may succeed, and I will do my best. Beyond that, there's none in Lanthi Ume, with the possible exception of Gless Vallage, more fit to attempt it."

For a moment, no one spoke. Even Grono seemed abashed. At last Karavise dispassionately changed the subject. "I am sure we've all considered the possibility of a connection between the legendary 'White Demons of the Caverns' and the vicious white creatures described by the Rider from Fenz."

"We may hope that no such connection exists, Madam," returned Wate Basef. "But it would be safest to proceed on the assumption that it does."

"Then they'll kill us if they find us in their caves."

"We can't know that, but it's a very real possibility. We must trust in the power of human Cognition over Vardrul zeal."

"But why should there be a link," inquired Devras, "between the Vardruls of the caves and the vengeful curses of Fal Grizhni? Grizhni may have been friend to the Vardruls, but that doesn't adequately explain it."

"No, it doesn't, and I can't enlighten you," confessed Wate Basef. "But we haven't leisure to ponder the question. Right now, if I may, I'm going to ask Grono to go downstairs and tell my retainers to ready the carriage and fill it with provisions to last six days or so. Tell them we're going to the Nazara Sin, and bid them include all necessary equipment. They'll know what to do."

"I do not take orders from you, sir." Grono's spine stiffened.

"Grono. *Please*," Devras urged.

"Very well, my lord. If *you* desire it." The valet turned and stalked rigidly from the room. Descending to the kitchen, he introduced himself to Wate Basef's household servants and began issuing orders. It was the first satisfaction he'd had all day.

During the valet's absence, the others plotted a furtive, Cognitively assisted infiltration of the caverns. Before an hour had passed, the discussion was interrupted. A quiet figure appeared in the doorway. Expecting the return of Grono, Devras turned casually to behold a short, slight person attired in gray merino. He started. Mistress Snarp stood on the threshold. Her hands rested in the pockets of her loose breeches. The quibbid twitched upon her shoulder, its little rodent face malevolent.

"Wate Basef," Snarp announced in her monotone voice, "I am taking you back to Lanthi Ume."

They stared at her, thunderstruck.

At last Wate Basef found his voice. "You came here alone, via ophelu?"

She ignored the question. "We will go now."

"I'm not going anywhere with you. Gless Vallage has no authority to order my arrest."

"'Authority' can take many forms." The flat quality of her voice did not alter, but an odd light glowed somewhere behind the yellow eyes.

"Snarp, you're trespassing on my property. I advise you to leave."

"We will leave together."

"You're wasting my time as well as your own."

"You have your answer, woman," Lady Karavise observed icily. "You may carry it back to your master Vallage. Now go."

"The rest of you do not matter," Snarp replied. She turned back to Wate Basef. "Must I compel you?"

Wate Basef looked at her and smiled. A close observer might have noted traces of perspiration upon the bearded face. Folding his arms, he leaned back in his chair. "Brave words. But your Guardsmen aren't with you now."

"I do not need them." Quick as sudden death, Snarp's right hand flashed out of her pocket, armed with something thin and glittering. Hardly pausing to aim, she threw. There was a fast shine of silver as a coil of Living Wire hissed through the air to settle about Raith Wate Basef's neck. Snarp's hand jerked, she spat a command and the noose tightened, biting deep into flesh. Wate Basef gasped for breath, and his eyes bulged. Deprived of speech, Cognition was also denied him. Clawing uselessly at the thing that choked him, the savant slid from the chair to his knees. His face swiftly darkened to purple-red, and a tracery of blood appeared upon his neck. The Wire sibilated, and the bristling quibbid shrieked.

Devras rose and sprang for Snarp. The woman saw him coming. Snatching her left hand from her pocket, she flung a second Living Wire with ambidextrous expertise. The Wire circled the young man's neck and tightened. Devras's hands flew to his throat, and he choked desperately. Dropping both Wires and detaching a pair of manacles from her belt, Mistress Snarp closed in on Raith Wate Basef.

Such was the scene that greeted Grono upon his return from the castle kitchen. The valet's response was prompt. Approaching Mistress Snarp from behind, he raised his cane to bring it thudding down upon the crown of her wide hat. Snarp pitched forward, hit the floor face down and lay still. As she fell, the quibbid sprang squealing from her shoulder and scuttled for the shadows under the table. With considerable effort Grono tore the Living Wire from his master's throat, while Karavise similarly aided Wate Basef.

Grono dashed the Wire to the floor. Instantly looping a noose at its anterior end, the creature coiled toward its victim. Grono struck with his cane—struck again and again until the Wire finally convulsed, corkscrewed and expired. The remaining Wire swiftly sought shelter beneath Snarp's prostrate body.

Despite the blood and welts that marked their throats, neither Devras nor Wate Basef was seriously injured. Recovery was swift, and the savant soon managed to inquire hoarsely, "Is she dead?"

Examining Snarp's inert form with distaste, Lady Karavise reported, "She's breathing."

"Good." Wate Basef's voice rasped painfully. "We'd best be out of here before she wakes."

Karavise threw him a startled glance, but her voice remained cool as she observed, "I see no need for such haste on this woman's account. Surely Castle Io Wesha possesses a secure chamber wherein she may be detained at our convenience?"

"No good." Wate Basef appeared regretful. "For one thing, she'll have informed the Selectic Guardsmen of her intentions. If Snarp doesn't return to Lanthi Ume within hours, Guardsmen will descend upon Io Wesha. My accomplices will be subject to Selectic prosecution. As daughter to the Duke, your Ladyship is beyond their power, but the same cannot be said of these other two—or, for that matter, of my household servants. The only way of immobilizing Mistress Snarp is to kill her, and that I am unwilling to do. All things considered, it's best we go at once. Grono"—he turned to the valet—"did you instruct my servants?"

"I did, sir. They seem a sensible lot, very sprightly fellows, but naturally they require time to complete the preparations—"

"They don't have it. Whatever they've got done at this point must serve."

"No, sir!" Grono faced the savant like a knight confronting a dragon. "It will not do! My master is ill and cannot travel yet."

"Yes I can," said Devras. His face was gray, but his eyes were bright.

"It is madness, sir! The carriage is scarcely equipped, the preparations aren't half complete—Oh, your Lordship, stop and think! This man is leading you astray, this man will be your ruin—"

"I'm going, Grono. Will you come with us?"

Quivering on the verge of impassioned reply, the valet paused to stare into the face of his calm but unwontedly resolute young master. Devras met the flaming regard pleasantly. Following an instant's electric silence, Grono conceded momentary defeat. "I will come. But under protest, your Lordship. Under extreme protest."

"If that's settled, let's look to the carriage," Wate Basef urged. At his feet Snarp stirred and groaned.

Together the four of them hurried from the chamber, down the stairs and through the great hall to emerge from the castle into blinding afternoon sunlight. Awaiting them in the courtyard was a battered, sturdy, inelegant carriage drawn by four horses. The groom was completing the final adjustments on the animals' harness, while the steward placed the last baskets of provisions inside under the seats. The luggage rack on the roof was piled with boxes and sacks.

"This is well done," Karavise approved, "but may we not save time by using the transportation device that carried us to this place?"

"No, Madam. We could only shuttle back and forth between the two sundered halves of the ophelu—that is the limit of the device's capability. The two halves are connected by a most extraordinary—but no, I'll explain it another time."

As Karavise, Devras and Grono entered the carriage, Wate Basef issued hurried last instructions to his servants. Twice he gestured toward the workroom window, but the others did not catch his words. Then the savant climbed to the box seat and took up the reins. The red mark still burned upon his neck, but his energy was unimpaired. He snapped the whip once, and they were off with a rattle.

The carriage passed under Io Wesha's great arched gateway, and out onto Morlin Hill, where the cold breezes blew and the passengers could see for miles in every direction. Weedy, deserted fields spread out below them. Not many leagues to the south rose Lanthi Ume, her towers and domes shining superbly in the sun; and beyond the city, the deep blue gleam of the sea. The road north unwound down Morlin Hill; circled the base of the Crags, continued on across the Gravula Wasteland, as far as the hills of the Nazara Sin.

The whip in Wate Basef's hand sang, and the carriage thundered down Morlin Hill like an avalanche.

The shadows were lengthening when the gray figure stretched out on the stone floor finally returned to life. Eyes wide open, Snarp lay still for a time. At last she sat up slowly, and the chittering quibbid approached to nose her booted leg. Snarp extended a clawlike hand, touched the creature lightly, then reached up and pulled the wide hat from her head. A few strands of scanty, almost colorless hair came straggling down. Pressing her skull experimentally, she soon encountered a lump. She winced as she touched it, and her face was ghastly then, the skin yellow-pale, the lips stretched tight over teeth clenched in a grimace of painful rage.

Briefly she paused, clammy forehead resting on death-cold hands, then rose and lurched to the table. She picked up someone's unfinished goblet of wine, and drained it at a gulp; then she doubled up as nausea hit her. The Enforcer retched a couple of times and vomited, the contents of her stomach spewing out over table and floor. For a few seconds she stood gasping, then vomited again.

The quibbid sidled near, huge ears twitching; sniffed the pool of vomit on the floor; started to lap and nibble. Snarp did not interfere. Pouring herself another glass of wine, she sloshed a little around in her mouth, spat it out, and drank the remainder without ill effect. Moistening a napkin with wine, she applied the cloth to her brow. When nausea subsided, she walked to the door, tried it and found it locked from the outside. She rattled the latch viciously, then paused as a new wave of dizziness struck her. Snarp stared at the barrier. Her face remained impassive, but the yellow eyes began to glow with a light of fanaticism.

"Run swiftly, Wate Basef." She spoke as if her enemy could hear her. "I will keep pace. Hide, and I will find you. Seek refuge in vain. I am taking you back to Lanthi Ume—alive or dead."

Having thus unburdened herself, she went to work. Her hatband concealed a very thin, flexible double-edged blade of steel. This implement in hand, Mistress Snarp attacked the locked door.

That evening, two significant personages in Lanthi Ume received messages.

It was past sunset when Duke Bofus's personal attendant announced the arrival of a courier from Castle Io Wesha.

"Io Wesha? Io Wesha? It must have something to do with that Wate Basef fellow again. Is there no peace?" inquired the Duke.

Upon admittance, the courier bowed profoundly and declared, "Your Grace, I convey the esteem of my master the Cognizant Raith Wate Basef, who bids me render assurance that your Grace claims his duty and respect to the extent that Ducal office warrants—"

"One moment," the Duke interrupted. "Didn't you come from Castle Io Wesha?"

"I did, your Grace."

"Then how can you carry word from Raith Wate Basef?" A frown creased the Duke's remarkably unlined forehead. "I thought he was under arrest in Lanthi Ume?"

"It cannot be, your Grace. My master and the others appeared at Io Wesha around midday."

"It's very strange." An idea struck him. "Maybe Gless Vallage released him after all. I do hope so. Kara will be so pleased." Bofus smiled his sweet smile.

"I have been dispatched to bring your Grace a message from her Ladyship Karavise Dil Shonnet."

"From Karavise!" Bofus was astounded. "But where is she?"

"Her Ladyship sends word from Io Wesha."

"Karavise at Io Wesha? But why? What is she doing *out there*?"

"I cannot answer for her Ladyship's intentions."

"But why would she go? I don't understand it. It doesn't seem right. She shouldn't be gadding around like this. Karavise and Wate Basef—" The Duke's blue eyes expanded. "Do you suppose—is it possible that they've *eloped*?"

"I believe not, your Grace. They were not alone. They were accompanied by a young gentleman and his man. Judging by the airs the servant gave himself, his master must be a very great lord indeed."

"A great lord! But who?" Bofus tugged worriedly at his goatee.

"The Lady Karavise expresses her duty and regard, bidding me inform your Grace that she and the others plan a brief excursion to the Nazara Sin. She expects to return to Lanthi Ume within the week."

"Karavise off to poke around the caves? With Raith Wate Basef? And somebody else whose name I don't know? Whatever

68

can she be thinking of?" When the courier did not reply, he prodded, "Didn't she say anything else?"

"No, your Grace."

"No. Oh, I do wish that girl wouldn't do such things. I do wish she wouldn't! What will people say? She has such strange ideas, and she's so very headstrong! And she couldn't have chosen a worse time to go. It couldn't possibly be worse!"

"Your Grace?"

The Duke's blue eyes were filled with perturbation. *"Gless Vallage is coming to dinner tonight!* Didn't she remember?"

Gless Vallage was looking forward to his dinner engagement, and had spared no pains to ensure a splendid appearance. For the occasion he had abandoned his customary robes in favor of a beautifully fashioned suit of muted silvery brocade, a masterpiece of richness and elegance. With his handsome features, thick silver hair and imposing figure, his Preeminence was a magnificent sight indeed. Nevertheless, Vallage's aspect was far from cheerful. He, like Duke Bofus, had received a visitor; one who came under cover of newly fallen darkness.

His Preeminence stood in the audience chamber of his private apartment on the third story of Vallage House, a mansion exceeded in size only by the Ducal Palace, and in beauty by none. Gless Vallage was a devoted collector of art and sculpture, antique furniture, manuscripts, expensive curios and thaumaturgical devices. His palace bore testimony to the strength of his acquisitive instincts as well as the perfection of his taste.

The visitor haunted the vicinity of the fireplace like a black ghost, evidently unwilling to venture more than a very few feet from the blaze. Although the evening was not particularly chilly, he was enveloped from head to foot in a dark, hooded cloak. His hands were hidden at all times beneath the folds of the wrap. His old-fashioned vizard remained firmly in place, although it was the general custom to doff such concealment within doors. Discernible beneath the edge of the hood was a faint, chill luminosity. When the stranger spoke, his voice was arresting—oddly accented and halting, as if ill-acquainted with the speech of Lanthi Ume. The musical tones were beautiful, but indescribably alien.

"There is dissonance. Why?"

"Not so. All is as I promised," replied Gless Vallage.

"They have received warning."

"But they did not believe it. They know nothing. There is no reason for you to be here, and you risk your own safety." Vallage spoke with an air of concern.

"One has spoken. This has happened . . .". The visitor paused and groped for a word or expression that eluded him, finally settling on one that only approximated his meaning. ". . . not as you promised."

"The speaker has been discredited. I have seen to that."

"He may speak again."

"No. He won't have another chance to speak in public. I'll use whatever means necessary to silence him. You have my word for that."

"Your—word?" There was movement behind the mask.

Vallage caught the gleam of very brilliant eyes fixed upon him. "My personal promise," he replied with urgent sincerity.

"The Select must not know."

"You needn't fear. The Select will learn nothing. I am their leader and they'll follow my directives, which are formulated with your benefit in mind. You may trust in me absolutely as your friend."

Another slight movement behind the mask. "We trust in our friend Vallage," the voice vibrated, almost hummed. "He has much to gain and much to lose."

His Preeminence gestured in graceful negation. "Now is not the time to speak of material reward," he murmured.

"I do not speak only of—reward."

Gless Vallage examined his guest as if searching for structural flaws. None were apparent beneath the enveloping cloak, and Vallage answered at last in a practiced, forthright manner, "I wouldn't deny that you've promised me much. Great favors, after all, merit great returns."

"Truly. Already you have received the Lightcrystals of J'frnial. You are the first human ever to possess such, and you know what they a to my kinsmen. Hereafter, all that belongs to the Select will belong to you. With such knowledge you may make yourself a—king—in some other place. Far from Dalyon."

"Perhaps. But it is not in hope of gain that I have agreed to aid you. It is because"—Vallage's fine eyes glowed with a fervent light—"I truly believe—I believe with all my heart—in the right and justice of your claim.

"For this reason—to serve justice by settling Man's debt to the Ancestors—you have by Cognition conferred with the kinsmen, in the manner of the savant-Patriarchs of old?"

"That is so, my friend. Your people have suffered at our

hands, and it is now up to some of us to make amends."

"So." The visitor's voice changed pitch, vibrating with a significance that escaped the listener, who did not recognize an alien vocal convention expressive of irony. "So."

"I believe," Vallage continued, "in your victory. I am convinced you will succeed."

"And therefore you serve us—that is easier to believe. You are wise, for it will be so. Our time has come. The very—skies—proclaim it. The new darkness opens our way. This realm is ours."

"And the Men?"

"They will not remain. But that does not concern you. You must earn your—reward. The Select must continue ignorant. You will—stop—their eyes and ears."

"You have my solemn assurance. I control the Select."

"All but one."

"The minor difficulty you allude to has been resolved." His Preeminence was rescued by the sudden glow of blue light beneath the bell-shaped crystal dome resting on a nearby gilt-and-onyx table. "Ah—the word reaches us, even now. One moment's indulgence, my friend." Vallage approached the dome. Under the crystal, wisps of vapor materialized and began to whirl like a tiny cyclone. As they spun the vapors thickened, slowed, and coalesced into a fist-sized lump of dull gray matter. The light faded. Vallage removed the lump and cracked it sharply against the edge of the table. The gray matter broke easily to reveal a message folded within. A swift expression of surprise and displeasure crossed the savant's face as he read:

Preeminence—
    Wate Basef has escaped. I will hunt him down and bring him back to Lanthi Ume. This I swear.
                                                                —S.

"Harmony has been restored?" inquired the visitor.

"Yes." Gless Vallage turned back to the hooded figure. His facial expression, once more under complete control, reflected nothing but satisfaction. "Excellent news. Raith Wate Basef has been taken. He is now in the custody of my most trusted agent, and he will not trouble us again."

"The news is good," returned the stranger inscrutably. "May it continue so. I will inform my . . ." He searched and at last used a word that did not appear to satisfy him. ". . . Patriarch."

"By all means." Vallage casually consigned Snarp's message

71

to the flames. "And now, my friend, may I offer you the hospitality of my house?"

"I am leaving now."

"My dombulis will carry you."

"No. I go by way of the lightless-tunnel-in-damp-soft-stone-that-runs-near-surface-through-wet-ground." The visitor paused, and added, "This language is . . . barren, expresses little."

"Convey my respects to your great king."

A brief dimming of luminosity beneath the visitor's hood was the sole response.

Comfortless silence.

"I bid you good evening, then," said Gless Vallage at last.

"Farewell. Do not disappoint us." The visitor retired as silently as night fading into morning.

Following the departure of his guest, Gless Vallage stood alone and brooding in the audience chamber. For some minutes he remained thus, inner tension mounting. Then, very abruptly, as if conquered by an impulse that could no longer be denied, the savant hurried from the room. Through the luxurious apartment he hastened, until he came to a stout locked door, behind which lay a small, plain windowless closet originally intended to lodge the master's personal valet or attendant. But the present Lord Gless Vallage had assigned the little chamber an altogether different use.

He unlocked the door and entered. The closet was sparsely furnished, containing nothing more than a table, chair, and a couple of very massive iron-bound cabinets, Cognitively secured. Carefully shutting the door behind him, Vallage approached and opened one of the cabinets, whose center shelf supported a great hollow cone of thin glass resting upon a glass plate. Although the glass was colorless, the cone appeared black as a rip in the web of space and time. In a hasty, almost furtive manner, Vallage removed the vessels and set them upon the table. For a moment he stared at the cone, then cautiously laid his hand upon it. The glass was warm, noticeably warmer than room temperature. Very gingerly he lifted one edge of the cone. At once a seemingly solid sliver of darkness thrust itself under the glass, protruding out into the room in an impossible curve. The hot darkness carried a stench of rotting vegetation, and the savant's nostrils twitched. Quickly he clapped the edge of the cone down, thus amputating a small crescent of Cognitive midnight. The crescent, wafting heavily over the edge of the table, dropped to the floor and lay there. After a moment its outlines softened, its shape changed,

72

and the liberated darkness began to spread, slowly at first and then with increasing swiftness.

Gless Vallage watched attentively. Then, unwilling to allow the process to continue, he stepped back to the cabinet, removed a number of Cognitive aids, and set to work.

Despite all his Preeminence's celebrated ability, Cognition was not easy to achieve, and the effort continued for long minutes. Vallage was breathing in gasps, his forehead was dewed with sweat, and the darkness on the floor had expanded to twice its original volume by the time he experienced the flash of comprehension and utter certainty that signaled success.

He opened his eyes slowly. He was still breathing hard, and his limbs were leaden. But the physical exhaustion inevitably attendant upon feats of significant Cognition could not suppress Vallage's thrill of triumph as he watched the ugly pool of darkness on the floor contract, shrinking in upon itself, lightening as it compressed, until at last a tiny faint blotch of grayish vapor was all that remained. An instant later, the last shred of vapor faded from view.

Vallage straightened. Victory exerted a remarkably revivifying effect, and his weariness receded. His step was elastic as he moved to restore the black cone to its cabinet. This done, he paused a moment to consider the game he played, weighing the risks against the prize.

For generations, rumors of the horrific Death of Light Cognition had haunted the Select. Reputedly the final and most dreadful accomplishment of the demonic Terrs Fal Grizhni, the secret had died along with its master, and from that day until the present, no man had rediscovered it. No mortal had proved capable of comprehending or controlling the complex, wildly unpredictable Cognition that induced a poisonous decay of light. Many had attempted the feat and all had failed miserably—all, that is, until the advent of Vaxalt Gless Vallage, greatest of modern savants, perhaps greatest of all savants, not excepting Fal Grizhni himself. Who but Vaxalt Gless Vallage could possibly have carried it off? His accomplishment, once revealed, would establish his greatness in Selectic history, but that was only a beginning, for the talents of Vaxalt Gless Vallage were by no means limited to Cognition alone.

It was an obvious fact, denied by no impartial judge, that Vaxalt Gless Vallage possessed a rare genius for diplomacy, combined with great intellectual force, vast knowledge, resolution, far-ranging vision, near-magical personal charm and charisma—

all the qualities, in short, of a great ruler. And a criminal waste it was that such abilities should confine themselves to Selectic administration, when Lanthi Ume herself stood in desperate need of inspired leadership. It was at this critical point in history that the genius of a single man might turn the fortunes of the city, halting her long decline and restoring her to former greatness. It was at this moment above all others that a mingling, a merging of Ducal temporal power and Selectic knowledge might best serve the city. This combination, so potent in itself, would surely prove invincible if embodied in one extraordinary man.

Vaxalt Gless Vallage was the man, destined Cognitive ruler and savior of Lanthi Ume.

The question yet remained, how best to effect his Preeminence's ascent? A straightforward coup d'état, while not altogether out of the question, was hardly apt to win the affection of his future subjects. A second possibility lay in the quiet elimination of the amiably simpleminded Duke Bofus. Upon the apparently accidental death of the Duke, Vaxalt Gless Vallage might have himself declared Regent for the youthful, inexperienced female Karavise. His position would be much strengthened were he to marry her. The weakness in that scheme lay in the character of Karavise herself. Youthful and inexperienced she might be, but neither weak nor stupid. Moreover, for reasons he could not fathom, she obviously hated him. Should he attempt, however gently, to force her compliance, the ice-blooded hellcat was perfectly capable of raising the entire city against ʰⁱᵐ Such an insurrection might be suppressed, but again, it was not by such crude methods that Vaxalt Gless Vallage desired to establish himself.

No completely satisfactory course of action had suggested itself—not until his secret mastery of the Death of Light Cognition, and the near-simultaneous activation of Terrs Fal Grizhni's ancient malediction, had presented his Preeminence with the opportunity of a lifetime. The spread of the poisonous darkness, disastrous though it might seem to most, appeared nothing less than providential to Vaxalt Gless Vallage, who now possessed the power to banish the danger at will.

That power, however, would be displayed to maximum effect.

The poisonous darkness must be permitted to advance at its own pace, unhindered. The resulting destruction of life and property was regrettable, but necessary in view of Lanthian interests. Those most capable of opposition—that is, the savants of the Select—must be kept as much as possible in ignorance. And therefore information concerning the true nature of the threat—information such as that offered by the repulsive Raith Wate Basef—must be suppressed at all costs. In this the purposes of Vaxalt Gless Vallage and the emerging, warlike Vardruls of the caverns appeared to coincide, and it was this illusory commonness that had inspired his Preeminence to raise the stakes by offering his services to the cave-dwellers in exchange for the priceless Lightcrystals of J'frnial—a stroke of such masterful cunning that he could hardly forbear gloating at the thought of it. The Vardruls would discover their error soon enough, while Vallage would retain possession of the crystals.

The darkness must advance to the very walls of Lanthi Ume. And then, when fear was at its height and the citizens had given themselves up for lost—only then and not before—would Vaxalt Gless Vallage singlehandedly break Fal Grizhni's Cognition, turning back the darkness and thus distinguishing himself for all time to come as a hero, sole preserver of his city.

Vallage unconsciously smiled as he pictured the scene in his mind—himself, a magnificent figure in his black robes, alone upon the ramparts of the Vayno Fortification, a solitary champion with the eyes of all the city fixed upon him in hope, fear and supplication; speaking the words of power that would pierce the darkness like missiles of purifying flame.

And afterward—afterward they would be half-mad with gratitude. All Lanthi Ume would be at his feet, and he would rule in fact if not in name. The hand of the Duke's daughter would be urged upon him then—they would beg him to take her, and the union would almost guarantee his swift succession to the Ducal throne. Even Karavise herself, whatever her true feelings, could scarcely object without appearing an ingrate.

At the thought of his prospective bride, some of the elation faded from the savant's handsome face. Incredible though it seemed, she clearly disliked him. It was not essential to the success of his schemes that the girl regard him warmly, but matters would be simplified if she did. Moreover, the challenge was piquant. He would win her over, he would charm her. It was a project that he was determined to carry through to a triumphant conclusion, and he did not for a moment doubt his ultimate success, for experience had confirmed the potency of the Vallage appeal. Karavise might affect an icy hostility, but she was a woman like others, and sooner or later, she would melt.

Yes, it was a difficult, delicate and dangerous game that he played, but the prizes—honor, sovereignty, fame and deathless glory—were worth any gamble. And, after all, were the risks truly so great? In view of the resources at his command, Vaxalt Gless Vallage was hardly apt to fail. With this thought in mind, Vallage squared his shoulders and strode from the room; a jolly, thriving wooer.

Chapter Seven

ᕡᘓᕢᘔᕡᘓᕢᘔ

Night and darkness. Clouds obscured the moon and stars. The deepest of shadows obliterated Morlin Hill and all the surrounding countryside. It was a prospect uninviting to any traveler, but Mistress Snarp was not dismayed.

She rode a swift and nervy black stallion bred for stamina, Wate Basef's favorite mount. Her saddlebags bulged with provisions furnished under duress by the terrified servants of Io Wesha. A couple of lanterns swung by her knees. The quibbid clung to the pommel of the saddle.

Before her the steep slope descended in blackness. The lanterns illuminated but a few feet of the road ahead, and she moved through the night enclosed in a small, dim bubble of light. Although the darkness, the sharp grade of the road and the unfamiliar terrain demanded caution, she sent the horse hurtling down Morlin Hill at breakneck pace, heedless of possible disaster.

At the foot of the hill, where the ground leveled out, she urged her mount to a gallop and sped across the fields and pastures like a spirit intent on suicide. For well over a mile they continued at the same reckless pace, the powerful horse bearing her light weight with little effort. At last the animal began to tire, his speed slackened, and Snarp's spurs drank blood in vain. With an impatient hiss, she hauled in on the reins. Snorting at the sudden vicious stab of the bit, the stallion slewed to a quivering halt.

Dismounting, Snarp rummaged swiftly through the contents of her leather pouch to bring forth a vial filled with green crystalline powder. She uncorked the vial, tipped a few crystals into the horse's distended nostrils, and rapped out the syllables of activation taught her by her mentor Gless Vallage. The effect was almost instantaneous.

With a screaming whinny of anguish, the stallion tore his halter free and reared, hoofs pawing the air. Lashing out with both hind heels, he bucked and twisted wildly. The quibbid clinging to the saddle was thrown clear to land in the soft grass several feet away. One of the lanterns crashed to the ground and

77

went dark. Still screaming horribly, the horse reared again, flinging his head from side to side in pain and terror. The watching
Snarp unhurriedly corked the vial and returned it to the pouch.
Then she leaped in, neatly dodging the lethal hoofs, regained her
hold on the reins and swung herself back into the saddle. As her
victim continued to plunge, she jabbed her spurs into the lathered
flanks, sawing savagely on the bit. The horse snorted, spewing
blood-flecked foam. As the subsiding pain in his nostrils was
superseded by new and more intense miseries, the animal quieted
and stood trembling. Snarp whistled sharply. At once the quibbid
emerged from the grasses, sprang to the stirrup and clambered up
its mistress' leg to its original place before her on the saddle. A
touch of the spur and they were off again.

The green crystals, whatever they were, had done their work
well. The stallion raced on through the night with all his former
vigor, and even greater speed. Snarp crouched in the saddle like a
jockey. Her bony face, with its tight, thin lips and long jaw, was
weirdly lit from below by the weak light of the one remaining
lantern. Across the quiet fields they flew, actually attaining the
base of the Crags before exhaustion once more overtook the great
black horse. He faltered, stumbled, and slowed to an uneven trot.

Snarp pulled up and leaped from the saddle to inflict a fresh
dose of crystalline anguish. This time the horse's reaction was
confined to whinnies and odd, choking moans. His eyes had
taken on a dull glaze, and his breath carried a new, acrid odor.
Ignoring these ominous signs, Snarp remounted and spurred on
relentlessly. Around the foot of the Crags she galloped at killing
speed, then up a long, stony incline to pause at the summit with
all the Gravula Wasteland spreading out before her. The night had
cleared somewhat, and a sickly gibbous moon contended with the
clouds. Pale rays touched the surrounding hills and rocky hollows. Snarp's pouch yielded a small, collapsible spyglass. Raising the instrument to her eye, she squinted out over the silent
Wasteland, and many miles away caught a faint gleam of orange.
She focused the glass, and the orange gleam resolved itself into
three distinct points of light. Nodding once, she put the glass
away and applied her reddened spurs.

The horse stood motionless, head drooping and eyes dull.
Snarp hissed, dismounted to slap a new dose of green crystals
into her victim's nostrils, and sprang back into the saddle. For the
next minute nothing happened, and she sat roweling her spurs to
no avail. Then, as the stimulant took hold, the stallion shuddered.
An uncanny equine scream echoed hideously over the hills.
Rearing, the animal threw himself over backward and rolled in a

frantic effort to crush his rider. Had Snarp's reflexes been anything less than excellent, the attempt would have succeeded.

Kicking free of the stirrups, she flung herself to the side, safely clear of the huge body and thrashing hoofs. She landed on her feet, and instantly whirled to face the horse as it rose from the ground. The one remaining lantern had been extinguished, and moonlight provided the sole illumination. The animal's ears were laid flat and his teeth were bared. Even in the uncertain light, the whites of his eyes flashed wildly. In a last burst of screaming strength, the stallion charged.

Snarp sought refuge behind a large outcropping of rock, one of the many that dotted the Gravula. Her face was expressionless, yellow eyes untroubled. Drawing a broad-bladed knife from its sheath, she waited, poised lightly on the balls of her feet. There were other, more sophisticated weapons at her command, but she did not judge them necessary. When the stallion circled the bulge of the rock, she took a step forward to meet him. The animal reared, iron-shod hoofs flailing, descended and collapsed to the ground, strength completely exhausted. The black flanks were lathered with bloody foam. The legs kicked feebly and the glassy eyes, frenzied no longer, reflected only bewilderment.

Snarp finished the horse with a single stroke of the knife, stepping back to avoid the rush of blood. Calmly she retrieved the lantern, relit it and surveyed her surroundings. The first thing to catch her attention was the red flash of lamplight on the beady eyes of her small companion. At the conclusion of the battle, the quibbid had emerged from its hiding place to crouch at its mistress' feet. Snarp knelt and restored the little beast to its accustomed perch upon her shoulder. One hand stroking the quibbid's furry back, she gazed frozen-faced toward the Nazara Sin, lost in darkness. Until such time as she overtook Raith Wate Basef and his accomplices, she would be forced to proceed on foot. The night was black, the road unfamiliar, and the stony ground treacherous.

"Tomorrow, little beauty," she promised aloud. "At the first light." The quibbid arched its back against her caressing hand.

A chilling wind swept the Gravula. Snarp returned to the dead stallion. From one of the saddlebags she withdrew a thin blanket. Retiring to the leeward side of a great boulder at the side of the road, she knelt and opened her tunic to bare her bosom. The exposed right breast was small but conventionally molded. Where the left breast should have swelled, her chest was perfectly flat. Extending her arm, she chirruped, and the quibbid scampered down into her hand, where it curled itself into a flesh-colored ball. Pressing the creature to her heart, she spoke a quiet word. Form shifted, outlines blurred, boundaries vanished as the quibbid merged with its mistress to restore nocturnal symmetry to her body. Familiar ritual completed, Snarp composed herself for slumber. She did not trouble with a fire, but merely wrapped herself in the blanket and stretched out on the ground, her back to the rock, head resting upon a tussock. Sleep did not come at once. For a long time she lay fully conscious, eyes wide open and glinting like crystals of sulfur under the moon.

The smell of bacon frying awakened Devras. He opened his eyes upon a misty early morning sky alive with migrating clouds. Around him towered the vast prism-shapes of the Granite Sages, those mysterious monoliths of unknown origin. The incessant cold breezes of the Gravula Wasteland played hide-and-seek among the Sages. The ground was cold and Devras's bones ached. He was not well rested. Disturbing visions had plagued last night's unquiet sleep. Ghostly, white, luminous figures peopled his dreams, and he couldn't rid himself of the suspicion that it hadn't been pure fancy. Nonsense, of course—the result of unsteady nerves, overactive imagination, or possibly indigestion; but surely not ghosts.

"Man's repudiation of the supernatural," Grif Zeezune had written, "marks the greatest victory of Reason over Reality..."

Devras shivered. No sense in lying there, prey to sinister imaginings. Throwing his blanket aside, he rose and emerged from the shade of the monoliths into the sunlight, where Grono and Wate Basef sat beside a small fire. Grono was frying the bacon. Thick rashers of streaky meat sizzled fragrantly. There was buttered toast, a bowl of assorted dried fruits, and a pot of orange-scented tea. Evidently Wate Basef chose to travel in comfort. Despite the unwonted plenty, Grono exuded disapproval, even outrage. His shoulders were hunched, lips compressed, eyes fixed fiercely on the skillet. Wate Basef sat on the opposite side of the fire. His brows were elevated, his lips curved in a smirk as he studied a large map spread out on the ground before him.

"'Morning," Devras greeted them.

Wate Basef grunted, without lifting his eyes from the map.

"Good morning, sir." Grono's acidulous expression vanished as he began heaping mammoth portions of bacon and toast onto a metal plate. "How did your Lordship fare last night?" He handed the plate to his master.

"Bad dreams." Devras glanced uneasily at the Granite Sages. "I could almost believe the old legends about this place—ghosts and white demons and whatnot. Amazing how real dreams can seem." He ate with surprisingly little appetite. "Where's Lady Karavise?"

"Her Ladyship has not yet graced us with her presence. It may be that your Lordship will be obliged to awaken her. There's many a gallant would envy your Lordship that task!" The valet peered hopefully over the rim of his spectacles to see if this remark had opened any new vistas, but Devras appeared oblivious. Grono sighed.

"Plotting our route, Raith?" Devras inquired.

"That's right. This old Selectic map notes the location of four entrances to the caverns of the Nazara Sin. The closest one is *here*"—his forefinger tapped the map—"and I don't think it's more than four or five hours away."

"I thought you said that the inhabitants sealed the entrances."

"Certainly they've sealed some, but they're scarcely apt to imprison themselves underground. Some of the doorways will have been left open, but no doubt camouflaged. That's what we're hoping to find. We'll try them all, and sooner or later we're bound to hit on a way in. I've been mapping the best path from entrance to entrance, and I think we can try them all, if need be, within a single day."

"Very good," Grono muttered bitterly, "if that were *all* he'd been doing."

"It is all I've been *doing*," Wate Basef asserted with a cackle, and added for Devras's benefit, "This time friend Grono takes exception to my intentions rather than my actions."

"And very dangerous intentions they are—dangerous and foolish!" Grono exclaimed with the air of one resuming an earlier argument. He turned to his master for vindication. "Your Lordship, this man plots an attack upon Preeminence Gless Vallage. Needless to say, it is an endeavor fraught with direst peril, not only for the perpetrator in his insensate arrogance, but also for those so misguided as to associate themselves with him. You understand me, sir?"

"An attack?" Devras inquired.

"Through legal channels," Wate Basef explained. "As I've mentioned more than once, Gless Vallage has greatly exceeded his authority as Preeminence. In his suppression of information vital to civic welfare, his attempt to imprison me in Lanthi Ume, his attack upon my property and my person—and yours, for that matter—he's violated five articles of the Selectic Charter, three provisions in the Principles of the Select, and four Lanthian ordinances. And does he imagine that he may do so with impunity?

He's gone too far, much too far, and this time I'm going to nail him. By the time I'm finished, he'll be the one up before the Council on charges, not I. He's given me all the evidence I need, including witnesses—"

A cry of outrage escaped Grono. *"We are not your witnesses!* His Lordship will not involve himself in your quarrels with the Select. It is not his Lordship's concern! It is not even *safe!"*

"Raith's got a point," Devras observed. "Vallage shouldn't be allowed to get away with it. My neck's still sore where that woman's Living Wire pinched it, and Gless Vallage is responsible. You're always thinking of the Fennahar dignity, Grono. Do you really feel that the Lord Har Fennahar ought to submit to such abuse?"

Grono considered his reply with care. "There is a difference," he decided at last, "between vile submission and prudent circumspection—"

"Vallage has broken the law," Wate Basef insisted. "Don't you understand that? He should be stopped. It's your master's duty to uphold the law, and yours as well—"

"I do not need you to tell me my duty, sir! I *know* my own duty, sir! Can you say the same? It is not my duty, sir, nor the duty of my master, to serve as the instruments of your vengeance upon the Preeminence who has not seen fit to advance you!"

"Grono, the man had me locked up and half-strangled for no just cause," Devras argued. "Does that mean nothing to you?"

"Ah, your Lordship, no doubt his Preeminence *thought* he had just cause—"

"What if he did? Do his intentions answer for all offenses? Nef Domeas writes—"

But the Domean wisdom was lost, for the discussion was cut short by the appearance of Lady Karavise, who emerged at last from the carriage wherein she had spent the night. Karavise was faultlessly groomed as ever—gray-green velvet gown unwrinkled, high-heeled shoes unspotted, hair perfectly ordered. An incongruously elegant figure on the Gravula Wasteland, she stepped forth from the shadows that gloomed at the foot of the Granite Sages and picked her way over the rough ground to the fire. Greeting her companions, she sat and reached for the teapot. Instantly Grono, all solicitude, filled and handed her a cup, then a plate of food, at the same time inquiring deferentially, "I trust these rude surroundings did not unduly trouble your Ladyship's repose?"

Karavise hesitated as if fearing to appear overly fanciful, then shrugged. "I slept badly," she admitted dryly. "I woke several times during the night, feeling that I was not alone. I thought I spied white creatures, but when I looked out, there was no one. Imagination, of course." She stirred her tea with care.

The three men exchanged uncomfortable looks. For a time they sat sipping their tea in silence, then rose to repack their gear. Once the horses were back in harness, little remained to be done.

Wate Basef had left a small telescope lying on the ground near the fire. Now Devras took up the instrument to survey the landscape. His idle gaze swept the Gravula from east to west and back again, then halted. He leaned forward, staring, and declared, "Something's moving out there. It's coming our way."

"An animal, sir?" inquired Grono.

"Can't tell yet. It's gray and blends into the hillside."

"Gray? Let me see that." Wate Basef appropriated the telescope. His obvious uneasiness caught the notice of his companions.

"Animal or human?" Karavise demanded.

"Human, more or less. It's Snarp," Wate Basef announced flatly. His companions clamored for the spyglass. When collective curiosity had been satisfied, the savant advised, "We'd best move now. She travels quickly."

"She's alone, and there are four of us," said Karavise.

"You are afraid of a lone woman, sir?" inquired Grono. "And what of your much-vaunted Cognition? Couldn't you throw her off the track? Transport her to another place? Render us invisible, perhaps?"

"Grono. I am a savant, but I can't work miracles."

"And is it a miracle to overcome a single woman?"

"You don't know this woman."

"Couldn't you incapacitate her?"

"Not at this distance, at least not without a focusing apparatus. In any case, disabling her in the midst of this wilderness would amount to murder, and I've told you I'm not willing to undertake that. Best that we simply go. For reasons I can't fathom, Snarp's traveling on foot. With our carriage and good horses, we'll soon leave her far behind, provided we leave right now."

They stowed away the last of their belongings, extinguished the fire and reentered the carriage. Wate Basef ascended to the box seat, and this time Devras climbed up along with him. Throwing a last uneasy glance back over his shoulder, the savant cracked the whip and the carriage rolled north. They maintained a smart pace, and soon the gray figure behind them was no longer visible, even with the aid of the telescope.

* * *

83

Time passed slowly. Long before the rolling terrain of the Gravula Wasteland gave way to the steeper, sharper hills of the Nazara Sin, Devras had tired of the dreary vista of rock, scrub vegetation, and rutted road. The blue-gray sky with its racing clouds was more interesting for a while, but eventually that too palled. Presently he no longer saw his surroundings, no longer felt the jolting of the carriage or the lash of the wind. His thoughts turned inward and he was forced to confront his own doubts. Had he indeed committed a blunder in allying himself with the notorious Raith Wate Basef? Would he have done better to remain in Lanthi Ume as Grono had so earnestly urged? Wate Basef's tale was fantastic, improbable in the extreme, yet there could be no denying the suggestive nature of Gless Vallage's actions, or the weight carried by the letter of his own ancestor Rillif Har Fennahar. Beyond that, deeply and instinctively, he believed Wate Basef—had believed him from the very start. That being the case, his participation in this endeavor had been almost inevitable from the moment he'd accepted the invitation to the Mauranyza Dome, but he still couldn't rid himself of the notion that it was all some lunatic accident. Such thoughts were unsettling, and Devras did his best to banish them. Turning to Wate Basef, he offered, "I'll take the ribbons for a while. You must want a rest."

"The horses need it more than I do," the savant replied, pulling up. "We'll stop for a few minutes." As they climbed down from the box, Karavise and Grono emerged. While the others stretched their limbs, Grono laid out biscuits and wine on a flat, sun-swept rock.

They had attained the high ground. Behind them the Gravula Wasteland lay cheerless victim to the wind. The Granite Sages were barely visible in the distance. Around them and ahead rose the jagged, uninviting hills of the Nazara Sin. The hills appeared to harbor neither human nor animal life, and only the stingiest of vegetation. The chill sigh of the breeze was daunting, and for the first time Devras actively regretted the loss of his one pair of gloves, sold weeks earlier when the landlord, howling for his rent, had threatened eviction. The young red wine from the cellars of Io Wesha would help to ward off the chill, and Devras gladly accepted a cup. As he drank, his eyes lifted to the sky, where the diurnal star of Lanthi Ume shone redly. Requesting the telescope, he studied the star at length and then, regard descending to the Gravula, he gazed for miles over the undulating landscape. In the far distance, almost upon the horizon, he could barely discern a tiny moving figure. In thoughtful silence he observed the figure's slow but inexorable approach, then returned the glass to its owner. Wate Basef likewise surveyed the landscape. The two men exchanged glances.

"Is it much farther to that first entrance, Raith?" Devras inquired casually.

"I think another couple of hours," the savant replied with equal nonchalance. "Come, we've dawdled long enough."

Grono and Karavise, faintly surprised, accepted the decree without demur. Resuming their journey, they traveled on in silence relieved only by the pounding of hoofs upon the road, the rattle and creak of the old carriage. The slopes were steeper now, and the air colder. Around them rose hills colorless and dreary. The thin covering of dirt and vegetation barely served to shroud the skeleton of rock, which often showed through the tatters of its flimsy garment. The place seemed barren and dead. It was hard to believe that such stark simplicity concealed a complex maze of caverns; harder yet to imagine that maze inhabited by intelligent beings.

The time passed and the travelers sat wrapped in their individual meditations. The hills marched by in wearisome succession. The road narrowed and roughened, at last dwindling to a near-invisible lane, distinguishable only by the faint rutted track of anonymous vehicles. Soon the tracks disappeared. The lane faded out of existence, and the carriage was clattering over bare, unmarked terrain. For a few hundred yards farther the way was navigable, and then the rocky incline steepened, the carriage slowed and the horses strained against their burden. Shortly thereafter Wate Basef drew the team to a halt, informing his companions, "From this point, we proceed on foot."

Karavise's dubious regard shifted from the stony slope to her own insubstantial, high-heeled shoes. She said nothing.

Wate Basef led them up the hill, paused to consult the map, then took a sharp swing to the northeast. Another twenty minutes of walking brought them to the entrance they sought. It was a sizable, fairly obvious hole in the side of the hill, a once-great gateway known to the inhabitants in former ages as the Mvjri Dazzle. No attempt at concealment had been made, for none was needed. The opening was plugged with several tons of stone. They stood regarding the barrier in thwarted silence, until Grono inquired, "Well, Master Cognizance? Can you open it?"

"Are you serious? It's blocked with solid granite."

"What of that? Are you not a savant? You keep telling us that you are. What's a little bit of rock to a great savant?"

"It's hardly a 'little bit' of rock," Devras observed.

A bark of laughter escaped Raith Wate Basef. "Grono never ceases to expect miracles of my Cognition."

"Not miracles, sir—only competence, if you've got it."

"I don't think you distinguish between the two. As it happens, my Cognition could open that gateway, but it might take me weeks to hit upon the proper method."

"Very good. You cannot open the door. If the caves are directly below, as you claim, then why not create your own pathway for us?"

"That would be about equivalent to opening the door."

"Ah, another excuse. Always there is an excuse."

"Grono, as your complaints are rooted in ignorance rather than malice, I take no offense," the savant smirked.

Grono's wattles quivered and he drew a deep breath. Noting the signs, Devras broke in quickly, "Your map shows other entrances, Raith?"

"Three of them."

"We'd better go now if we're to reach them today."

"Yes, we waste time," Karavise agreed.

"So I have said from the first," Grono muttered under his breath. "From the very first." His companions feigned deafness.

Returning to the carriage, they resumed their journey. The barely visible road snaked among drearily inhospitable hills. The steep way taxed the strength of the horses, who required periodic respite. And the shadows were lengthening by the time they reached the second entrance; an opening once known, although not to humans, as the F'jnruu Batgate.

The F'jnruu Batgate was thoroughly sealed. The weathered old stones had stood in place for years.

It was a two-mile hike back to the carriage. By the time they arrived, Karavise was limping. Her high-heeled shoes, absurd in the wilderness, were perilous as well as painful—twice she had slipped on the uneven ground. Her trailing velvet skirts impeded every step. She made no complaint, but her expression was grim as she reentered the vehicle.

The afternoon wore on swiftly, and the sun was reddening on the horizon when they finally came to the supposed site of the third doorway. The opening was nowhere in sight, and it was too late to begin a search. They made camp for the night upon the windswept hillside. The provision sacks furnished a store of dried meat, beans and root vegetables with which Grono concocted a creditable stew. That night they slept soundly, their dreams unvisited by tall white beings.

Morning dawned damp, dim and clouded. The wind had died

for the moment and a thin milky fog veiled the Nazara Sin, blotting out the sky and pooling in the hollows. The weather did not favor their endeavor as they wandered from slope to slope in search of the third doorway. Wate Basef's map was old, and a number of landmarks had vanished or altered. The travelers' present position was somewhat uncertain, and the location of the entrance even more so. The minutes slipped away, they found nothing but rock and gorse, and it began to seem increasingly likely that they had missed their target altogether.

Devras was down on his hands and knees, studiously pawing the scrub. He was tired, sore, frustrated, and at that moment inclined to share in Grono's doubts of Raith Wate Basef's Cognitive competence. How much might be expected of a savant who couldn't even find his way into the reputedly enormous caves of the Nazara Sin?

Why can't he just—transport us, or whatever it is these savants are supposed to do? His Cognition doesn't seem so much, and if he doesn't have that, then this entire expedition is a waste of effort. 'A hopeless cause is the favorite recreation of the nobly ineffectual,' Heselicus wrote.

Maybe Grono had been right all along. A short distance away, the valet stalked back and forth, stabbing the ground with his cane and muttering to himself. He met the eyes of his master, and the stabbing gestures grew more violent. An outburst would have followed shortly, had not Wate Basef chosen that moment to admit defeat.

It was with mixed disappointment and relief that the four returned to the carriage and clattered off in search of the final doorway. The journey was long, but this time there was little difficulty in locating the entrance. A full day of travel brought them at last to a jagged rise unnavigable by carriage. Another half hour of walking took them to the foot of a sheer cliff of chisel-sharp angles. Some subterranean convulsion of past eons had split a great fissure in the granite face of the cliff, and for countless ages it had gaped like an idiot's jaws. Now it gaped no longer, for the fissure was filled with stone, blocking forever the entrance once known as Great Kf'rj. In silence the travelers confronted defeat, and in silence made their way back to the carriage.

There was little conversation around the campfire that evening, but Grono's heart was light as he set about preparing dinner. He was generous, almost lavish with the provisions, for it was clear that they wouldn't have to hold out much longer. It would take only three or four days to complete the journey back to Lanthi Ume, and there was more than enough food for that. He went about his work in silence. Magnanimous in victory, he permitted no expression of unseemly satisfaction to escape his lips. But the gleam in his eye, the swing in his step and the ripe curve of his mouth proclaimed his triumph more clearly than any words.

The valet's elation lasted through the meal, at the conclusion of which Wate Basef produced another of his cursed maps, along with the ominous invitation, "I'd like all of you to look at this."

Foreboding chilled the heart of Grono. The sensation intensified as he noted the eagerness with which young Master Devras peered over the savant's shoulder. Her Ladyship Karavise appeared equally interested—a great disappointment, inasmuch as he had hoped that *she* would show better judgment. Grono himself pointedly ignored the map.

"Here we sit on the northwestern slopes of the Nazara Sin." Wate Basef tilted the parchment to catch the jumping firelight. "We've visited all the known entrances in this vicinity, and we've found ourselves blocked. We could continue to search the hills in the hope of stumbling across a concealed entrance, but that might take weeks. In any case, there's a more promising alternative. These caves are immense, and the Nazara Sin is by no means the sole point of entry. Notice the two additional gateways marked inland—there and there." Wate Basef's finger flicked the map twice.

"Quite a distance from here," Karavise observed.

"It is, and that's an encouraging sign. At that distance, the inhabitants have probably never been troubled by the humans of Lanthi Ume, and the doorways may remain unsealed to this day. Rather than wasting any more time here, I suggest that we proceed inland to look for them."

Devras and Karavise were silent. Grono narrowly surveyed the face of his master. At last Devras inquired, "Raith, if there's a way in close at hand but hidden, can't your Cognition reveal it?"

"I shouldn't have thought that so very difficult for a savant," Karavise added.

"All Cognition is difficult—always—even for a savant. Moreover, it's very particular." Wate Basef's habitual smile sometimes seemed nothing more than an unconscious tic. "In order to discover a hidden doorway in a granite hillside, I'd require a procedure specifically designed for that one purpose, and I don't happen to know one. Certainly I could devise such a thing—quite likely some variation on Tasm's Revelation of the Void would do it—but I'd have to rely on trial and error, and it's

88

difficult to guess how long it would take, particularly in the absence of my books, Cognitive records, and most of my equipment. All things considered, I think we'd do best to try the inland gateways."

"How long would it take to get there?" Devras asked.

"Your Lordship surely would not consider it?" Grono's foreboding transmuted to hideous certainty. "Your Lordship is not in earnest?"

"Would you want me to give up at the first setback?"

"I would desire you to exhibit wisdom and maturity. Oh, sir, this mad folly must come to an end. For days now I have followed you through the wilderness in uncomplaining patience. For days I have conducted myself with the restraint and decorum appropriate to a retainer of the noble House of Har Fennahar, but I cannot continue in silence forever. Is the truth not yet apparent? This Wate Basef person has misled your Lordship. We have searched the barren hills in vain at his behest and discovered no gateway here. The time we have spent in this place has been wasted, and there's no help for that, but surely you will not compound your error? You will not continue with this frivolity? Wate Basef has been given every chance to prove the truth of his tale, he has repeatedly failed, and now it is time to make an end. Your Lordship—and you, your Ladyship—you must see now that it is time to return to Lanthi Ume!"

Devras and Karavise traded undecided glances. Wate Basef's habitual smirk remained locked in place. At last Devras replied, "I'm not ready to give up on it." Until the words came out, he hadn't known what his answer would be. Once voiced, the decision became final, and internal questioning ceased.

"There is no point in pursuing the impossible!"

"Oh, I don't know. 'The greatness of a man,' Heselicus writes, 'is the sum of his abilities to aspire to the impossible, to perform the improbable, and to accept the unspeakable.' Sorry, Grono."

"Pox on Heselicus!" The valet turned to Karavise in desperation. "Your Ladyship—?"

"Will bear with the Cognizance, for now," she returned.

Grono's shoulders sagged. Plagued with guilt, Devras turned back to the map. "We should travel northwest from the Nazara Sin to the River Yl," he suggested with spurious indifference. "We can follow the river inland, and we'll never get lost."

"There are settlements along the Yl," Karavise observed. "We'll be able to buy food."

"Quite right; our stores will soon run low," Wate Basef

agreed, with a quick glance at Grono. Sunk in gloom, the valet did not respond.

"These entrances," Karavise added thoughtfully, "are not far from the settlement of Fenz. If the Rider's account was accurate, then the region is now in darkness. By the time we reach the caves, we'll encounter the dark."

"Long before we reach them," Wate Basef replied. "Remember, the darkness spreads quickly."

They sat up for hours making plans in which Grono did not join, before retiring for the night. They slept soundly and arose refreshed at dawn, three out of the four eager to push on. Following a substantial breakfast of salt fish, meal cakes and soapfruit, they sought the carriage and resumed their journey. It was with a sense of relief that they abandoned the hills, descending from the Nazara Sin to emerge onto the quiet Dask Grasslands that sloped down gently to the Daskyl Race, a tributary of the River Yl. The carriage rattled northwest. Its occupants did not look back to the hills behind them, nor did they note the small gray figure gliding along in their wake.

Chapter Eight

The northwest border of the Dask Grasslands impinged upon
straggling woods—the outermost limits of the great inland for-
ests. Through the woods ran the Daskyl Race, brisk tributary of
the Yl. A narrow lane hugged the water's edge. Along the road
came Mistress Snarp, the quibbid on her shoulder, a pack upon
her back. Despite the burdens, Snarp's gait was swift and
buoyant. Her whipcord muscles carried her across the land at a
pace that never flagged. Two days earlier the light provisions she
carried in the pack had given out. Since then she had lived on
what she could trap and kill. The diet agreed with her. Her yellow
eyes glittered metal-bright, and the color deepened in her normally pallid lips.

The smudged track of carriage wheels scored the dirt lane.
Snarp studied the ruts, and her brows contracted. She was not
gaining on Wate Basef's carriage.

At the crest of the next shallow rise, she stepped forth from
the trees into strong midday sunshine. Shading her cat's eyes
against the light, she gazed off into the distance, but failed to
locate her prey. For a moment she paused, lightly rubbing the
quibbid's huge ears. "A horse, little beauty," she told her companion. "We need another horse."

The quibbid chittered softly. Snarp delayed no longer, and her
thin gray form was soon lost among thin gray trees.

In the late afternoon she came to a settlement hard by the
Daskyl Race. The settlement, almost too insignificant to be
called a village, comprised a handful of cottages and sheds; a
couple of barns; assorted vegetable gardens, and a graveyard.
The construction of a dam upon this site had created a deep pool.
It was likely that the villagers depended in part for their liveli-
hood on the fish of the Race.

Snarp advanced, ignoring the countryfolk who gaped at her in
frank curiosity as she passed. Her eyes were fixed on the few
small carts and wagons that toiled along the road. They were
drawn by slow-moving miskins, which could be of no use to her.

Then she spied what she sought—a horse, most likely the only horse in the village, running loose in a fenced enclosure behind one of the larger cottages. It was a tolerably young and active animal; probably not very swift, but it would have to do.

Snarp strode to the cottage and knocked on the door. The door opened and a woman looked out. She was stout, matronly, drab. Interest and faint suspicion tightened the skin around her eyes as she took in the visitor; the travel-stained masculine garb, the quibbid, the strange yellow eyes.

"Fetch your man to me," Snarp directed.

"What would ye be wanting with Jarn?" The visitor did not trouble to reply, and the housewife's eyes narrowed. She hesitated as if contemplating disobedience, then shrugged. "Come in, then."

Snarp entered. As the door closed behind her, the vigilant children in the street scattered to spread the news of the stranger's arrival. "Fetch Jarn," she commanded.

Hostile brown eyes countered indifferent yellow. A momentary pause, another shrug, and the woman shuffled out, leaving Snarp alone in the cottage. She took a quick survey of the single large room, noted the rustic furnishings, the simplicity and the cleanliness. Nothing of interest. The door was equipped with an unusually heavy bar. A wooden ball and paddle sat on a shelf near the hearth; Jarn and his wife must have at least one child. Snarp crossed to the window and peered through the slats of the bolted shutters. Out in the garden her hostess stood with a man, presumably Jarn. In the paddock the brown horse grazed. Snarp's attention was fixed on the animal. She had little to spare for the humans.

A moment later Jarn and his wife came into the house. Jarn was burly, bearded and sly-eyed. Inspecting Snarp briefly, he observed, "The woods're full o' strangers these days."

"I want the horse," said Snarp. "How much?"

"Ye're a woman." Jarn was clearly nonplussed. "What kind o' decent woman runs around by herself, dressed up like a man and looking to buy horses? Who are ye, Mistress?"

"How much?" asked Snarp.

"Only horse in the village." The rustic's eyes gleamed. "Don't know that I want to sell 'im. Hard to come by a horse in these parts. Have ye thought about a miskin?"

"Two shorns," Snarp offered without expression.

Jarn's wife grinned.

Eyeing the visitor shrewdly, Jarn shook his head. His wife stared at him, aghast.

92

"Three," said Snarp.

Jarn's wife gasped audibly. Jarn threw her a warning glance and ordered, "Fetch us some ale." She obeyed with glaring reluctance. Jarn turned back to the customer. "'Tisn't like ye'd be a-carrying that much money," he probed.

Snarp fearlessly displayed a handful of silver. Jarn's eyes bulged at the sight of it, and he bent to ask with the air of an accomplice, "Did ye come by it honestly, then?"

"Three shorns." Snarp was impassive as ever, but the quibbid upon her shoulder, whose attitude was at times a barometer of its mistress' mood, bristled and bared minute fangs.

"Don't know." Jarn's cunning waxed. "Have to think it over. Don't really want to part with the horse, I don't. Maybe ye'd best look fer a miskin." His wife brought the ale. He accepted a tankard and sat, leaning back in elaborate indifference. Ignoring the proffered refreshment, Snarp watched her host unblinkingly, and Jarn's eyes fell beneath the feral stare. "Have to think it over," he repeated. "Come back tomorrow."

"Today," said Snarp.

"Softly, Mistress. I haven't said I'd be selling 'im at all, have I?"

"Four shorns," said Snarp.

The jaw of Jarn's wife sagged. "*Take it*!" she hissed.

"You keep out of this, woman!" Jarn fondled the tankard, deliberating importantly. "Come back tomorrow," he decided at last. "Can't hurry things like this. But," he added as an afterthought, "don't try to spend the night outdoors."

Snarp's lips thinned. "I am Enforcer of the Select. I require the horse."

"Ye're sayin' ye're a member o' the Select?" Jarn surveyed the visitor's small figure in disbelief.

"I am Enforcer. I offer four shorns. Surrender the horse, or I must compel you."

Jarn rose to his feet. He towered over Snarp. "Ye'll do that, will ye, Mistress? Take me and my wife on? All by yourself, eh?" He smiled down indulgently.

Jarn's wife did not share her husband's amusement. "Why, of all the bold-faced creatures—" she began.

"Your answer?" Snarp asked.

"I told ye I'll think it over. Come back tomorrow and bring money." He looked into his visitor's face and something prompted him to add, "And if ye be dreaming o' mischief, don't try it. Folk here help their neighbors and mislike strangers. Ye wouldna' get far."

She glanced outdoors. A sizable group of villagers had gathered before Jarn's house in hope of glimpsing the stranger. Whatever immediate scheme had formed in her mind was abandoned then and there. In silence Snarp walked to the door.

"She must be a loony," opined Jarn's wife. "Dressed up like that and talking like that! Loony enough to spend the night out of doors, I'll warrant!"

"Shut up, woman!" Jarn commanded without success.

"No, *you* shut up! She offered four shorns fer that oat-burner, and ye're too smart to take it. Ye're so sharp, ye'll outwit yerself!"

As Snarp exited the cottage, a violent quarrel broke out behind her.

It was chilly outside, and the sun was sinking toward the horizon. The hour was late and Snarp's belly was empty. At least a score of villagers loitered curiously in the street, and she might easily have purchased a meal and shelter for the night. Preferring to fend for herself, she wandered down toward the Daskyl Race, with a dozen townsfolk drifting silently in her wake. Agitation stirred their ranks as she neared the pool behind the dam. Their uneasiness increased as she seated herself upon the bank and brought forth a fishing line and hook.

The villagers paused for a hurried consultation, at the close of which they advanced upon the stranger. Snarp's attention seemed fixed exclusively on the tackle in her lap. She almost might have been unaware of the approaching rustics. But every muscle was tensed, and her hand lay but inches from the hilt of her knife.

The villagers, however, were pacific. "Going to do some angling, are ye, Mistress?" one of the men asked pleasantly enough.

Snarp inclined her head.

"Bad spot fer it." His companions nodded in fervent agreement. "Bad spot. No sense in stirring 'em up, there isn't."

"Them?" asked Snarp.

"Aye. Them." There were murmurings of trepidation and perhaps sorrow among the villagers. For the first time Snarp lifted her eyes to aim her sulfurous gaze directly at her unwanted companions. The townsfolk returned the regard with curiosity and some concern. "Best come away, Mistress. We'll see that ye don't go hungry. Come away."

"Why?" asked Snarp.

"I tell ye 'tisn't safe, especially not fer strangers. They ben't used to strangers, 'twill stir 'em up for certain. That little beast

94

upon yer shoulder makes it worse. They might even come out to look."

"Explain."

"No need! Just look ye down and see fer yerself. Look down into the pool!"

Snarp complied, narrowing her eyes against the surface glare. At the bottom of the pool bulked dozens of still, gray forms. At first they seemed to be rocks. Closer inspection revealed the human conformation, identifiable despite decomposition, despite grotesque bloating. Corpses, then. The villagers did not bury their dead, but simply dumped the bodies into Daskyl Race. A slight flare of the nostrils signaled Snarp's contempt. She was about to turn away when a swirl of motion arrested her attention. In the clear depths of the pool a silvery fish darted. One of the reclining gray figures stirred; raised a long, algae-slimed arm; extended a bony hand from which the tatters of skin streamed like carnival ribbons; made a languid grab for the fish. The terrified fish flashed out of reach. The cadaver-creature seemed to watch it go, slowly turning its head on a neck whose naked vertebrae shone white. Then the corpse looked up, lifting the remains of its face toward the humans standing beside the pool. For a long moment it sat staring up at them with its eyeless sockets. Both arms slowly rose, floating skyward in supplication. The fingers flexed and the arms swayed. And then the other cadaver-creatures began to wake, to move, to watch. Most were in various stages of disintegration, some verging on the skeletal, others monstrously swollen. But some remained nearly intact; fully dressed, features still distinct, with hair waving gently in tendrils. One young girl's long raven locks had come unbound to float about her face in a dusky cloud. Some of them still had their eyes, and these were perhaps the worst. The blank, pearly orbs were more terrible by far than empty sockets. Most dreadful, those dead faces altered as they gazed up through the water. Those rotting features reflected incongruous and pitiable expressions of longing. The arms reached up toward the living; a multitude of arms that swayed like a forest of reeds.

Staring impassively into the faces of the animate dead, Snarp awaited explanation.

"Now d'ye see why it ben't safe, Mistress?" asked the man who had first addressed her. "The sight o' the living, and more so a stranger, will always stir 'em. 'Tisn't unlike they'll come a-climbing out to see ye close up, and a sorry coil that be. I told as much to the strangers t'other day, and I say the same to you, Mistress."

"Strangers? When?" asked Snarp.

"Yesterday morning. They wouldna' tarry, and just as well, I say. Four of 'em, there were."

"Aye," broke in an eager young girl. "Two gentlemen, a servant and a lady, all city-bred. You should've *seen* her clothes! All velvet, with feathers and embroideries, and her shoes—with heels *that* high! She must be a duchess at least. D'ye know 'em, Mistress?"

Snarp's gaze was fixed on the submerged corpses. The dead eyes still watched, the uplifted arms still yearned. "What are those?" she asked.

"Them as died o' the sickness," replied the first speaker. "Died yet didna' die." Snarp glanced at him briefly and he continued. "The sickness come upon us weeks ago, nigh the time the new star that shines by day and night was birthed. The star so changed the look o' the sky at night that some folk'll have it that the old Lion constellation was become a great serpent, and took to callin' it the Dragon. And these same folk put forth that the Dragon breathed a vaporous humor o' pestilence upon us. No matter fer all o' that, 'twas then that the sickness came. Those it struck burned with fever and their flesh was covered with crumbling patches. They died quick enough, and we buried 'em deep."

"But they didn't stay buried," the young girl interrupted.

Snarp eyed her in cold distrust.

"'Tis so," insisted the first speaker, interpreting the look. "Those that died couldna' rest in peace. Each night when the moon come up, they'd dig their way out o' the ground and rove through the village in search o' their friends and kin. Ye could see 'em longing for those they'd cherished in life. Sometimes they found 'em, and woe betide us then! The dead embraced the living, the living fell sick and died, and so the sickness spread."

"'Twas a fearsome thing to see 'em walk by night with the earth o' the grave still upon 'em and their dead eyes a-shine," the girl interjected with a certain air of exhilaration. "Many a night I peeked through the shutters and saw it all, I did!"

"It seemed that we were lost," the man continued. "The dead grew bolder and even ventured abroad in daylight hours. And as fer the night—mewed up in our cottages we were, with the doors barred and shutters bolted—"

"And each night the dead ones knocking at the doors and scratching at the windows until the break o' dawn!"

"Thought we were finished fer sure. Until one day the corpse o' poor Nula walked, a-searchin' fer her child. The boy fled

96

along the bank o' the Race until he stumbled and fell into the pool afore ye. Nula came after. The child swam out safe, but Nula sank to the bottom, and there she sat. Days passed and still she sat without stirring. 'Twas plain that the water soothed her spirit and gave 'er peace. When we saw that, we made haste to lead the others o' the dead to this same pool. There they bide quiet until the flesh drops from their poor bones, and then 'tis finished and they be truly dead at last."

"But until that time comes," the girl concluded, "'tisn't safe to mess with 'em."

"They should be destroyed." Snarp studied the cadavers dispassionately. "Burned, crushed, or dissolved."

A mutter of collective distress greeted the suggestion.

"Ah, ye doesna' understand, Mistress," replied the man. "These be our own folk—our parents, sisters and brothers, sons and daughters. How could we destroy them? See down there?" He pointed at a recumbent corpse with a few strands of silver hair still clinging to its scalp. "That be Livil's mother. Could Livil crush her? That black-haired lass over there—'tis young Crevin's wife. Died last week, and he thought she was the sun and stars. And that little one below—'tis Jarn's only son. Ye think Jarn would burn 'im or suffer others to do it? Nay, Mistress. I tell ye we canna' destroy 'em. I say let 'em sit down there, 'twas meant to be." Snarp did not reply, and he added, "Best come along with me, then. There's a place fer ye at our table, and ye can sleep in our lean-to. Ye mustn't spend the night out o' doors."

Snarp permitted herself to be led away from the pool, up the street to one of the cottages where, as she had been promised, she received a hot meal, with barley mash for the quibbid. She spent the next couple of hours disregarding well-meant questions. At the end of that time her rustic host admitted defeat, abandoned the interrogation and showed her to her pallet in the lean-to. Within the dark little enclosure, Snarp sat listening. For a while she heard footsteps passing to and fro. Then—nothing. Time passed, and the sound of snoring arose. Snarp waited in preternatural stillness. At least two hours passed and still she sat motionless, the quibbid asleep in her lap.

In the dead of night, when all the village slept, Snarp finally moved. She assimilated the quibbid, strapped her pack to her back, and settled the wide hat upon her head, then passed silently from the lean-to into the cottage. Moonlight leaking in through chinks in the bolted shutters furnished the faintest possible illumination, but it was enough for Snarp's cat's-eyes. A big cupboard bed stood in the corner. Her host and his wife were safely immured therein. The children slumbered on pallets at the other end of the room. One of them tossed and whimpered, but did not wake. Snarp glided to the door and softly, very softly, lifted the massive bar. Iron hinges moaned as the portal yielded, and she slipped out into the night.

White moonlight bathed the sleeping village. The road, the darkened houses and gardens were all easily visible. Not far away stood the cottage of Jarn; behind it, the paddock and shed containing the horse Snarp had marked for her own. Skirting the cottage, she went straight to the paddock and began to climb the fence. Before she reached the top, a low snarl arrested her. She looked down into the gleaming eyes of Jarn's four watch-dogs—great, gaunt, wolflike creatures, pointed of snout and fang. Normally the dogs were stationed about the cottage. Tonight, fearing special danger to his horse, their master had set them to guard the shed.

One of the dogs snarled again, lips writhing back from its teeth, and a faint expression—something almost resembling amusement—passed over Snarp's face. She could kill the dogs, but in so doing would inevitably rouse the attention of the entire village. Another approach was indicated. It did not take her long to devise one.

Dropping from the fence, she made her way back along the road, down the brambled slope to the bank of the pool. The rippling water reflected changing glints of pale light, quivering stars, a distorted moon. In vain Snarp strained her eyes for a glimpse of the gray ones dreaming beneath the water. The depths were shrouded in darkness and deceptive tranquility.

Her attention shifted to the dam—a clumsy affair of rock and wood, plugged with moss and leaves; crude, but sufficient to create the corpses' pool. Below the dam the Daskyl Race flowed on much diminished, its power leashed as it hurried to meet the Yl. Heavy wooden posts sunk deep in the ground shored up the wall of rock. The posts were very strongly reinforced; built to defeat the attack of the elements, but hardly designed to defeat the attack of Mistress Snarp. Within her pack reposed a stoppered flask, another contribution of the ever-generous Gless Vallage. She rarely resorted to this flask, but sometimes its contents proved invaluable. Such an occasion had now arisen.

Snarp selected three supporting posts at the center of the dam. Removing boots and stockings, she waded out into the water. The bottom was soft with frigid ooze, treacherous with algae-slicked rock, and it took some care to maintain her footing. The Race rose up around her as she advanced until she stood chest-deep in icy water. Snarp ignored the discomfort. Inspecting Vallage's flask, she saw that little remained of the liquid content; barely enough, in fact, to accomplish her purpose. Very carefully she removed the stopper and poured a few drops onto each wooden post. What was left she sprinkled on the stones of the dam, then tossed the empty bottle aside. This done, she left the water as quickly as possible.

Snarp sat on the bank, watching the dam as she donned her stockings and boots. At first nothing happened, and her jaw muscles hardened. A moment later a dense, strangling vapor arose. The waters of the Race seethed and boiled fiercely. Snarp's keen ears detected a faint crackling, and then the wooden posts burst violently into flame. The stones of the dam softened, bubbled, melted and flowed. Dribbles of molten rock slid down into the water. The trickle increased to a stream, and then to an incandescent torrent. Tremendous clouds of steam and smoke billowed skyward. Steam was everywhere, glowing orange in the light of the flames. As the stones dissolved, water poured through the dam. The blackened posts cracked, gave way, and crashed down into the Race. Shattered rock came rattling down like hail. A gap opened in the center of the dam and the waters of Daskyl Race, released at last, burst through in roaring triumph. The pool behind the dam began to empty. At this time, lights appeared in the windows of the neighboring cottages.

Snarp's gaze shifted from dam to pool, where the water level was sinking swiftly. Down it went, and warring eddies fluttered the formerly placid surface. And then a fleshless, clutching hand rose slowly out of the foaming Race.

Springing to her feet, Snarp sought the shadows. The water continued to sink. A second hand rose up, trailing scraps of muscle and tendon. A ghastly head broke the surface, and a corpse dragged itself from the Daskyl Race to stand hesitating upon the bank. The cadaver's height suggested that it had once been a man. By no other sign was its gender evident. It must have been dead for some time, for most of its flesh was gone. The eye sockets were empty, and only a smear of a face remained. A silver chain and medallion still hung upon its neck, and the medallion knocked against the exposed clavicle with a horrible clinking sound each time the creature moved.

The corpse loitered aimlessly, regarding the ruined dam in what might have been wonder. It seemed to have no idea where to go or what to do with itself. Its dilemma was resolved when confused villagers began to converge upon the dam. The corpse stretched forth its arms to its former compatriots and tottered forward to meet them. The approaching townsfolk beheld the cadaver, turned tail en masse and fled screaming for the safety of their respective homes. The corpse followed. More lights appeared in the cottage windows.

The waters shuddered, and then the newly awakened dead emerged, a ghastly throng of them; men, women and children with filmy eyes and distended flesh. One after another, singly and in groups, the dead lurched dripping from the pool to stagger toward the beckoning lights. Snarp followed discreetly in their wake. She could see the faces of some of them as they walked— pathetic dead faces of love and longing and even hope. The dead hands reached out as if to clutch at the vanished warmth of life.

Lights were burning all over the village now, and they shone upon a wandering horde of corpses. Scores of cadavers roamed the street in search of their family homes. Snarp heard a dragging scuffle and whirled to face a dead woman who lurched toward her, arms spread wide. Recalling the tale of lethal contagion, Snarp turned and ran, easily distancing the creature. She headed for Jarn's house, and as she ran she passed corpses, beating on locked doors, rattling at bolted shutters, scratching at keyholes with their livid fingers. Wails of mortal fear issued from the besieged dwellings. One of the corpses managed to discover a window insecurely fastened, and the shutters gave way beneath the assault. Slowly the corpse climbed through the window, and screams of horror arose within.

A little farther on, the black-haired, ice-white female identified as Criven's wife stood knocking on a barred door while a young man, presumably Criven, watched her through the shutters. After a time, Criven opened the door and admitted the girl.

Jarn's cottage was locked, and a light burned at every window. The inhabitants were obviously awake and aware. But no cadavers roamed the premises, and the only intruder seemed to be Snarp herself.

Not troubling to conceal her intentions, she rushed to the fence, scaled it nimbly and jumped down into the paddock. The dogs set upon her at once, and the night resounded with their clamor. The boldest of the canines leaped forward to seize her elbow in its jaws. As if by magic a knife appeared in Snarp's free hand, and the next moment the blade was buried to the hilt behind the animal's shoulder.

As she wrenched her elbow free another dog rushed at her ankles, snapping furiously. She dispatched her attacker with an almost negligent stroke, and the remaining two wisely retreated.

100

Circling the trespasser at a safe distance, they bayed in mounting frenzy. Snarp took no notice. Gliding without haste to the padlocked shed, she removed the steel from her hat, and with that tool she deftly picked the lock.

As the canine uproar in the paddock continued, one of the cottage windows banged open and Jarn's bearded face appeared. He gazed out searchingly, spotted the intruder, and uttered a yell of fury. Snarp did not trouble to glance in his direction. The padlock in her hand clicked open. She pulled it from the staple and threw it aside.

The cottage door flew open with a crash. Jarn rushed forth bellowing invective and brandishing a staff. No sooner had he left the house than a short white figure toddled from the shadows. A cadaverous child, no more than two years old at the time of its death, lurched slowly forward, cerements slapping wetly against its ankles. Jarn froze, staring. The child extended its small, still chubby arms. Jarn stood petrified. The child advanced and wrapped both arms around its father's leg. It gazed up into his face with its eyeless sockets, and Jarn gave a hoarse cry that drew his wife to the doorway. When she beheld her husband and her son thus entwined, her screams soared in hysteria.

Flinging wide the shed door, Snarp slipped inside to take possession of Jarn's brown horse. Seizing a handful of the animal's mane, she swung herself onto its back and spurred vigorously. With a startled snort, the horse bolted out of the shed. Guided by the pressure of its rider's knees, it cleared the paddock fence at a surprisingly creditable bound and thundered up the road.

Straight through the stricken heart of the village Snarp galloped, past lighted houses, trapped townsfolk and wandering corpses. Her jaw was set, her eyes alight, her thin lips set in a curve. She was clear of the area in seconds. The sound of screaming died behind her and soon it was gone.

Chapter Nine

They had left the Nazara Sin far behind, and now they followed the curve of the River Yl that ran like a great silver artery from the heart of Dalyon to the sea. For years the river had served as a highway for settlers, traders, explorers and outlaws, providing transport across territory virtually impassable by other means; and did so yet, now more than ever. In the course of their journey, Devras Har Fennahar and his companions had encountered a polyglot variety of fellow travelers, from whom they often purchased provisions. The refugees—most of them simple folk from the inland settlements—were heading for the coast. The majority traveled in family groups. They came in miskin-drawn carts laden with scanty possessions; in small boats and rafts; or else they walked, belongings bundled upon their backs. Their faces were drawn, their demeanor weary, and their tales instructive. They spoke at length of the darkness marching across the land— intense, suffocating blackness lethal to body and spirit; domain of the terrible White Demons, pitiless killers devoid of restraint.

Not many, as it happened, had personally encountered either darkness or demons. Forewarned of approaching disaster, most had lingered in their villages only long enough to see the shadow loom upon the horizon before fleeing for their lives. A minority of skeptical or stubborn settlers had stood their ground to experience the darkness at firsthand, but they had not endured it long. The heat, the near-unbreathable atmosphere, the horrid sensation of blind helplessness—these things had swiftly broken human resolve. The indomitable few remaining to defend their homes had suffered the invaders' fury, and all but a handful had died.

But more than simple settlers fled the dark. All manner of odd beings inhabited the inland regions. There were Eatches, descendants of the primitive twelve-fingered sorcerers who abused their power in Lanthi Ume and her sister-city of Hurba prior to the rise of the Select. There were violet-haired Vemi in their filthy rags; their religion forbade them to wash or to drink water, and they had developed a vampiric thirst for blood. There were shy, large-eyed Bexae, who dwelt in a moving city in the depths of the forest, and customarily shunned the sight of men. There were Zonianders, who lived in the marshes of Jire, developing so perfect a rapport with the local vegetation that their children were chlorophyllous of skin, with tendril fingers able to draw moisture and nourishment directly from the soil. There were swindling Turos, androgynous Denders, dwarfish Feeniads, webfooted Swamp-Splatters, cannibalistic Burbies, and flame-eyed Fugitives of the Zoushe. These last two represented genuine danger, and it was therefore with some alarm that Devras, out by himself gathering firewood upon an otherwise featureless evening, reacted to a rustling in the bushes close at hand.

He froze, all senses straining. The sound was tentative, surreptitious, and therefore all the more suspicious. For a moment he listened before pinpointing the origin and then, Wate Basef's hatchet in hand, he pounced. The rustling quickened to a frenzied scuffle. The bushes convulsed, and a small drab form broke from cover. Devras flung himself upon the fleeing figure. He found himself clutching a small, bedraggled, long-haired creature. The mite squirmed and squeaked; and the helpless, despairing quality of those cries banished Devras's fears. His grip relaxed a trifle, and the shrieks subsided. He stared down into wide eyes glazed with terror. He sat up, still grasping the other's wrist, and examined his captive.

He held a girl-child—tiny, filthy, tearful, no more than five or six years old. She had long, disheveled black hair; white skin beneath the dirt; and long, down-slanting brown eyes shaded by unusually thick lashes, casting so dense a shadow that pupil merged indistinguishably into iris. She was skinny and clad in rags. But the most unusual aspect of her appearance lay in her hands, each of which carried two thumbs.

"What are you doing here?" asked Devras.

She stared at him blankly.

"What's your name? Where are your parents?"

No answer. The tears flowed faster.

"Where do you come from?"

"Go away!" the child commanded, struggling valiantly. She spoke a provincial variant of Old Umish, a dialect with which Devras was reasonably familiar. "Go *away!*"

"It's all right." Devras soothed the litle girl in her own language. "No one will hurt you. Calm down."

Responding more to the tone of voice than the words, she gradually grew quiet. The tears evaporated and the facial contraction relaxed.

"What's your name?"

"Glindi," the child returned. Her terror had already vanished. She stared at him in open curiosity.

"Mine's Devras."

"That's a funny name."

"Not where I come from. Why are you out in the woods by yourself, Glindi? Are you lost?"

Glindi shrugged, ducking her head.

"Do your parents know where you are? Are they far from here?"

"They're dead. Everyone's dead." The black eyes filled again. "The white things that live in the caves came and killed them."

"The white marauders are the same as the folk of the caverns? You're sure of that?"

She nodded.

"They killed your people? When?"

"I don't know. I ran away to the river and then I walked beside the water. After a while, it wasn't dark any more."

"You've been alone all this time?"

Large-eyed silence.

"You've been a very brave girl." Devras found himself extraordinarily touched by the child's story. Her plight would have awakened almost anyone's sympathy, but his reaction went beyond that. Perhaps it was because she was an orphan, all her family dead, and he knew exactly how that felt. "But now the worst is over—you won't be on your own any longer. Are you hungry?"

"*Yes.*" She nodded so vigorously that the tangled black locks fell over her eyes.

Devras smoothed them aside. "Come along, then." He extended a hand to receive her grubby little paw, and together they set off through the trees. She followed with unquestioning trust. "I'll take you to meet my friends."

"Are they Ten-Fingers like you?"

"Why, yes." Devras glanced at the six-fingered hand nestled in his own. "I suppose others of your family have hands like yours?"

"All my people," Glindi returned proudly. "All. We live in the Ring and we are Friends of the Soil."

"Friends of the Soil?"

"Yes. All of us are."

There was no time to request an explanation, for they had reached the camp, set up on a flat open space beside the narrow lane that followed the River Yl. The child's eyes widened at the

104

sight of the carriage. Most likely she had never before encountered such a vehicle. Of at least equal interest were the four tethered horses. Not far from the carriage a fire burned within a stone circle, and there Grono stirred the contents of a pot suspended above the blaze. A seductive odor wafted from the pot, and Glindi's nostrils twitched. Beside the fire the heiress of Lanthi Ume sat peeling boiled potatoes, to Grono's obvious distress. Atop the carriage, Raith Wate Basef fussed with the bags and bundles. The three paused in their respective tasks to stare in surprise at the new arrivals. Wate Basef descended at once.

Devras led his small charge to the fire. "This," he announced, "is Glindi. She's apparently sole survivor of a massacre. She's identified her people's killers as Vardruls of the caverns, and seems very certain of that. She's an orphan, all alone and hungry. Oh yes, and she only speaks Old Umish." He turned to address the child in her own tongue. "Glindi, these are my friends, and now they're yours as well. This is Karavise. Raith. And Grono."

The little girl looked up at Karavise. "You're pretty. I thought Ten-Fingers were ugly," she said.

"Thank you, Glindi." Karavise replied in stilted Old Umish. She could read the dialect tolerably well, but had never before been called upon to speak it. "You are pretty too."

"Yes, because I'm a Friend of the Soil." Glindi hesitated, then recited carefully, as she had evidently been taught, "I greet you in the name of the Ring. May your kindness be returned one hundred thousandfold."

Even Grono, the only one present entirely ignorant of Old Umish, was charmed. All traces of disapproval vanished from his face as he ladled her out a large portion of stew.

"That's a lovely greeting, Glindi," said Devras, "but I'm not sure what it all means."

"It means she's an Eatch, that's what it means," Wate Basef explained. "See her hands, with the extra thumbs? The Eatches are a race of twelve-fingered magicians once dominant in Lanthi Ume. They possess a certain—how shall I put it—instinctive understanding of a few natural phenomena that grants them some influence over their physical surroundings. Their power is not to be compared with the Cognition of the Select, who supplanted them in Lanthi Ume generations ago, but it is sometimes astonishingly effective. The surviving Eatches live in gatherings known as Rings, which generally consist of several families. Each Ring specializes in some particular object of influence. When this little girl calls herself a Friend of the Soil, she probably means that her people exert their power over the land—a very useful accomplishment, obviously, for farmers." Turning to the little girl, Wate Basef switched over to Old Umish. "Glindi, I've been telling them that you're an Eatch, and the folk of your Ring have power over the soil. Have I got it right?"

"Yes. Raith." She pronounced the foreign name carefully, with an accent that made them all smile. Accepting the bowl of stew from Grono, she thanked him in her polite Old Umish, without once releasing her hold on Devras's hand. Evidently marking Devras as her particular friend and savior, she remained glued to his side as he took his stew and seated himself by the fire. Only when he was sitting as close to her as possible, and certain he didn't intend to move, did she relinquish his hand.

When all had been served, they ate in silence as the darkness gathered to blot the world from view. At last Karavise observed, "We've already met several Eatches along the way, and it's likely we'll meet more. Perhaps we'll find someone who can take the child."

Glindi caught the word "Eatches," and glanced questioningly at Devras, who provided translation. The little girl appeared bewildered. "Can't I stay with you?" she asked.

"We couldn't look after you properly," Devras explained gently, meeting her wounded eyes with difficulty.

"I don't care!" Glindi exclaimed, her expression willful.

"But we care," Wate Basef told her. "For your own good, you should be with your own people."

"I want to stay with you." Glindi's eyes filled.

"We'd like that too," Devras consoled her. "But we're going into the darkness from which you escaped. You don't want to go back there, do you? We're going into the caverns themselves, and we can't take you with us."

"It's far too dangerous," Karavise concurred. "Do you understand, child?"

There could be no doubt that she understood. Hungry though she had been, she set her dinner aside unfinished. Her face screwed into the grimace of a child poised on the verge of howling grief, but the tears didn't come. In a voice that quivered, Glindi warned, "You can't go there. The white things are in there and they'll get you."

"We'll keep out of their way," Devras promised with hollow conviction.

"You can't. They can see in the dark—they're magic. *Please* don't go in there!"

"The Vardruls aren't magic, child," Wate Basef said. "That I can promise you."

106

"They are!" Glindi insisted. "The Ring all called upon our friend the Soil to help us, and the Soil did, but the white things got in anyway. So they're magic."

Her listeners were uniformly uncomprehending. "Could you tell us what you mean, Glindi?" Devras asked.

"We were home, and night came and morning never came," the child explained. "It was all hot, and it smelled bad, and everyone felt bad. Vundi kept throwing up, but I didn't, because I'm too big."

"Why didn't your family run away?" Karavise asked.

"Daddy said that everyone who trusted the Soil would stay."

"In such darkness?" Wate Basef inquired. "You couldn't live in it for long."

"Daddy said we could, if we were brave and trusted the Soil. There were lots of fires everywhere, so we could see. Everyone in the Ring got together near the big fire, and everyone spoke to the Soil. Then the Soil built us up a high wall, all around the houses. It was so high that nobody could climb it and it had no door."

"The Soil built them a wall? She must be speaking figuratively," Karavise remarked in Lanthian.

"Not necessarily," Wate Basef replied in the same language.

"Then what happened?" Devras prompted. "Did the white creatures climb over the wall?"

"No, the Soil wouldn't let them. But they tricked the Soil, and came underneath. They're magic, they've got tunnels through the stone, and the stone's stronger than the Soil. There was a tunnel that came up in Pulni's smokehouse, so they got in."

"Did your people try to fight them?" asked Karavise.

"Some did, but most were too sick. There were lots of the white things and they were strong. They had pointed sticks and swords, and they killed everyone. The biggest one was leader, and he killed Daddy. Then there were white things all over, and Daddy, Mother and Vundi were dead. I was running and it caught me."

"The leader caught you, you mean?" Wate Basef inquired.

"Yes. He had blood all over him. His skin was shining through and he was all bright and red like a coal in the fire. I thought he'd kill me, but he didn't. He looked at me a long time. His eyes were black. The other white things had light eyes, but his were black. Then his skin stopped shining so much. He put me in the barrel beside the shed and put the lid down."

"Prefers to leave the actual slaughter of infants to his subordinates, evidently," Karavise murmured in Lanthian. "We are dealing with a creature of delicate conscience."

"I hid in the barrel until they were gone," Glindi continued. "When I came out, everyone was dead. I asked the wall of Soil to let me through, and it did. I went down to the river and ran away."

"Poor child, it's a miracle you survived," said Devras.

"Then you won't go back there? *Please* don't go!" Her tears broke forth anew.

"What ails the poor little lass?" inquired Grono, who had not understood a word of the story. "Grieving for her parents, is she?"

"That, and afraid that all of us will die in the darkness."

"Well, give her some more stew, your Lordship. That's bound to cheer her up."

"I don't think food will work."

"It usually did for *you*, Master Devras."

"Hush, Glindi," Devras soothed the sobbing child. "Don't be frightened. No one's going to get us, I promise."

"They will," Glindi insisted. "They're magic."

"Well even if they are, it doesn't matter. Raith's got magic too." *Although we've seen little sign of it.* "Now be a brave girl. Everything's going to be fine."

Reluctantly her sobs subsided. She pleaded no longer, but her tragic expression revealed the futility of Devras's attempted reassurances.

"That child is exhausted. She needs sleep," Grono announced with the air of an expert. "And a bath," he added under his breath.

"Tired, Glindi?" Devras asked.

"No!"

"Well, I think you'll soon find that you are, but you can sit up a little longer."

And sit up she did, straining to follow conversation largely incomprehensible to her, until her head began to nod and her lids drooped.

"Put the child in the carriage," Karavise directed. "She can sleep there until we find someone to look after her."

Devras lifted Glindi and bore her toward the carriage. As he went, her arms stole about his neck, and already half-asleep she murmured, "Don't go back there!"

He placed her on the tufted leather seat, covered her with the woolen rug ordinarily reserved for Karavise's use, deposited a kiss upon her cheek, shut the door and returned to his companions. For a while longer they sat by the fire analyzing the child's narrative, which confirmed one significant point—the proximity of the darkness. It would not be long before they'd meet it.

"And we must first see to the child's welfare," Grono proclaimed righteously. "For I trust that even the Cognizant Wate Basef, so willing to work the ruination of a promising young lord, would not stoop to the destruction of a helpless little girl. Particularly if he has nothing to gain by it."

The fire was beginning to sink, and the shadows encroached. It was time to retire, if they were to rise at dawn. The night was mild and they had no need of the tent packed away in a roll atop the carriage. Without further conversation, they prepared themselves for slumber. Devras stretched himself upon his makeshift bed, and sleep took him in seconds.

He had no idea how long he rested, nor what it was that finally woke him—perhaps the thud of horses' hoofs, perhaps simple instinct. Some time must have passed, for the moon had set and the fire was dead. Not so much as a handful of glowing embers remained. How was he able to see so clearly? Devras sat up abruptly.

The night glowed violet. Large, dark forms crossed his field of vision. It took him a moment to identify them as horses. The four animals were loose and heading away from the camp at a nervous trot. Devras jumped to his feet with a shout that simultaneously roused his companions and sent the horses stampeding into the night at full gallop. Their departure was hardly noted, for the incredulous attention of all was fixed upon the carriage, or rather the ground on which it stood.

The soil was bathed in violet luminescence. Waves of heat rolled off its violently churning surface. The carriage stood at the center of a glowing, seething circle some forty-five feet in diameter. At the edge of the circle stood a tiny figure with outstretched arms, visible in black silhouette against the violet radiance.

"Glindi! *What are you doing?*" Devras ran to the child's side.

She turned to gaze up at him, dark eyes unfathomable in the odd light. "I asked the Soil for help."

"Help? What kind of help?"

"The Soil will choose."

He was unlikely to get anything more out of her just then, and in any event it was not the time for an interrogation. The heat from the ground beat at his eyes. For a moment he turned his face away from it, and saw that his three companions stood near, regarding the scene in disbelief. The ground at his feet writhed and heaved. The soil itself had altered in consistency, taking on the heavy plasticity of lava. In this state it mounded and hollowed, spun in brief whirlpools and broke in slow waves, its motion apparently random. Gradually, however, the most vigorous activity began to center itself about the carriage. There the soil was rolling itself into long ridges, swelling and flattening, long bulge indenting, rocks shifting busily as a definite outline started to take shape. The exact nature of the construction as yet remained unclear.

"My Cognitive gear!" Wate Basef found his voice at last. "It's on the luggage rack!" He started for the carriage. The instant his foot touched ground within the circle, the bubbling soil gave way beneath him and he sank to knee level. A squawk of pained surprise escaped him. The soil was viciously hot, roasting him through his boots and stockings. As he stood there floundering, the violet glow in his vicinity intensified, the temperature rose, and a muddy excrescence heaved itself high to clutch at his leg. Wate Basef tottered, and Devras caught his outstretched hand. With Grono's assistance, he hauled the savant back to solid ground.

At the center of the circle, the curved shape forming about the carriage acquired pointed extremities. The large stones were surfacing to line themselves up in two rows.

"Don't walk on the Soil!" Glindi begged. "You'll make it angry!"

"Glindi, *what are you doing?*"

"Nothing! It's the Soil!"

"Tell it to stop!" Devras commanded.

"I can't! It wants to help!"

"I've got to get those things back, we can't do without them." Wate Basef's tic of a smile flickered.

"Why assume they're in danger?" Karavise inquired coolly. "What we see is unfamiliar, but not necessarily threatening."

"We can't afford to take the chance. There's no telling what this Eatch-child has unleashed." Wate Basef took a step toward the circle. His companions' protests overlapped.

"I'll get them," Devras offered, secure in his youth and agility.

"Good lad. The leather satchel at the back of the rack. And the carpetbag, if you can carry it."

"Master Devras, what are you thinking of?" Grono demanded.

"Please don't tread on the Soil now! You can't!"

Without responding to either, Devras backed to the end of the clearing, took a long running start to the edge of the circle and leaped for the carriage. As he left the ground, he heard Glindi's

110

shrill cry of alarm, and simultaneously the heat from the agitated ground rose to strike him. His jump carried him high above the glowing ooze, and his outstretched hand caught the carriage frame as he descended.

He landed on his feet, and the impact drove him calf-deep into the softened dirt. It took but a moment for the heat to make itself felt. The soil was scorching his flesh and the pain increased as he sank. So swiftly was the mud sucking him down that he almost could have credited Glindi's quaint belief in the Soil's sentience. Devras's hold upon the swinging carriage door arrested his descent. Little by little he dragged himself toward the vehicle until at last he lifted one foot clear to set it upon the passenger step, and in so doing aroused the spite of the Soil. The hot violet light brightened and the turbulence increased. The carriage itself was pitching giddily, and it took all of Devras's strength to maintain his grip. One foot still remained upon the ground, half-sunk, and as he struggled to pull it free, the Soil's hold tightened. A shaft of softened clay reared itself, bulging at the tip. The bulge swelled, budded, sprouted clay shoots that quickly lengthened to six large-knuckled digits. A moment later the clay replica of a double-thumbed human hand and arm was complete. The hand lunged forward to seize Devras's ankle. It pulled strongly and Devras slid backward a couple feet. As he felt the mud rise to engulf him, he clutched the door and kicked convulsively, breaking his enemy's hold. Quickly he drew his leg up out of the clay hand's reach. For the moment he was free, but other spears of clay were lifting, budding, sprouting fingers—dozens of them, all around him. The hands were reaching for him, clutching and pulling at him, smearing traces of their heavy substance along his limbs as they dragged him struggling down to the boiling mud. Abruptly his hold on the carriage was broken, and then they had him and he tumbled full length.

He could hear the cries of his friends only a few feet away, but couldn't make out the words, if any. He couldn't see them, for his view was obscured by a field of crazily weaving, swaying, uplifted arms. He was wallowing on his belly in the mud, his body buoyed up on the dense, rolling surface. The stuff was burning him—not lethally, only enough to cause pain. Of far more real danger were the hands that strove so eagerly to pull him under. He felt one on the back of his neck, wandering upward to clog his hair with clay as it pressed his face to the ground.

With a violent effort Devras managed to flip over onto his back. He could breathe again, and he caught a flashing glimpse of the stars before a dank palm clapped itself across his eyes and

111

nose. He tore at the hand, obtained a grip on the many-jointed second thumb and bent the digit backward. The clay, endlessly malleable, curved back to touch the clay wrist. He twisted hard, and the thumb came away in his grasp. Mashing the clay into formlessness, he threw it aside. The mutilated hand jerked away from his face and he could see again, see the lank arms snaking over his body. One of the arms was clamped across his chest, its hand crawling up toward his throat. He grabbed the middle fingers, bent backward, twisted and pulled. The fingers came off, and he could feel them wiggling like worms in his grasp before he squashed them. The hand clenched, shuddered, withdrew a little; and then began to sprout two new fingers to replace those lost. Conquering his repugnance, Devras twisted the entire hand off at the wrist, whereupon the stump of the arm shot away from his chest to plunge down into the mud.

More of them now. One at his shoulder. Another at his knee; his chest; his thigh. Again at his throat. Working at desperate speed, Devras twisted clay hands from clay wrists, one after another. The hands he squashed and tossed aside did not return, but others took their place. Faster now, destroying faster than the hands could regenerate. The struggle that seemed to continue for agonizing minutes was actually over in seconds. A last member at his shoulder mutilated and discarded, and then he was free to flounder across the few heaving feet that separated him from the carriage. Grabbing the passenger step, he hoisted himself from the muck, scrambled up to the box seat and thence to the roof, where he crouched exhausted, filthy and smarting all over, but out of the Soil's reach.

A moment's pause to catch his breath, and then to work again. The carriage was pitching and wobbling beneath him. With difficulty he made his way on singed hands and knees to the rear of the tossing luggage rack, located the leather satchel containing Wate Basef's Cognitive aids, and stood to throw the bag to safety. At the edge of the circle, his companions screamed and gestured incomprehensibly. No time to puzzle their meaning now. Devras threw, and the satchel flew to the arms of Raith Wate Basef. He paused to see the bag land safely, and in that brief moment heard the voice of Grono rise frantically:

"Master Devras! *Save yourself!*"

Grono was always prone to melodrama.

Devras turned away, knelt and pawed through the luggage, soon locating Wate Basef's carpetbag. Once again he stood and threw. The bag sailed out of the glowing circle, and he turned back to eye the remaining bundles. Which of them most merited

112

salvation? The painted casket with the double lock looked significant. As he stooped to raise it, the carriage suddenly stopped pitching. A slight shock vibrated through the frame, and then the vehicle rested motionless, listing a little to starboard. Another vibration, a grinding crunch, a creak of tortured wooden joints, a breathless sense of imminent catastrophe, and then the explosive crack of shattered timber.

The carriage was lifted, shaken like a toy, and dropped sickeningly. Devras was thrown forward on his face. For a moment he lay prone, one hand clenched upon the rail of the luggage rack as the carriage descended in a series of spine-snapping jerks. The noise was louder now, an incessant rhythmic clashing punctuated by the crackle of demolished woodwork and human screams from the edge of the circle. Raising himself on his elbows, Devras glanced down at the ground, and understood at once the cause of his companions' hysteria.

The form taking shape around the carriage was at last complete. The Soil had chosen to mold itself into an immense human mouth, complete with full, curving lips; a fat, forked, prehensile tongue; and teeth composed of jagged rocks lined up in a double row. The mouth surrounded the carriage. A leisurely ingestion was in progress. Already the four wheels were gone—bitten clean off, chewed, and swallowed down to unknowable depths. As Devras watched, the mouth gaped, the Soil snapped like a hungry fish, and granite incisors crushed the axle. The carriage shook as the Soil masticated; molars chomping, muddy saliva dribbling from the corner of the smiling lips. The vast forked tongue emerged to lick saliva and splinters away. The tongue rose, slid up the carriage frame to the window in the swinging door; curled about the window frame; and with a sudden yank tore the door off its weakened hinges. The door vanished into the giant maw. The granite teeth clashed with gusto, the wooden fragments were gulped down, and the smile on the giant lips broadened to a grin. The tongue reappeared to snake its way up to the roof, where it darted this way and that in search of a tempting morsel. Several canvas sacks were considered and rejected in quick succession. Then the tongue encountered Devras's leg, whipped around the ankle and pulled.

Devras slid backward on his belly to the edge of the roof and there he halted, caught on the railing of the luggage rack. The pull on his leg increased, and the flimsy rail—all that stood between himself and grinding granite—was already bending under the strain. Devras wriggled, kicked and struggled to no avail. He could feel his leg and spine stretch, hear the teeth crunching a few feet below. His groping hands encountered a twine-lashed bundle of tools from which he pulled a shovel. Turning, he sat up, leaned over the rail and drove the shovel's blade deep into the tongue. The pressure on his leg did not slacken, and he twisted the shovel, digging out a large chunk of wet clay. Flinging the clay aside, he repeated the operation three more times to create a deep and oozing canker. Pained at last, the tongue released his ankle and dove underground.

Devras shrank to the far side of the roof, looked down to see the great lips spread, and felt the shock as the gray teeth closed on wood. The carriage was disappearing rapidly. Unless he moved, he would disappear along with it. The shrieks of his companions confirmed this opinion. Devras stood. For a moment he balanced on the edge of the roof and then, shovel still in hand, he leaped.

His jump carried him high above the hungry mouth, more than halfway back to the edge of the circle. He came down hard, feet driving deep, and started to sink. Around him the muck bubbled and the lank gray arms rose up like weeds. Devras plied his shovel with vigor and the arms gave way beneath the assault. Slowly he slogged toward solid ground, swatting the six-fingered clay hands aside as he went. As he neared the edge of the circle, Wate Basef and Grono floundered forth to meet him. Their hands closed around his arms and they dragged him from the mud.

Devras sank to the cool ground. His flesh burned and his breath came in gasps. For a moment he rested, until the sound of a splintering crunch spun him around to face the carriage.

The vehicle had nearly disappeared. Only the top section and roof were left, and they would not remain much longer. As Devras watched, the mouth gaped, the forked tongue curled, and the last fragments of the carriage disappeared. A subterranean gulp, a rumble of satisfied hunger, and it was over.

Its purpose accomplished, animation deserted the Soil. The surface smoothed and quieted. The great mouth closed, its lips set in a smile of satiation. One by one the clutching hands slowed and froze, clawing air. The luminescence faded until nothing remained but a faint violet glow. By that ghostly light, Devras could see the faces of his companions—Grono, white and glassy-eyed with terror; Wate Basef, gnawing his lip bloody; Karavise, hard-jawed and composed; and little Glindi, quivering in mingled fright and relief.

"I'm all right," Devras assured them. "A little sore, but all right."

"You'll be burned all over like a neophyte sun-soaker," observed Wate Basef, "but I've a salve that will help. Right here, in this satchel you saved. It also contains the Cognitive articles without which we couldn't hope to continue our expedition. Well done, lad!"

"Better to have let them sink! And the expedition along with them!" Grono turned fiercely on Wate Basef. "What are your cheapjack gewgaws, sir, compared to his Lordship's life? Had Master Devras died, it would have been *your* fault! Yours no less than this—this *wicked*, unnatural infant's!" He glared down at Glindi.

Glindi did not understand the valet's Lanthian, but his expression and angry tone required no translation. She burst into tears. "I was helping!" she wailed up at him.

Grono's scowl faded as he regarded the weeping villainess.

Karavise knelt beside the child. "What were you trying to do, Glindi?" she inquired, not harshly, but in a tone that brooked no evasion.

"I didn't want you to send me away. I didn't want you to go back there in the dark. You'll get lost and the white things will get you. So I let the horses go and asked the Soil to stop you."

"By destroying Raith's possessions and nearly killing Devras?"

"I didn't know the Soil would do it that way! I didn't want to hurt Devras or ruin things! I was helping!"

"You have not helped. You have harmed us greatly. You may have meant well, but that does not alter the case."

"I'm sorry! Don't be mad!" The flow of tears increased. "I'm *sorry*!"

Karavise relented, and her expression softened. "Glindi, you have special gifts, and you must be very careful how you use them, or you will hurt yourself and others. Do you understand?"

Glindi nodded. "I'll be careful. I promise." She turned to Devras, her head hanging, and muttered, "I'm sorry. I'm sorry the Soil hurt you."

"I'm not really hurt. I know you meant no harm. It's all right, Glindi."

"I'm sorry about the carriage, Raith."

"Think nothing of it, child. Accidents will happen."

Her eyes were fixed firmly on the ground. Impossible to judge their expression. "Now you can't go anyplace. You have to stay here."

Wate Basef laughed briefly. "No such thing. In the morning we'll resume our journey on foot. We'll keep going, child. Of that you may be certain."

She would not look up at him.

Wate Basef rekindled the campfire, and by its light Devras made his way down to the river, where he washed the clinging mud from his body. The shock of cold water on his skin set his burns to stinging fiercely. Blisters already spotted his limbs, and his hands were noticeably swollen. While Devras bathed, Grono washed his master's filthy clothes, then carried the garments back to the fire and spread them out to dry. By the time Devras returned, wrapped in a blanket, Wate Basef had located the promised salve. Devras applied the soothing stuff to his burns, and relief was immediate. Shortly thereafter they returned to their beds, Glindi crawling under the blanket beside Karavise. Devras, sore and exhausted, was swallowed into dreamless sleep as if into the black maw of the Soil.

In the morning, when they woke to take inventory of their much-diminished possessions, Devras discovered the efficacy of Wate Basef's Cognitive salve. His blisters were gone, along with the swelling, and all that remained was a faint redness and slight discomfort that the savant assured him would soon vanish. In the meantime, there were more pressing issues to consider.

The horses, the carriage and nearly everything it had carried were gone. All that remained was the bedding, one sack of provisions, the cooking utensils, a few tools and rudimentary weapons, their clothes, including Grono's walking stick, the contents of their pockets, and the mysterious but vital contents of Wate Basef's rescued satchel and carpetbag. These burdens were proportionately distributed. Wate Basef obligingly chopped down the high heels of Karavise's ridiculous slippers and then they set forth, all of them glad to abandon the site of misfortune.

The weather was fine, the sun was bright, and the burdens manageable. For hours they walked in the dappled shade beneath the trees by the side of the River Yl, pausing to rest from time to time, mostly for the child's sake. Glindi breathed no word of complaint. Chastened by her experience, she offered little comment. But as the sun climbed, midday approached, and the trek continued, her manner reflected growing uneasiness. They paused at last for lunch—a frugal meal, in view of their reduced supplies—and the little girl's nervousness abated, only to reappear when the journey resumed. As the hours passed and Glindi's obvious discomfort mounted, the cause became apparent. Her companions were leading her back into the darkness of ghastly memory, and fear was already eroding newfound loyalties. Her steps began to lag, and her requests for rest stops increased in frequency.

In the midafternoon they encountered a party of Eatches, from whom they purchased bread and lentils. The Eatches, refugees from a threatened Ring of forest-dwelling Friends of the Soil, were heading for the coast. Should the darkness follow, they explained in their countrified Old Umish, they would set sail for Strell, where the Soil was said to be exotic but not unsympathetic. When the Eatches departed, Glindi went with them—sad to part from her Ten-Fingered friends, but on the whole relieved; as were they all.

That afternoon they encountered another group of Eatches, a caravan of Turos, a refugee farm family and a brace of Vemi, incomprehensible of tongue but eloquent of gesture. These people were only too willing to recount their misfortunes. By all accounts, the darkness was close at hand. At the end of the day's march, however, they had not yet glimpsed it.

Some twelve hours following the flight of her quarry, Mistress Snarp reached the clearing. She reined in her tired brown horse —bridle and saddle hers at the expense of a hapless farm family so unfortunate as to encounter her on the road—dismounted, set the quibbid upon her shoulder and lowered her yellow gaze to the wheel ruts marking the ground. The tracks led to a circular, anomalous patch of soil some forty-five feet in diameter. The ground there was peculiar in appearance—its surface wavy, the waves broken by many vertical shafts of hardened clay, each shaft inexplicably sculpted into the likeness of a human arm and six-fingered hand, complete down to knuckle ridges and fingernails. At the center, a long mound curved. The wheel tracks crossed the clearing, ending abruptly at the edge of the circle. Snarp walked the entire perimeter, noted the prints of the fleeing horses, but discovered no sign of the fugitive carriage. It was as if the ground had swallowed it up.

For some moments she eyed the circle expressionlessly, without attempting to touch it. At last she moved to a nearby tree, ascending with the agility of some arboreal weasel. From the vantage point of the lower branches she could discern the overall shape of the mound at the center. Incuriously she studied the full lips, the satisfied smirk, the single protruding granite fang.

Snarp descended, returned to her original position, and tested the ground, which proved firm and hard. Slowly at first, and then with increasing assurance, she picked her way through the petrified garden of arms and hands until she stood beside the lips of soil. From her pocket she drew a rag of black fabric, torn from a savant's robe belonging to Raith Wate Basef and discovered at

Castle Io Wesha. Raising the cloth to the quibbid's nose, she allowed the creature to sniff.

"Find him, little beauty." She lowered the quibbid to the ground. "If he is below, we will rip him from the grave."

The quibbid ran in tight circles, weaving in and out among the clay limbs, nose lowered to the soil. Periodically it paused to sit up on its haunches, bat's-wing ears quivering at full extension. Gradually the circles widened until the animal was clear of the arms, past the edge of the clearing and back to the road, where it picked up the fugitives' scent. The huge ears furled, the quibbid sat up and chittered shrilly to its mistress.

Joining her pet, Snarp knelt to study the faint trace of footprints in the dust of the road. "So. It will not be long now, little beauty. You are lovelier than fame, more beautiful than triumph. Come."

Replacing the quibbid upon her shoulder, Snarp returned to the horse, remounted, and whipped the luckless animal to a tired trot.

Chapter Ten

The Yl was heavily traveled these days, its silver surface high-way for a host of refugees. They came in a variety of boats, floats and rafts, many of exotic design. The Feeniads, for example, employed miniature galleys, perfectly scaled down to reflect their owners' dwarfish proportions. The Denders came in rafts equipped with thatched cottages, complete with lace curtains at windows whose roundness was the sole concession to nautical custom. The ingenious Children of the Lost Illusions fled the darkness in tiny floats equipped with clusters of inflated bladders, from which the controlled release of air propelled the odd crafts forward. After a time, Devras Har Fennahar thought himself in-ured to marvels and incapable of further astonishment. On the second morning following the departure of Glindi, he discovered otherwise.

Along the Yl glided a great square-rigged vessel, built high at gilded stem and stern in the massive antique mode. Her sails were green and silken. Her rigging and railings were golden, and the mainmast was inlaid with sculptured jade. She had much in common with the venerises, those pleasure crafts of the Lanthian nobles. But venerises, treasured playthings of the great, were flawlessly maintained; while this ship was ancient, battered and soiled. The emerald sails were torn and stained, the fringed pen-nants tattered, crisp carvings dulled by age. The name, painted in faded letters of black and gold, was still distinguishable: *Subli-mity*. The vessel's sails were furled. Without the aid of oars, in seeming defiance of natural law, she proceeded inland against wind and current.

Devras and his companions paused to stare. Even as they watched, the boat slowed. On deck a bearded man shouted fran-tically useless orders. *Sublimity* faltered, halted, wallowed dead in the water. Shortly thereafter, a large port just above water level snapped open, and three long objects were ejected. In the brief instant before they sank, they were recognizable as human bodies. The port closed. Elbows propped upon the golden rail, the bearded captain moodily surveyed the shore. His gaze caught and fixed upon the four spectators. He shouted fresh orders, and several of his underlings appeared on deck. Following hurried, frenetic preparations, *Sublimity*'s boat was lowered and its occupants rowed for the bank.

The boat touched land, and its six occupants sprang ashore. Their leader—*Sublimity*'s captain—was a brawny man of middle years with long limbs, soft belly, lank grizzled hair, and a cleft nose. He was dressed in filthy finery of fawn satin, with topaz buttons and earrings; old-fashioned knee-sparklers; and a wealth of golden chains, beads and paste jewels threading his thicket of beard. His followers greatly resembled him in face and stature, all of them boasting the same cleft chin and soiled satins.

In silence, with an efficiency born of practice, the sailors spread out to surround the four astonished pedestrians. One of them, a big blemished youth in red gauds and ersatz rubies, seized Lady Karavise, swung her clear off her feet and bore her to the small boat, depositing her therein without ceremony. Pale with outrage, Karavise leaped to her feet and slapped her assailant smartly across the face. Without hesitation, he cuffed her hard in return, knocking her to the floor of the boat. She sat up slowly, one palm pressed to her stinging cheek, eyes glittering with anger and wide with amazement.

"Ruffians!" A yell of fury burst from Grono. The sunlight glanced off his spectacles like flashes of lightning as he laid about him with his heavy walking stick.

Seizing a hatchet, Devras rushed to the valet's aid.

While the others shouted and struggled, Raith Wate Basef stood quietly twisting the ring on his finger. His head was bowed, eyes closed, face almost eerily empty. When the ring began to glow, he spoke in a low voice—but never reached Cognition.

Almost before the first words had left Wate Basef's lips, one of the marauders dodged nimbly under Grono's flailing stick, smashed an earthenware egg on the ground at their feet, and leaped clear. A cloud of blue vapor rose to the nostrils of the three victims. Wate Basef's voice slurred, stumbled, and died. He swayed briefly, gasped for air, and toppled headlong. A moment later, Grono collapsed.

Devras observed the disaster with glazed eyes and dimming vision. Twilight descended upon his mind. His muscles liquified, and the hatchet dropped from his hand. He tottered, slumped to the ground, and twilight swiftly darkened to night.

Roughly dumping the three unconscious men, together with their meager belongings, into the boat, the marauders pushed off from the shore. Soon they reached *Sublimity*, and the small boat was hoisted to the deck. As the limp prisoners were unloaded, a thin gray figure astride a long-suffering brown horse broke from the cover of the trees. Snarp directed her mount to the edge of the water, pausing there to watch expressionlessly as her quarry disappeared belowdecks. For several minutes the venerise rested motionless in the middle of the broad Yl, then began to move upstream at a leisurely pace, against the wind. For a moment Snarp sat watching, then set off along the river's bank on the trail of *Sublimity*.

The mists dispersed reluctantly as consciousness returned. His head ached, but he couldn't lift a hand to it. He could not stir at all—he was paralyzed. Panic rose like milk boiling over, and Devras's eyes snapped open.

He lay supine on a flat, hard surface. He could hear the creak of ancient timbers, and he sensed the motion of a ship under sail, familiar yet somehow unlike any other ship he had ever known. By dint of much effort, he managed to lift his head, to behold his body closely bound with thin white cords. The cords—glistening, soft but horribly strong—squirmed upon his breast and brow, pulsed to the rhythm of his heartbeat, clustered with avidity at his neck and wrists, and he knew in that instant they possessed a hungry life of their own. They were sickening to watch, and he quickly averted his eyes, glancing around to discover himself prisoner in a nightmare nest. The small chamber in which he lay was alive with vermiculate strands. They slithered up and down the walls, across the ceiling and over the floor in a twining, shifting, wormy tangle. Pale fibers joined him to the walls, and as they pulsed he felt a coldness steal over him.

Not far away lay Grono, awake but clay-faced, bound by white fibers to a bierlike block. Similarly bound, and tightly gagged, lay Raith Wate Basef. His eyes were open, but still glazed. Among the four prisoners, only Lady Karavise remained unfettered and unharmed, though much disheveled. Her hat was gone and her long hair had come unbound. The lace at her throat hung in shreds, and ugly bruises splotched the fair skin along her jaw. Despite her obviously recent participation in a losing struggle, she had lost none of her composure. The bruised chin was up and the blue eyes were icy. Beside Karavise stood two of the cleft-nosed kidnappers; the pimple-faced youngling with red glass earrings to match his frayed red silks, and the bearded, fawn-clad captain.

Noting Devras's return to consciousness, the captain addressed his captives. "No doubt you are wondering why we have brought you here today." He spoke Lanthian with a provincial accent and an air of gracious condescension. "Your concern is natural, and thus we consent to satisfy your curiosity. Imprimis know—we are his Majesty Pusstis Whurm Didnis. Here stands our beloved son and heir, the Crown Prince Krotz Whurm Didnis. We, the direct descendants of Lanthi Ume's greatest lords, are sovereigns of great Jobaal, famous land of Prugid's Green Tower. Yes, Gentlemen and Madam, it is true—you have fallen into the hands of royalty. Therefore be at ease and fear nothing."

"Royalty—pah!" spat Grono fiercely. "Pirates! Brigands! Kidnappers!"

Seizing a handful of white hair, Crown Prince Krotz elevated the valet's head, shook it until the teeth rattled, and let it fall again. "You'll address his Majesty with *respect*, dungheap," the Prince advised.

"Never!" Grono fired back, undaunted. "He's no monarch, for he isn't listed in Vornivoe's *Blood of Kings*. He's no lord of Lanthi Ume either, for there's no Whurm Didnis mentioned in Prenn's *Peerage*. He's nothing but a common hooligan, and you are the same, sir!"

The Crown Prince doubled his fist with a snarl.

"Peace, Prince," King Pusstis soothed his fractious heir. "You will damage him, and that we can ill afford. In any case, the lackey is not altogether culpable, for how could he know that the name of Whurm Didnis was stricken from Prenn's *Peerage* by the enemies of our House?"

His prisoners regarded him with varying degrees of hostile skepticism.

"In the days of my great ancestor Lord Yans Whurm Didnis and his famous daughter Josquinilliu Tiger-Heart," his Majesty confided, "it was the desire of the Lanthian populace that our family assume sovereignty within the city, and so it would have come to pass had not the Lanthian Duke Povon prevailed upon the sorcerers of the Select to employ their magic against our kinsmen. Yans Whurm Didnis, backed by an army of loyal partisans, fought his way to the Ducal Palace itself before the black magic of his enemies overcame him. Yans was banished, for they did not dare to slay him. His name, despite its greatness, was struck forever from the *Peerage*. His followers were slaughtered in a great massacre that still lives on in legend and nightmare. Fleeing in the magical vessel *Sublimity*, gift of the loyal populace, Yans Whurm Didnis made his way inland to carve out a kingdom in the wilderness. There he created a nation, and his descendants rule in wisdom and splendor to this very day. Now do you know us?"

"No, but the name of the ship is familiar," Devras recalled. "It's recorded that the Duke Povon Dil Shonnet died under mysterious circumstances. Upon the night of his death, Duke Povon's Select-crafted venerise *Sublimity* disappeared, never to be seen again. It was thought that the crew had mutinied, murdered their master and stolen the ship. If so, perhaps that murderous crew included a Whurm Didnis."

"They fear us still." King Pusstis shook his head in wonder, the gold chains in his beard jingling. "And thus they resort to lies and calumny. No matter. They will learn the truth upon the day that we return to Lanthi Ume in glory to reclaim the ancient rights of our House, treating with the Lanthian Duke as one prince to another."

Karavise's lip curled.

Grono lifted his head, all that he could move. "And all this does not explain why you have assaulted and kidnapped us, dragged us aboard this most unnatural vessel, bound us to these accursed blocks and gagged the Cognizant Wate Basef." His wattles quivered ominously. "We are free people, sir! What right have you to imprison us? How dare you restrict us, sir? How dare you?"

"You do not address us with the respect due royalty," King Pusstis observed, "but mindful of your present confusion, we in our mercy will pardon your impertinence, up to a point. Know, Master Lackey, that we and our royal family have embarked upon a great mission of mercy. In our benevolence, and at the risk of our own lives, we brave the spreading contagion of darkness. Boldly advancing to the brink of destruction, we pick the desperate refugees from between the very teeth of Death and then, for a trifling financial consideration, bear the grateful wretches to safety aboard the good ship *Sublimity*."

"And if they cannot pay you?" asked Devras.

"Ah, we are not heartless! We do not insist upon a golden remuneration! If our passengers are flat-pursed, they are encouraged to offer alternate forms of recompense. In the face of the incentive afforded by the approaching darkness, the levels of ingenuity attained by our clients are often astonishing. Why, the sheer originality of the hunchbacked ventriloquist with the mechanical duck—but I digress. Suffice it to say," King Pusstis concluded, "that *Sublimity* will transport the refugees in comfort and safety, provided she is properly maintained. You see, this magnificent craft bestowed upon our ancestor Yans Whurm Didnis is a ship unlike others. She is more than a floating hulk of wood and metal. She has nerves, emotions, perhaps a spirit. She is alive and, like all living things, requires sustenance—not of a gross material sort, no, but emanations—the invisible humors deriving from the mind and heart of Man. Such emanations lend her the will to lift her prow above the floods and fly! Without them, she is lifeless, unremarkable. And that, good people, is why we have brought you here. Your emanations will nourish our *Sublimity*. See, she feeds even now!"

The moist white tendrils clinging to Devras throbbed, and the prisoner shuddered with loathing. They were shifting now, twining like worms upon his breast, and the sensation was intolerable. Briefly he struggled, head thrashing from side to side, while the tendrils imbibed voraciously. It was not painful, but he could feel the cold, drowsy weakness steal along his limbs as the life drained out of him. He felt too the immense greed and appetite of the vessel, felt the hunger that would suck every last vestige of vitality before discarding the empty husk of his body. He was cold, and fog dimmed his vision, obscuring the faces of friends and enemies alike. A sigh that was almost a moan escaped him, and his eyelids drooped. The rise and fall of his chest was barely visible.

Grono screamed. *"What are you doing to my master?!"*

"It is nothing," King Pusstis soothed. "*Sublimity* feeds, that is all. She feeds, and she is strengthened. Do you note her new vigor?"

The venerise's speed increased perceptibly. Devras lay white and spent, his lips bloodless.

"You're killing him! You're killing my master!"

"No fear," King Pusstis assured his horrified captive. "We've no desire to harm the young gentleman, or any of the rest of you, for that matter. To do so would be to harm ourselves, for *Sublimity* needs you, and we need *Sublimity*. Therefore we shall do aught in our power to prolong your lives as best we may."

"What do you mean by that?" Grono strained uselessly against his bonds.

"Your good health is our treasure. The next time *Sublimity* requires nourishment, she will obtain it from you or from the other gentleman, thus affording your master a term of rest and recovery prior to his next contribution. Such rotation preserves the resources of all, and thus your lives are significantly extended. This is wise husbandry."

"Husbandry!" Grono choked. "You call it—"

"From what source did this ship derive nourishment before you took us aboard?" Karavise finally broke her frozen silence.

"Our brave crew members were recruited from the ranks of the homeless wandering the shore."

"What became of them?"

"They wore out," Crown Prince Krotz explained, "and had to be replaced."

Karavise nodded as if expecting as much.

"Murderers!" Grono accused. "Savage murderers!"

"Enough," warned King Pusstis, affability fading. "We are magnanimous, but our patience is not inexhaustible. Do not seek to exploit our good nature, Master Lackey. Do not forget that you address a king."

"A king? Bah! A pirate, a killer, a monster, and plebeian to boot!"

"Royalty," mused his Majesty, "is to be used with reverence. You will learn that soon enough, as the peasantry of our own land learned under the tutelage of our ancestors. In the meantime we advise you to save your energy. You will need all of it."

"Want me to teach him some manners, sire?" Prince Krotz offered hopefully.

"No, Prince. In your enthusiasm you are likely to damage our valuable acquisition."

"So what? We've got a spare, haven't we?" The Prince's eyes turned significantly to Karavise.

"What, you mean the lady? Ah, Krotz, Krotz, Krotz..." King Pusstis shook his head. "Your education has been neglected, and you have much to learn. The lady must be used with all consideration. We of royal blood are distinguished by unfailing gallantry to fair ladies!"

"But, sire," protested the heir apparent, "what about all those cottage wenches we—"

"Krotz. Those were not *ladies*."

Grono could no longer remain silent. "We are not your acquisitions!" he burst out. "We are free people! What right have you to imprison us? You've no right!"

"As *Sublimity* is a vessel unlike others, so is a monarch unlike other men," King Pusstis replied with a hint of melancholy. "His station is high, his aims are great, and he cannot be bound by the restrictions of lesser folk. Sometimes, Master Lackey, it happens that the very laws protecting the common citizenry may disastrously limit the essential efficacy of a king in times of national emergency. A monarch, like a mighty eagle, requires his freedom to ride the winds of Chance and Opportunity. What right have we

125

to demand your service? The necessities of a king are his rights."

"Feeble sophistries, you hairy ruffian! Your arguments fall flat. Do you know why, sir? Because we are not common folk, and therefore you are not justified in treating us as such, that's why. Do you know who we are, sir? Would you like to know whom you have kidnapped?"

"Indeed." King Pusstis nodded sociably.

A warning croak filtered through Wate Basef's gag.

Grono charged ahead undaunted. "The young gentleman," he proclaimed, "is his Lordship Devras Har Fennahar, scion of the best and noblest blood of Lanthi Ume, last of an ancient and honorable line. The other gentleman is the Cognizant Raith Wate Basef, also of an ancient House; a famous savant, and a senior member of the Select of Lanthi Ume. Beware how you trifle with him."

"I told you, didn't I, sire?" Prince Krotz broke in. "I told you he was up to something tricky when he stood there twisting his ring and mumbling to himself! I told you he was up to no good, and I was right, wasn't I? Well, if he's one of those savant boogeymen, then I say he's too dangerous to keep around, and I'm right about that too. Gagging him isn't enough. Let's get rid of him now, before he makes trouble."

Wate Basef's eyes widened above the gag.

"Have we not made it clear to you, Crown Prince, that we need him for the moment?"

"We don't need him, sire," Prince Krotz insisted. "If we're smart and dispose of the wizard now, *Sublimity* can still use the wench."

Noting his Majesty's meditative demeanor, Grono broke in, "You cannot! This lady you have kidnapped—this lady before you—" Karavise shook her head imperatively, but the valet did not heed the signal. "This lady is none other than her Ladyship Karavise Dil Shonnet, sole daughter to his Grace Bofus Dil Shonnet, Duke of Lanthi Ume! Now what have you to say to *that*?"

Karavise stood motionless as her captors turned to inspect her with new interest.

"Is this true?" demanded his Majesty.

Silence.

"Speak up, girl!" Prince Krotz raised his hand to strike, and the watching Grono gasped in horror.

"Youth is impetuous," King Pusstis sighed. "Patience, my son. There are gentler ways." Seizing Karavise's right hand, he bent to inspect the massive ring upon her middle finger. "Ah,

126

see! The old man speaks the truth! Here is the Dil Shonnet crest!"

"That ring's worth something," Prince Krotz observed. "Hold her still and I'll take it off her."

"Nothing of the sort. Son, how shall we ever make clear to you the vast difference between a common wench and a lady?" King Pusstis released the prisoner's hand.

"I don't see much difference," muttered the Prince. "Lady, wench, strumpet, it's all one. Shrill voices, finicking airs, and a hole to swallow a man alive. Blow out the candles and they're all—"

"Enough, Prince Krotz," King Pusstis admonished with a touch of paternal sternness. "We will tolerate no vulgarity in our presence. It offends our royal dignity. As for the lady—and she is a great lady, Prince—she will be treated with the courtesy her station merits. The Duke's daughter!" His tone grew thoughtful. "This puts matters in an entirely different light. It is a great stroke of fortune—a very great stroke indeed. We must consider this new development with care."

"But sire—what will we do when the gaffer wears out? At his age, it won't take long. And there's no telling what the bald trickster might not do, given half a chance."

"The savant cannot move or speak. He's safe enough for the present. But as we value our beloved heir's peace of mind, we give him our word, upon the splendor of our crown, to install two replacements at the earliest opportunity."

"And the wench—the *lady*?" Crown Prince Krotz still looked dissatisfied.

"She will be treated with all due respect, Prince. She deserves it. She is the daughter of a reigning duke, and therefore almost your equal." Turning to Karavise, King Pusstis addressed her with an air of gallantry. "Madam, we regret the inconvenience to which you have been subjected, and we hope to make amends. In token of our good faith we offer you the hospitality of the royal vessel *Sublimity*." With a deep bow, he extended his arm.

The eyes of Grono and Wate Basef turned expectantly to Karavise. In vain they awaited the blast of her scorn.

"Sir, our encounter is unconventional as it is unforeseen." Karavise met the King's regard squarely. "Although your claims have not been proven, I can doubt neither the sincerity of your convictions nor the strength of your resolve. Moreover, it is certain that a flexible adaptability to changing circumstances is a hallmark of the mature intellect. Wisdom demands acceptance of current reality, together with a recognition of future possibilities. Therefore I accept your offer of hospitality, placing my trust in your chivalry." Ignoring the shocked stares of her fellow prisoners, she took his Majesty's proffered arm.

"Madam, your pragmatism delights me. It is similar to my own."

Arm in arm they exited, followed by the glowering Crown Prince Krotz, who carefully barred the door behind him.

A terrible time followed. Nourished by the life-forces of the fresh captives, *Sublimity* ploughed her stately way upstream, ragged pennants flying and battered gilt turrets shining in the sun. Many a wanderer along the river bank paused to stare in wonder as she passed. Despite King Pusstis's promise to his son, no replacement prisoners were taken aboard.

For the victims it was an endless nightmare. Devras, Grono and Wate Basef remained perpetually anchored to their ghastly beds in the midst of the writhing white jungle. The appetite of *Sublimity* was insatiable, and several times a day, she fed.

Devras had never experienced anything so dreadful. As he lay there helpless, the moist tendrils throbbing above his heart, feasting upon his strength and life, his sensations were unimaginable. Nothing in all the works of his beloved philosophers had prepared him for the horror of this prolonged execution. For he would not leave his bier, he knew, until *Sublimity* had finished with him.

He spent many hours sleeping—the sole escape from an unendurable reality in which fits of intense anguish alternated with periods of utter boredom. Each loss of vital emanations left him weary and sick to death. Sleep restored some strength and alertness, but not enough. Always exhausted, faint and feeble, he was far too weak to plot escape; far too sick to contemplate anything beyond approaching dissolution.

Grono and Wate Basef fared no better. Grono spent the first few hours of captivity struggling, shouting, and denouncing his kidnappers. Later, as *Sublimity* drank his vigor, he grew quiet. His lids drooped over empty eyes and his jaw sagged loosely. It was impossible to gauge his level of awareness.

Wate Basef was undoubtedly conscious most of the time. The mental discipline of a senior savant enabled him to continue comparatively alert. But weakened, gagged and immobilized as he was, Cognition lay beyond his power. As the hours passed, his strength dwindled until escape became too troublesome to consider.

The only brief respite came in the evening, when King Pusstis cast anchor for a couple of hours to rest *Sublimity*. It was at such times, when the ship lay quiescent, that she lost her appetite. It was then that the prisoners received their evening meal, delivered by King Pusstis himself; or by his younger brother, the unwashed Duke Cheedle; or by any of a dozen ill-favored lords and princes, all members of the royal House of Whurm Didnis. There were no women on board other than Karavise, who would or could not visit. At mealtime Wate Basef's gag was temporarily removed and the savant ate with a Didnis lord's steel hovering inches from his throat. Cognitive utterance was thus discouraged. Under other circumstances Wate Basef might have chanced an attempt, but leaden exhaustion sapped his will.

As the hours lengthened into days, the prisoners deteriorated steadily. Five times Devras watched the sky visible through the porthole deepen from blue to black, and even in the midst of his wretchedness, he was conscious of faint curiosity. By all accounts, *Sublimity* must surely have borne her masters and victims to the very verge of Fal Grizhni's darkness. Any moment they would confront it, and then what? Presumably his Majesty Pusstis would approach as near as he dared, in the hopes of securing the most desperate refugees from whom the largest payments might be extorted. Passengers aboard, *Sublimity* would turn her prow downstream and fly at her best speed, at which point the demands upon the resources of her three victims would probably render the miseries of the last five days trivial by comparison. It would be a miracle if they all survived it. *Sublimity* could scarcely have been planned, Devras reflected, to consume her human victims so quickly. A design necessitating disposal of corpses and installation of fresh prisoners every few days was clearly impractical. Most likely, the Selectic creator's original Cognition had slowly spent its force over the years. That, or else the fault must be laid to the charge of the current owners' ignorance. In either case, correction of the malfunction was unlikely, and if any hope existed for the prisoners, it lay in Karavise, who had not been seen in days. Had the King, clearly an indulgent father, allowed his son to brutalize or kill her? The question was answered that evening, when *Sublimity* paused for her customary brief repose.

The scrape of a bolt, the creak of hinges, and Devras turned his face to the door. The King's younger brother Duke Cheedle loomed upon the threshold. Beside him stood Crown Prince Krotz, dagger in hand. Duke Cheedle much resembled his brother in form and feature, possessing a cleft nose, bedizened beard, filthy bravery of sky blue satin, and an air of exuberant affability.

"Dinner, gentlemen!" Duke Cheedle flourished a bowl of

grayish gruel. "Rest. Refreshment. Life can be beautiful!"

No reply.

"*Sublimity* makes good time," the Duke informed them. "Appreciative of your contribution, the King sees fit to reward you. His Majesty has therefore decreed a full three hours of rest this evening." He looked encouragingly from face to face in search of gratitude. Finding none, he shrugged. Placing the big bowl on the floor, Cheedle produced three flexible tubes, the ends of which he sank in the gruel. Prince Krotz removed Wate Basef's gag, and the free ends of the tubes were inserted into the mouths of the prisoners, who now sucked their sustenance in a process unpleasantly reminiscent of *Sublimity's* own feeding methods. Prince Krotz's blade gleamed inches from Wate Basef's throat. For the next several minutes the prisoners consumed their gruel in silence finally broken by the gurgling sound that signaled the end of the meal.

Devras allowed the tube to slide from his mouth. Turning his head, he encountered the wide-open eyes of Grono, staring out in dull despair through the mesh of white tendrils that crisscrossed withered cheeks and forehead.

I brought him to this. Devras looked away quickly. On the neighboring bier, Raith Wate Basef lay ungagged but judiciously silent. The savant's alert, unbroken, speculative expression appeared to trouble the scowling Prince Krotz. Following a period of cogitation, the scowl smoothed itself.

"Your Grace—Uncle—I've a thought," Prince Krotz announced.

"Yes, Prince?"

"I don't trust this bald trickster. He's sneaky, you can tell by those eyes. I don't like having him on board."

"I know it, Prince. However, the wishes of his Majesty your father—"

"Right. So we don't kill him. But there's another way to make him safe."

"What is your plan, Prince?"

"We cut out the wizard's tongue, that's what. That way he won't be speaking his filthy spells and mysteries, but he's left alive to feed *Sublimity*. What d'you say, Uncle?"

Devras gasped, appalled. Wate Basef's face was blank.

Duke Cheedle considered the suggestion with care before replying mildly, "It's a good thought, Prince, an enterprising thought, a creative solution to our immediate difficulties. One drawback, however."

"Well?" The Prince was impatient.

"If we cut out the savant's tongue, he'll lose a quantity of blood, which will weaken him, possibly to the point of death."

"So much the better, I say."

"Ah, Nephew, I understand your concern, but you must think of the greater good, the ultimate objective. That is a mark of maturity."

"You're getting off the subject, Uncle."

"Not at all. The savant must live as long as possible. *Sublimity* needs him, and therefore so do we all."

Wate Basef spoke up for the first time. "If you're so anxious to keep us alive, you're not doing a very good job of it," he observed in a hoarsened voice. Prince Krotz's dagger twitched at the sound.

"How so?" Duke Cheedle turned to the savant in surprise. "Your welfare concerns us, your health is precious. We wish only the best for you. What could be wanting? Explain, sir."

Wate Basef's eyes jumped to the dagger.

"Let him speak, Prince," the Duke instructed. "But watch him." Krotz nodded grimly.

"You deny us the necessities of life," Wate Basef told them. "No exercise, no sun or air, inadequate diet, our vital forces sapped and plundered—we won't last long."

"You exaggerate." The Duke spoke reasonably.

"No. Stop and think—how long have your victims before us survived?"

"Victims?" The Duke was affronted. "Victims? We have no victims, sir. Such a description is unbecoming, even offensive. Your predecessors were patriots, loyal to the House of Whurm Didnis and eager to lay down their lives in defense of their sovereign's birthright. It was their duty, and now it is yours."

"Are we your subjects?" Wate Basef inquired with a ghost of his old sarcasm.

"You are now," Prince Krotz informed him.

"Never!" Grono managed a weak, defiant wheeze.

"My princely nephew lacks diplomacy. A failing of extreme youth," Duke Cheedle confided. "In answer to your question, Master Savant, I can only point out that true, innate royalty finds natural subjects everywhere."

"Royalty will not keep them long," Wate Basef insisted wearily, "without adequate food, rest and exercise."

"It is sometimes necessary to sacrifice greatly upon the altar of historical inevitability. Now is not a time for spiritual parsimony, Master Savant. A vast change is in the making. The common good is all. The last thing that should concern you at such a moment is the loss of a few personal luxuries. That is the sign of a small and selfish nature."

Raith Wate Basef did not choose to waste his remaining strength in useless debate. His silence mollified Duke Cheedle, who, like his royal brother, possessed a genial disposition. "Enjoyed your dinner, gentlemen? Feeling better? Feeling stronger, I hope? Vigorous and resolute?" No response. "That is well, that is well. Rest assured that your service is greatly valued. You have earned the personal gratitude of a king—and I salute you for it with all my heart! And now, gentlemen, before I leave you to your well-deserved leisure, is there anything you would ask?"

Grono's jaws were working, and Devras wisely forestalled the valet's reply. "Where's Lady Karavise?" he asked.

"Her Ladyship? She is very well indeed, bless her pretty face! There's a sweet lady!"

"Her Ladyship possesses many sterling qualities," observed Wate Basef, "but I would not number sweetness among them."

"Ah, you are no judge of character," returned the Duke. "You've not perceived the womanly tenderness beneath the cool facade. Her Ladyship is sweet. And kind. High, but not haughty. Soft, but no weakling. A little meager, but fair. And clever—perceptive! She understands our ambitions, she sees the justice of our claims. And she is the daughter of Duke Bofus himself! If her Ladyship recognizes our rights, then all the world must concur!"

"Your 'rights' to what?" asked Devras.

"To the honors and privileges due the royal House of the land of Jobaal—as well as the more tangible benefits ordinarily accruing to Lanthian nobility. In brief, we seek redress for the wrongs suffered by our great ancestor Yans Whurm Didnis. We demand full restoration of the Whurm Didnis titles and fortune. We demand property, a Lanthian estate, and all income attached thereto. Rumor along the river has it that the great palace known as Fennahar House currently stands empty. That one should do nicely."

Grono strained furiously against his bonds.

"Until recently," Duke Cheedle continued, "the prejudice of the Lanthian Duke appeared insurmountable. But now that his Grace's only offspring has fallen into our hands, the situation has providentially altered. In fact, our state is transformed! Not the least delightful aspect of the entire affair is her Ladyship's free and spontaneous sympathy to our cause."

"Karavise supports your claim to the Fennahar estates?" asked Devras. Out of the corner of his eye, he caught the convulsive quiver of Grono's wattles.

132

"She does. She is logical, for a woman. Clever—and yet a fair lady." The Duke's eyes took on a roguish sparkle. "It may well be that our warlike venture will ultimately prove a source of universal satisfaction. A union of the two great Houses of Whurm Didnis and Dil Shonnet would heal all wounds."

"A union?"

"If I don't miss my guess, the lady has a weakness for his Majesty. In her maiden modesty she strives to conceal her partiality, but we have all observed it. The King has always had a way with pretty women! When he sets himself out to captivate, he does not fail. This very night his Majesty and her Ladyship dine by moonlight. And therefore, gentlemen, be of good cheer. A joyful announcement is imminent!"

Crown Prince Krotz spat on the floor.

Face wreathed in smiles, Duke Cheedle collected the empty bowl and tubes, while the Prince replaced Wate Basef's gag. Both men withdrew, barring the door behind them.

Fury had renewed Grono's strength. "Master Devras," he appealed in feeble but passionate tones, "tell me it isn't true! Her Ladyship hasn't abandoned us for that bandit! She wouldn't lower herself thus!"

"Grono—" Devras attempted.

"She can't believe his lunatic tales! She wouldn't bestow your own Fennahar House upon that excrement!"

"Grono—"

"My cup of bitterness is full!"

"Grono, consider. She's clever, cool and resolute. She'll use the weapons available to her, and use them well."

Wate Basef nodded.

The effort of conversation was exhausting, and the three prisoners soon sank into oblivion less slumber than swoon.

Sublimity rocked gently in the water, at rest for the moment.

Chapter Eleven

"Do you believe in Destiny, Madam? Do you believe in Fate?" inquired his Majesty Pusstis.

"I believe in the Man of Destiny who shapes Fate according to his own desires." Lady Karavise's eyes held the King's a split second longer than custom dictated. "Such a man captures my imagination."

"Only your imagination, Madam?"

"My respect as well. My admiration."

"And what of your esteem?"

"Respect and admiration are the natural parents of esteem."

"You fire our hopes."

"And you my curiosity, sire. You were about to tell me of your ambitions."

Karavise and King Pusstis sat at ease upon *Sublimity*'s poetically moonlit poop deck. They had just finished dinner, and the dishes had been cleared away by Lord Xen, second son to Duke Cheedle. Nothing remained on the linen-draped table but a tarnished silver candelabrum, a carafe of Weo on a warming stand, and the implements of the traditional Weo ritual.

Her three hours of repose concluded, *Sublimity* ploughed steadily upstream. It was the fifth evening since Lady Karavise had come aboard. During that period, despite the fulsome gallantry of her captor, she had never been left unguarded save at night, when the tiny chamber set aside for her use was securely barred from the outside.

"How did you embark upon this present mission of mercy?" Karavise persisted. "When did your altruism first manifest itself?"

"Do you really wish to hear about that now?" King Pusstis leaned forward to gaze ardently into her eyes.

"Indeed, sire. How could I not? Were it not for your philanthropy, we two should never have met."

"A pretty sentiment! You shall hear, then. Know, Madam, that the monarchs of the House of Whurm Didnis have for generations

134

ruled in wisdom, strength and splendor, much beloved of the people. But always the kings of our House have chafed under double injustice. Treachery deprived us of our Lanthian greatness, and misfortune consigned us to provincial obscurity galling to the proud spirit. Enduring greatly throughout the years, we have looked to the day that we return to claim our rights in Lanthi Ume. And then at last it came to pass that a new star appeared in the sky, a star that was visible during the daylight hours. Permit us to observe that you, Madam, are a star of like nature."

"Your Majesty honors me. But the story, sire?"

"At the time the star appeared," King Pusstis resumed, "it came to our attention that a great darkness arising inland was spreading outward toward the sea. Many travelers fleeing the darkness sought our protection, and these fugitives thrust all manner of gifts, tribute and treasure upon us."

"In token of gratitude, I presume."

"So we regarded the matter, Madam, and therefore we accepted the gifts and listened to the strangers' tales. All of them spoke of dread white creatures inhabiting the darkness—beings like men and yet unlike, merciless killers and enemies of humankind. They spoke too of a certain white king possessing the strength of twenty men and the ferocity of forty demons. This King of Demons, so they claimed, was a savage warrior and an inspired general—cunning, fearless and ruthless. There were tales of bloody massacres, attacks, pursuits, villages burned to the ground, corpses piled up like firewood and left to molder, slaughter, mutilations, dismemberments, butchery and carnage— Madam, your eyes are delightful."

"Your Majesty will make me vain," Karavise murmured. In the warm glow of candlelight it was difficult to judge, but surely she blushed. Her low voice was tremulous with emotion.

"Madam, we speak only the truth. Dear Lady Karavise, since you came aboard *Sublimity*, our life has changed in so many ways—"

"So has mine, sire, I assure you. But pray continue your story."

"If you insist," he conceded in disappointment, and resumed. "It soon became apparent that the travelers' tales contained some measure of truth, for the darkness appeared one morning on the horizon. By late afternoon it had advanced appreciably. During that day, the refugees flocked to our gates, seeking succor. They pressed gold, jewelry and valuables upon us," Pusstis recalled, fingering one of the chains threaded through his beard. "How could we in our mercy refuse the poor wretches? Thus we took

135

them aboard *Sublimity* and carried them to safety."

"What, all the way to the coast?"

"No. Even with all the resources of *Sublimity* at our command, the distances involved would have been too great. Therefore we carried our passengers beyond sight of the darkness and then set them ashore, despite the plaints of those selfishly reluctant to disembark. This done, we returned to rescue others. And so our work continued until our three junior crewmen expired— brave lads! That was the day we met you, Madam—the happiest of days!"

"And now, sire? Does your work continue?"

"Not for long. Your sweet presence alters all things, Madam. We shall collect one last cargo of refugees, this time bearing them as far as Lanthi Ume, where we negotiate with your father the Duke for restoration of the Whurm Didnis titles and fortunes. This done, and our presence in Lanthi Ume perhaps superfluous, we invest our new fortune in the expansion of our inland empire."

"And if the darkness engulfs your inland empire?"

"In that event, *Sublimity* carries us across the sea. All contingencies have been anticipated, for care and foresight mark the strategy of the victor. Even a Man of Destiny, however, may be conquered by the power of a woman's beauty. His care and foresight are then set at naught. His genius does not shield him." Gently he took her hand. She did not withdraw it. King Pusstis leaned forward. At the last moment she turned her face aside and his kiss landed on her cheek. "You are cold, Madam," the King complained.

"Sad experience has taught me to distrust the stirrings of a heart perhaps foolishly soft." She lowered her eyes.

"A woman's heart is her surest guide," his Majesty argued.

"And what is a man's, sire?"

"His eyes, Madam, which teach him what is beautiful. His honor, which tells him what is good. His mind, which illumines the possibilities of the future. Lady Karavise, have *you* ever contemplated such possibilities?"

"Possibilities—sire?" Timidly she returned the pressure of his hand.

"Possibilities, Madam—for the two of us."

"Ah, your Majesty, you confuse me, you trouble me. You are too hasty."

"Dear lady, can a man be too hasty in doing what is right and good?"

136

"We are strangers, sire. How can I trust? How can I be sure?" Sighing a little, she withdrew her hand.

"We offer you the first and only love of a true heart. Believe in us, Madam. Our love and our crown are both pure gold."

"Oh, sire—you overwhelm me. I can't think—I can't speak—"

"I will pour you a glass of Weo. It will restore you." Solicitously his Majesty reached for the carafe.

"No." She halted him with a gesture. "Allow me."

Karavise performed the traditional Weo ritual with graceful economy of motion. Holding the carafe high, she allowed the warm green liqueur to stream down into a pair of bubble glasses. Setting the carafe aside, she passed a lighted splint like a magic wand across the mouths of the glasses. The alcoholic fumes ignited at once, and transparent, ghostly blue flames blossomed. The cold light ascended to her face, lending it a sinister cast that King Pusstis did not observe. Deftly snuffing out the flames with the silver lid provided for that purpose, she stirred the Weo vigorously with a tiny silver whisk. As she stirred, head slightly bowed, she lifted her gaze, to potent effect. King Pusstis was caught, transfixed. He stared as if mesmerized into eyes warm with promise. While he was thus occupied, a quick pressure on a hidden spring flipped open the hinged lid concealing the recess in Karavise's massive ring, releasing a quantity of white powder into his Majesty's glass. The powder foamed and disappeared. A pinch of sugar in each glass, and it was done.

"You do that beautifully, Madam." The King's fingers brushed hers unnecessarily as he accepted his glass. "And now—a toast! To a glorious future!" The glasses clinked. They drank. "Excellent!"

"I fear I've added too much sugar, sire."

"Not at all." His Majesty took a swallow, eyeing his companion appreciatively. "Perfect. Quite perfect."

"Are you certain, sire? Better try again."

His Majesty complied. "Exquisite."

Karavise regarded him attentively. Presently the King's eyes glazed and the glass slid from his hand to shatter on the deck. He fell forward, forehead clunking on the table. For a moment she waited, but he did not stir.

She looked around her. No Whurm Didnis lords were in evidence, for the King had desired romantic seclusion. With caution, Karavise descended from the poop deck and made her stealthy way down to the hold, pausing en route only long enough to secure Raith Wate Basef's leather satchel, whose location she had ascertained days earlier.

Sublimity fed. Her victim was Grono. Weak lantern-light illuminated the horrible scene. Grono lay stretched upon his bier, the white tentacles throbbing at temples, throat, chest and wrists. The valet's eyes were shut, lids twitching spasmodically. He was unconscious, or nearly so. As his strength ebbed, *Sublimity*'s vigor waxed.

Devras watched, guilt and despair festering in his mind.

The door opened and Karavise entered. Rushing to Wate Basef, she dropped the satchel and stripped the gag from his mouth. "You won't have much time," she told him.

The savant's head jerked affirmatively. "As I speak, twist the ring on my finger."

Karavise obeyed. As she rotated the ring, the metal and stone began to glow with a sickly light. Eyes shut, Wate Basef spoke in a weak voice, almost too low to be heard. The white cords binding him shivered, but didn't let go.

"What's wrong?" The first tremor of alarm shook the even coolness of Karavise's voice.

"Weak. Tired." Wate Basef's eyes remained closed. "Try again." He did so, brow ridged with effort. Once again the ring glowed, this time brightly. *Sublimity*'s white tendrils writhed, convulsed and went limp, releasing their hold on all three prisoners. The venerise slowed, and shouting broke out overhead.

"They'll be down here in seconds." Karavise was pale but composed. "Can you three move?"

Slowly and with difficulty, Wate Basef hauled himself to a sitting position. For a moment he rested, then dropped his legs over the edge of the bier and attempted to stand. Dizziness overcame him and he sat abruptly, breath coming in gasps. Karavise fidgeted as she watched.

Devras was young and resilient. His first effort to rise was successful, and he staggered to Grono's side. The valet lay motionless, eyes closed and forehead clammy with sweat. When Devras shook him, he did not stir.

"Wake up! Try!"

Grono moaned and opened blank eyes.

"Get up. Lean on me." Sliding an arm about the other's shoulders, Devras found the valet dead weight. "Grono can't walk."

"Then carry him. I'll help." Karavise slipped a surprisingly strong arm around Grono. Together she and Devras lifted the valet to his feet. His body was limp as *Sublimity*'s Cognitively stunned tendrils. His eyes were open but unaware.

On the deck above, frantic footsteps boomed like cannon fire. A shout rang out, shocked and wrathful, "The King is dead!"

Devras stared at Karavise in awe. "You killed him?"

"Drugged him," she replied impatiently. "A weak potion and he took very little. He'll be well enough too soon."

"Where is that woman?" The furious voice belonged to Crown Prince Krotz. "I'll have that murdering harlot whipped to death! I'll feed her to *Sublimity* for breakfast! *Where is that woman?"* Confused cries and exclamations overhead. Footsteps clattered down the wooden stairs, and the three conscious prisoners froze. Grono drooped, mercifully oblivious. Releasing the valet, Devras slammed the door and threw the bolt home, locking the room from within.

"That's it. We won't get past them now." Karavise was still and cold as a wintry graveyard. "Unless Raith's Cognition will serve us."

Wate Basef shook his head. It was all he could do to remain on his feet. "Tired," he muttered. "This boat has drained me dry."

Pounding and thumping upon the bolted door. Cursing, just outside.

"How come it's locked?" came the voice of a Whurm Didnis lord.

"Because that bitch is hiding in there," the avenging Crown Prince explained. "Break it down!" His kinsmen did their best, and the door rocked beneath their assault.

"Raith!" hissed Devras. "You're a savant—do something!"

"You won't have another chance," Karavise observed coolly.

Just outside, the Crown Prince Krotz screamed hysterical imprecations upon her head.

"Couldn't you stun or paralyze them?" Devras appealed.

"Can't," Wate Basef muttered. "No strength to act on solid flesh. Shadows—illusions—that's all, at most, for now."

"Then do it," urged Karavise. "Do it."

Outside, the hammering waxed in ferocity, but the stout door held.

"Get an ax!" commanded the Crown Prince Krotz.

Within the chamber, Raith Wate Basef shut his eyes and bowed his head. For a long moment he remained thus, as if searching within himself for strength and resolve; then he began to speak. His words were inaudible, drowned out by the strokes of the ax on the door. Sweat dewed his temples. By the time he reached Cognition, he was swaying on his feet. He finished and sat down heavily, massaging his forehead with both hands.

A splintering crash, and the door gave way. Crown Prince Krotz burst through, ax in hand. With him came Lord Xen and a couple of anonymous princelings.

"Regicide!" accused the Prince.

"Your father is not dead. He sleeps," said Karavise coldly.

"You'll sleep too, when I strike that scheming head off those scrawny shoulders." Prince Krotz raised his ax, and Karavise shrank back. He struck at her and missed, blade whooshing down to sever one of the vessel's larger tendrils. The white cord expired, and began to shrivel. *Sublimity* quaked.

"Here now, Cousin," Lord Xen expostulated. "Have a care, you'll damage the boat."

"That bitch killed my father, and now she pays. I start by chopping off her feet, one at a time and not too fast, and then I work my way up the legs nice and slow." The Crown Prince struck and missed again. Once more he severed a great white fiber, and *Sublimity* trembled.

White-faced, Karavise dodged back. Her eyes raced about the chamber in vain search of a weapon.

"One of you—grab her!" Krotz commanded.

Lord Xen leaped forward, only to trip over Devras Har Fennahar's well-placed foot. He staggered, recovered, and whirled, dagger in hand. "You're a dead man, whey-face," Xen promised, and advanced. Devras, debilitated and unarmed, hastily retreated.

"You—Drep! Help me here!" Prince Krotz commanded. With the aid of his brothers he backed Karavise into a corner.

Bowing his head, Wate Basef attempted Cognition—without success. *Sublimity* had drained him indeed. Now, absurdly weaponless, he lurched toward the ax-wielding Krotz.

"Lay her down on one of those blocks," the Crown Prince directed, and his followers hastened to comply.

Karavise stiffened as she felt their hands upon her. Frozen with contempt, she made no resistance as they bore her to the nearest bier and spread-eagled her upon it. Prince Krotz hesitated, weighing delectable alternatives. Before he had reached a decision, fresh shouts and screams broke out on deck. Frenzied footsteps thundered to and fro. The shrieks mounted in volume and frenzy. Audible above all others was a voice calling, "Lords and Princes! To us, noble kinsmen!"

"His Majesty's voice!" exclaimed Prince Drep in awe. "He's *alive!*"

"What's that?" demanded Prince Krotz.

And once again the shout: "Attend us, noble Lords and Princes! Danger!"

"Alive!"

"He wants us."

"And—?" Prince Drep cocked a significant eyebrow at Karavise.

"Later, Prince. Later."

Abruptly loosing their captive, the Whurm Didnis kinsmen hastened from the room.

"What is it?" Green-white but unharmed, Karavise rose from the bier.

"You'll see when we get up on deck," Wate Basef told her. The savant was faint and shaky. Depletion notwithstanding, he did not forget to scoop the satchel from the floor, slinging the leather strap around his neck and over one shoulder.

"Grono needs help," said Devras.

The valet, only semiconscious, lay on the floor. Gently lifting the old man, Devras and Karavise half-carried him from the room, along a narrow passageway to the foot of a carven, inlaid ladder. The hatch above the ladder was open. By dint of collective feverish effort, they managed to hoist Grono up the ladder and through the hatch. Another narrow passage, another ladder to climb, and then they were out on deck, beneath the starry sky, there to confront the source of the Whurm Didnis panic. The air was mild and the moon glowed through a whispery veil of mist. But straight ahead loomed a vision that killed all the beauty of the night.

Sublimity had come upon the deathtrap known as Frejeeria's Teeth, where the River Yl ran shallow and the water foamed among jagged boulders. In the middle of the river sat a huge and naked woman, so tall she seemed crowned with a diadem of stars. The bloated form, an explosion of flesh, bulged from shore to shore. The greenish hair, like strands of lank aquatic weed, dripped down over pendulous breasts. The face, with its pig nostrils and imbecile eyes, reflected a weird green glow. Between the colossus's widespread knees bobbed a fleet of ruined boats, barges and rafts. She played with them idly as a child sports with toys in the bath, her mindless smile revealing algous tombstone teeth.

"What is *that*?"

Devras's query was answered by the cries of the terrified Whurm Didnis lords:

"Frejeeria! Frejeeria!"

Sublimity ploughed steadily toward the monstress. Frejeeria lifted her idiot eyes, beheld the venerise and slapped the water in glee. The river flinched. The wrecks danced between her knees.

"Is it real?" asked Devras.

"Shadows. Illusion," Raith Wate Basef replied.

Frejeeria beat the river with her heels, and *Sublimity* rocked in the resulting eddies. Icy spray drenched the decks.

"Bring her about!" roared King Pusstis, vigor fully restored by terror.

Duke Cheedle obediently wrenched the tiller, and *Sublimity* veered aport—too far. There was only a sense of mild impact, a slight shock as a submerged point of rock opened a long gash in the hull. Water poured into the hold, and Frejeeria clapped her hands in vacant pleasure. *Sublimity* slowed, but continued her doomful progress upstream. Frejeeria extended Olympian arms in greeting.

"*Bring her about*!" the King howled in impotent frenzy.

Laughing soundlessly, Frejeeria kicked her heels, and smacked the river with an open palm. Seizing the hulk of a shattered boat, she flung it playfully, and the missile crashed down within yards of *Sublimity*. The water exploded, and the foundering venerise pitched sickeningly; whereupon her masters conceded defeat.

"Abandon ship! Jump!" the King commanded, and his kinsmen dove from the deck, pelting the river with lords and princes.

"We'd best follow them," said Karavise.

"Not yet," Wate Basef told her. "Not yet."

Dead ahead, Frejeeria spun a vast finger in the water to create a whirlpool, sucking *Sublimity* on toward the lethal harbor between her gaping legs. The last of the Whurm Didnis tribe, including the King himself, flung themselves overboard to swim for the shore, while Frejeeria drooled and giggled.

"Jump for it. Now!" urged Devras.

"Stay!" Wate Basef commanded. "It's an illusion. Stay where you are!"

Doubting, they obeyed.

Sublimity forged on. Frejeeria's legs rose up like greenish cliffs on either side.

Consciousness returned to Grono, and he lifted his head to behold Frejeeria. His eyes bulged. "Master Devras—!" he appealed.

"An illusion," Devras promised, praying that he spoke the truth. "Nothing's there. Nothing."

At the last moment, her prow verging upon the mammoth body, *Sublimity* picked up speed and Devras clutched the railing, bracing himself against the inevitable collision. It never came. And suddenly he couldn't see Frejeeria as an entity any longer. The air turned cold and murky as *Sublimity* plunged deep into her. The illusory monstress rose on all sides, her bones, vessels and organs visible but insubstantial. It was cold in the depths of Frejeeria—cold, silent and uncanny. Devras could see the ghostly six-chambered heart pumping, tentlike diaphragm rising and falling, tremendous lungs swelling—all transparent, spectral. Briefly marking the spasmodic contractions of the surrounding passageway, his attention shifted to the misshapen fetus distending the monstrous womb. Through it all he could still discern the river, trees and moon. Beside him, Grono gaped in bewildered horror.

The fog lifted and the air warmed as *Sublimity* passed on through to emerge at Frejeeria's back. For a moment the monstress lingered, immense and ghastly; then faded to nothingness. Downstream, Whurm Didnis heads bobbed in the river.

Low in the water and listing perilously, *Sublimity* floundered on until a bone-shaking jolt arrested her progress. The venerise had struck another submerged rock. Water was flooding in. The wet deck tilted sharply, cargo and passengers sliding aft, as *Sublimity* began to sink.

"We swim for it." Devras clung to the rail. The stern was already awash. "Else she carries us down."

Wate Basef and Karavise nodded. Only Grono, conscious but disoriented, voiced an objection. "I cannot."

"No choice. We're sinking," Devras told him.

"Then I must sink with her, for I do not know how to swim. Athletics are not the province of a gentleman's gentleman. Farewell, Master Devras. Farewell."

"Not quite yet. Somebody help me." Already seated astride the deck railing, Devras grasped the valet under the armpits and hauled him up. Karavise assisted from below.

"Your Lordship—your Ladyship—what are you—"

"Ready, Karavise?"

"Ready."

Together they swung the dazed valet out over the water and let him go. Grono fell with a choking cry. He hit the river on his back, went under and rose, arms flailing wildly. Devras dove, and the chilly waters closed over his head. Karavise and Wate Basef followed.

The current was swift where the river battered itself against Frejeeria's Teeth. Devras surfaced with a gasp, shaking the water from his eyes. The lanterns still burning atop *Sublimity*'s tilting castles cast their ruddy light upon the turbulent Yl. A few feet away, Grono splashed and struggled and choked. Devras struck out for the drowning retainer; reached him, seized his collar and headed for the bank. Drained though he was, desperation lent him strength to fight the current. Master and servant made it to solid ground, considerably downstream of the stricken ship. Collapsing face down in the mud, Grono lay still. Devras turned back to survey the water, and what he beheld was disheartening.

Raith Wate Basef was all but spent. Slow and sluggish, he seemed barely able to lift his arms. Lady Karavise was in a worse state yet. Her heavy, trailing skirts and multiple petticoats had wound themselves around her legs. The tight lacings that reduced her waistline to fairy proportions were cutting off her breath. Gasping for air, she inhaled water. Shocked, she floundered, thrashed, and went under. A moment later she surfaced, coughing and choking. The long, wet hair was plastered across her face, blinding and suffocating her. While Karavise clawed at her hair, the current bounced her against a rock. She cried out, swallowed water, and sank.

Devras agonized briefly.

I can only help one of them. Raith is indispensable. But Karavise is drowning; she's dying before my eyes.

He threw himself into the Yl, and a few strokes carried him to the failing woman. Despite his own increasing exhaustion, he managed to drag her to shore. Karavise sprawled full length, long hair straggling, legs still encased in a cocoon of sopping velvet, former cool perfection a thing of the past. A hundred yards downstream, Raith Wate Basef—bruised, dripping, debilitated but whole—crawled from the water. And the Whurm Didnis pirates? There was no sign of King Pusstis or his kinsmen. Out in the middle of the river, *Sublimity* shook in her death agonies. Racked with convulsions, her nervous fibers flailing wildly, the venerise was tearing herself apart. As Devras watched, the forecastle vibrated—lanterns swinging in wide arcs, fitful light flaming on gilded sculptures, fanciful turrets and tattered pennants. Flakes of loosened gold leaf rained down in a magically glittering shower. Great fissures split the ancient wood, and the frivolous carven top turret toppled. Amidst a final furious rattling the ship went down, loftiest silken banner dipping at last to meet the black waters. The lanterns drowned, and only moonlight illuminated the brief agitation that marked *Sublimity*'s passing. A few moments later the bubbles arose, a last rush of escaping air, and then the Yl flowed on untroubled.

For a time the castaways lay where they had fallen, scattered along the bank like dead fish cast ashore. Devras was distantly aware of freezing mud, sharp rocks pressing his flesh, filthy moisture, bleeding cuts and curious insects. Pain and cold notwithstanding, the moon was sinking toward the horizon before he could bring himself to move. He sat up slowly. Beside him, Karavise was stirring. A few yards distant, Grono lay ominously still. Heartbeat quickening, Devras crawled to the valet's side. Grono lay prone, motionless and colorless, eyes closed behind miraculously preserved spectacles. Devras turned him over gently, and the old man's lids lifted.

"You're well, Master Devras?" Grono whispered.

Devras nodded.

"Her Ladyship? Cognizance Wate Basef?"

"Both safe."

"The ship?"

"Struck a rock and sank."

"The giantess?"

"Never existed. A Cognitive illusion."

"The pirates?"

"Abandoned ship. I don't know what's become of them."

"Good riddance to bad rubbish. As for the Pusstis person's claim to noble rank, I scorn it. I say they were common, and nothing will change my mind. Help me up, your Lordship."

"Are you certain you want to move yet?"

"I am certain. I am a retainer of the noble House of Har Fennahar. Such a retainer does not disgrace his livery with unseemly wallowings. I leave that to riffraff such as the Whurm Didnis brigands. Please assist me, sir."

Devras helped the valet to rise and the two of them made their halting way along the bank to Lady Karavise, who sat untangling her skirts. She appeared calm, but the chill night air upon her damp skin raised gooseflesh, and her teeth chattered with cold or tension. Wate Basef soon joined them, and it was then that the value of the satchel still slung around his neck became fully apparent. The satchel yielded a flat charcoal disk, which, at the command of its owner, radiated heat. The heat swiftly drove the moisture from a hastily gathered pile of dank vegetation and wet twigs. Presently the fuel burst into smoky flame, and the wet, exhausted castaways huddled gratefully near—all save Karavise, who for some minutes retired quietly from view. When she reappeared, the Duke's daughter was transformed. Gone were the stays that impeded her breathing. The filthy froth of petticoats had been discarded, and the trailing velvet skirt had been torn off at calf level. Her hair was loosely braided into a single massive

145

plait that hung to her waist. Wordlessly, Karavise joined her companions beside the blaze. The warmth and jumping light exerted an almost narcotic effect on the four of them. They nodded, their lids drooped, and sleep found them almost at once.

Instinct alone must have wakened Devras, for the approach of the enemy had been soundless. He opened his eyes to behold three damp figures glowering at the edge of the circle of firelight. King Pusstis Whurm Didnis, Duke Cheedle, and the Crown Prince Krotz had arrived. All were armed and clearly hostile. Prince Krotz, still bearing an ax, grinned unpleasantly.

"Surprise," said the Crown Prince.

His voice roused the three sleepers, who started up rigid with alarm. Wate Basef took a deep breath and Duke Cheedle sprang to his side, purloined cavalry saber unsheathed. "Not a word, Master Savant," the Duke enjoined. "Not a solitary word, Master Treachery."

"So." King Pusstis spoke with an air of almost melancholy accusation. "We find you at last. Traitors, destroyers, ingrates, your crimes have overtaken you."

"What do you want?" asked Karavise coldly.

"Justice," returned his Majesty. "Nothing more. Although the wound that you above all, Madam, have inflicted upon our soft and trusting heart cries out for vengeance, we shall content ourselves with simple justice."

"Justice swift and irrevocable," added the Duke.

"How dare you speak to us of justice, you scrofulous pirates?" demanded Grono. "The very word shrivels upon your lips!"

"Peace, lackey," advised the King. "Impudence will not help you now. We advise you to think on your crimes. Repent them while you may."

"Crimes? You kidnap and enslave us, you torture and exploit us, you trample upon our natural human rights, and you speak of *our* crimes, you putrid scum?" cried Grono.

"Silence. These wild and pointless accusations shall not serve to cloud the issue. Do not think to hoodwink or mislead us. Such insolence only adds to the sum of your offenses."

"Of what specifically are we accused?" inquired Karavise.

"You have betrayed the trust of a king," returned his Majesty. "You have betrayed the faith of all humankind by subverting our great mission of mercy and rescue. You have broken a sensitive masculine heart. More to the point, you are responsible for the destruction of our vessel *Sublimity*, together with the property aboard, which destruction constitutes an attack upon our royal

146

person and all our House. After all, we could have drowned. Did you think of that? Did you think what such a loss would have meant to our subjects? Do you begin to comprehend the enormity of your transgression? You have hindered, thwarted, damaged and obstructed us, which is to say, you are guilty of treason."

"Punishable by death," the Crown Prince Krotz observed.

"The heir apparent is correct," his Majesty agreed. "We regard ourself as a liberal, progressive and merciful monarch, innocent of personal malice. Nevertheless, the hope of the populace resides in us, and therefore the preservation of Whurm Didnis lives is our own greatest obligation to the state. Our decisions in that regard, harsh though they may appear to the superficial observer, are in a larger sense sanctified by philanthropy. In certain sad instances, drastic defensive measures are dictated by political necessity. Alas that such an instance now confronts us."

"So we're going to finish what we were just starting aboard *Sublimity*." The Prince's avid gaze pinned Karavise. "Remember, girl? But first—your Majesty, your Grace—I say we get rid of the wizard. I said so from the beginning and if you'd listened to me then, we wouldn't have lost *Sublimity*, would we?"

"You can scarcely add to the reproaches we have already heaped upon our own head, Prince."

"Then don't make the same mistake twice. We don't need the wizard—we don't need any of them. So I say we do him right now, before he pulls something else on us."

"I agree, your Majesty." Left hand clamping Wate Basef's bearded jaw, Duke Cheedle pressed his blade firmly to the savant's neck.

"Then I defer to your wisdom. Master Savant"—King Pusstis addressed Wate Basef directly—"you are guilty of treason, and the sentence—alas—is death. The matter is not open to discussion and thus there is little point in soliciting your commentary. In the interests of efficiency we shall likewise dispense with your final farewells. Duke Cheedle, you may carry out the sentence."

Wate Basef flopped and struggled, striving in vain to wrench his jaw free of Duke Cheedle's grasp. Devras, Grono and Karavise leaped up to confront the Prince's ax and the King's dagger. With a cunning twist, the Duke forced Wate Basef to the ground. Setting his foot firmly upon the savant's neck, Cheedle raised his saber. The blade was quivering on the verge of descent when a flat monotone voice spoke from the shadows:

"Release that man. He is mine."

All froze, staring, as a short, slight figure stepped into the light.

"In the name of the Select, I claim the prisoner," said Mistress Snarp.

"It's female, I think," said the Prince.

Ignoring the comment, Snarp addressed Duke Cheedle. "Release him."

"We do not know who you are, Madam, but you ask the impossible," King Pusstis informed her. "The traitor has been condemned, and justice will be served. Resign yourself. He dies this instant."

"I am taking him back to Lanthi Ume," said Snarp.

"You are welcome to transport his corpse, if you so desire." His Majesty turned to the Duke. "Your Grace, proceed with the execution."

"Release him," Snarp repeated.

Duke Cheedle chose to obey his brother. Once again the sword rose. Simultaneously a knife winged from the hand of Mistress Snarp. The blade flashed over the fire and buried itself to the hilt in Cheedle's bosom. The saber dropped from a suddenly nerveless grasp. The Duke tottered and fell, dead before he hit the ground.

A scream of fury broke from the Crown Prince Krotz. Ax swinging, he leaped for the murderess, who sent a Living Wire hissing through the air to meet him. The Wire landed, looped and tightened. Suddenly airless and in pain, Prince Krotz dropped to his knees.

As Pusstis rushed to the aid of his purpling heir, Snarp launched herself in a kicking leap. Her flying foot crashed into the other's chest, and his Majesty staggered backward. A second kick took him full in the groin, and he sank to his knees, mouth wide open and face blank with shock. Without difficulty, Snarp twisted the dagger from his grasp, yanked his head back by the hair and cut his throat from ear to ear.

The sight lent Prince Krotz strength to tear the Living Wire from his throat. Flinging the hissing creature aside, he rose to advance upon Snarp. Poised and wholly expressionless, she spun to confront him.

Devras and his companions did not wait to view the outcome of the battle. Pausing only long enough to pluck Wate Basef's satchel and Duke Cheedle's saber from the ground, the four of them fled into darkness. The branches whipped them as they ran, and behind them rose the hoarse shouts of the Crown Prince. The shouts shrilled to a single loud scream that cut off abruptly, and then there was nothing.

Instinctively the fugitives quickened their steps, hurrying in silence away from the river and into the sheltering woods, through midnight shadow and patches of luring moonlight; circling the edge of a silvered clearing where the night-blooming ghostlilies shone luminously white beneath the open sky; then under the trees again, across a moonlit rill and along a narrow trail. Often they glanced behind them as they went, but if Snarp pursued, she followed undetectably. Of greater immediate concern was the surviving Whurm Didnis royalty.

Footsteps sounded behind them on the trail, and voices that made no effort at concealment. Impossible to judge how many. The fugitives abandoned the path, running now, fighting through the undergrowth, stumbling over roots and rocks; the voices swelling behind them. On they went, hearts hammering, breath rasping, until without warning the night clenched like a fist around them. The moon and stars blinked out of existence; all traces of light vanished. Absolute, ineffable darkness reigned; blackness beyond comprehension, pressing upon them with almost tangible weight. The air turned hot and moist. A vile odor fouled the heavy atmosphere, a nauseous stench of mold or rotting vegetation. Devras felt his stomach churn. Within seconds he was bathed in tepid sweat. He was blind, slightly dizzy, and breathing seemed to require conscious effort. But that was not the worst of it. Beyond the physical discomfort was something more —some nameless quality of sick, helpless, hopeless fear breeding like pestilence in blackness.

"What is it, Master Devras? What is it?" Grono's shaking voice was near at hand but muffled, as if the air killed sound as well as light.

"It is Cognition turned against humanity," Raith Wate Basef answered for Devras. "It is the funeral pall of all Dalyon. Now do you understand?"

Thus they came to the region of Terrs Fal Grizhni's darkness.

Chapter Twelve

❧❧❧❧❧

Dawn was breaking when Mistress Snarp reached the edge of the Cognitive darkness. Her encounter with the Whurm Didnis royalty had proved inconclusive and generally unrewarding. His Majesty, his Grace and the Crown Prince were all dead, but Snarp herself had sustained a gash upon her upper right arm, courtesy of the ax-wielding Krotz. The wound was long and deep. A makeshift linen bandage was slow to stanch the flow of blood, and now the length of her merino sleeve was splotched with red. The limb would be impaired for a time, but this was no great matter. Snarp's total ambidexterity was one of the many natural attributes that suited her so exactly to her profession. Of far more significance than the wound was the disappearance of her quarry. Wate Basef and his accomplices had vanished into the silent woods, and Snarp had pursued in vain throughout the night. Now as early morning grayed the air, and the range of visibility increased beyond the circle of light cast by the lanterns swinging from her saddle, Snarp sawed unnecessarily on the bit. The horse had already halted, unwilling to advance another step toward the horror yawning dead ahead.

Just beyond the nearest stand of trees, the darkness rose in a seemingly solid wall. Impenetrable, impossibly black and almost palpably malign, it smothered the land like a flow of nightmare lava. As Snarp sat motionless, stolen mount trembling beneath her, the shadow approached at the pace of a walking man. A couple of oak trees were swallowed. A cluster of elms disappeared; and on it glided in relentless silence, devouring all in its path. For a moment longer Snarp watched, then lowered her gaze to scrutinize the footprints, fresh and clear in the soft dirt before her. The tracks led on into darkness. Requiring no additional evidence, she straightened and kneed her horse. Muscles bunched, the animal balked, and the rider roweled her spurs until the brown flanks streamed with blood. The horse bucked and plunged beneath these persuasive ministrations, but nothing could induce it to move forward. A weary breeze sighed from the darkness, and the horse snorted violently at the scent of it. Shuddering, nostrils aflare, the animal danced sideways.

Venting a brief hiss, Snarp dismounted. Under other circumstances she would have remained to pursue the contest of wills to its inevitable conclusion—the horse's subjugation or its death. Just now, she did not wish to spare the time. Swiftly she transferred most of the contents of the saddlebags to her own pack; detached one of the still-burning lanterns from the saddle; then administered a final stinging slap that sent the horse off at a gallop.

"You will not have him." Mistress Snarp spoke aloud to the towering darkness as if addressing a sentient foe. "He is mine."

Forward she strode to meet the oncoming tide of black, pausing only once to stroke and soothe the terrified quibbid before resuming her march. Her step never faltered, and soon her gray form was lost in fantastic shadow.

"How will we eat? Where is our shelter? How shall we live in this dreadful place? What hope have we now of finding our way into those accursed caverns? Isn't it time to go home?" Grono's voice was fervent but weak. His face, in all its tired gloom and sickly pallor, was visible by the light of a pile of rocks Cognitively invested with a pure, hard, blue-white radiance. In that sweltering, stifling atmosphere, the heat of a campfire would only have enhanced the general misery. Moreover, there was no food to cook. Therefore Raith Wate Basef had resorted to Cognition, and the resulting brilliant illumination pushed the darkness back a few grudging feet. The cold light drained the color from four already pale faces, and the company resembled a gathering of sweaty corpses. The appearance of ill health was not misleading. Since entering the realm of Grizhni's darkness, each of the travelers had suffered illness beyond the discomfort of breathless heat, moldy dampness and loathsome odors. There was nausea, lassitude and giddiness; beneath these things there was fear, primal fear tapped from the depths of mind and body; blackness within rising to meet and merge with outer blackness of like nature. It was always there, often suppressed but never banished.

In hopes of containing the inner blackness, Devras answered, only partly joking, "We'll manage, Grono. Have you never read Klam Leboid's *Delicacies of Dalyon*? Did you know that there are over one hundred varieties of nonpoisonous fungi native to this island? There are all sorts of roots, nutritious weeds, edible slugs, maggots, beetles and grubs. We'll not starve."

"Does my Lord Har Fennahar intend to dig for grubs and

151

maggots?" the valet inquired with elaborate restraint.

"Grono, sometimes I wish you wouldn't be so stiff-necked."

"Stiff-necked—I? There is no stiffness troubling my neck, I do assure you. I thank your Lordship for your concern. While your Lordship is burrowing for maggots, does your Lordship also intend to investigate the nutritive properties of carrion, decayed vegetation and fecal matter?"

"Not today. But I shouldn't rule out that possibility if I were you."

"That is coarse and revolting, Master Devras!" Outrage stiffened Grono's spine. "Where is your breeding?"

"Lost in the dark, I suppose. Still, we must eat."

"We'd eat well enough if we returned to Lanthi Ume, the sooner the better."

"You know better than that. Surely you don't imagine we've come this far only to give up?"

"Well, what choice have we? Consider, sir. We've lost our belongings as well as our bearings, we're lost and starving in a hideous place—*hideous*! We are weakening, ailing, dying by inches—and all in vain. We cannot find our way to those caverns in the dark. Without maps to guide us, and all landmarks hidden, our efforts are useless. You cannot argue that point, sir. It is folly to pursue a hopeless cause. You cannot argue that either. By all standards of sound judgment, but one course remains to us now —retreat. And I suggest we move without delay, while we've yet the strength to walk."

"There is a flaw in your reasoning, Grono," Wate Basef observed, smile broadening at the valet's scowl. "We still have a map." Reaching into the satchel—his only surviving possession—he withdrew a packet of treated fabric from which he removed a parchment map, none the worse for its recent immersion. He unfolded the map and spread it to catch the blue-white glow of the stones. "See," the savant pointed, "there's the entrance we want, and it can't be far away."

"How do you know?" Grono demanded. "We've no idea where we are, no way of measuring time or distance, no means whatever of navigation. How do you presume to tell us we are near the entrance when in truth you cannot know?"

"A fair estimation of *Sublimity*'s speed, continued over a period of five days and nights, gives me a reasonable approximation of distance covered."

"Pah, that is sheer guesswork. But let us suppose you are correct—what then? We might pass within ten feet of the entrance we seek without ever finding it. In this ghastly darkness, it is useless to attempt a search. Useless and, if I may say so, very foolish."

"There's where you're wrong, Grono. There are certain guides that even Cognition can't obscure. One of them is the river itself. You see"—Wate Basef consulted the map—"our route takes us along the bank of the Yl. We need only follow the river, and that we can manage even in darkness."

"Follow it how far, and how long? We can't know! We don't even know if it's day or night! We won't know when to sleep— not that there's any shelter to sleep beneath!"

"In this heat we don't need shelter. In answer to your first question, we proceed along the river until we reach the Icy Ambition, a deserted glass tower of unknown origin whose reflective surface will be readily identifiable, even in darkness. Not a hundred feet from the base of this construction, equidistant from tower and river, lies the entrance."

"Which will doubtless be sealed, as all the others were."

"Well, there we must hope for good luck. We are certainly due some."

"Luck, Master Wate Basef, rarely keeps balanced account ledgers. Nor does the Goddess Fortune favor the foolhardy who ignore her warnings. She smites them for their hubris."

"Or rewards them for their valor."

"The point is open to debate, sir. Unfortunately, the wisdom of my judgment can only be confirmed by disaster, and I would prefer to avoid so unrewarding a victory."

"Bravo, Grono! But surely you can't maintain that it is impossible for us to proceed?"

"But surely *you* can't maintain that it is advisable?"

"For ourselves, no," Wate Basef admitted. "But there are other considerations, remember."

"I do not require instruction, sir! As for Lanthi Ume and her sister-cities, our lonely demise in the midst of darkness will not benefit them in the slightest."

"Have you never considered—even considered—the possibility of our success?"

"A remote possibility at best, and not worth the risk of his Lordship's life."

"No? Don't his Lordship's prospective title and wealth lie in Lanthi Ume?"

"I do not care about it!"

"But I care about it. I care about Lanthi Ume," Karavise broke in unexpectedly. She lay on her side, propped up on one elbow, inches from the coldly glowing rocks. Her grayish face shone with sweat, and the tendrils of chestnut hair had glued themselves to her damp forehead. Her bloodshot eyes glittered diamond-bright, and the words issuing from her cracked lips were curiously headlong and breathless. "I'll do whatever must be done to save the city, no matter what the cost. If need be, I'll do it alone. Flee the darkness, all of you, flee Dalyon altogether if you choose, and I'll go on by myself. Now that I've seen this darkness, now that I know what's in store for Lanthi Ume, nothing will stop me. I swear it."

The others stared at her in amazement.

"Your Ladyship—" Grono attempted.

"I hope that Terrs Fal Grizhni suffered before he died," she continued. "Suffered for what he's inflicted upon thousands of innocent people—*my* people, Lanthians. I'm sorry he's dead, for I'd like to kill him myself. I only wish that somehow I could strike at him."

Her companions exchanged uneasy glances.

"Your Ladyship, I implore you—" Grono tried again.

"He won't win, though. He won't destroy my Lanthi Ume." Tossing restlessly, Karavise flung the heavy braid of hair aside to clear the back of her sticky neck. But the black air lay upon her flesh like hot glue, bringing no relief. She resumed her babbling monologue. "We'll break Grizhni's Cognition. But even when we've done that, there are many problems, many problems. Lanthi Ume's decline must be reversed. We must make good our debts somehow, and we must eject those Lammish soldiers. Above all things we need money, lots of money. We can't raise the taxes. The people are miserable already—poor, hungry, ignorant, overburdened and angry. Father won't tap the resources of the nobles; he's afraid of offending personal friends. When I'm Duchess, *I'll* do it, though—I don't care whom I offend. But you needn't worry, Devras, the Har Fennahar fortune will be left nearly intact for you. Oh yes, you'll have it. Because I believe your story, you see. I don't think you could lie if your life depended on it. I could, of course. Lie, I mean. Cheat. Steal. Murder, even, if the welfare of Lanthi Ume depended upon it. Sometimes such measures are necessary, just as that pea-brained pirate claimed. I'm not proud of it, but there it is." Her unfocused smile was oddly wistful. "An effective Duchess, you see, cannot be a woman of gentle character."

"Karavise, stop," said Devras.

"Oh, it's all right, I accepted it long ago, and I can live with it, I suppose, although sometimes I wish—" She was panting. "But don't worry, Devras, you're a good person and you'll have what's rightfully yours. My father would say it was meant to happen. Poor Father! How I miss him now! And he must be sick with worry on my account. He's the sweetest, dearest, most innocently loving of mortals, and that's why he's not a successful Duke. When I speak of betrothing myself to the Duke of Hurba in order to gain Hurbanese military backing—or of fomenting war between Gard Lammis and Rhel, to Lanthi Ume's obvious advantage—he doesn't understand, he simply does not understand. Oh, often he speaks of retirement—of abdicating in my favor— and I wish he'd do it. He'd be much happier, and Lanthi Ume would benefit greatly."

"Raith, she's feverish," said Devras. "I think she's delirious."

"Yes." Leaning forward, Wate Basef pressed his fingers to Karavise's forehead. Accepting the familiarity without protest, she closed her eyes and expelled her breath in a sigh. "Yes. Sooner even than I expected."

"Expected?"

"I'm afraid it was inevitable. How do you and Grono feel?"

"Tired. Queasy. Weak, a little lightheaded. You too, Grono?" Devras asked.

The valet nodded.

"We're not unprepared," Wate Basef told them. "I was hoping we wouldn't have to resort to this so soon, but—" His voice trailed off and he turned to his satchel, which yielded a pouchful of opalescent tablets. "Here is our remedy. It is—I'd like you all to listen, please." Karavise opened her eyes reluctantly. "These tablets will counteract most of the darkness' debilitating effects. You will take one each day—or under these circumstances, as you sense you need them—and you'll remain moderately vigorous, for a while. Here." He shook the tablets into the outstretched palms of his companions, distributing them evenly. "Chew one now." He popped one into his own mouth, and the others did likewise.

Devras crunched down tentatively, and his mouth was flooded with tumultuous warring flavors. He swallowed, and his veins tingled—a sensation peculiar but not unpleasant. A moment more, and his giddiness was gone. He was stronger, more alert, and suddenly ravenous. Beside him Grono sat bright-eyed and vital. Wate Basef was similarly invigorated. Karavise slumped to the ground. Within seconds she was fast asleep.

"She'll be better when she wakes," Wate Basef promised. "The tablets will break her fever, for a while."

"If they're so effective, why did you say you hoped we wouldn't have to resort to them so soon?" Devras inquired.

"They inflict a certain shock upon the system," Wate Basef explained. "They're somewhat addictive, and prolonged use results in cumulative deterioration of the body, character and intellect. Other than that, they're quite safe."

Grono's wattles quivered. He said nothing.

Devras's newfound contentment died a quick death, but his newfound hunger remained. "I'm going to see about finding us some food," he announced. "Want to help, Grono?"

"Your Lordship does not intend to dig for grubs? I'll countenance no such activity."

"Berries, roots and mushrooms. That's all."

"Truly, sir?"

"I promise. Maybe a little edible moss and lichen. Perhaps a snake, if we can find one."

"No! No snakes, sir!"

"Oh come on, Grono. Klam Leboid says that snakes are wholesome, nourishing and delicious."

"Klam Leboid has degraded and repulsive appetites."

"We must see to it that you two don't get lost," Wate Basef interrupted the argument. "To begin with, you'd each better take a rock from the pile and use them to light your way. They're cool to the touch and you can carry them comfortably, but whatever you do, don't lick them or try to put them into your mouth."

"Are we infants, Cognizance?" Grono demanded.

"Certainly not, but the response to this particular sequence of assorted radiant effluvia varies according to the mental organization of the individual thus bombarded. Moreover, I would advise you to wash or at least wipe your hands after you have touched the stones, particularly before you eat anything."

His listeners regarded the rocks without favor.

"You mustn't rely on the rocks alone," the savant continued. "For one thing, their light is apt to fail without warning. Even were that not the case, you won't be able to see more than a very few feet in any direction, and you'll require an alternate tool in guiding you back to our camp. But see, I've provided for that." He pushed back his right sleeve to reveal a loop of colorless cord knotted about his wrist. From the loop dangled a short tail of thread the approximate weight and thickness of fishing line. "Just take the end of the thread," Wate Basef directed. "Wrap it around your finger or fasten it to your belt, wander where you will, then follow the line when you wish to return." Noting his companions' twin expressions of disbelief, he added, "It stretches." Pinching the loose strand between thumb and forefinger, he pulled. The thread lengthened effortlessly. When released, it hung motionless for a few seconds, then snapped back to its original length faster than the eye could follow.

"How far will it stretch?" Devras asked.

"Several leagues, at least."

"What if it breaks?"

"I suggest you take care that it doesn't. And don't let go of it, or it's gone."

"I'll tie it around my wrist." Devras did so, linking himself to the savant. The taut bond exerted a light pressure. When he took a couple of steps backward, the thread stretched but its tension did not increase. The line was drawn straight and tight. He touched it and it sang like a harp string. A thin, pure tone knifed the heavy air. Devras jumped slightly, and Wate Basef smiled.

"Once you get used to it, you can use that tone to judge the approximate length of the line."

"Did you invent this, Raith?"

"Hardly, lad. The device has been in use among the members of the Select since the days of Nes the Eyes."

Even Grono was grudgingly impressed. Without further conversation, Devras and his valet selected a pair of fist-sized rocks from the lucent pile. Rocks in hand, they ventured forth.

The swiftness with which the Cognitive atmosphere devoured light was intimidating. Having advanced no more than a few long paces, Devras looked back to behold a smudge of blue-white luminosity, all that marked the campsite. Wate Basef and Lady Karavise were already invisible. A few paces more and the glow vanished altogether. Then they were alone in the midst of a black universe, with only the light of the two small rocks to hold the malignant darkness at bay. Devras could see Grono beside him, his drawn, perspiring face reflecting faint blue highlights. He could see the surrounding patch of weedy soil, vegetation already pining away for the sun. Beyond that—nothingness, a midnight void. The world and its inhabitants were gone without a trace. Only the slight, comforting pressure of the thread at his wrist assured him of Wate Basef's existence. On impulse he plucked the line, and the string sang. An instant later he felt an answering vibration, and the note was repeated. Wate Basef was still there.

"Well—what now, Master Devras?" Grono's hearty tone rang appallingly false.

"Now we find something to eat." Devras's assurance was equally hollow. "According to Klam Leboid, there are edible fungi everywhere. Could you do with some mushrooms for dinner?"

"They are preferable to maggots, I suppose. How do you

know it's dinner time, sir? Perhaps it's morning or noon."

"Perhaps. The last meal we had was the gruel aboard *Sublimity*. Judging by the state of my appetite, at least a night and a day have passed since then, but that's only a guess and I could well be wrong. As Heselicus wrote, 'Pain and privation retard the passage of time. The hours spent in woe stretch interminably. It is therefore logical to conclude that grief prolongs life, that absolute misery prolongs life absolutely, and thus in wretchedness lies the secret of eternal youth.' "

"No doubt the drivelling buffoon fancied himself amusing. Let's find those mushrooms, sir."

The wilderness scarcely proved the garden of abundance promised by Klam Leboid. The berries, if there had ever been any, were gone from the bushes. The edible roots so eloquently praised in Leboid's treatise could not be located. Fungi, however, flourished in the humid warmth. Mushrooms and toadstools sprouted everywhere. A few varieties were certainly poisonous; many others possibly so, and these were left untouched. Then Devras discovered a patch of the familiar, wholesome Living Pearls. Eating as they worked, he and Grono soon gathered a respectable bundle of fungi, enough to stave off the worst pangs of hunger. But mushrooms, though plentiful, would not satisfy, and the foragers chose to prolong the hunt. Through the darkness they wandered, their world reduced to the tiny volume of space illuminated by two small flares of Cognitive radiance. Slowly they went, for mishap in that place would have spelled disaster. Above all, Devras feared for the safety of the fragile line binding him to Raith Wate Basef. If the thread snapped, they would never find their way back.

They were walking uphill and Devras could sense the shallow slope of clear, once cultivated land. The ground underfoot was whiskered with dead grass. Presently a barrier of horizontal logs rose athwart their path. For a moment they wondered, then recognized the obstacle for what it was—the wall of some small farmer's cabin or outbuilding. Feeling their way along the wall and around a corner, they found the entrance. The door gaped wide, but the light of the stones failed at the threshold. Devras hailed the inhabitants in confident tones. Receiving no reply, he opined, "Deserted."

"Take care, Master Devras."

"There may be food."

"Your Lordship's decision."

"My stomach's decision." Devras entered the cabin, carefully maneuvering the thread around the doorjamb. Grono followed close on his heels. He found himself in an empty wreck of a room, rude furnishings overturned and scattered.

"Anyone here?" Devras's shout drew no response.

"It's surely abandoned, sir. There is no danger at hand. And you were right about the food." Grono pointed. In the corner, a shattered hutch disgorged its contents. Sacks of flour and meal spilled forth, along with broken cannisters of salt, sugar, tea, dried fruits, beans and lentils. The bins lined up along the wall contained assorted root vegetables. Sausages hung from the hooks sunk into the rafters. "*Meat*, sir! And ours for the taking. Surely the owners have fled."

"It would seem so. I wonder why they didn't carry their belongings with them when they went?"

"Perhaps they hadn't the time. In any event, this abandoned property must not go to waste. We will *eat*, sir! All four of us. Think what this will mean to her Ladyship!"

"That's true. Very well, you can collect the food while I look for weapons, cooking utensils, lanterns, blankets and so forth." Devras commenced his hunt. Despite the cabin's reassuringly lifeless air, his uneasiness mounted as he searched, peaking as he reached a curtain of rough weave apparently concealing a niche or storage compartment. Half unwillingly he thrust the curtain aside, and icy light pushed into the closet beyond to reveal a collection of corpses. A man, a woman, and two adolescent boys lay there, blood-soaked and wide-eyed. All of them were armed. Their respective weapons—an ax, a harrow, a cleaver and a carving knife—were slick with a nearly transparent colorless substance. Pools of this same material had clotted on the floor, where it mingled with the dark stain of human blood. Devras stood very still, staring.

"Master Devras?" Grono's voice issued from the blue-white smear of light glowing at the far end of the room. "Master Devras, there is more here than the two of us can carry. It is my opinion that we should take what we can, and then plan on coming back—"

"We won't come back," Devras said flatly.

"How, sir! Master Devras, what's happened?" Without awaiting reply, Grono hurried to his master's side. He saw the corpses and a gasp of sick dismay escaped him. When he spoke again, it was in a whisper. "The White Demons, sir?"

"So I believe."

"Demons indeed. Do they kill for the pleasure of it?"

"I don't know. They were here recently and they may be back. Let's go."

"Do you think they are near, sir?"

"Yes, Grono. I've a feeling they are very near."

Some two hundred feet directly below Devras and Grono lay the room known to the Vardrul cave-dwellers as the Chamber of White Tunnels. Small and austere, devoid of stalactite, stalagmite, or colored crystalline growth, the room was almost featureless save for a number of dark, polished, hexagonal slabs set into the natural stone floor. These slabs—product of the self-taught Cognition of the legendary human/Vardrul Fal Grizhni Terrs, Patriarch-progenitor of Clan Grizhni—were similar in appearance to the ophelu of Raith Wate Basef, and served an identical function. Each slab constituted one half of a matched set. Their respective mates were scattered throughout the huge caverns. A few had even been installed in camouflaged form at various strategic points Surface. Thus it was theoretically possible for the clanmembers to travel from point to point instantaneously. In reality, however, the procedure was so alien, so disharmonious—and the device itself so disturbingly human in concept and execution—that few Vardruls other than the Grizhni kinsmen had ever cared to avail themselves of the convenience. The members of Clan Grizhni, of course, were peculiarly insensitive to dissonance and always had been. This was scarcely surprising, in view of the ancient human taint of which the clan had never managed to cleanse itself.

Among the hexagonal slabs was one of anomalously small size, set in the center of the chamber. This slab—the only one bordered with bands of variegated stone—was mate to the Gnrfrl K'frazh, or in human terms, the Wandering Flat. The Wandering Flat—whose relatively light weight and resulting transportability had been achieved at the cost of some Cognitive potency—was carried in the train of the Grizhni Patriarch, thus affording that great general immediate access to his home caverns, any Coloration of the Small Ven. No matter where his victorious campaigns might take him across the length and breadth of Dalyon, the Grizhni Greater Patriarch possessed power to return to the Chamber of White Tunnels in the blink of an eye. He was expected to utilize this power at the turn of the Purple Coloration, now close at hand.

Awaiting the appearance of their Greater Patriarch, whose title reflected acceptable influence over clans other than his own, stood three Vardruls of note. There was the youthful but highly competent F'tryll'jnr Drzh; the Zmadrc Lesser Matriarch, who had twice experienced and survived Cold Stupor; and Dfjnr'l

Gallr, ultraproficient in human languages and recent unwelcome visitor to Vaxalt Gless Vallage. The three were typical of their kind in appearance, possessing lithe, hairless, emaciated bodies, humanoid in conformation, but with little obvious differentiation between the sexes; boneless tentacular fingers; lambent flesh brighter than the rock-lit walls of the caverns; and huge, palely brilliant eyes ringed with triple ridges of muscle. Over the course of the Great Vens, their race had undergone little visible alteration. However, an Ancestor of an earlier age would have noted the qualitative change in the ruu (an expression describing a Vardrul's state of self-knowledge, serenity, harmony with the environment and with the race past and present) of his modern kinsmen. Subsequent to the self-transformation and final acceptance of the Fal Grizhni Terrs, Vardrul character had altered. Gone was the old tranquility. The timidity and pacificism had likewise vanished; and with them the essential innocence. The profound sense of racial unity was considerably diminished, and Knowledge of Ancestors was no longer easy of access. The decline of these gentle qualities had accompanied the development of vigor, resolve, courage, initiative, and a kind of restless turbulence that could only be described as human. The change was fundamental, marked by sacrifice as well as gain. The net profit or loss to the race as a whole as yet remained open to question.

Melody stirred the warm air. A Vardrul conversation was in progress. Translated into wholly human parlance, it would have run approximately:

"This is the Greater Patriarch's second visit within six Small Vens." F'tryll'jnr Drzh was the speaker. The flickering of his lambent flesh and the dilation of his ocular ridges communicated doubt, even disapproval. "How shall the kinsmen presently Surface fare in the absence of their Patriarch?"

"Such absences are brief," replied the Zmadrc Lesser Matriarch. "And they are justifiable. Not many Colorations remain before the old Grizhni Inrl joins his Ancestors."

The collective diminution of fleshly luminosity signaled the Vardruls' sorrow at the impending demise of Grizhni Inrl, esteemed artist/teacher and last surviving kinsman of the Greater Grizhni Patriarch.

"Upon the departure of Inrl, the Patriarch is entirely bereft of his clan," hummed Dfjnr'l Gallr, arrhythmic flicker conveying his concern. "He will be alone, with no kinsmen of his own name. It is a terrible thing—almost beyond comprehension—to live without a clan."

"Clan Grizhni never throve," observed the Zmadrc Matriarch.

161

"Dissonance sapped vitality and oneness, finally rendering the Grizhni kinsmen almost unfit to inhabit our caverns."

"Harsh sentiments, Matriarch," F'tryll'jnr Drzh replied, ocular ridges expanding. "Clan Grizhni has furnished our most brilliant artists and engineers, our greatest Patriarchs. Their disharmony, if such it must be termed, furnishes strength."

"But destroys unity, thereby killing serenity," returned the Matriarch. "The present Grizhni Greater Patriarch is perhaps the greatest leader we have ever known, in all ways fit to fulfill the prophecy of the Ancestors. He is also the loneliest and most discordant of all his clan. His disharmony manifests itself in a manner all too recognizable—The Grizhni resembles his human forebears."

The erratic variation of her listeners' luminosity communicated distress at this open expression of an observation common to all, but hitherto unvoiced. The Zmadrc held her hiir steady and her ocular ridges immobile.

Following an uneasy, flickering silence, Dfjnr'l Gallr replied, "All of us carry the human blood within us. All of us suffer discordancies the Ancestors never knew."

"But we retain our identity as clanmembers, kinsmen and Vardruls." The Zmadrc's deliberate control of hiir to suppress open communication of her emotions to fellow Vardruls belied her own assertion, for such suppression had been almost unknown among the Ancestors. "Can the same be said of The Grizhni? He is discordant. He knows no unity, no oneness with others of his race. His ruu is eccentric and incomprehensible, his nature alien and remote. He is not like us. He is separate from us as Men are invariably separate from one another, knowing no deep harmony with race or with environment. His fingers are jointed rods. His eyes are black. He is very like a Man."

"Matriarch, he is no human."

"Neither is he quite a Vardrul."

"He drives Men from the land, thus fulfilling the promise of the Ancestors."

"It is a measure of his discordancy that he is capable of doing so."

"It is also a measure of his greatness. The Surface itself is his gift to the clans. Soon we shall walk aboveground without fear."

"What manner of creature will tread Surface?" the Matriarch demanded, luminosity plunging. "In venturing from the caverns we must change, and I fear the effects of that change. Aboveground, how shall we retain what is left of our harmony, our mutual comprehension, our essential being? Shall we not inherit the violence and loneliness of the humanity that we supplant? In gaining this so-called victory, shall we not lose ourselves and all that we are—as The Grizhni loses?"

"Triumph and freedom are not to be dreaded," Dfjnr'l Gallr opined. "These caverns are a place of exile. Have we grown so inured to confinement that the prospect of liberty arouses our fear? Do we not desire justice? Satisfaction of Man's debt to the murdered Ancestors?"

"And vengeance?" The Zmadrc Matriarch's warble rippled with irony. "Do we not desire vengeance?"

Dfjnr'l Gallr dimmed in silence.

"Perhaps the Zmadrc Matriarch fails to differentiate between The Grizhni's personal afflictions and those disharmonies besetting the race as a whole," suggested F'tryll'jnr Drzh.

"Are the two not inextricably bound?"

"Not always. The Grizhni Greater Patriarch suffers extraordinary misfortune. The departure of Grizhni Inrl marks the loss of the last of his kinsmen, and this follows close upon the death-without-issue of the Patriarch's sister/consort. The personal grief of the Grizhni Patriarch inevitably affects the communal ruu, but remains the Patriarch's alone."

"Even yet, Clan Grizhni is not lost," hummed Dfjnr'l Gallr. "A new consort for the Greater Patriarch—"

"Would matters change?" The Zmadrc's finger-tentacles curled backward in negation. "The lost Grizhni Nine bore the Patriarch no offspring. A new consort would fare no better. The blood of Grizhni is tired and sterile, neither human-red nor Vardrul-clean. The last of the Grizhni vigor expends itself in heroic accomplishment; but the simpler things, the truest treasures— peace, harmony, the clan—are lost. Such is The Grizhni's misfortune, but the remaining clans need not suffer a similar fate. There is still time to change our course."

The Matriarch's companions regarded her without expression, ocular ridges relaxed inscrutably. Before anyone replied, a slight vibration drew collective attention to the mate of the Wandering Flat. The tropical air shimmered and danced. A puff of foam-white vapor spun above the hexagonal slab, then came a wailing rush of white wind, the howling Cognitive whirlwind from whence the term "White Tunnels" derived. For a moment the rock-light glanced from the ice-polished walls of a seemingly solid vertical column. Then the scream of the gale died; the whirlwind slowed and lightened, faded and vanished. In its place stood a lone, still figure. The Grizhni Greater Patriarch was home.

Quietly he stepped from the hexagonal slab. His step was firm and he seemed uninjured, but his subjects could hardly repress their trills of alarm at the state of their Patriarch's hiir. The luminescence of his flesh was all but quenched—a sign of the most profound terror, grief, or morbidity. Only in death was the light altogether extinguished, but The Grizhni's natural radiance was now depressed nearly to the point of invisibility, lending him the pasty opacity of humankind. To the watching Vardruls, their Greater Patriarch appeared as an animate corpse.

"Patriarch, you are taken ill?" F'tryll'jnr Drzh could not control the abrupt, sympathetic dimming of his own flesh. Despite an uneasy awareness of The Grizhni's oddities, all clanmembers of the caverns were bound to their Greater Patriarch by ties of the greatest loyalty, respect and affection.

"No. I am in good health. I regret the unnecessary reduction of the young F'tryll'jnr Drzh's light." The Grizhni shrugged in the traditional Vardrul gesture expressing acknowledgment of another's concern. His manner, composed and unrevealing, discouraged inquiry.

His compatriots regarded him, baffled and at a loss—again, conditions almost unknown among the Ancestors in dealing with one another. At last the Zmadrc Lesser Matriarch sought refuge in formality. "We are here on behalf of the Clans to greet our beloved Greater Patriarch," she hummed with an impassive tranquility equal to The Grizhni's own.

"I thank the Matriarch and her companions. I ask her to extend my greetings and affection to all belowground. I may not embrace the clanmembers upon this Coloration, for my stay is necessarily brief. I have come to visit the ailing Grizhni Inrl, and then I will return Surface to the banks of Mfra Living Water where the clans ready an attack. Briefly, then—what news of the caverns?" The Grizhni's address was calm, if somewhat hurried. Only the ghastly dullness of his flesh gave evidence of distress, but it was enough to send the collective hiir of his companions plummeting.

"Little has occurred in the past six Small Vens, Patriarch," replied Dfjnr'l Gallr. "The tunnels, caverns and excavations rest quiet in your absence—quiet and all but abandoned. The few among us remaining behind draw strength from the Ancestors to maintain harmony in the absence of our kinsmen. All await the announcement of final victory that marks the Coloration of reunion with the beloved kinsmen. The condition of the Grizhni Inrl continues to deteriorate, and his final union with the Ancestors is imminent—but this you already know. A fissure has split a Bellyscraper in the Hllsreg Net, and the passage is decreed unsafe until such time as repairs are effected. The infant Lbavbsch Eleven in her ignorance wandered from the caverns, but was swiftly located and restored to her kinsmen. And this is all the news to relate."

"The infant Lbavbsch Eleven suffered no mishap?"

"None, Patriarch. In this happy time of spreading warmth and darkness, the awful threat of Cold Stupor has been eliminated. Moreover we may all venture Surface freely, without fear of dazzlement, blinding, or injury to the eyes. A fortunate thing for Lbavbsch Eleven—and indeed, for all the kinsmen."

"Perhaps," The Grizhni hummed in a low tone betokening a thoughtful mood. "The origin of this darkness remains obscure?"

"Yes, Patriarch. F'tlyrlbsch K'fl's close study of the old shadow-sculpture friezes uncovers evidence suggesting this darkness to be the magical work of your great human Ancestor, the First Fal Grizhni, savant of Lanthi Ume and benefactor of the race. Insight afforded by several R'jnrllsch kinsmen's Knowledge of Ancestors tends to support this theory, but the matter rests uncertain."

"More significant by far is the prophecy of the Preamble to Knowledge," interjected the Zmadrc Matriarch. "It is promised that the skies will proclaim our ascendancy and the Surface will ready itself for our coming. The forces of Nature will extend a welcome, and Man will flee before us. Now all befalls as promised. Surely the Surface has readied itself. The present darkness is stimulating, salubrious and indescribably invigorating, is it not?"

"Yes," F'tryll'jnr Drzh warbled, hiir rising. "There is something wonderfully beautiful there—a kind of harmony I should never have thought existed outside our caverns. There is courage, strength, comfort, oneness. It is easier to know the Ancestors in the shelter of that shadow, and it is easier to know oneself. Surely this is the world we were meant to inhabit. Our home has extended beyond the caverns."

The Grizhni's two inner ocular ridges relaxed and the outer band of muscle contracted in the Vardrul equivalent of a smile, but his hiir did not rise, and his flesh remained cadaverous. "If so, then our 'home' has extended farther than you realize," he replied. "As the shadow expands, its speed increases. Ever faster it overspreads Surface. If it continues thus, we now stand within a few scant Small Vens of the sea."

"And then, Patriarch?"

"And then our choices are varied. The cities of Men ring the coast, and we shall take them all in time. It is fitting, and much in accord with the designs of the distant Grizhni Ancestors, that we turn our steps first to Lanthi Ume."

"What of the human settlements that stand between our soldier/kinsmen and the city?" inquired The Zmadrc.

"Largely deserted, now."

"Are there not human fugitives roaming the darkness? They are vicious, and we must take steps to protect ourselves."

"They do not threaten us. The darkness that sustains Vardruls destroys Men. The human fugitives must depart or die. In any case, they are bereft of home, health and kinsmen. So much have we accomplished, we need hardly do more." A lowering of vocal pitch, a slight expansion of the ocular ridges, were all that conveyed The Grizhni's emotion.

The others regarded their leader wonderingly, and F'tryll'jnr Drzh inquired, "You pity them, Patriarch?"

"Even to this Small Ven, the pain and terror of the slaughtered Ancestors reverberates in our blood," hummed Dfjnr'l Gallr. "To know the Ancestors is to share their grief. And you, the promised leader, pity the oppressors of the race?"

"We will not speak of it," stated The Grizhni. "Time is short, and I must visit the chamber of the ailing Grizhni Inrl."

"Grizhni Inrl lies no longer in his chamber," The Zmadrc informed the Patriarch. "At his own request, he has been conveyed to the Grizhni death-pool, there to await final Ancestral joining."

The Grizhni undulated his boned digits in assent. His hiir, already deathly low, did not alter. Without another word he turned and exited the Chamber of White Tunnels through a gaping fissure. None of his companions offered to accompany him. Neither Connections nor members of Clan Grizhni themselves, they could not in courtesy approach the Grizhni death-pool uninvited.

Following the departure of their Patriarch, the three remaining Vardruls traded significant flickerings. Young F'tryll'jnr Drzh spoke for them all in observing, "His dissonance makes me doubt."

"With reason," the Zmadrc Matriarch agreed.

"In reclaiming Surface, we right ancient wrongs, restoring peace and order to the world," said Dfjnr'l Gallr. "We must believe that our cause is just. If it were not so, why should Surface itself extend so warm a welcome? Nature and all the elements work on our behalf, and this must reassure us."

"Nature is subject to the influence of human Cognition," hummed the Zmadrc Matriarch. "Artificial and possibly temporary alterations must not dazzle our judgment. Nor can we trust altogether in the wisdom of the Ancestors, for our own human blood mutes their voices. Our forebears walked Surface, but we are different creatures now. We cannot abide the cold winds, the punishing sunlight, the empty open spaces of the unmodified Surface. We love the security of our rock-lit walls, surrounding, enclosing and shielding us. Is it not time to recognize ourselves for what we most truly are—creatures of the caverns? Therein lies the only lasting harmony."

"For generations, Matriarch, the kinsmen have cherished the dream of emergence. And now, when the promised leader has finally risen to lead us Surface, you would abandon that dream?"

"The blood of the human/Vardrul Terrs transformed us all. We have lost much Knowledge of Ancestors, and with it much understanding of ourselves," returned The Zmadrc. "And the Grizhni Greater Patriarch is perhaps the most unfortunate among us."

The misgivings of his followers had shown as clearly in their eyes, their pitch and their hiir as in their words, but The Grizhni could not spare the time to dwell upon such matters. Swiftly traversing the nearly deserted maze of corridors, he came at last to the Grizhni death-pool chamber, where the moribund Inrl lay on a pallet beside the rocklit, funnel-shaped reservoir. Inrl's head rested on the flat Speaker's Stone. Food and water lay untouched within reach of his hand. The old Vardrul's aspect was serene. If he suffered pain, he showed no sign of it. Only the dull opacity of his flesh proclaimed his nearly exhausted vitality. Inrl turned his face to the entrance. His ocular ridges contracted in welcome, and he even managed a very faint, ghostly brightening.

"Greetings, Patriarch," Inrl fluted in tones weak but clear.

"Greetings, beloved kinsman/teacher," responded The Grizhni. "Are the Ancestors near?"

"They approach too slowly. Their voices grow clearer with each Coloration, but still they loiter. I call to them, but they come at their own pace."

"The waiting assails your ruu?"

"Somewhat. But the presence of my kinsman mends all."

In response to the unspoken request, the Grizhni Greater Patriarch glided forward to clasp the hand of Grizhni Inrl. As his jointed fingers met the other's tentacles, the Patriarch experienced the familiar surge of clan warmth and understanding of which the racial unity was but a weak reflection. Blood spoke to blood in a manner that no other contact could equal. With the death of Grizhni Inrl, last of his kinsmen-in-name, all such unity would be lost. And the Grizhni Greater Patriarch, whose greatness had cost so dearly, would soon find himself alone, cold and unbearably solitary, last of all his disharmonious line.

"A kinsman's touch is comfort indeed," trilled Inrl, unwittingly inflicting fresh wounds. But perhaps not so unwitting after all, for his ocular ridges writhed, his great eyes focused, and he observed, "You are altogether lightless, and seem closer to the Ancestors even than I. Does the struggle Surface dismay you? Do you mourn the loss of the sister/consort Grizhni Nine, the decay of our clan? Or are you simply discordant as always, my brilliant pupil/Patriarch Grizhni T'rzh? Which of these things consumes your hiir?"

"All," replied The Grizhni. "The first above all." As he spoke, a trace of light enlivened his flesh. The luxury of self-expression was rare indeed.

"The opposition of Men is too strong?"

"Quite the contrary. They hardly resist. I had expected challenge, strength and defiance. But the darkness has already conquered, and I meet only sickness, dismay and despair. They are defeated before we attack. Is this our great destiny—to slaughter the helpless, to kill the farmers of Surface, their infants and old ones? You need not remind me of the murdered Ancestors, kinsman/teacher. I know their grief and it is my own. Does that excuse us?"

"There is more," observed Grizhni Inrl.

"You know me too well, kinsman/teacher. Yes, there is more. You have known the will of the First Grizhni?"

Inrl curled his fingers backward in negation, without lifting a hand from the pallet. "Never. Has any among us traveled back so far?"

"I have done so. In fact, it is often easier for me to know the distant human Ancestors than those more immediate and more essentially Vardrul."

Inrl's ocular ridges expanded uneasily.

"Kinsman/teacher," The Grizhni continued, "the First Grizhni Patriarch—the human savant of Lanthi Ume—urges us most strongly to kill the others of his kind. I have sensed his will many times."

"A man desired the death of his own kind?" A weak flickering brightened Inrl's flesh. "I do not understand."

"I cannot altogether interpret the motives—they are alien and profoundly violent. I sense indescribable disharmony—tumult—anger as cruel as sunlight—the thirst for vengeance. I do not

168

know the cause. Always I have trusted in the wisdom of the Ancestors, for that is our way. As for the First Grizhni, he is the benefactor of our race, creator of the Cognitive fires without which our caverns would be largely uninhabitable. Surely it is fitting and appropriate to honor the will of such an Ancestor. Such a course I have always followed unquestioningly."

"And now, Grizhni T'rzh?"

"Now I must question. I wage war Surface—I destroy, I kill —and I question the justice of the Ancestors. I can speak of this to you alone, Grizhni Inrl, for you are my last kinsman and only a kinsman will understand. In taking the Surface, we merely recover what was torn from the Ancestors in the distant past, and that is surely just. But such justice necessitates the slaughter of an innocent population, and I cannot still the outcry of my conscience."

"An innocent population, Grizhni T'rzh? You speak of Men."

"Tell me, Grizhni Inrl—have you never felt a sense of connection to humans?"

"That is unavoidable. We are tainted with their blood."

"More than that. We are very like them, so like that a human Ancestor was able to sire offspring upon a Vardrul consort. To me, waging war upon the humans is like turning a sword against the fellow clanmembers. Do you understand me, Grizhni/kinsman? If you do not, no one will."

Inrl lay silent for a time, his great black Grizhni eyes closed. At last his lids lifted and he replied, "You speak of things I have always striven to put away from me. At this moment, upon the very brink of my final joining, I have not the strength of body or mind to confront these issues. Patriarch, your conflicting impulses are irreconcilable. You must choose one path or another."

"Choosing is easy. Constancy is difficult."

"Then apply to the Ancestors for reassurance. Know them, and your resolve is strengthened. Alongside the death-pool of our clan, Knowledge is readily available."

The Grizhni undulated his fingers.

Inrl's flesh lightened infinitesimally. "And intercede with them on my behalf, Grizhni T'rzh. Tell them I tire of waiting."

"Kinsman/teacher, I will bid them hurry to you." Without further conversation, the Grizhni Greater Patriarch commenced his internal journey backward in time. His ocular bands were slack, his features blank, his concentration rigorous. It was difficult, even upon the bank of the Grizhni death-pool, to meet the Ancestors. But the Patriarch's need was great, his efforts intense, and the Ancestors took note. At last The Grizhni's corpse-white flesh took on a pale glimmer. Moments passed and the light waxed, waned, struggled fitfully for life. Then all at once The Grizhni's hiir leaped and light blazed from every pore, signaling the onset of Knowledge. This time, the voices of the gentler Vardrul kinsmen were all but stilled, and the Patriarch sensed more strongly than ever before the will and ferocious intent of his human progenitors. Their violent determination boiled in his blood, their incomprehensible impulses possessed his mind.

Incomprehensible? Alien? Not entirely. Even in the midst of Knowledge, some small citadel of inviolate identity yet existed, and deep within himself The Grizhni acknowledged the familiarity of the human instincts and desires. He knew them; somehow he had always known them.

Communion with the Ancestors continued some eighth of a Coloration. At the end of that time, the Grizhni Greater Patriarch emerged from his trance, still troubled but nonetheless strengthened in purpose. Pausing only long enough to wish Grizhni Inrl a prompt and joyous joining, he hurried back to the Chamber of White Tunnels, sought the mate to the Wandering Flat, and by this means returned to the Vardrul troops, now massed upon the bank of Mfra Living Water, known to Men as the River Yl.

Chapter Thirteen

"Where is my daughter, Vaxalt?" Duke Bofus pleaded. His blue eyes brimmed. "Where is my Kara?"

"No doubt safe, your Grace," Gless Vallage soothed.

"But how can you be certain? My darling Kara has left the city, and who knows what disaster might not befall her—*out there*? Oh, Vaxalt, these are dangerous days!"

"Not so dangerous as all that, your Grace. Certainly the reports and rumors that reach us are sadly distorted."

"Oh, I hope you are right! I do hope you are right!" Duke Bofus wandered the private Audience Chamber, trudging endlessly from wall to wall and back again. For a moment he paused by the window to stare down at the Lureis Canal, whose embankment was more than ordinarily populous, before resuming the futile trek. "But there is something out there, Vaxalt! Something terrible! There's no use trying to pretend it isn't so!"

"There is indeed something," the savant conceded. "I have never denied it. I do not doubt the existence of some more or less uncommon atmospheric phenomenon approaching Lanthi Ume. Does its mere existence warrant such widespread alarm? My dearest lord, the ignorant always fear the unknown, usually without justification. I am certain that you in your enlightened erudition despise all such idle terrors." His tone was warmly persuasive, deferential, reassuring. Nothing in his aspect revealed the tension seething within him, and nothing revealed his almost intolerable irritation at the other's incessant pacing.

"Well I am sorry, Vaxalt, but I must disappoint you—for I don't despise them, and I *am* alarmed, very alarmed indeed. After all, what of the inland refugees? Every day they arrive in Lanthi Ume, by the hundreds. They are wretched and homeless, poor souls. They are also voracious. There is not enough food in the city to feed them all, and matters grow worrisome. Most are foreigners and strange. Many are peculiar, to put it kindly, and some—those horrid Fugitives of the Zoushe, for example—are downright unsettling. They crowd our streets and walkways, they do not know the canal rules, they gibber in foreign tongues, they thwart and offend my Lanthian citizens. They should be turned away at the gate, I suppose, but I haven't the heart to order that, they seem so desperate. When those possessing civilized tongues are questioned, their stories are all alike. They speak of the dreadful spreading darkness, and they speak of the white monsters who live in it. They can't all be wrong, can they?"

"Not altogether, but their fears have warped their perceptions," returned Gless Vallage. "Being simple folk, uneducated and foreign or at best provincial, they are confused and fearful of the unknown. The darkness can and will be averted. As for the 'white monsters'—when all is exposed to the light, we shall discover a meager tribe of albino cutthroats, seizing the opportunity to prey in darkness upon the unfortunate settlers. Such criminals —fierce, perhaps, but quite human—will prove no match for your Grace's faithful Guardsmen."

"You really think so, Vaxalt?"

"I am certain of it. Your Grace, did I not promise you weeks ago that we of the Select would focus our attention and energy upon this matter?"

Bofus nodded, eyes wide.

"We have done so, and I am in a position to promise my Duke that his loving Selectic subjects will prove entirely capable of dealing with this darkness at such time, if any, that it reaches Lanthi Ume."

"Truly, Vaxalt?"

"You've my personal assurance. I will deal with it myself. Therefore be at ease, your Grace, and trust in your loyal servant." Vallage's confidence was unfeigned. Armed with secret knowledge, he spoke in perfectly clear conscience.

"That restores my spirits, indeed it does! Dear Vaxalt, your loyalty and diligence do you much credit, and you will not find me ungrateful. Now that I know Lanthi Ume is safe, I am much easier in mind. And yet there still remains the question of my daughter. Where can she be? Why has she not sent word? Is she sick or hurt? Is she in trouble and does she need her father's help? What if she has died, alone or surrounded by strangers who do not love her? My heart would break, I think. I cannot bear the uncertainty. Vaxalt, I must know! I beg you for Cognitive aid."

Gless Vallage stirred uncomfortably. He did not like to acknowledge limits to his Cognitive power, but in this case there was no alternative. "Your Grace, my previous investigations yielded no clue as to her Ladyship's whereabouts. If the Lady

172

Karavise has left the city, I cannot locate her for you. Even the strongest Cognitive vision fails over distance."

"But what if she has returned in secret to Lanthi Ume? What if she is here now and we don't know it?"

"Would she not send word?"

"What if she has lost her memory?"

"The possibility seems remote."

"What if she is a prisoner?"

"Who would dare lay hands upon his Grace's daughter?"

"But it's not impossible, is it?" Bofus appealed. "It is at least a chance! And therefore I implore you to search for her one more time. See, Vaxalt, see—all is prepared for the Diver!"

The Duke's gesture embraced a large, flat-bottomed tank of perfectly transparent glass, filled to the brim with distilled water.

"It is ready, Vaxalt." Bofus offered an anxious smile. "I ordered it brought in here and filled. You need only dispatch the Diver, that is all. I will stay to watch; you need do nothing more."

Vallage's answering smile beamed sympathetic fervor. "I will do aught in my power to aid my dearest lord." So saying, his Preeminence crossed to a pedestal whereon reposed the ornate casket carried from Vallage House. Opening the casket, he withdrew a handful of glass vials together with a wide-mouthed lidded jar. He moved to the tank, unstoppered the vials, and dumped the contents into the water. Instantly, sprays of color zipped across the tank—plumose curls of crimson, yellow, deep ultramarine, black and a burning colorless radiance that passed for white. The sprays softened, blurred and spread. Within seconds the primary colors blended to produce green, orange and purple. Additional combinations occurred, and soon a hundred different hues swirled in confusion. Vallage gestured, and the chaos began to resolve itself. Colors thickened and coalesced, pastel hues darkened, and recognizable forms began to emerge. Nose pressed to the glass, Duke Bofus watched in childlike wonder as the darkening shapes settled to the bottom of the tank, where they took on a spurious solidity. Tiny activity continued for some moments longer. Bumps and nodules extruded themselves, ridges rose and channels opened. Presently the entire city of Lanthi Ume lay submerged in miniature. The contours of the famous Nine Isles were perfectly reproduced, together with the patch of mainland territory bounded by the city wall. Every canal was accurately represented, and certain landmarks were readily identifiable—the foursquare Vayno Fortification upon the mainland side; the needle spire of Ka Nebbinon Bell Tower; gold-glinting Ducal Palace upon the Lureis; domed Shonnet Arena; the Victory of Nes, a shadowy blot in the middle of Parnis Lagoon; and many others, all complete and perfect down to the last visible detail and beyond.

"And the Diver?" inquired the Duke. "Now, Vaxalt?"

"Now, your Grace." Gless Vallage spoke rhythmically, confidently, achieving Cognition almost without effort. Sudden light glowed within the lidded jar. Opening the container, Vallage released the inmate into the water. For a moment an amorphous glowing blob darted just below the surface. The blob sprouted radiant tentacles, a knob of a head. Its body lengthened, and briefly it resembled a shining homunculus. The resemblance lessened as hairline antennae sprouted from the head, each stalk terminating in a naked eyeball. Arms and legs widened into webbed flippers. Eyeballs popped up like pimples along the back and belly. Lateral fins flared. The Diver's outlines, initially indistinct, sharpened and defined themselves. For a few moments the sprite circled, testing its flippers and fins. Suddenly it dove, streaking down through the water like a falling star, diminishing in size as it neared the bottom as if receding into vast distance. Briefly it twinkled above the miniature canals, then descended to vanish altogether into the model metropolis.

"And now the hunt commences," Gless Vallage explained, concealing his boredom. "The Diver will search the city through, leaving no unshielded jot of ground unexplored. If our sweet Lady Karavise has returned to Lanthi Ume, your Grace will soon know it."

"If only that may be! But Vaxalt, can we not see through the Diver's eyes?" Having witnessed this form of Cognition in the past, Bofus already knew the answer.

"As your Grace wills, now and always. Moreover, we may dispatch the Diver to any specified locale within the city, at your Grace's pleasure."

"True. True. A marvelous device, my friend, marvelous. Then let us see, if you please, where the Diver wanders."

Vallage bowed his silver head, whispered and gestured discreetly. As usual, Cognition followed with elegant promptitude. The city spread out at the bottom of the tank smudged itself into nothingness. The colors, released from constraint, diffused throughout the water, spinning wildly in momentary celebration of freedom before resolving themselves into new images. The scene in the tank changed, and Bofus saw what the Diver saw, or rather, part of what the Diver saw. His mind could neither accept nor interpret the superabundance of simultaneous images recorded by multifarious eyes, and therefore he witnessed the scene as a human would, with only moderately augmented scope of vision. The picture shifted and slid disconcertingly, sometimes breaking apart to form separate images at either end of the tank as the flexible antennae that carried the primary eyes bent and diverged.

The Diver glided through the Destula, along a wynd lined with ancient, crumbling tenements. Each of the buildings was investigated in quick succession, all proving drearily similar—filthy, foul, overcrowded and indescribably squalid. Within the wretched rooms huddled the most miserable of Lanthians—the sick, the hopeless, the criminal, the destitute and degenerate. Duke Bofus fidgeted as he watched, and his face flushed guiltily. He imagined what Karavise would say if she could see, and the flush deepened. Fortunately for his Grace's peace of mind, Lady Karavise was not to be discovered within the tenements.

Back out in the wynd, a family of refugee Bexae, identifiable by their large eyes, uncut golden-brown hair and fawnlike mannerisms, grilled vegetables on skewers over a small brazier. The smell of cooking peppers and onions had attracted a group of hungry Destulans, who now surrounded the foreigners. The underwater scene was silent, yet it was certain that the alley therein represented rang with shouts and catcalls. Lanthian jaws gaped wide, and Lanthian expressions were ugly. The Bexae, shoulders hunched and great eyes downcast, huddled together for mutual comfort. Their pacificism failed to mollify the Destulans, and the crowd closed in. Backed by his prancing, taunting cohorts, a feral ragamuffin swooped down on the brazier, seized a slice of red-fleshed squash and fled. Others followed, and the vegetables disappeared one after another. At last the Bexae protested, gesturing excitedly. The gestures were deliberately misinterpreted. An instant later the crowd attacked; shoving, spitting, and striking with clenched fists. The Bexae took to their heels, abandoning all their belongings. Some of the Destulans pursued, while others remained to loot.

Along the wynd fled the terrified Bexae, the Diver close behind. Presently all emerged into Old Market Square. The Bexae ran south toward the Straightwater Canal. The Diver continued on into the Square, where many of the merchants' booths were shuttered and locked. Suppliers having already fled their farms, few merchants now dispensed food. The lines of stalls ordinarily overflowing with vegetables, fruit, meat, fish and poultry now stood deserted. Among the booths loitered the sullen townsmen, their pent frustration finding no outlet.

Back and forth, side to side—the Diver inspected all corners of Old Market Square simultaneously. The Lady Karavise was nowhere in evidence, which was all to the best, in view of the public mood. One of the townsmen hurled a stone in aimless protest, striking the bolted shutters of an empty poulterer's booth. Bored fellow idlers followed suit, soon broadening the attack to include neighboring stalls. For a time stones whizzed through the air to bang against wooden walls, and then a party of Lammish soldiers, part of the hated Vayno garrison, entered the Square. Approaching the restive citizens, the Lammish men appeared to issue orders, thus drawing upon themselves the wrath of every Lanthian citizen within earshot. Flying rocks pelted the Lammish soldiers, who turned and fled for the safety of the Vayno Fortification, the Lanthians raging upon their heels.

"That is ugly." Duke Bofus averted his eyes. "I do not like to see it. Was anyone hurt, do you think? If his soldiers are injured, the Keldhar of Gard Lammis will be deeply offended, and I will be forced to face his anger. Why can my people not help one another in times of adversity? Why can they not treat one another gently and with kindness? Then all would be well, would it not, Vaxalt?"

"Beyond doubt, your Grace is herald of a new Golden Age."

"If only my darling, clever Kara were here to advise me! We shall not find her in such a low place as Old Market Square, Vaxalt. Send the Diver somewhere else. What about the Victory of Nes? Perhaps my daughter seeks aid of your fellow savants."

"Impossible, your Grace. The Victory is shielded from Cognitive observation. Attempting entry, the Diver would lose himself in a maze of shadows, from which he might never emerge." It did not suit the purposes of Gless Vallage to permit his Duke a view of the Selectic stronghold where the exhausted savants toiled in vain to solve the riddle of Fal Grizhni's Death of Light Cognition. They would never succeed, of course, for Vaxalt Gless Vallage alone possessed the power and skill to save Lanthi Ume. That fact should be revealed to the world at the appropriate moment, and not before.

"The harbor, then," suggested Bofus. "Perhaps she has returned by sea. Perhaps she disembarks even now. Let us see the harbor!"

Vallage spoke and the watery image darkened. When the tank cleared, the great Lanthian docks stood revealed. The harbor was suggestively depleted of vessels.

"Where have all the ships gone?" Frowning, Bofus tugged his goatee.

"They have set sail for foreign ports, your Grace. There are fortunes to be made carrying refugees from Dalyon."

"They are running away!" The Duke chewed his lip. "They abandon Lanthi Ume! Have they no care for their city?"

"They care more for their lives."

"But Vaxalt, you have said there is no real danger."

"The fainthearted do not believe, your Grace."

"Ha! How foolish they'll look when they discover their error! Eh, Vaxalt?"

"Very foolish, your Grace."

"They will have brought it on themselves, though. Who are all those odd characters crowding the dock?"

The wharf teemed with would-be emigrants. Here wealthy Lanthians mingled with inland settlers, with Denders, Feeniads, Swamp-Splatters and sinister Burbies. Here the blue-blooded rubbed elbows with the plebeian, with the criminal, and in some cases with the semi-human; necessity having murdered social distinction. The Diver swiftly surveyed the scene, gliding past the clans of violet-haired Vemi encamped beside the water; past the tents of the Zonianders and past the boat-shaped caravans of the Turos; all of these hopefuls awaiting the opportunity to purchase passage upon some merchantman bound for Strell or Szar. But the prosperous Lanthian tradesmen flashed their silver shorns in vain; berths were so dear and passengers so plentiful that greater inducement than coin was needed to rent so much as a patch of empty deck. As the days passed and the killing darkness advanced, fear was giving way to desperation.

Along the docks slid the Diver, multiple eyes goggling in all directions at once. Lady Karavise was not to be seen. On swam the Diver, past knots of haggling humanity. The Strellian bark *Golden Talgh* was due to set sail within hours. Berths aboard had quadrupled in value within the space of a day, and now commercial enterprise reached its feverish peak.

Swiftly the Diver surveyed the ships, then moved on toward the warehouses rising at the far end of the wharf.

"She is not there, Vaxalt." The Duke was growing restless. "I am almost sure of it."

Gless Vallage suppressed a shrug. "Your Grace must not lose hope."

"I shall not do so. I must believe my Kara will return. Perhaps, even as we speak, she approaches Lanthi Ume from the mainland side. Perhaps she now draws near the city gate. Vaxalt, send the Diver to the city wall! Let him gaze out along the highway, and then we shall see!"

Vallage complied. Within the tank the images changed, and the harbor gave way to the city wall. The Diver followed the line of the wall, pausing at last at the Northern Gate to survey the surrounding countryside. Bofus stared, and his breath caught in his throat. For a few leagues the fields and pastures lay tranquil beneath an untroubled sky. Beyond them the Cognitive darkness loomed like a hungry nightmare.

Following the departure of Preeminence Gless Vallage, whose reassurances had provided inadequate comfort, Duke Bofus cogitated long and hard. Twilight lay cool upon the canals when he finally reached his decision. Summoning a messenger, the Duke issued orders. Presently his private dombulis was readied and Bofus embarked from the Ducal moorings, attended by a couple of sendillis-squads of his green-and-gold Guardsmen.

The Lureis Canal seemed untroubled, her surrounding palaces glorious as always. To the left shone Vallage House, most elegant of Lanthian mansions. Straight ahead, the four blue spires of masterless Fennahar House rose straight and proud as ever. Here and there the golden lights of evening bloomed, and along the Prendisant—a walkway known in earlier times as the Prendivet Saunter—the lamplighter was already at work. Somewhere nearby there was music, the light strains floating upon sea-scented air. The earliest stars blinked in the sky, and only the single red point of light still burning directly overhead belied the appearance of total normalcy.

The Duke tugged his goatee. At last he recognized the falsity of that appearance. Having glimpsed an image of the Cognitive shadow but a few short hours earlier, he began for the first time to comprehend the magnitude of the menace. Gless Vallage, of course, had displayed the most comforting confidence and optimism. It reflected a certain shameful lack of faith and friendship to question the savant's abilities, much less doubt them. Yet Bofus couldn't help himself. The ghastly darkness waited just *out there* beyond the wall, poised to descend upon the city—a prospect so horrifying that reassurance above and beyond the promises of Gless Vallage were needed to banish the dread. Such reassurance was not easily available, for the Selectic Preeminence's arcane insight was exceeded by that of no living Lanthian.

Which left only the dead to consult.

On the near side of the old Shonnet Gardens stood a crystal image of the Eatchish savant Jun, said to be a self-portrait. Predating the rise of the Select in Lanthi Ume, the statue had endured throughout the ages; but showed no trace of cracking, chipping, discoloration or deterioration. This uncommon resistance to time's onslaught was generally attributed to the extraordinary nature of the artist/subject. According to popular belief, the image of Jun had been known to speak at widely separated moments of extreme civic peril. In the opinion of many, another such moment had arrived, and expectant crowds were gathering about the statue. Bofus intended to join them.

On the dombulis glided, past Ka Nebbinon Bell Tower, past palaces and mansions quiet in the fading violet light; past the grotesque Croino Deth Monument, and into the Channel of Vho, which in turn fed the Straightwater Canal. Beneath the Bridge of Beggars they slid, passengers deaf to the pleas of the massed mendicants; on past dwellings of decreasing magnificence, to the near edge of the Shonnet Gardens. They moored at Jun's Pier. From there it was but a short walk to the famous crystal image.

Hopeful Lanthians had haunted the spot for days. Little by little the crowd had grown, and now there were hundreds assembled there. The ground was strewn with blankets, food hampers, empty bottles and gnawed bones. Some, tiring of the long vigil, slept on the grass at the base of the statue; but most were intent and alert. Throughout the preceding hours, occurrence of certain signs and portents had signaled the imminence of Jun's utterance. Around noon, several members of the crowd had noted a ghostly aura surrounding the statue. Later on, the crystal eyes were said to have glowed with light. And not an hour earlier, many claimed to have seen Jun's lips and chin vibrate. The arrival of their ruler and his Guardsmen confirmed the beliefs of the Lanthian citizens. Perhaps reluctant to address the Commons, Jun would surely unburden himself to the Duke.

A murmuring ran through the crowd, and the ranks parted to permit the Duke and his retinue passage. Bofus advanced, pausing often to shake his subjects' hands. Soon he arrived at the foot of the statue and there he stopped, wide blue eyes fixed upon the crystal visage of Jun. The colorless eyes yielded nothing and Bofus hesitated, somewhat at a loss. What now? What if Jun disdained to speak? To be scorned by a statue before his watching subjects—how embarrassing that would be! If only Kara were here to tell him what to do! But she was not, and he had to do something. Moistening his lips, Bofus spoke in a tolerably steady voice, "Great Jun, we greet you, extending our compliments, admiration and respect. We wish you joy of your eternal crystalline serenity."

The statue did not respond.

"Knowing your benevolence, we have come in search of your counsel," the Duke attempted. "We implore you to share your wisdom in this hour of civic need."

The statue was mute and the watching crowd muttered.

Bofus shifted his weight uncomfortably. "As Duke of Lanthi Ume, I beseech your assistance. In the name of all your fellow Lanthians of the past, present and future, I make this appeal. Great Jun, your Lanthian brothers and sisters await. I beg you to speak to them." The Duke concluded, imagination exhausted. Fortunately for his public dignity, nothing more was required.

Light glowed from the statue, and the spectators gasped. Many, including a number of Guardsmen, hastily retreated. Bofus stood his ground, hands clasped and face wreathed in a smile of delighted wonder. Jun shone moon-bright in the darkening air. A radiant nimbus encircled the crystalline head. A slight tremor shook the ground, and many a Lanthian fled screaming. Almost to a man, the Guardsmen drew their weapons. Duke Bofus, however, perceived no danger. One chubby hand reached out as if to touch the statue, then drew back shyly.

Intelligence beamed from the colorless eyes. The transparent jaw dropped open. Arcs of force crackled along the rigid limbs.

"Advise us, Jun," Duke Bofus urged, encouraged. "Guide us."

Another tremor shook the ground. Before the vibration had fully died, the voice of Jun rang from motionless lips:

"TIME IS."

The silent crowd awaited elucidation.

"TIME WAS," the statue added.

Confused rumbling from the crowd.

"TIME IS PAST."

The tremors ceased. The crackling aura began to fade. Perceiving the retreat of his advisor, Duke Bofus cried out in alarm, "Great Jun, do not leave us yet! Advise us!"

A pause, as if the statue pondered the necessity of further communication, and then the reply:

"LANTHIANS, SAVE YOURSELVES. FLY."

"Abandon our city?"

"YOURS NO LONGER."

"Our homes?"

"DOOMED."

"Our possessions?"

"FORFEIT."

"Isn't that a little pessimistic? I mean, are you sure?"

"SUFFICIENTLY."

"Where shall we fly?"

"ACROSS THE SEA."

"Great Jun, we cannot. We've not enough boats to carry all. What is the fate of those who remain?"

"DEATH."

"That can't be true!"

"YOU WILL DISCOVER OTHERWISE."

"What of the innocent?"

"CONDEMNED ALONG WITH THE GUILTY."

"It is unjust, it is dreadful!"

"BE COMFORTED, DUKE. DEATH IS NOT A WHOLLY UNSATISFYING STATE. YOU WILL GROW USED TO IT. I HAVE."

The Duke's distraught reply was drowned in a sudden roar of voices. Through the Shonnet Gardens came racing a quartet of maroon-clad men, identifiable by their pot-shaped headgear and steel-tipped epaulets as officers of Gard Lammis. Hot on the heels of the foreigners stormed a furious Lanthian mob. Overtaking the fugitives not a hundred feet from the statue of Jun, the mob attacked with sticks, rocks, fists, clubs, and broken sendillis oars. One of the officers drew a flintlock pistol and fired. An oar-wielding citizen fell dead. For an instant the dead man's companions stood bewildered, almost stunned; then frozen shock gave way to white-hot rage. Howls of execration arose, and the offending Lammish were surrounded, engulfed.

From his vantage point beside the statue, the Duke looked on in helpless confusion. "What has come over them? What are they doing? Have they gone mad?" Bofus appealed in desperation to Rish Frayner, Commander of Guardsmen. "Go over there! Put a stop to that! And find out what is going on!"

Commander Frayner saluted smartly. Leaving a contingent of Guards behind to shield the Duke, he and his remaining men started for the heaving, screaming rout of humanity. Before they reached it, a piercing two-note whistle split the air. Moments later, a patrol of maroon-clad soldiers appeared. Unable to fire into the mob without harming their fellow Lammish, they charged with leveled bayonets, and a dozen Lanthian Commons fell within seconds.

Incensed, Commander Frayner ordered his men forward. They needed little urging, and the passionate ferocity of the Guardsmen's attack overwhelmed the Lammish almost instantly. The maroon line broke like rotten thread. Shouting fiercely, the Lanthian Commons surged forward. The surviving Lammish soldiers turned tail and ran for their lives. The Ducal Guardsmen did not follow, but a pack of enraged civilians pursued the fleeing Lammish through the streets to the very gates of the Vayno Fortification.

While the brief combat raged, Duke Bofus stood watching in wet-palmed anxiety. Around him rose a protective wall of loyal Guardsmen. Beyond the wall reigned violence and confusion. Many of the citizens clustered around Jun's statue now rushed to the aid of their battling compatriots. Many fled for safety, while others lingered to watch from the sidelines. Bofus caught flashing glimpses of riotous humanity; running figures, falling bodies, the occasional white face twisted in rage, fear, anguish or exultation. Screams of pain and hatred battered his eardrums. And then, as the Guardsmen charged and the Lammish fled, the sound swelled to a roar of Lanthian triumph. The tangle of flesh shifted and broke, components scattering in all directions.

"I want to talk to one of them," Duke Bofus informed the nearest Guardsman.

The soldier stepped forward to catch the arm of a flying figure. The adolescent captive flopped and struggled like a snared rabbit. As recognition dawned, his struggles ceased.

"You oughtn't handle the boy so roughly," the Duke remonstrated. "Don't you think you might release him now?"

The Guard complied with reluctance.

"No need to be frightened, lad," Bofus assured the prisoner kindly.

"I'm not frightened," the youth replied with patent conviction. Exalted rank notwithstanding, Bofus Dil Shonnet rarely, if ever, inspired fear.

"Then perhaps, if you would be so kind, you might explain the cause of this dreadful disturbance?"

"It's the Chamberpots, your Grace! Those Lammish swine should be torn to pieces."

"What happened?"

"We caught their officers down at the shipyards, trying to hire passage for the entire Vayno garrison."

"Is that so bad?" Bofus inquired. "Naturally they wish to save themselves."

"You don't understand, your Grace! They were going to grab every last ship in the harbor and send 'em down the coast to Gard Lammis for their own use, leaving us Lanthians here to rot in the dark."

"Are you sure of that?"

"That's what I heard," the boy returned defensively. "That's what everyone's saying."

182

"Selfish, even unjust of the Lammish," Bofus mused. "And yet it's natural for them to think first of their own people—"

"Your Grace *defends* them?" cried the boy.

"No, no, no. I'm not defending them, only trying to see things from their point of view, trying to be fair—"

"Fair, you say? Those foreigners go swaggering around our city like they owned it, lording it over us all, and now they're shooting us down in the streets like dogs. Are you going to let them get away with it, your Grace? I'd like to use their guts for sausage casing. That's what I'd call fair."

"Ah no, boy, you do not understand—"

"I understand those Lammish pigs are killing Lanthians. Your Grace may be willing to swallow that, but the rest of us aren't. And we're going to give the Chamberpots just what they've been asking for." Without awaiting dismissal, the youth flung off in the wake of the fleeing Lammish soldiers.

"Want me to bring him back, your Grace?" inquired the Guardsman.

"No, what good would it do? I cannot fathom such rage and violence. I do not understand it." Tears rose to the Duke's eyes. "This is not the way men should behave, it cannot be. It is senseless and horrible. Why do they do it? Don't they understand it isn't right?"

His Grace's queries were doomed to go unanswered. At that moment Commander Frayner returned to deliver the curt command, "Get the Duke out of here."

Bofus protested in vain. Gently but inexorably the Guardsmen herded their lord back to the waiting dombulis. Moments later the boat shot away from the pier, bearing his Grace toward the Ducal Palace. Commander Frayner and a number of his subordinates stayed behind to direct the disposition of corpses, and to discourage by their presence a fresh outbreak of rioting. They in turn came under the scrutiny of the Eatchish sorcerer Jun. For some hours following the battle, the statue continued to glow with eerie inner light. Changing colors haloed the crystalline head, bright arcs snapped along the limbs. The intensity of the dead sorcerer's mental activity was obvious, but its nature remained mysterious, for Jun did not speak again.

The hours lengthened and the Cognitive darkness flowed on toward Lanthi Ume; sometimes racing, sometimes inexplicably dawdling. Following the engulfment of Morlin Hill and Castle Io Wesha, the shadow lingered for a time as if to savor absorption of a particularly tasty morsel before resuming movement at renewed speed. The advance was erratic but inexorable, and presently, despite the frantic efforts of the Select to halt its progress, the bulging blackness bumped experimentally at the stones of the old city wall; and there it paused.

The populace watched in growing fear. It was impossible to ignore now, impossible to deny. Ghastly midnight towered upon the very verge of Lanthi Ume, annihilating half the noonday sky. Impossible to pretend it did not exist, impossible to pretend that it would spare the city, and now—all but impossible to escape. The last of the boats had left the harbor. The more philanthropic, adventurous or avaricious of the captains might return to ferry additional passengers to safety, and then again, they might not. All that remained were fleets of dombuli, sendilli, racing jistylli and a very few venerises. But for the possible exception of the last, none of these crafts were remotely seaworthy.

The darkness, overspreading all the island of Dalyon, now hurried to meet the sea. Lanthi Ume was the last refuge, and now there was nowhere left to run.

The streets of the city were thronged day and night. The polyglot refugees, fleeing the interior, had converged by the thousands upon Lanthi Ume and her sister city-states scattered along the coastline. Now the babble of foreign voices assaulted Lanthian ears. The sight of strange, sometimes questionably human faces and bodies offended Lanthian eyes. The scent of alien flesh and breath outraged Lanthian nostrils. Outsiders competed for Lanthian food, space and air. Even more unacceptable, these same outsiders vied for precious shipboard passage. More than once already, space aboard an outgoing vessel had been snapped up by the wealthy, chlorophyllous Zonianders. It was unjust that decent Lanthians should be supplanted upon their own soil by foreign lucre, and the citizens made their displeasure plain. Immigrants—particularly those of conspicuously exotic appearance or language—were often subject to sudden rough justice. Floating foreign corpses polluted the canals, and strangers of even moderately nonhuman persuasion were subject to varied persecutions. Unfocused, near-senseless rioting broke out all over the city; the most bitter demonstrations taking place in the square before the Vayno Fortification, with the detested Lammish soldiers peering down from the ramparts and the darkness looming just beyond. These minor uprisings provided limited gratification at best. Little was accomplished and the level of popular terror did not subside—quite the contrary. As the hours passed, fear mounted to the level of delirium. Lanthi Ume, desperate and demoralized, stood in dire need of a savior.

It was the moment Gless Vallage had long awaited.

Thus it was that the Selectic Preeminence found himself confronting the darkness at last. He did not address the menace from the ramparts of the Vayno Fortification, for the alarmed Lammish soldiers immured therein steadfastly refused admittance to all Lanthians. Instead he stood alone atop the city wall, itself a continuation of the ancient fortress' defenses. In all other particulars, the scene was as he had so often envisioned it.

Gless Vallage was swathed in voluminous robes, cleverly cut to emphasize his grand height and broad shoulders. The golden double-headed dragon insignia of the Select gleamed at his throat. The rest of the costume was dramatically unrelieved black. His thick silver hair was burnished and perfectly ordered; his expression, calm and exalted. Beneath and behind him the square was packed with worshipful Lanthians, their faces uplifted in fear and supplication—uplifted to Vaxalt Gless Vallage, their sole champion, their only hope. Before him loomed the ineffable darkness. At his feet, invisible to the crowd below, lay the assorted aids and thaumaturgical devices designed to facilitate high Cognition. There was no need, in the opinion of Vaxalt Gless Vallage, to advertise the full extent of his reliance upon mechanical assistance. Such self-revelation could only dim the effulgence of his public image, doubtless to the sorrow of his admiring future subjects.

For a long moment Vallage stood perfectly motionless, and perfectly aware of the picture he presented to the spectators massed below. They would see him against a background of unutterable blackness. His own stygian robes would blend into the dark. Yet the sunlight beating down upon his head would throw his bright hair and strong, pale profile into magnificent relief. His hands, too, with their long, fine white fingers would be highly visible. They would appear to float disembodied in midair, rendering every graceful gesture doubly effective.

Vallage let the Lanthians gaze their fill. Then, at the precise instant dictated by a finely honed showman's instinct, he broke the tableau. Raising his arms high amidst an impressive swirl of dark draperies, he began to speak, or rather, to chant. His voice was superb, as he well knew. The mellifluous tones rose and fell in solemn cadences of studied beauty; a sound to set the listeners dreaming. For some minutes the serenade continued, mounting in speed and urgency until at last Gless Vallage gestured sharply with his upraised hands, four times in quick succession; whereupon four great bursts of jewel-toned radiance exploded into being. Briefly they bloomed in defiance of darkness and then, discrete existence ending, they sent a thousand threads of colored light shooting across the blackened sky. The filaments crossed, recrossed and interwove to form a blazing Cognitive net, lifting itself high, beyond the range of human vision, to hold the menacing darkness at bay. Cries of excitement and joy arose from the square. Only those Selectic savants standing among the spectators remained inert and expressionless; for they alone recognized the utter irrelevance of Vallage's theatrics. The blazing net was pretty as Hurbanese fireworks, and in this case approximately as useful.

Cries of approbation from below. Gless Vallage affected not to hear them. With head thrown back and face uplifted to the black heavens, he chanted fervently. As the syllables poured forth richly, one unobtrusive foot pressed assorted activating mechanisms. Then an answering chant arose, as if a spectral host sang from the air around and above him. The notes, impossibly pure and mournful, brought tears to the eyes of many listeners. The effect was masterly, and the crowd suitably admiring. Only the savants in the audience remained dourly unappreciative. The Cognizant Nem Kilmo folded his arms, lips thinning. Cognizance Jair Zannajair turned aside in unconcealed disgust. Vallage did not trouble to heed them, for the great moment had arrived.

And now at last, with the eyes of all men fixed upon him, to perform the feat of high Cognition for which he had prepared so long and hard.

Gless Vallage's stance and demeanor altered. Abandoning theatricality, he moved and spoke with the forceful, practiced economy of the gifted savant that he truly was. Marshalling all his mental resources, he addressed the darkness, his own powerful forces challenging the Cognition of long-dead Terrs Fal Grizhni. The resistance was immediate and intense. Vallage felt the toxic darkness pressing upon his mind, hammering at his will. This was familiar and predictable, entirely consistent with the sensations he had so often experienced during the long months that he had struggled to master the Death of Light Cognition. This, in fact, was the critical point in the entire procedure. Once past this initial barrier, difficulty would decrease sharply. Therefore Vallage hurled his concentrated strength into a fierce, impetuous attack designed to smash all barriers at the outset. The darkness that he dealt with now was immense, overwhelming. The tiny slivers of Cognitive shadow he had vanquished in his workroom were absurd by comparison. Yet the same principles of Cognition applied to both. He had studied long and hard to perfect his technique, and success would not elude him now.

Hovering upon the very brink of Cognition, he thought he felt the darkness begin to give way before him. This belief was supported by the motion of the rainbow web of light, which now started to billow outward from the city wall. Fresh shouts arose from below, and even the watching savants, former skepticism forgotten, watched in breathless suspense.

It was moving, he was certain. The giant darkness was weakening, surrendering to Vaxalt Gless Vallage. He felt the power stir and rise within him. And then without warning, everything changed.

As if his efforts had ripped a mask from the face of Fal Grizhni's great Cognition to reveal the demon's leer beneath, Gless Vallage found himself confronting a force he had never experienced and certainly never anticipated. At last the true might and dread of the Death of Light were revealed to him, and the revelation was shattering. For the first time he recognized both the nature of his enemy and the magnitude of his own folly. Gless Vallage, Preeminent of the Select and greatest savant of Lanthi Ume, was puny, ineffectual, a helpless nonentity in the face of the Death of Light. There was no question now of counterattack, or even of self-defense. Vallage felt himself crushed, overwhelmed, effortlessly obliterated. His flickering Cognition was snuffed in an instant. Reeling, he pressed his temples as if to contain an explosion. A thin wail of astonished despair escaped him.

It took the citizens a few moments to comprehend the failure of their champion. Their first inkling came with the dissolution of the web of light that rose above the wall. The glowing strands unraveled, shrank, and abruptly faded from view. Vaxalt Gless Vallage, that omnipotent Preeminence, slumped heavily to his knees. Silver head bowed, he buried his face in his hands.

Perhaps stimulated by the opposition, the darkness chose that moment to advance. Over the city wall it suddenly poured in a swift, irresistible torrent. Vallage looked up at the last moment to see the blackness crashing down upon him. His face twisted in horror and remorse, and then he was gone, blotted out. The citizens fled screaming, and the tidal wave of darkness pursued wherever they ran. Over the streets and canals it swept, devouring mansions and monuments and gardens. Palaces and parks, hovels and tenements, cookshops and taverns, barges and venerises—all vanished within minutes. The black tide spread to the edge of the mainland, and there many prayed it would halt.

It did not. Across the Water of Tren it slid to Jhannetta, first of the city's Nine Isles; from Jhannetta, on to Faneel; and so from

187

island to island. The Lanthians fled in their dombuli and sendilli; fled as far as Jherova, outermost of the Isles. And there, with their backs to the open sea and no place left to run, they huddled helplessly upon the strand to watch the darkness rushing toward them. Within the hour, Jherova was overwhelmed.

It was midafternoon, and somewhere the sun was shining. But Lanthi Ume lay buried alive beneath poisoned shadow blacker than mortal hatred.

Chapter Fourteen

❧❧❧❧❧

They were not alone in the dark. Unseen presences walked the night, and Devras heard them often. There were large bodies shuffling through the undergrowth; dragging footsteps; voices whispering across black space; and more than once, the sound of sobbing. The grief of those invisible sufferers was pitiful to hear, and Devras was initially sympathetic. Once or twice he sought without success to locate the source of the sound, and his third such attempt brought near-disaster. It happened one steaming night or day when the rain came thudding through the reeking air to splash against his face with a touch as warm as blood. He was off by himself hunting mushrooms. The Cognitive line bound him to Raith Wate Basef. Over one arm hung the iron loop of a lantern carried from the home of the slaughtered farmer's family. Despite the lantern's unwelcome heat, its natural light was infinitely preferable to the toxic Cognitive radiance of Wate Basef's blue-white stones. The lamp itself was plastered over with translucent moths. They came by the hundreds, attracted by the light —great, delicately green creatures with jeweled eyes, feathery antennae, and wings broad as saucers. Affixing themselves to the glass panes, they quickly expired there, and the warm light filtering through their exquisite corpses took on a nacreous shimmer.

Devras walked slowly. His head was bowed, eyes fastened on the ground, thoughts fixed upon the elusive mushrooms. Without warning, his vision swam and dizziness rocked him. Sweat bathed him from head to foot, and he tasted bile. He recognized the signs readily enough. It was time to take another of Wate Basef's tablets. The pills were wonderfully effective in suppressing the symptoms of illness. One of them could banish giddiness and queasiness, restoring equilibrium within seconds. He could not help but notice, however, that the intervals of strength and vigor were shortening. More and more pills were required to maintain the illusion of health, and even then, the spirit suffered. A false sense of physical well-being could not overcome pervasive gloom, dread and cancerous despair. Moreover, the supply

of tablets would soon be exhausted. And when they were gone—
what then?

Don't think about it.

He crunched a tablet between his teeth and swallowed, exper-
iencing the now-familiar riot of flavors. At once his dizziness
abated. He stood still, breathing deeply as the black world righted
itself and the ringing in his ears was replaced by an urgent simian
chatter interspersed with wails and groans. Devras loudly hailed
the unseen neighbors. Raising his lantern high, he signaled. Instantly all conversation ceased. Midnight silence reigned. He repeated the signal and call. The darkness stirred and rustled about
him. Moments later a band of squat, bandy-legged figures leapt
into the light to grapple for the lantern. Devras glimpsed swart,
flat, hairy faces; deep-set ember-colored eyes; barrel chests from
which the black hair hung in hundreds of tiny plaits. They seized
him, shook him, and flung him to the ground. While two knelt
upon his chest, a third ransacked his pockets, and a fourth
wrenched the lantern from his grasp. Bruised, breathless and
half-paralyzed with astonishment, Devras scarcely struggled. The
pockets were empty. Venting shrill chatters of frustration, the
bandits sprang up, kicked the victim's ribs soundly with their
bare feet and departed, bearing the lantern. The light vanished.
Devras was alone in the stifling dark. For a few moments he lay
still, until the blackness began to bear down on him, pressing him
flat against the ground, crushing him beneath its weight, and the
fear iced its way along his nerves. Then he felt the pull of the
cord at his wrist, and the pressure upon his heart eased, for he
knew that he was neither alone nor lost. Raith Wate Basef and the
others waited out there, and the line would lead him straight to
them. Scrambling to his feet, Devras felt his way back to the
camp, where he was obliged to report the loss of the lantern. And
after that the four of them walked warily.

The new caution stood them in good stead not long thereafter.
They were walking close beside the river, the only dependable
landmark left in a horribly transformed world. The light from
their two remaining lanterns barely served to illuminate a few
square feet of soil littered with dead vegetation; the nearest of the
moribund trees; and the water lapping against the bank. The
black air was alive with giant moths. The insects fluttered about
the lanterns; darted at pale human flesh; clung to human hair and
clothing; drove human minds to distraction.

All preoccupation with the moths ceased when the sufferers
beheld a hazy luminosity streaming along the river bank. The
glow, long and trailing as a comet's tail, approached swiftly. As it

190

drew near, the light intensified and the overwhelming size of the anonymous phenomenon began to manifest itself. The soil underfoot vibrated. Trilling notes of intensely alien music filled the air. Instantly extinguishing their lanterns, the four humans drew back, removing themselves from the path of the oncoming glow. Hands linked, they felt their way through a few yards of blackness to a stand of dying brambles, behind which they crouched in silence. The glow streamed on apace. Presently the amorphous light resolved itself into a collection of individual lambent figures—tall, emaciated, pallid and great-eyed. Devras stared, entranced. There must have been thousands of them—an army of hairless humanoids with flickering lucent flesh and euphonious otherworldly voices. So brightly did they shine that even the Cognitive darkness gave way before them. Here then were the fabled White Demons—healthy and vigorous in the midst of an atmosphere deadly to humans. The army, lacking the rigid regimentation of human soldiery, marched in a loose formation comprising clusters whose varying size and composition were governed by principles obscure to the hidden observers. At the head of the great column walked a being distinguished by unusual height and huge black eyes. A light tunic, probably some indication of rank, also set him apart. More striking yet, the flesh of the leader was noticeably duller than that of his followers; in fact, he appeared more nearly human than anyone else in the column. Devras's heartbeat quickened. He found he could not tear his eyes from the leader. Crouched there behind the bushes, he fought an inexplicable urge to leap forth, impressing the fact of his existence upon the black-eyed commander. The leader passed, and so did the impulse. Thereafter Devras waited, pulses racing, as the long column glided by. He noted the lithe longlimbed bodies, flowing movements, musical voices, intelligent eyes and sensitive features. In the glow of the enemy he perceived Grono's awe; Wate Basef's scholarly interest; and Karavise's indecipherable intensity. The Demons marched on, unconscious of human presence. The leader had already vanished into blackness, and the glowing legion followed. The minutes passed and the weird parade continued, until the last of the shining figures passed from view. Once more the world lay smothered in blackness.

There was silence, until Devras spoke almost dreamily. "They are really quite—beautiful."

"How can you say so, Master Devras?" Grono was astonished. "They are monstrous!"

"Did you see their grace?"

"Yes, like snakes. They're hideous."

"Devras is right," said Karavise, adding under her breath, "But it doesn't matter."

For a while they lingered there, not daring to stir, then relit the lanterns and made their way back to the river. On they plodded along the bank, walking in single file. Often they heard voices, but these they learned to ignore. Sometimes they saw ghostly lights glimmering close at hand, and these they altered course to avoid. Occasionally there were screams, and once they heard prolonged, disquieting laughter that followed close behind them for what seemed like hours. Grono, walking at the end of the line, swore he felt the touch of fever-hot fingers upon the back of his neck. Only by snuffing the lanterns and sneaking in silence away from the bank did they manage to evade The Giggler, as they dubbed the eerie companion.

In that lightless universe, time passed unmeasured. The travelers soon found that they tired, hungered and thirsted at significantly dissimilar intervals. Sleep was impossible to regulate, and one or another of the four was invariably deprived. It grew difficult to judge which of their frequent bouts of weakness and queasiness were Cognitive in origin, and which the result of simple fatigue. In the latter case, Wate Basef's pills were useless; ingestion a waste of a scarce commodity. The tablets were disappearing too quickly. Soon they would all be gone.

Impossible to judge the passage of black hours and days, but their total was considerable—the diminishing food supply gave evidence of that. The sacks of provisions carried from the ruined cottage were all but empty. When the stores were exhausted, the travelers would be forced to live as best they could upon the land; and Grono, former culinary standards forgotten, was already experimenting with boiled bark and toasted moths. So far, his efforts had yielded little success; the attempts themselves suggested desperation.

Featureless time crawled on; and nothing in all the philosophy of the ancients had prepared Devras to deal with the tedium of that journey. Conversation among the travelers all but died. It was prudent to proceed as much as possible in silence; moreover, there was little of value to communicate. Observation was impossible; the land was altogether invisible. Expressions of discomfort, hunger, somnolence, apprehension, boredom, frustration or general pessimism were valueless and usually went unuttered; which left almost nothing to say. Even Grono had ceased all complaint. Periods of rest were short, infrequent, plagued with heat, vile odors, inquisitive insects and unidentifiable crawlers.

Miseries were assorted but repetitive, and spirits unvaryingly low.

Collective gloom intensified as the food supplies diminished, finally dwindling to a single small sack of pebble-hard lentils. When Grono presented his smoked moths, the atmosphere did not improve. Despondency reached new depths as it became apparent that the glass tower known as the Icy Ambition was not to be found. Recognition of this fact dawned slowly. It took many weary miles of sightless wandering along the bank of the Yl before the doubts arose, and then the first reluctant questions. Wate Basef managed to banish such doubts for a while. The Icy Ambition was always just around the next bend of the river, just beyond the next stand of trees. River and trees flowed by in an endless tide. Time passed, and the tower did not materialize. Perhaps they had passed it in the dark, perhaps it no longer existed at all. Doubt blossomed into trepidation, then fear that no one acknowledged openly. Queries ceased, but the trek continued; mile after spirit-numbing mile. Wate Basef walked at the head of the group. His step was firm, his demeanor assured, but one telltale sign revealed his uncertainty; the characteristic smile had disappeared.

No one panicked when the last of Wate Basef's tablets was consumed. There were no lamentations, no recriminations. The general atmosphere took on a certain subtle aridity, and that was all, at first. For a little while the loss of the tablets seemed to make no difference; collective discomfort, already intense, hardly increased. But gradually the weakness and nausea held barely at bay for so long began to make themselves felt. Devras grew light-headed. No longer feeling the ground beneath his feet, he stumbled often. Perpetual haze fogged his vision, and he perceived the lantern he carried as a smoky orange blur. His companions were similarly afflicted, all of them mildly feverish. Footsteps dragged, heads drooped, eyes went glassy. Hours passed and the wretched progress continued, but the Icy Ambition remained elusive. Despite the misery and mounting hopelessness, no one spoke of giving up. No one spoke at all. The profundity of the silence provided dramatic contrast to the eccentric high-pitched laughter of The Giggler, who had managed to overtake them in the dark.

At first The Giggler employed some restraint. Its laughter shrilled in their wake for miles and hours on end, but it maintained its distance. Then when they finally paused to boil their lentils, restraint began to evaporate. The cackles danced around the campfire in ever-tightening circles. They resumed progress,

193

and The Giggler followed close behind. Its initial discretion gave way to insolent familiarity, and its victim of choice was Karavise.

She felt the fiery fingers plucking at her hair and skirts. Hot breath scorched her cheek and neck. Angrily she spun on her heel to encounter empty darkness. Crazed cachinnation rattled out of the void. Karavise glared this way and that, but her assailant was nowhere to be seen. Exchanging places with Grono, she walked flanked by two allies, and The Giggler's frustration was loudly manifest. The laughter turned menacing, and shortly thereafter Grono cried out in pain. Blood spotted his livery, and a thorn protruded from his shoulder. At the same time Karavise felt a burning hand slide lingeringly down her back. Once more she whirled to confront nothingness. Just beyond the circle of lamp-light, shrieks of glee resounded.

The creature was intolerable. Evasive tactics would cost precious time, but the expense was worthwhile. Accordingly they doused the lights and struck off in a new direction along a path that led to the charred remains of a village leveled in the recent past. The Giggler's mirth died away behind them, and they relit the lanterns. For a time they wandered aimlessly among the ruined cottages, barns and outbuildings, noting with gloom the signs of Vardrul visitation—widespread destruction and a profusion of corpses adding their taint to the familiar Cognitive fetor. Progress halted when Grono's legs gave way beneath him. The valet tottered, then sat down abruptly. Amidst profuse apologies he made as if to rise, then sank back, gasping for breath. His giddiness might have been due to illness, or perhaps simple malnutrition. Then Devras thought to search the village for fresh supplies to augment the lentils and smoked moths. Perhaps a change in diet might banish the ever-increasing weakness.

The others elected to remain with Grono. Devras left them sitting together in the midst of the rubble. Lantern in hand, farmer's basket over one arm, and Cognitive thread at his wrist, he ventured forth alone, stumbling from ruin to ruin until he had wandered far from his friends. At the outskirts of the village he came upon an isolated storehouse left entirely intact. Entering, he discovered a cache of root vegetables; enough to stave off hunger for days to come. His stomach rumbled at the sight. Kneeling, he set the lantern aside, reached for the vegetables—and then the sweat was pouring down his face, he was dizzy, and his stomach was heaving.

Will the food help, now that Raith's pills are gone? How long can we live without them?

He sat very still, breathing deeply. Minutes later, nausea temporarily conquered, he set to work. When his basket and pockets were full to overflowing, he took up the lantern, stood and moved toward the door. Halfway to the exit he paused to stare, for the feeble orange rays played upon a hitherto unnoticed hole in the dirt floor. Intrigued, he approached the cavity, leaning over the edge to cast lantern light into the depths. A startling odor wafted from the pit, a mingling of floral sweetness and carnivore pungency, strange even to nostrils accustomed to the stench of Fal Grizhni's darkness. He sniffed, nose wrinkling. The odor told him little, and the dim glow of his lantern revealed nothing beyond an old wooden ladder whose lower rungs were lost in blackness.

He listened intently, but heard nothing. Curious, he descended without caution, and one of the ancient rungs broke beneath his weight. The ladder teetered and Devras fell. Yelling, clutching wildly at the black air, he plunged into nothingness. The lantern flew from his grasp, crashed to the floor and blinked out. He slid down the length of the ladder to land at the bottom of the hole, alarmed but unhurt. For a moment he sat still, senses straining in vain. The surrounding darkness was absolute. A sense of major disaster oppressed him, and it took a moment to pinpoint the source. The pressure at his right wrist was absent. The flesh was bare and the thread gone, torn from his wrist by the fall. With it went the Cognitive link that bound him to his companions. The fear rose almost uncontrollably then, and he called upon the wisdom of the philosophers to fight it.

'*Fear deprives the mind of reason, making Man less than a beast. Thus in surrender to its influence lies an inevitable relinquishment of humanity morally equivalent to self-slaughter. As suicide is reprehensible, so unbridled terror must be deemed unethical.*' The Venerable Disitch—nobly intolerant, incorruptibly inflexible.

'*The fearful mind is shrouded in darkness blacker than the shadow of a thousand crypts.*' Good old Omee Nofid. How succinct he was, and in this case how very apropos.

Alone in the dark, Devras took a deep breath and thought fast. The Cognitive thread was irrevocably lost, by this time returned to the wrist of Raith Wate Basef. The savant would note the disconnection at once. He would begin searching for his vanished companion, resorting to Cognition if necessary. Thus the situation, while alarming, was not really dangerous. Devras need only remain where he was, and Wate Basef would quickly find him. Moreover, there was no need to sit in the dark. The lantern lay nearby. He would find and relight it.

Somewhat heartened, Devras crawled forward, groping with outstretched hands. He encountered neither lantern nor wall. The lantern, surely not more than a few feet distant, was surprisingly difficult to locate. The darkness confounded all perception, particularly perception of space and distance. Extraordinary, for example, how spacious the hole seemed—he had not yet found the end of it. Either the subterranean space was far larger than he could have guessed, or else he was moving in circles; probably the latter. The odd pungent-sweet odor heavied in the air as he advanced. He judged he was nearing the source, and the prospect was not reassuring. His face was tingling. Brushing a hand across his brow, he dislodged a collection of fine, clinging threads. They were sticky, resilient, and almost as strong as fine wire. When he tried to toss them aside, they clung to his fingers. Devras shrugged and kept searching. The hole seemed to go on forever. The heat, blackness and silence of the place were fraying his nerves. He deliberately paused to compose himself, and in that instant thought to hear the ghost of a sound; a faint click, a tiny scrape, the suspicion of a hiss. He froze, breathlessly alert, but the noise was not repeated. Imagination, then. Stupid, fearful, irrational fancy battening upon darkness. Light would send the bogies flying; speaking of which, where was the lantern? He couldn't afford to give up on it. How, after all, could he face the others and confess that he'd lost such a valuable possession—*again*? No, he couldn't afford to give up.

Devras crawled on, and the sticky threads fastened themselves over eyes, nose and mouth. Impossible to remove them all. Soon he was covered with a tough gossamer layer beneath which his skin tingled and itched. The stuff was incredibly adhesive. When he tried to peel it away, his fingers stuck as if coated with glue. The threads were falling across his eyes. He blinked, and his eyelids stuck together. In the midst of blackness this scarcely affected his vision, but the sensation was nonetheless unbearable. He knuckled his eyes to no avail. They were glued shut. His heart beat fast; nor could the philosophy of the Venerable Disitch slow his racing pulses. Every instinct urged flight.

Abandoning his quest for the lost lantern, Devras turned to feel his way back to the ladder. His outstretched hands and arms slashed through cloudlike suspensions of sticky threads. Surely they had not been there moments earlier? He was moving in the wrong direction. The exit must lie to the left. Or was it the right? He paused to regain his bearings, and as he knelt there in the dark, he heard it again—a click, a scrape, a barely audible hiss. Genuinely frightened now, he moved away from the sound.

Crawling, scuttling through the sultry dark, confused and disoriented, he blundered into a forest of threads. They were all around him, clinging to his face, his back, his limbs. He was wrapped in a growing cocoon of the stuff. His arms were sticking to his sides and his legs were bound. He struggled vigorously, lost his balance and fell sprawling. His elbow cracked sharply against stone, but the cry of pain that escaped him was muffled. Adhesive matter tightly sealed his lips. For a moment he lay still, listening for the scrape, the hiss. He heard nothing. Had he imagined them? He attempted to rise, and found himself glued to the floor. Violent struggles only attached him the more securely.

Devras lay spent and gasping, heart hammering and breath labored. He could not move and he could not shout for help. He was blind and sickeningly afraid. The black minutes crept by and his fear mounted as he contemplated a slow death alone in darkness. His friends would search, but they might never find him in the depths of this subcellar. He would lie here blind, mute and paralyzed, racked with the thirst that would finally kill him. Terror lent hysterical strength to his struggles, but he succeeded only in exhausting himself. Limp and defeated, he subsided. Only his head continued to twist from side to side in a useless effort to evade the sticky strands drifting over his nostrils, soft and quiet as gentle assassins.

Endless, helpless waiting. Then he heard the voice of Grono overhead, calling out his name. Devras strained desperately, but his muffled squeals did not ascend to ground level. Grono's anxious voice receded, and Devras's head dropped back. His cheek touched the floor and stuck there. The welling tears did not dissolve the adhesive that bonded his eyelids shut.

And then his fears took on a new and more dire immediacy as he felt a stirring in the air, heard a click, a scrape, a faint rustle, and sensed an alien presence at his side. A low groan fought its way out of his throat as he felt a light, inhuman touch wander coldly over his body. The member—tentacle or proboscis, it surely was not a hand—traced the outline of his face and jaw, slid over his chest and shoulders. The touch was icy, and Devras shuddered.

A voice spoke out of the darkness—a slow and hissing voice, identifiably female. "A man. What does he do here? He is warm."

A reply, an appeal, rose to Devras's lips and was stilled. Something passed like a wintry breeze across his face, clearing the threads away. His eyes opened, but he saw nothing.

197

"What does he do here?" the voice repeated. The cold touch rested on his chest over his heart.

"I was exploring." Devras managed a creditably composed reply. "I fell down the ladder, lost my lantern, and I—"

"Exploring. Ah. What do you seek?"

"I seek the caverns of the Vardruls."

"Have you searched within your own mind, where all the world may be found?"

"You do not understand. I seek a specific place, of the world and not of the mind."

"If it is not of the mind, then it is not of yourself, and there is little purpose in searching."

"The Vardruls possess certain information—"

"Which will not serve you."

"Why not?"

"All that the white Vardrul-folk impart, all that they are, cannot reach your understanding save by way of your senses, which distort and falsify, mislead and deceive. Better by far to ignore the traitorous senses, dwell in darkness and silence, searching for true knowledge within yourself. You are warm."

"Your views are similar to those of the philosopher Vu Bubash. In my opinion the argument possesses flaws. I'd be honored to discuss the matter with you, but under the present circumstances find it difficult to marshal my thoughts." Devras shivered. The icy touch still rested upon his breast.

"You tremble," the voice observed.

"Who are you? What are you?"

"I am that which occupies this space."

"What is this place? What is down here?"

"Everything that you see."

"I see nothing."

"You have answered yourself."

"Will you help me?" Devras demanded in desperation.

"What troubles you?"

"I'm caught, bound, covered with sticky stuff. I can't move."

"Ah. You are trapped in the web of Chul. It is useless to struggle. Perhaps this restriction of physical movement will assist you in directing your thoughts inward in search of true knowledge."

"It doesn't seem to have that effect. Who is Chul?"

"She exists. She occupies this space. She builds webs."

"She's another like you?"

"Yes, but younger and hungrier."

"Does Chul intend me harm?"

Devras, listless but clearheaded, related the entire tale. He spoke calmly and plausibly, but failed to convince the savant.

"You cracked your pate when you fell, lad." Wate Basef shook his head kindly. "It's confused you."

"I am not confused." A trace of angry color mounted to Devras's ashen cheeks. "If you don't want to believe me, please yourself." He sat up.

"Don't try to move yet, Master Devras," Grono pleaded. "Don't excite yourself!"

"Stop fussing, Grono. I'm fine."

Protests and queries from valet and savant.

While her companions argued, Lady Karavise explored. She carried a lantern and by its light she studied the stone walls, floor and ceiling. All were naturally formed, showing no sign of human workmanship. The cellar was improbably vast. She wandered until the others' voices began to fade, then returned to find Devras on his feet, shaky but determined.

"It looks as if Devras may be right about this place," Karavise announced. "The cellar goes on forever."

"If she told the truth, we're in the caverns now," said Devras.

Wate Basef hesitated, and Grono proclaimed, "The Lord Har Fennahar does not lie!"

"Nobody said he did. Still, it seems unlikely—"

"We'll see for ourselves," said Karavise, "as soon as Devras is well enough to walk."

Devras, unwilling to delay them further, feigned complete recovery. With an effort he disguised all sign of sickness as the group pressed on through the subterranean night.

The small, dim bubble of lantern light enclosed two figures. One of them was human; short, slight, quiet and relentless. The other was tiny, four-legged and huge-eared. Mistress Snarp's sojourn in darkness had visibly affected her. She had lost weight. Her body, always lean, was now skeletal—collarbone knife-edged, cheeks cadaverous. Her yellow eyes, sunk in shadowed sockets, glittered fever-bright. The wounded right arm was puffed and festering, with dirty-white matter seeping through the makeshift bandage. In the face of pain and sickness, however, her determination continued intact. Her step was firm, demeanor assured as ever.

The quibbid pattered along the ground before its mistress. Its coat was falling out in great patches, and its naked tail jerked in continual nervous agitation. Its nose was lowered to the dying soil, nostrils flared to catch the quarry's scent. Devotion to duty, however, could not overcome the little creature's dread. Presently it halted, sat up on its haunches, bat's-wing ears quivering at full extension, and chittered woefully.

Snarp dropped to her knees, her movements uncharacteristically ponderous. For a moment she knelt motionless, too-bright eyes shut. Then she reached out and stroked the quibbid's trembling back. "Do not fear, little beauty," she advised. "We will find him. We will bring him back to Lanthi Ume. Soon it will be over. Soon." Gradually the animal's terror subsided. Its trembling ceased and it arched its back against her caressing hand. Snarp stood with an effort. As she rose, a light shower of pebbles and clods pelted her. She whirled, knife already in hand, to face an invisible assailant. Gales of high-pitched laughter yammered out of the dark. Motionless, full vigor temporarily restored, she waited in slit-eyed readiness. The shrill laughter danced just beyond the circle of light, but the attack was not repeated. Presently Snarp uttered a whistling command and the quibbid, eager to leave the ill-omened spot, set its nose to the trail.

The Giggler, however, was not easily discouraged. For miles it followed them through the dark, its manic laughter rarely stilled. Along the bank of the Yl they went until the trail diverged from the river, inexplicably angling off into the woods. At that point the quibbid hesitated, casting about in search of the scent. Snarp stood waiting, and as she watched, a hot breath played on the back of her neck; fiery fingers tweaked her flesh and plucked the hat from her head. She spun, half-crouched and ready to leap. Despite her cat's reflexes, she was not fast enough; The Giggler was already gone. Laughter howled through the woods.

Lips thinning, Snarp retrieved her hat. Beneath the hat lay a fist-sized rock. For a moment she paused to listen, then grabbed the rock and threw. A solid thump followed by a squeal signaled the accuracy of her aim. The laughter cut off and deadly silence reigned. The seconds passed and the sound did not resume.

The quibbid had picked up the scent. Now it ran back and forth, inviting its mistress to follow. Snarp did so, and the two struck off through the woods. Among the dead and dying growths they wandered, the beast occasionally uncertain, but never thrown off the scent for long. As they trailed their quarry, so they in turn were stalked. The Giggler, much offended, cackled malevolently in their wake. Around and about them the sinister hilarity echoed, first to one side, then the other; sometimes distant, sometimes ominously near. Twice rocks whizzed from the shadows to part the air a handspan above Snarp's head. Each time the giggles retreated hurriedly, the ensuing silence discouraging retaliation. Snarp's eyes were fixed on the ground. She appeared unconscious of insult and danger alike.

The trail led to a lifeless village where the charred remains of cottages and outbuildings marked the site of a recent massacre. Here the quibbid encountered difficulty, for the stench of the decaying dead all but smothered the scent of the quarry. Progress was slow, the trail leading from ruin to ruin, as if the criminal savant Wate Basef had for some reason conducted a search of his own. Through the village, past piles of blackened rubble, past corpses animal and human on which the flame-eyed night creatures fed without fear, Snarp made her inexorable way. The Giggler, if present, was voiceless; a possibly threatening alteration. Once or twice the Enforcer paused, hand on the hilt of her knife, to listen intently. She heard nothing. Heat, decay and silence ruled the insalubrious night.

The buildings were widely spaced now. The quibbid was leading her to the outskirts of the village. Here the bare ground rippled in shallow swells and hollows. At the crest of an incline Snarp came upon a storehouse left entirely intact. Three wooden steps flanked by a rough railing led to a small landing and an open door, upon whose threshold the quibbid sat chittering. Snarp mounted the steps. Halfway up, she felt two searing hands close about her ankles. A sudden sharp jerk swept both feet from under her. She fell face forward, ribcage striking the angle of the topmost tread. Pain knifed through her, and for a few moments she could not catch her breath. As she lay gasping, shrieks of mirth tore out of the dark.

Her breathing eased, and the air found its way to her lungs. Snarp sat up slowly, hand pressed to her fiercely aching midriff. Pain stabbed with each breath. It was more than likely she had cracked a rib, but there was no help for it now. Carefully she reached out to right the upended lantern, which providentially continued to burn. With the same outstretched hand, she stroked and soothed the trembling quibbid, which pressed itself against her thigh.

"Softly, my beautiful delight. Do not fear for me."

A few feet distant, The Giggler racketed in triumph. Head bent, Snarp listened for a time. Without haste she drew her knife, aimed at the sound and threw. The knife flew from sight. An instant later, a scream of mortal agony arose. A heavy, unseen body crashed to the ground. Frenzied thrashing struggles convulsed the darkness. The screams gave way to perishing moans which receded, finally fading away altogether.

Snarp waited. The minutes passed uneventfully. At last she

rose with caution, took up the lantern, and retraced her path. A few yards from the steps she discovered a great pool of fresh blood, pitch black in the dim light. The Giggler was gone, however, and with the creature went her knife—a matter of little importance. She carried several other blades, in addition to armaments of far more exotic description.

Returning to the storehouse, she followed the quibbid inside. The trail must have been warm, for the little animal scampered directly to a hole in the earthen floor, where it crouched in ear-quivering excitement. Snarp examined the hole at some length before placing the quibbid on her shoulder and descending the broken ladder with care. The cellar beneath proved a source of unexpected interest, extending apparently immeasurable distances. Snarp paused only long enough to bind her aching ribs with strips of linen before resuming the hunt. Parched lips compressed, feverish eyes incandescent, she pushed on into the dark.

Chapter Fifteen

It was unclear how long the march continued. Far away in the depths of the caverns, the Bleeding Stalactite measured out the Great and Small Vens, but Surface offered the clanmembers no corresponding temporal standard. The sun, moon and stars that guided mankind were obscured by Cognitive shadow. Refreshing and delightful though that shadow was, it fostered a certain confusion, and the Small Vens blended, distinguished from one another by incident alone. Certainly the trek was prolonged, and the distance covered considerable. Little hardship was involved, for the atmosphere was invigorating, foodstuffs abounded, and the opposition of the enemy was almost negligible.

For the Grizhni Greater Patriarch, the journey was marked by a steady decline in personal harmony, loss of unity and a perceptible distancing of the Ancestors. His conquests did little to strengthen the general's spirits. The very ease of Surface victory was demoralizing, and the great campaign begun in such a spirit of oneness and idealism had in his mind sunk to the level of squalid butchery, unredeemed by motives of self-preservation or self-defense. Death and destruction lay in his wake. His path was strewn with human corpses. More, much more of the same lay ahead, for the coastal cities were yet to be taken. And The Grizhni sensed himself polluted by his own deeds, lost forever to peace and harmony. The personal dissonance of a lone Patriarch was a small price to pay for the triumph and vindication of all the Vardrul race; or so The Grizhni assured himself, as this consideration alone restored some measure of harmony. The clans would gain new life, new hope; and perhaps the long process of decay, the decline in vigor and ordinary vitality so fatally apparent in Clan Grizhni, but common to all the clans—perhaps that general deterioration might be reversed at last. If so, the price was not too high—or so it was necessary to believe, if The Grizhni Greater Patriarch was to lead his people Surface.

The comfort provided by these reflections did not serve to

raise The Grizhni's hiir. Dull-fleshed he marched at the head of the glowing horde. The doubts so disruptive of the Greater Patriarch's harmony did not appear to trouble the various clanmembers, whose luminosity waxed in the face of consistent victory. Following the destruction of the last human settlement of note standing between themselves and the human city of Lahnzium—or as the inhabitants termed it, Lanthi Ume—Vardrul optimism was reflected in a level of hiir rarely attained outside the confines of the home caverns. The army shone with an intensity that cut the darkness, creating a lucent environment soft and bright as the rock-lit walls of home. The living light glowed pearl-white against the black backdrop of Cognitive night. It shone upon great eyes clear and brilliant, ocular ridges contracted in confidence, tentacle-fingers vivaciously undulant. Activity along the column was varied and incessant, for the clanmembers did not march with the inflexible precision of human soldiers. Many nibbled fungi as they walked, some sang, others broke formation to seek out kinsmen. Trained bats bearing messages continually fluttered up and down the line. No longer did the Vardruls steal their way across Surface with the timidity of hunted trespassers, as in Great Vens gone by. Now they strode forward with the assurance of conquerors. Discipline and circumspection might manifest themselves once more beneath the walls of Lanthi Ume. Until that time, freedom, hope and clan solidarity reigned supreme.

The Grizhni Greater Patriarch's depressed hiir had not gone unnoticed. The clanmembers observed their general's lightlessness, but attributed it to the burdens of leadership combined with the shock of recent personal losses. Even now, the last Grizhni kinsman hovered upon the verge of final Ancestral joining. Was it any wonder that the Patriarch's flesh bespoke dissonance? Eventually, he would recover. In the meantime, The Grizhni's private woes, though a source of concern to all, could not be permitted to damage the communal ruu.

The Vardruls' ruu was in little danger of depression as the triumphant clanmembers surged over Surface. The novelty, excitement and success of the great endeavor promoted exhilaration. Not more than a very few of the least harmonious among the kinsmen shared The Grizhni's doubts concerning the wholesale slaughter of human beings. For most, Mankind represented the traditional enemy of the race; destroyer, oppressor, and murderer of the Ancestors. Fulfillment of the ancient Ancestral prophecies —an obvious manifestation of cosmic justice—necessitated human death. Moreover, not a single Vardrul in all that great force shared or comprehended The Grizhni's sense of kinship with the foe.

Collective hiir continued high as the advance devoured time and distance. Progress was swift and almost unimpeded. Energy, spirits and hiir soared to new heights as the Vardrul force traversed the Gravula Wasteland; bypassed the ancient Granite Sages, traditional site of the ritual mass Knowledge of Ancestors; turned its back on the Master—largest of monoliths, within whose belly the ancient observation post had been modified by the addition of a Flat, or component of the White Tunnels transportation system—proceeded on across the barren hills, over the granite rise known to humans as the Crags, across the lifeless fields and pastures until the wall of the human city rose to bar their path. And there, on the plain before the wall, beneath the cannon weighting the Vayno Fortification ramparts, the Vardruls paused to gather strength and oneness prior to the final attack. There they massed by the thousands and there, for the first time since the campaign began, they donned the black hooded cloaks and vizards carried from the caverns. Natural luminescence obscured, the kinsmen faded from view, blending invisibly into the darkness. Undeterred by walls, weaponry, or past disasters, they readied themselves for the great assault. High on the ramparts they beheld the signal fires of the defenders, flames intended to hold the darkness at bay. The light appeared pathetically small and feeble as the waning strength of the human inhabitants. The moment to strike was at hand. Despite his ambivalence The Grizhni realized as much, and yet he hesitated beneath the wall, withholding the final command that would send his troops hurtling across the Nine Isles. Far beyond the span that reason and prudence demanded, he hesitated; so long that his followers began to trill and hum amongst themselves. And then, when the passing Colorations squeezed him in viselike jaws, The Grizhni was granted a very temporary respite.

White vapor spun and groaned above the Wandering Flat. The pale whirlwind slowed, and presently a messenger appeared, bearing word of the Grizhni Inrl's imminent Ancestral joining. The Grizhni Inrl desired the presence of his one remaining kinsman. The request, absurdly negligible at such a time by human standards, carried immense weight with the Vardruls. No Vardrul would question the force of such a plea, and no one could question the Grizhni Greater Patriarch's compliance. Traveling by way of the Wandering Flat, the Patriarch would absent himself briefly. The diversion would be minor and justifiable, the clan-members patient until the moment of their leader's return.

The Master Suite at Vallage House contained a rich and exquisite bedchamber wherein towered a vast four-poster swathed in silver brocade and pearl-gray satin. Behind the lustrous hangings reclined a pallid figure. Vaxalt Gless Vallage lay faint and listless, prey to heat, noxious atmosphere, and paralytic melancholia. For days he had rested nearly motionless in a chamber whose poisonous darkness was relieved by the glow of two hundred candles. The warmth of the flames added immeasurably to the chamber's discomfort. Gless Vallage, ordinarily the image of cool perfection, was bathed from head to toe in sweat. The silk sheets clung to his body, and the moisture beaded on his forehead. A modicum of rudimentary Cognition might have altered matters, but Vallage did not attempt it. Crushed by the shock and humiliation of his recent public defeat, he had sequestered himself, passing the weary hours in dull-eyed sleeplessness. Misery, shame, and unwonted sickly pessimism had chained him to his bed. But Nature had blessed his Preeminence with much resiliency, and now his spirits were beginning to revive at last.

Vallage rose with an effort. He was languid and a little giddy; infirmities born of the Cognitive darkness. He recognized them as such, and at once sought appropriate remedy. A shelf concealed behind a sliding panel yielded a flask of opalescent tablets similar to those devised by Raith Wate Basef. Vallage swallowed a pill, and his symptoms abated within moments. Vigor restored, he surveyed his surroundings with reawakening interest. The familiar bedchamber appeared faintly exotic in the unnaturally muted light. A full two hundred candles could only lighten the Cognitive shadow to a dull orange murk. So it must be over all Lanthi Ume, over all of Dalyon itself. Vallage strolled to the window and looked out upon a world of blackness dotted here and there with the feeble blurry lights of what must have been tremendous bonfires. Directly beneath the window, out on the Vallage moorings, the hostile crowds loitered muttering. Surely they did not blame Preeminence Vaxalt Gless Vallage for their misfortunes? Surely they recognized Vaxalt Gless Vallage's generous sympathy? An angry outburst below, a barrage of stones pelting the facade of Vallage House answered both questions. Vallage withdrew without haste from the window, repaired to the nearest easy chair and seated himself to reflect in comfort.

Lanthi Ume was altogether uninhabitable, and the condition

208

was clearly permanent. If Vaxalt Gless Vallage's inspired Cognition lacked potency to banish the darkness, then the darkness was here to stay. Extraordinary, almost inconceivable, that the Cognition of the ancient demon-savant Terrs Fal Grizhni should prove so formidable. Grizhni, of course, had access to many stores of arcane knowledge unavailable to modern savants. In view of that advantage, all comparison between the present and former Selectic Preeminences was rendered invalid, and the abilities of Vaxalt Gless Vallage could not by any reasonable standard be adjudged the inferior. Vaxalt Gless Vallage had nothing with which to reproach himself, and yet—it did not bear thinking of. That way lay acute emotional discomfort.

Vallage shook his head, banishing disagreeable fancies. No point in dwelling on past disappointments; it was time to look to the future. He must leave Lanthi Ume, and quickly. Despite the dearth of seaworthy vessels, Cognition opened many possible avenues of escape. He need only choose the most convenient method, the most alluring foreign refuge. The matter deserved careful consideration, presently impeded by physical discomfort. Vallage rang for a servant, of whom but a handful remained, and ordered a cold meal and a bath. A short time later—clean, shaven, freshly dressed and much improved in spirits—his Preeminence sat sipping chilled wine, nibbling shellfish salad and fresh fruit. As he ate, his eyes roamed the chamber, lingering in turn upon the priceless paintings and statuary; the intricate hand-knotted rug; furniture so beautifully conceived and executed that each piece stood as a work of art; the hand-wrought gold flatware, unique long-stemmed iridescent crystal, and china whose pattern he himself had designed. Mentally he wandered through the various rooms, taking inventory of their irreplaceable, much-beloved contents. He contemplated the splendor of the building itself—the perfect proportions, the noble grandeur—and wondered how he could ever bear to leave his ancestral home. Then the answer came to him; he would not leave it at all. He would take it with him, wherever he chose to emigrate. Vallage House and everything in it would be transported across the sea.

Having resolved that immediate dilemma, his Preeminence ate with renewed appetite. His mind continued to whir. The relocation of Vallage House was a feat of some magnitude, demanding advanced Cognitive technique. Needless to say, the abilities of Vaxalt Gless Vallage were more than equal to the task. Vallage, however, had never in his life attempted transference of a building. As a senior savant of the Order, he understood the basic principle well enough. Whorlo's Winged Conveyance was a method particularly suited to the transport of large objects. Cognition sought by Whorlo's means often eluded the inexperienced, but Vallage had mastered the technique long ago. The particular variation required to modify the Winged Conveyance to the Cognitive specifications of a mansion, he did not know offhand. Such obscure information was generally buried in the depths of the archives that filled an entire floor of the Nessiva, the old Selectic stronghold on the Victory of Nes in the middle of Parnis Lagoon. To the Nessiva he would go.

A fresh volley of rocks flung from below recalled him to the problems at hand. Down on the moorings roiled the angry crowd —senselessly hostile and hungry for a scapegoat. In their mindless frenzy they were apt to seize upon the first victim at hand, and thus it was best not to call attention to his departure. Recourse to the most elementary Cognition of illusion transformed Vallage, simultaneously altering his appearance and influencing the perceptions of all who might behold him. Darkened hair, a slightly shortened, thickened figure, a resculpted nose and jaw; thus fortified, he might pass through the riotous mob unrecognized. A final set of instructions issued to the loyal major domo, a lantern selected to light his way and then he was off, exiting through a side door to avoid the majority of restive citizens.

Afoot, Gless Vallage circled a line of mansions, his goal the Fennahar Wharf some distance to the south. Despite all precautions, his Preeminence's journey was unsettling. The streets were black and airless, the darkness intermittently relieved by great bonfires pumping their heat and smoke into the already torrid atmosphere. By that sickly light he viewed the crowds—more numerous now than in the time of light, and infinitely more miserable. He had not realized prior to that sortie the number of refugees trapped in Lanthi Ume; so many that they littered his path even here, in the finest section of town. He saw now the legions of the desperate and destitute whose flight from darkness had been halted once and for all by the sea. The boats were gone. For the ordinary mortal devoid of Cognition, escape was impossible. Those remaining behind, doomed to suffer the horrors of the dark throughout the short and wretched remainder of their lives, differed in their reaction to disaster. All showed signs of illness. The dim fires cast their orange light upon feverish, sweat-drenched flesh, eyes glazed or glittering, colorless lips parted to gulp the poisoned air. But those sickly faces, so alike in misery, varied widely in expression—some calm and resolute; others fearful, despairing; dully resigned or angry, rebellious; even a few tight smiles of defiant gaiety. Vallage walked with his eyes fixed on the ground before him. He did not wish to observe those faces, he did not care to meet those hungry eyes. The sight woke within him a certain sense of—what? Remorse? Responsibility? Guilty knowledge that he might have warned the populace of the approaching menace weeks earlier; might have employed his Cognition to effect the escape of thousands? Ridiculous, of course. The intentions of Vaxalt Gless Vallage, always large-minded and humanitarian, had been thwarted by a cruel stroke of fortune. Vallage had done his best for Lanthi Ume and her inhabitants. No living man could have done any better. It was not his fault that the graceless fates conspired against him, and in no way was he culpable. Vaxalt Gless Vallage had meant well.

Exalted intentions notwithstanding, Vallage was prey to continuing uneasiness. He wished now that he had traveled by closed sedan chair; he could have drawn the curtains against the distressing sights that now confronted him. Eager to shorten the journey, he lengthened his stride. Past the grandest of mansions he hurried, eyes persistently downcast. From time to time, however, he encountered scenes too bizarre to ignore. It was impossible to overlook, for example, the revival of the cult of Ert. The primitive rituals and grisly sacrifices demanded by the Queen of the Nightmare Realm had fallen into disfavor generations earlier, and it was thought that the old superstition had died out. But the descent of darkness had proven that Ert only slumbered. Now she was wide awake, clamoring in the hearts of the ignorant and fearful. Here and there about the city rose makeshift altars where the ancient ceremonies were reenacted by gilded zealots calling themselves priests. Out in the open, of course, the sacrifices were limited to goats, sheep, and similarly luckless beasts, as Ert's well-documented thirst for human blood could not be publicly assuaged. In private, behind closed doors—who could say? Corpses bearing the telltale triple wounds of the sacrificial victim floated face down in the canals, but there could be no investigation; in this time of darkness, all manner of crime flourished unchecked. Now, as Gless Vallage walked the alley behind Beffel House, he came upon a knot of Cru Beffel's household servants. Nearly naked, flesh gilded, their voices rose in singing chant as they readied a cageful of unsuspecting songbirds for sacrifice. Vallage cast a glance of disdain upon them as he hurried by. All things considered, however, he might have encountered far worse things in a dark alley; many a starving refugee or citizen, driven by fear and hunger, had turned predator. Murder was endemic, even more widespread than suicide, which was saying a good deal, as organized mass suicide pacts now provided a popular means of exit. Foreigners, especially those of questionable humanity, suffered the most. The Zonianders, known to carry wealth upon their persons, were often targeted for attack, and the web-footed Swamp-Splatters—all but helpless upon the cobbled streets—fared little better. The timorous Bexae were born victims, and it was said with some truth that the Burbies, self-indulgent of their own cannibalistic appetites, deserved death. But ordinary Lanthian citizens were almost as much at risk, and many had taken to traveling in fairly sizable groups. Such a group was now approaching, its members linked hand in hand, each bearing a lantern. Their movements were sluggish; their heads bowed, white faces dully apathetic. Vallage stepped out of their path, eyeing them with disfavor as they passed. He found those sickly, shuffling, hopeless creatures profoundly distasteful; and inwardly he blessed the Cognitive talent that preserved him from similar degeneration.

The group dragged off into darkness, and Vallage resumed his advance. On he went without mishap until his progress was once again arrested, this time very briefly by a roistering gang of drunken merrymakers—self-consciously raucous, laboriously profane. Forced hilarity could not disguise the pallid cheeks and fearful eyes. Vallage looked on, deeply contemptuous. Where was their Lanthian spirit, their dignity? Had they no fortitude, no *pride*? True, their circumstances were depressing. For all that, Vaxalt Gless Vallage had no patience with arrant laxity. The gang roared down the alley, their torches and lanterns vanishing within seconds. Vallage's own journey was all but over. Another couple of minutes of walking brought him to Fennahar Wharf, where he was able to hire one of the few remaining public dombuli to carry him to Parnis Lagoon and the Victory of Nes.

Once out upon the canal and clear of the doom-ridden crowds, Gless Vallage breathed a sigh of relief. The voyage was slow, for the dombulman nosed his craft tentatively through the dark. Lanterns affixed to the high-curving prow and stern barely illumined the surrounding water. A few potent syllables would have increased the light a hundredfold, but Vallage, reluctant to draw attention to his own Cognizance, did not utter them. His caution appeared justified as the dombulis reached the junction of the Lureis Canal and Parnis Lagoon. There on the old Vezhni moorings the crowd had gathered to scream imprecations across the water at the Victory of Nes. Irrational as always, the citizens evidently fastened blame for their misfortunes upon the savants of the Select. Perhaps they imagined the savants had power to banish the darkness at will? There was no telling what the hysterical fools thought.

Fortunately, the dombulis escaped notice. Minutes later the craft bumped Victory Pier and Vallage stepped ashore. Bidding the dombulman await his return, the savant departed, pausing only long enough to restore himself to natural appearance before marching on to the Nessiva.

The halls of the Nessiva were dimly alight, and perceptibly cooler than the outside air. The difference in temperature was minimal, for the Cognitive energy required to maintain it was urgently needed elsewhere. The cooling was sufficient to create more or less bearable working conditions for the savants, nothing more. Vallage was astonished at the number of his compatriots present and hard at work. He had assumed that the majority of them would have employed their powers to carry themselves to safety long ago, but such was by no means the case. The workrooms were filled with grim-faced, ceaselessly toiling men and a few women. Throughout the black hours they had worked, never pausing for food or rest. Their experiments were diverse and far-ranging, the shape and thrust of each dictated by the highly individual talents of the separate investigators. Days and nights of intense effort, however, had yielded little insight into the nature of Fal Grizhni's Death of Light. The Cognition employed, a tribute to the power and genius of its creator, was evidently complex, demanding, unpredictably volatile, and subject to a host of internal variables. Years of experimentation might be required to rediscover Terrs Fal Grizhni's method, and they did not have years. Long before they found the answer, Lanthi Ume and her people would be lost, prey to the darkness and the beings that inhabited it. They could only work on in the hope of miraculous good fortune.

Gless Vallage's arrival was deliberately unobtrusive, yet it did not go unnoticed. His swift progress toward the Archives was intercepted by the Cognizances Nem Kilmo and Jair Zannajair, who seemed to spring from nowhere. Both savants were sweaty and exhausted, with dilated pupils reflecting the effect of the Cognitive medication temporarily shielding them from the worst ravages of the darkness. Their aspect brightened at sight of Vallage.

"Preeminence, you are greatly needed," Kilmo announced without preamble. "The Cognizant Rom Usine believes he's hit upon a method of reducing the toxicity of the darkness, but desires to consult you before proceeding. Zannajair and I have obtained results suggesting that the shadow may undergo a constant

213

process of self-renewal, but at present our combined abilities are unequal to the task of subversion. Caus Zellacaus wants your advice on the subject of—"

"Gentlemen, I am eager to confer with each, and will do so at the earliest opportunity," Vallage assured them. "However, the urgency of the matter at hand admits of no delay."

"The matter at hand, Preeminence?"

"I stand upon the very brink of a discovery whose significance may well alter the course of all our lives. Prudence, however, necessitates immediate verification of certain facts, and therefore I must seek the Archives, where I prefer to work undisturbed and in solitude."

"Preeminence, surely you realize—"

"Gentlemen, I shall join you as soon as may be. In the meantime, do not slacken your efforts." Vallage turned and stalked off down the hall.

Kilmo and Zannajair traded glances of disbelief.

"Did he not understand us?" asked Zannajair.

"Better than we understand him, I think," said Kilmo. "I'd give much to know the nature of Vallage's research."

Kilmo's sentiment was shared by many, and Gless Vallage found the Archives uncomfortably populous. Technically his demand for solitude was honored, for none of the savants addressed or approached him; but collective curiosity was intense. The nature of the folios sought by his Preeminence was noted, and the whispers flew. Vallage's investigations remained a source of interest until superseded by a matter of infinitely greater import and immediacy. Word reached the Nessiva that a luminous army of Vardruls had gathered on the plain before the city wall. Attack was undoubtedly imminent.

Drained by sickness and exertion, the savants knew themselves incapable of massive Cognitive resistance. Lanthi Ume was beyond salvation, her citizens doomed. Thus despairing, they turned their collective attention to the one last essential task that remained within their power to perform—preservation of the priceless Selectic Archives, treasury of Cognitive lore since the days of Nes the Eyes.

Within his nearly deserted palace, Duke Bofus wandered forlorn and forsaken. Down the gloomy corridors he trudged, golden candelabrum clutched in one chubby hand. His pace was slow, his expression despondent, his progress purposeless. Ever so often he paused to survey his surroundings—as much of them as he could see—with an air of incredulous, uncomprehending misery. Presently he neared an open window, and his attention was caught by the shouts of the crowd gathered upon the Ducal moorings two stories below. The Duke squinted down through the dark. He could make out a faint glimmer of lantern light, a vague swirl of agitated humanity. The voices rising to his ears were unmistakably hostile, and a frown furrowed the Ducal brow. His subjects were angry! Fear and distress at such a time he could well understand, but anger? And at him, their Duke?

It did not occur to him to summon Commander Frayner and the few remaining Ducal Guardsmen. Without an instant's hesitation Bofus turned and sped along the gallery, down the central staircase, through the entrance hall and out the great front portal. At the head of the broad canalside stairs he paused, somewhat at a loss.

The Ducal presence was quickly noted, and a roar of passionate protest arose.

"Good people—my dear friends—" Bofus shouted to make himself heard above the din. "How have I incurred your wrath? Tell me my offense and I'll make amends as best I may. I'll repent and reform within the hour, I promise." The uproar began to subside, and the Duke continued, "I understand your suffering, in which we all share, but not your anger. Surely you don't hold me responsible for this plague of darkness, when I'd do anything in the world to set matters right? Dear friends, I'd give my life gladly if I thought it would do any good!"

This plea appeared to appease the crowd somewhat. The cries died away and, following a moment's confused silence, one of the men at the foot of the stairs spoke up. His figure was short and sturdy. His features were all but lost in the gloom. "Your Grace, you've done nothing to rouse our anger. You've done nothing, period, and that's the trouble. We want a leader and we want action. Now, while we've still got the strength to move at all, before the sickness lays us all so low that we can't lift a finger to defend ourselves. You're Duke, you should do something."

"But what's to be done?" the Duke inquired earnestly.

"Fight back, that's what! We don't plan to sit around twiddling our thumbs until they come to slaughter us like sheep. Fight back now!"

"Fight the darkness?"

"Not the darkness, your Grace. The White Demons."

"White Demons?" Bofus opened his blue eyes wide. "I don't understand you."

"They're here, your Grace. The Demon army's waiting at our gates."

"An army at our gates? How do you know? I mean, you can't *see* anything out there, can you? Even if there is an army, what makes you think they're demons and not men like ourselves?"

"You can see for yourself, sir. They glow even in this darkness, and you can see them from the city wall."

"What's more," another man spoke up, "a couple of the lads snuck out to get a look close up at them, and they come back and tell us the creatures aren't any kind of men. They're White Demons."

"I wouldn't want to question the veracity of the lads," Duke Bofus answered mildly. "I'm sure they believe that everything they tell you is true. But sometimes young people get excited and make mistakes—"

"There's no mistake, your Grace. But you don't have to believe us or the lads if you don't want. Just come with us to the wall and take a real good look."

"Yes. Yes, that sounds reasonable." Bofus nodded with increasing conviction. "Yes, I'll come with you. Right now, if you like."

A ragged cheer went up. The Duke's pliability appeared to have reestablished his popularity. A moment later Bofus was hurrying toward the city wall at the head of a crowd of his torch-bearing subjects. It was a long walk, and Bofus—pudgy and sedentary at the best of times, and now additionally debilitated by the darkness—soon wearied. His face reddened and his breath shortened. Much as he longed for rest, he did not dare to slacken his pace. The march continued until at last he arrived, footsore and puffing, at the base of the city wall. A flight of stone steps led to the summit, where the great bonfires blazed. The Duke ascended, and the citizens surged in his wake. Bofus stopped short at the top of the wall, and his breath caught in his throat. Before him on the midnight plain spread a great amorphous pool of soft light. For a moment he gaped in wonder, astonished by the strangeness and beauty. Then he became aware of a voice at his shoulder:

"The White Demons."

The Duke did not attempt reply. His eyes remained fixed on the subtly shifting luminosity, and as he watched, it seemed to him that he could discern the individual graceful, lambent figures occasionally detaching themselves from the main mass of light, to enjoy brief independent existence before merging once again with the whole. The report was true. An army waited at the wall.

And still Bofus stared as if enchanted, until the voice at his shoulder inquired:

"I wonder what it takes to kill them?"

"Kill them?" A shocked refusal rose to the Duke's lips, but died unspoken. With a pang, he recognized before him the enemies of Lanthi Ume, of all humanity. For a moment longer he stared almost yearningly, then tore his eyes from the weirdly beautiful spectacle. Taking a deep breath, he spoke with an effort. "Well, you know, the Vayno Fortification was built to defend Lanthi Ume against landward attack, wasn't it? There are the cannon and all. I think we might explain the situation to the Lammish fellows still holed up in there. Once they understand, I believe they might let us in; then the cannon can be used against that army out there—"

"We were hoping your Grace would say that!"

"If those Chamberpots try to keep us out of the Vayno, they'll learn what we can do!"

"The White Demons will learn the same!"

"Do you think the cannons will do any good, though?" someone in the crowd inquired. "Against demons? Can they die?"

"They may be demons," came the confident reply, "but they can die, all right. Our cannon will do for them."

And even as the optimist spoke, the glowing army out on the plain faded completely from view. It was at that moment the Vardruls donned their cloaks and masks, extinguishing their own light, but the human spectators could not know that. One moment the White Demons were there, shining in plain sight; the next, they were gone as if they had never been. Cries of consternation arose, followed by dreadful silence finally broken when someone opined:

"We're finished."

"Oh, you mustn't say that," Duke Bofus pleaded. "You must not give up hope, my dear friends! We're still alive, aren't we?"

"Yes, but for how long, your Grace? How can we fight an invisible army?"

"Our cannon are useless."

"We're almost too sick to fight anyway."

"We're helpless."

"Not yet, we aren't." The speaker was the short, sturdy citizen who had confronted Duke Bofus upon the Ducal moorings. "Here's what I think. Our chances aren't good. We're few, we're sick and getting sicker by the hour, we've darkness and invisible Demons to deal with. All things considered, it's likely we're cooked. Be that as it may, I think that most of us want to strike a blow for our homes, and that doesn't mean sitting around waiting for the White Demons to finish us off at their leisure. It means pulling ourselves together as best we can, going out there and hitting them before they're ready. We're not apt to win, but we'll go down fighting, and we'll take plenty of them with us. At the very least, those twinkle-skinned maggots will know they've been in a fight. I think that's about the best we can do, and we'd better act now, while we can. Are you with me?"

A roar of confirmation arose. Duke Bofus watched with parted lips and astonished eyes.

"Then let's get started," urged the anonymous demagogue. "First we'll give the Demons a taste of our cannon. Even if they're invisible, that'll throw a scare into them. For that we've got to get into the Vayno. With any luck the Chamberpots will listen to reason, so we need to send a delegation over there. Secondly, we need to scour the town for every able-bodied citizen willing to fight. Next, let's try talking to the Select. They may be strange, but they're Lanthian and they're smart. No telling what they may come up with."

A storm of disapprobation greeted this suggestion. Even desperation could not quell the distrust of citizen for savant. While the arguments raged, Duke Bofus stepped forward and spoke timidly. "Some of Commander Frayner's men are still here. We could ask the Guardsmen for help."

"That's good, your Grace, that's excellent!"

Bofus beamed.

"Then let it be done," the other commanded.

"Let it be done!" Bofus echoed, adding masterfully, "And no more delay!"

Chapter Sixteen

They had stumbled into a gigantic maze. The stone walls glistening with slime; the stalactites sprouting overhead; the shy, demon-faced bats; and above all, the awesome size of the place: these things convinced them they had found the caverns at last.

Once accepting this, they paused in the dark to consider their course. Quietly they huddled around the single lighted lantern, conferring in voices pitched discreetly low.

"So. We have arrived at last, thanks entirely to his Lordship's perspicacity. Now what? Now where?" demanded Grono.

"Legitimate questions," replied Wate Basef. In the weak orange light his face was haggard and unsmiling. It would seem he no longer chose to waste precious energy upon sarcasm. "We've two concerns. The first is locating the records we need. The second—escaping the notice of the inhabitants. In these endeavors Cognition will aid us, and this time you won't find me unprepared. Now. Don't distract me." Without further explanation he opened his leather satchel and withdrew a small bronze figure, crude but recognizably human. Bowing his head, he spoke almost inaudibly. Despite his look of sickly exhaustion, his strength of mind and will must have been nearly unimpaired, for he achieved Cognition swiftly. Success was signaled by the gradual lessening of the bronze figurine's substantiality. As the group watched raptly, the little figure lightened, took on a smoky translucency, and faded to the threshold of visibility. By the time Wate Basef raised his head and opened his eyes, he seemed to hold a bit of captive fog. Carefully he returned the transformed figurine to the satchel, then took a moment to compose himself before announcing, "We are veiled in Heejin's Glamor."

"You don't mean you've worked your mumbo jumbo on *us*, Master Wate Basef? What have you done to us *this time*?"

"Grono, please keep your voice down," Devras requested quietly. "From now on, whisper."

"Heejin's Glamor," Wate Basef explained, "epitomizes misdirection. It will deflect the attention of all whom we encounter."

"You mean, you've made us invisible?" asked Devras.

"No. You mustn't think it. We aren't invisible, we are simply inconspicuous. With a little care, we'll escape notice."

"Care?" asked Karavise.

"We walk lightly," Wate Basef told her. "We speak in whispers and infrequently. If we meet anyone, we stand motionless, preferably in shadow. Given these precautions, we'll attract little attention, if any."

"I do not feel any different," declared Grono. "What's more, I see the three of you quite clearly. None of us seem changed."

"We aren't changed," replied Wate Basef. "The Cognition shrouding us alters the perceptions of others. In effect, they simply won't look at us, provided we take care. But make no mistake, this is weak Cognition—all I can afford right now, and easily penetrable. A misplaced word, a cough, a sudden gesture, and we'll be seen, right enough. And in any event, the Glamor is temporary, lasting only few hours."

"Can a senior member of the Select do no better for us?"

"I must conserve my Cognitive energy, Grono. I'll need it all when we find what we're looking for."

"How shall we know where to begin searching?" asked Karavise.

"There's Rillif Har Fennahar's bracelet," Devras suggested. "Raith says it warms in proximity to Cognitive articles. It will take some time, but eventually—"

"Too slow," Wate Basef interrupted. "I'll use Cognition to seek Cognition. That much I can spare." The procedure that followed mystified the observers. At the conclusion of his ritual the savant opened his eyes to declare, "I've located a Cognitive force—a strong one. In fact I don't understand how a mere collection of old writings could possibly send forth so powerful a—well, no matter. I've a sense of the direction and distance that we want, and a hazy image of our destination."

"Is it far from here?" asked Karavise. Her face was expressionless, but the signs of sickness and exhaustion were plain to see.

"Quite. We face hours of walking. The best I can tell you is that I've sensed no major obstacles in our path."

"Then let us start at once," she returned steadily. He hesitated, evidently gauging her strength, and she added, "Come, there's no point in delay."

Wate Basef inclined his head. "Follow close behind me, then. Walk softly. Don't speak unnecessarily. Above all, if you see or hear anything of the inhabitants, stand perfectly still and trust in the Glamor."

They obeyed, and the dark time that followed was nerve-racking but essentially uneventful. Through the tunnel they glided in silence, senses probing the blackness ahead. A multitude of tunnels branched, twisted, met and diverged before them, inviting confusion; but Wate Basef seemed blessedly sure of his way. Rarely did he hesitate, and never for long. The minutes lengthened into featureless hours. The moist stone walls plodded by. The tunnels appeared deserted, and there was no sign whatever of the inhabitants. Only twice in as many hours was their progress briefly arrested, once by a sudden vigorous whirring, once by an erratic thudding sound. In each case Wate Basef snuffed the lantern and the group froze into motionless silence until the noises were respectively identified as a solitary bat and water dripping from the ceiling. In the face of prolonged tedium, their vigilance gradually relaxed. Their pace quickened, and occasionally they conversed in muted tones. Thus it was that Grono, walking at the end of the line, did not hesitate to inform the others of his observation:

"Gentlemen, your Ladyship—the air's glowing."

It was true. The hot, moist air was charged with a whisper of pale luminescence—the ghost of a light, so faint that they doubted their own perceptions.

"Reflected lantern light?" Karavise spoke doubtfully.

"Reflected off what, your Ladyship?"

"Something in the air? Dust? Vapor?"

"Illusion?"

"Dangerous?"

"What isn't, in this place?"

The questions were momentarily unanswerable. Reluctantly they moved on, their path leading down along steep inclines, ever deeper into the bowels of the caverns. As they went, it seemed that the glow intensified. A little farther and there could be no doubt—the humid air was softly brightening all around them.

Devras studied the walls, the floors, the dripping ceiling. "It isn't the air," he observed. "The rock shines with its own light."

"Why should it do so, Master Devras?"

"Don't know, Grono. It's just characteristic of this type of stone. The natural philosopher Mas Ravileen calls the phenomenon 'Cold Fire,' and names it as the source of moonlight." Devras considerately forbore mentioning Mas Ravileen's belief in the power of rock-light to drive men mad.

The tunnel broadened and brightened. The pale radiance

strengthened by the moment and presently, for the first time since they had fled into Fal Grizhni's shadow, they were able to extinguish the lantern. Devras took a deep breath of warm air free of the stench of Cognitive darkness, and even in the depths of that alien, inimical place, felt his spirits rise. The misery began to lift, and for the first time in all those uncounted black hours, something akin to hope stirred in his mind.

They emerged from the tunnel into a wide chamber where countless stalactites dripped from the ceiling in translucent clusters, mineral lace frilled the stalagmites, and violet puffballs ballooned underfoot. There they stopped to rest briefly. Seating himself upon a mica-flecked stone, Devras surveyed his surroundings with reawakening interest. Most of the floor was covered with puffball colonies interspersed with silvery octahedral crystals, black nightwort, circular patches of parti-colored toadstools and lavish tufts of white hagsbeard. The natural contiguity of such disparate species was unlikely, the regularity of their alternation even more so.

"It's a garden," he realized.

"This poisonous hodgepodge?" Grono frowned in disbelief.

"I'm sure of it. Look at the way those crystals line up in rows, and see how each black stone is always surrounded by white fungi. That never happened by accident."

"Then the inhabitants must be very near," said Karavise.

As if in response to the observation, a Vardrul glided into the chamber through one of the fissures that gashed the opposite wall. The four shocked humans froze.

It was a very small, immature Vardrul of indeterminate gender, obviously too young to fight Surface with its kinsmen. The child was a miniature of the soldiers they had seen beside the River Yl—same lambent white flesh, tentacular fingers, fleshless features and huge sea-foam eyes. Upon its wrist crouched a brace of tiny albino bats.

The child's gaze swept the chamber, passing over the motionless humans. Obviously the alien presence had gone undetected by the Vardrul, but the bats, immune to Heejin's Glamor, noted the intruders at once. With a flutter of snowy leathern wings they took to the air, swooping in wide, distraught curves, circling hysterically above the intruders' heads. Often they dived low, passing so near that Devras felt the breeze through his hair. With effort the humans sat motionless, neither flinching nor blinking.

The Vardrul child watched closely in what was probably puzzlement. Its two inner ocular ridges expanded, and the brightness of its flesh faded. Advancing to the middle of the room, it halted a few feet from the Cognitively self-effacing intruders. Its great eyes were fixed upon the agitated bats. Its flesh brightened, dimmed, flashed twice and dimmed in what was evidently a signal. The bats responded promptly, returning to their owner's wrist. Again the child's searching gaze swept the room, and a soft trill of unknowable import broke from its lipless mouth. Turning, it hurried back to the fissure through which it had entered, and with a last bright backward glance, slid lithely through the narrow opening.

For a few moments following the child's departure, the humans sat breathlessly still. Paralysis passed, but a renewed sense of caution remained. They rose, and Wate Basef led them quietly from the chamber, through an archway studded with crystalline clusters, along a gallery lined with massive natural columns, and into a passage so narrow that they had to advance sideways. There was no more conversation, for now they stole through the tunnels with the stealth of the hunted. Emerging from the narrow passage, they found themselves walking a broad, high corridor with curving walls curtained in richly hued slime. They had arrived at the height of the Crimson Coloration, and the rock-light filtering through the flora glowed red. Here they began to discover obvious signs of Vardrul habitation. The tunnel had been artificially widened and leveled, the walls artificially smoothed. The great standing stones placed at regular intervals along the corridor were carven, and friezes of shadow-sculpture decorated the walls.

Farther and deeper. On they walked through a silent gallery of wonders, along a twisted path that carried them ever downward. The pale rock-light played upon marvelous natural fretwork, spears of golden crystal, frozen cataracts and draperies of stone. Twice more they encountered isolated Vardruls, and each time Heejin's Glamor preserved them. The Vardruls passed by unseeing, for all the brilliance of their great eyes. The infrequency of these encounters revealed the scarcity of remaining inhabitants. Nearly all the population had followed the Patriarch to Surface.

On and deeper along a low and twisting corridor, through a succession of small jeweled chambers strung together like beads, and out into an unadorned, undistinguished tunnel thrusting down through the rock. The tunnel narrowed to a puny bridge arching above a fanged chasm. Beyond the chasm, the trail led through a maze of passageways so convoluted that Devras wondered how, if ever, they would find their way out again. And with that thought came the first conscious recognition of escape's improbability. They had already ventured too far and too deep to expect a safe retreat. They had buried themselves alive.

Doubt receded temporarily when the Har Fennahar bracelet began to heat. Devras felt the first flush of warmth at his wrist and he looked down. The familiar silver band glinted in the rock-light. Never before had he understood its seemingly spontaneous changes in temperature. Now, thanks to Wate Basef's explanation, he knew the cause—proximity of some Cognitively influenced object. The heat increased with every step; another few minutes of walking, and his wrist was smarting painfully. He slid the bracelet off and dropped it into his pocket.

Another few yards down a sloping corridor, as far as a wide arched opening flanked by a massive stalagmite, behind which they sought refuge. Their path led through the arch, but the chamber beyond was occupied by a pair of tall, unusually muscular Vardruls armed with steel-spiked staves and heavy blades sized somewhere between knife and short sword. Evidently a few able-bodied inhabitants had remained behind to guard the caves. Both guards stood near a curious device occupying a low dais in the middle of the room. The device—an opaque boxlike structure surmounted by four bright hemispheres—appeared indefinably alien in that place. The rigidly symmetrical design, uncharacteristic of Vardrul tastes, somehow suggested human manufacture.

What is that thing? Devras wondered. *And how do we get past it?* His questioning gaze jumped to Raith Wate Basef.

The savant stood mouthing inaudible arcane syllables. His sense of urgency must have been profound, for him to expend a portion of his priceless Cognitive energy at such a time. Within the chamber, the two Vardrul guards went inanimate. The light drained from their flesh and the intelligence from their great eyes. Motionless and cloudy-orbed they stood all unaware.

"I've slowed their lives to a snail's pace," Wate Basef explained in a quick whisper. "For them, we now move too quickly to perceive, but that effect won't last long. Come, there's our way." He pointed at a fissure on the far side of the room.

Through the arch in single file, then past the oblivious guards they hurried, skirting the edge of the dais whereon stood the device that bore such a puzzlingly human stamp; somehow speaking of Surface and of Men. The sight of human handiwork in such a place stirred emotions so compelling that Devras could not forbear asking, "What is it?"

"A heating device," Wate Basef told him. "Select-crafted and very ancient. Perhaps created by Terrs Fal Grizhni himself—it

224

looks old enough for that. I didn't know this was here, but I knew that something like it must be. Nothing else would explain the warmth of these caverns."

"If the device is as old as you say, it could malfunction. What then?"

"Then woe to the White Demons, for Nature will reassert herself with a vengeance. The Cognitively banished cold will return with a rush, all the frustrated chill of centuries striking back at once to freeze and paralyze these tunnels. The Vardruls would be devastated, for they can't abide the cold; it stupefies them. But there's little chance of that—a well-constructed Cognitive device doesn't spontaneously fail."

"No wonder they station guards here." As he spoke, Devras glanced over his shoulder to check the condition of the decelerated sentries, and what he saw drew a gasp. The two guards stood motionless and unseeing. But framed in the entry were three more, armed and fully aware. No question that the newcomers saw straight through Heejin's Glamor. Their brilliant eyes shifted from humans to unconscious kinsmen and back again, their skin flickered erratically, and their fluting cries echoed weirdly.

The humans spun to face the sound. For a confused moment the two groups locked astonished eyes. In that instant Cognition buckled, and the lives of the two ensorcelled sentries regained their accustomed velocity. The sentries' luminosity leaped, and their ocular ridges writhed. Following an exchange of melodious warblings the five Vardruls glided forward, steel-tipped staves raised and ready. They handled the weapons with easy expertise. No hope at all of fighting the creatures.

"Through the fissure," Wate Basef commanded, and sprinted for the opening.

Run? What use, now we've been seen? Raith will have to use his Cognition, no choice. Even as these thoughts flashed through his mind, Devras was already running as fast as prolonged debilitation allowed. Karavise gasped along beside him, Grono stumbled close behind. The Vardruls fanned out to intercept them and Wate Basef changed course abruptly, angling off toward a low, jagged gap in the wall. Ducking low, he vanished through the hole, and the pursuers fluted aloud.

Another ten paces, head down, back hunched, down low and Devras was through the gap and into a narrow gallery. Karavise still beside him, footsteps hurrying in his wake, and the eerie music of the Vardruls singing through the tunnel, shivering in the air around him. Along the gallery, breath scraping now, until the tunnel opened like a flower, with half a dozen passages shooting off in all directions. Raith Wate Basef was nowhere to be seen. He had disappeared down one of those passages, impossible to say which. No time to think about it. Six long paces, veer to the left and slide through the gap, with Karavise right behind him. A quick backward glance and there came Grono, pale and panting; just behind him, the tall and luminous forms of the guards.

How to lose them? In such a maze of a place, it ought to be easy to throw them off the track. The passage was narrow and tall, little more than a crevice with walls sheer and featureless. No gaps, no crannies, no hiding place, and the walls pressed in closer with every step. Then the stone jaws widened and again there were niches, excavations, diverging corridors and choices. The path zigzagged sharply a couple of times, interposing baffles of stone between hunters and fugitives. The sound of pursuit faded.

Straight down the corridor sped Devras and Karavise, as far as a fork in the path, where they looked back to discover that Grono was no longer with them. Somewhere along the way the valet had fallen behind, and now he was gone. They halted, breathless and shaky.

"I'm going back for him." Devras turned.

"No. Wait." Spent though she was, gasping as she leaned on the wall for support, Karavise remained cool. "If he's behind us, he'll be here in a moment. If's he's not, there's nothing the two of us can do for him."

Devras nodded grudgingly.

A moment's silence; then the thud of hurrying feet, and a luminous quintet burst into view. The humans fled.

Deadly tired now, lost and drowning in the hot, humid air, they stumbled along a branching tunnel; turned to the left, then left again, and found themselves in a narrow little finger of a passage ending in a blank stone wall. Turning to retrace their steps, they met the Vardrul guards grouped at the head of the passage. The creatures' flesh shone moon-bright. Their melodious voices vibrated with incomprehensible emotion. Daggerpointed staves leveled, the White Demons advanced.

The rock-lit caverns held no interest for Mistress Snarp. Immune to the glories, indifferent to the wonders, her bloodshot gaze anchored on the quibbid pattering along the floor before her. The animal followed the quarry's trail through the corridors with relative ease. Indeed, in comparison to the darkness above, the caverns provided a wholesome atmosphere, and the quibbid was already recovering its health and spirits. The same could not be said of its mistress. Feverish and festering, juiceless and skeletal, Snarp resembled a refugee from the tomb. Her right arm hung puffed and oozing. Her back was hunched to favor the fractured rib. Her face, fungus-pale, was the face of a dead thing. Only her eyes, burning with a yellow light of fanaticism, reflected unconquered vitality. Her pace was steady and relentless as ever. Pausing to rest only when the quibbid showed signs of fatigue, she stalked the caves like a corpse possessed by a demon.

Throughout the course of her subterranean explorations, she had encountered no living creature, but that good fortune could not continue indefinitely. She had long since lost track of the corridors, galleries, chambers and excavations. She had not marked the twists and turns, the protracted, spiraling descent. Her attention was fixed exclusively upon the tracking quibbid, or so it might have appeared. But Mistress Snarp was never truly unaware of her surroundings.

A stirring in the air, an infinitesimal flash of movement behind the nearest column, and Snarp leaped sideways to confront a flickering White Demon. It was her first clear, close view of a Demon, but she did not pause to marvel. The creature was fleeing, no doubt to warn its cohorts of her presence. Instantly the knife sprouted from Snarp's left hand, the good hand, and she thrust deep. Colorless blood gushed, and the Demon fell without a sound, the light swiftly fading from its flesh. Snarp bent to retrieve her weapon. Reassured by its mistress' gesture and intrigued by the nature of the victim, the quibbid sidled near. Tail jerking in excitement, huge ears fully unfurled, it sniffed at the feebly twitching Demon. Confidence mounting, the quibbid hopped onto the Demon's back to nose the wound and lick the limpid blood.

The Vardrul, not quite dead, uttered a desolate cry. Its flesh blazed with a light like the last great effulgence of a dying star, and a final violent convulsion racked the spare white form. The quibbid, flung from the heaving body, flew through the air to strike the tunnel wall head-on. Down it fell and lay still, neck broken.

Snarp did not change expression. Not a muscle in her face moved. Only one word escaped her. "No," she said calmly, as if denying an obvious impossibility. She waited. The quibbid did not stir.

A minor turbulence passed over Snarp's features, but still she spoke calmly. "Come, little beauty, we must go. Up, lovely lazybones."

The quibbid lay still. A few spots of blood matted its fur.

227

Kneeling, Snarp extended an unsteady hand, lifted one of the flaccid ears and let it fall again. With two fingers she raised the tiny head on its too-limp neck, then gently laid it down. There was something wrong with her breathing. The air had to force its way past some obstruction in her throat. Her eyes were dim and swimming in acid. Tremors shook her from head to foot. For this brief moment, she was helpless. While waiting for her body to right itself, she softly smoothed the quibbid's rumpled fur.

Her vision cleared at last. The quibbid lay a few feet from the White Demon, both creatures indisputably dead. Snarp spoke shudderingly aloud. "It is his doing. He has murdered you, my heart's delight. I will carry his bald head back to Lanthi Ume in a sack."

Carefully she lifted the quibbid, placing the little cadaver in her pack. Perhaps she intended future rites of burial, or perhaps she simply could not endure a parting. Pack refastened, she rose to shoot a searching stare up and down the corridor. Deprived of the quibbid's tracking ability, she would have to rely upon her own particular arts to locate the quarry. Of her ultimate success she had not the slightest doubt. Without another glance to spare for the dead Vardrul, Snarp resumed the hunt. Through the pale rock-light she stole, alert to the faintest sign of Raith Wate Basef's passing. Her feral glance stabbed restlessly this way and that. The stony corridor told her nothing, and gradually the blaze of fanaticism kindling the feverish eyes took on a red tinge of madness.

"In a sack," said Snarp, and went her way.

On the shore of his clan's death-pool, the Grizhni Greater Patriarch watched the light fade irrevocably from the flesh of his last kinsman. Grizhni Inrl's final Ancestral joining was gentle, painless, warm with peace and fulfillment. One could only rejoice in so sweet a union, or so it should have been. The Patriarch, however, could not rejoice.

Inrl was last of the kinsmen. From this Coloration onward, Grizhni T'rzh was alone in the world. The other clans remained, of course. The race of Vardruls continued, and that was much, for the sense of racial unity lent great comfort. But never again would the Patriarch know the sense of belonging, the burst of inner light or the current of feeling that passed at a touch between kinsmen. With the death of Grizhni Inrl, those joys were lost forever. Clan Grizhni, dissonant from the beginning, had consumed itself at last, and the world no longer held a place for it. And as for the last Grizhni Patriarch, he must somehow muster the fortitude to endure a clanless existence until the Small Ven of his own Ancestral joining.

Inrl lay at peace and lightless. The beloved kinsman/teacher surely merited the most reverent obsequies, presided over by the Patriarch he had tutored. But the clans were assembled Surface, even now awaiting the return of their general. The Grizhni himself could not remain to celebrate the joining of his only kinsman, and Inrl must sink beneath the waters of the death-pool all but unattended—a discourtesy to the welcoming Ancestors, but unavoidable.

A muted thunder of wings broke The Grizhni's reverie. He looked up to behold a great brown bat circling below the vaulted ceiling. He extended his wrist and the bat descended. The tiny pouch on the animal's collar yielded a set of pebbles whose colors communicated an urgent summons.

The Grizhni emerged with reluctance. In the corridor outside the death-pool chamber he encountered Dfjnr'l Gallr, who carried incredible news. There were human beings in the caverns. Two of them had been captured alive.

Chapter Seventeen

The room was bare and bleak, devoid of furnishings, vegetation or mineral formations. Its appearance suited its present function —prison cell—save for the absence of a locked door. There was no door at all, locked or otherwise, such appurtenances hardly existing within the caverns. A broad split in the wall offered sole means of ingress or egress. In the corridor outside the room stood three armed Vardrul guards.

Devras sat on the floor, his back to the wall. Beside him sat Karavise, motionless and seemingly inert. So they had sat in silence throughout the period of their captivity. Devras studied his companion's profile. She appeared indifferent, and he wondered what lay behind the expressionless mask. Her pale face disclosed nothing, and he could only hope that his own was equally unrevealing; but it was hard to pretend indifference in the face of disaster. With discovery came defeat and destruction— Lanthi Ume's, together with personal destruction, for by all accounts the White Demons took no human prisoners. It was astonishing that he and Karavise still lived. He could only assume that they had been preserved for questioning, and who could guess what methods of interrogation the creatures might employ?

What's happened to Grono and Raith? Is there any chance they'll escape this place? Forget Fal Grizhni's records, Raith, he urged silently. *Just get yourself and Grono out alive, if you can.*

A slight commotion in the corridor outside; a musical hum of conversation; then a new figure appeared in the doorway and Devras repressed a start of surprise. He remembered the tall, straight, spare form with the all-but-lightless skin; the unusual jointed fingers; and above all the intelligent, intensely black eyes. He recognized the Vardrul general first glimpsed leading his army along the bank of the River Yl. It could be no other, yet what was the general doing here, back in the caves? The sight of the nameless leader exerted a peculiar effect, at once fearsome and appealing. The force and sentience beaming from those midnight eyes might have been partially responsible, but that wasn't all of it. Nothing adequately explained Devras's sense of connection between himself and the general—of shared emotion, instinctive mutual comprehension. A ridiculous delusion, of course. The being before him was enemy to all mankind. His thoughts and impulses would be alien, inimical; and if his black eyes possessed some power of fascination, it was a lure designed to paralyze the judgment of his prey, nothing more. For all that, Devras could scarcely look away, nor could he rid himself of the notion that a bond existed; not physical, but very real. Did Karavise experience anything of the sort? With an effort, he tore his eyes from the general to glance at her. She was watching the newcomer with cold, concentrated animosity. Probably she recognized him, impossible to be sure. Both prisoners stood.

The general walked into the room, paused and addressed his startled captives in perfect, if careful and oddly accented Lanthian. "Questions. Who are you? Why have you come to this place? How many have accompanied you? Answer."

His voice was low, resonant, inhumanly melodic. Devras's sense of inappropriate empathy intensified at the sound of it, and a truthful answer rose quite naturally to his lips. Deliberately he repressed it. Karavise similarly maintained grim silence.

The ridges of muscle surrounding the general's eyes expanded slightly in a manner whose significance escaped the observers. "It is known that others of your kind have come to our caverns. How many?"

There was something resistless in the music of that voice. Unable to withhold all response, Devras replied unrevealingly with a question of his own. "Where have you learned the language of Men?"

"Many of us know it, to some degree. For those of my clan in particular, it is the language of the Ancestors." The apparent openness of the answer surprised both listeners, perhaps surprised the general himself, who had little reason to confide in a human intruder whose execution was a foregone conclusion. "We are at war, and it must be assumed that your intent is destructive. Yet I am informed that you were found to be unarmed. Have you secreted weapons somewhere about the caverns? What is your purpose here? Answer." There was no reply, and the general produced an exhalation something like a human sigh. "Come, will you force me to resort to the methods of your own kind? Must I compel your answer by means of cruelty? Ugly and discordant beyond measure that would be, but if necessary I will do it."

Underlying the threat, Devras heard or thought to hear a note

231

of pain; a kind of bleak, disillusioned emptiness approaching despair. Why he should have thought so was unclear, for the Vardrul vocal conventions expressive of emotion were altogether unfamiliar. Why he should respond with more sympathy than fear was equally mystifying. It was as if his perceptions were warped, and he had lost the capacity to recognize an enemy.

Such was not the case with Karavise. Her blue eyes were icy as she replied, "Do as you wish, but spare us your hypocrisy. You and your people have proved yourselves capable of every cruelty. Without provocation you have slaughtered the innocent and the inoffensive. You yourself are as bloody and rapacious a killer as any human ever born."

The Vardrul's flesh brightened slightly. The equivalent human reaction would have involved a rush of blood to the cheeks, but the prisoners did not know that. Devras divined something of it, but did not trust his own interpretation.

"Take care," the general advised, voice as melodic as ever.

"Why?" Karavise's brows rose. "You will kill us, whatever we say. That being so, why shall I not indulge myself?"

The general's fingers undulated in a gesture of assent, performed awkwardly by Vardrul standards. The light faded from his flesh and he replied, "Woman, there are many things you do not understand. You speak of our crimes, our violence, our disharmony—those things that are the traditional province of mankind. You forget the sufferings we have undergone at the hands of Men, the outrages and injustice."

"I am aware of none," returned Karavise.

"Not in your lifetime, perhaps, for I perceive you are young. Learn now of the misery you humans have inflicted upon us—the terror, death, and unutterable grief. You have driven us from our Surface home in Great Vens past. You drove us underground and even there you persecuted us, sending your soldiers with their steel blades to decimate the clans. You harried us, you hunted us and killed without mercy, when we had offered no offense. We suffered greatly, and the suffering reverberates through our minds and bodies to this very moment. But always the Ancestors promised reparation, and now the time of reckoning has come. By our deeds is harmony restored." The general ostensibly addressed Karavise, but his eyes rested as often on Devras, and their expression was indefinable.

"You puzzle me," Karavise replied after a moment's thought. "You cite offenses of which I know nothing. They are not men-

232

tioned in our histories. I am aware of no Lanthian attacks upon your caverns—nor Hurbanese, Lammish or Rhelish military action, for that matter."

"Be certain they occurred."

"What proof have you of that?"

"The agony of the Ancestors."

"I do not understand you, but let us say that it is true. It happened then in the dim and distant past."

"By our reckoning, the past is neither dim nor distant," replied the general. "It is with us always."

"Perhaps. But that does not alter the fact that *we* have not harmed you," replied Karavise. "We humans now living have offered no offense, no more than did your innocent ancestors. Must we be held responsible for the misdeeds of our forebears—people we never knew, dead these many generations? Where is the justice in that?"

"And now I do not understand you," the Vardrul told her. "Do we not speak of your clans, your blood kin, your own Ancestors? Are they not of your flesh, part of you and with you always? Why distinguish between your own deeds and those of your Ancestors, when you and your Ancestors are one? How distinguish between past and present, guilty Ancestors and innocent Descendants? There is no separating them, the one blends with the other; the joys and sorrows, crimes and virtues of each are inseparable. We know the pain and terror of our Ancestors. Do you not know the guilt of your own?"

And Devras answered, "It is not like that for us."

The eyes of the general turned to him and the ocular bands expanded slightly.

"I am not the best qualified to speak of human families," Devras continued, "as I possess none of my own."

A pronounced dimming of the general's flesh communicated his reaction to a disclosure that was by the standards of his people dreadful, unutterably sad and empty.

"But you must recognize the difference between our races. I think you may understand, for I think there's something of humanity in you." Devras saw the general flicker at that, saw the ocular ridges writhe, and wondered. "We humans are not as closely bound to our forebears as you appear to be. When all is said and done, we have little knowledge of them. There's distance, vast separation even within a single generation, and the blood that they have shed in the past does not stain us. If you punish the humans of our time for the crimes of their ancestors, you commit injustice."

"We commit none. It is only just that we reclaim the Surface home stolen from the Ancestors. Our cities are fallen and our death-pools are long since dry, but all shall we rebuild."

"The land above, the city upon the Nine Isles, these belong to my people," said Karavise.

"Stolen from the clans."

"No. It has come to us by means of legitimate inheritance, down through the generations. If our ancestors truly stole it, and that has not been proven, then our long centuries of care, tending and building have made it rightfully our own. It is our home and you shall not have it, not for all your magical poisoned shadow. Drive us out and we shall return. Kill us and others will take our places, for Lanthi Ume is ours and we shall fight to the last drop of our hearts' blood to keep her."

"And we shall fight to the last drop of our hearts' blood to take her. It is our obligation to the Ancestors. It is just. And it is necessary for the good of the race. Can you imagine what it is to think of the good of an entire people? Do you comprehend me?"

"That is something I can understand." Karavise nodded slowly. "If I were in your position, I would do as you do. I can admire your people's spirit, even sympathize with their wrongs. But that is irrelevant. Your justification—the legitimacy of your claim to the land above—that too is beside the point. Whatever the ambitions of your people, right or wrong, they will not be achieved at cost of human lives and property. We will defend ourselves and we will stop you."

"Lahnzium is all but taken. Sheltered in darkness, the clanmembers gather before the gate, awaiting the order to attack."

"*Your* order?" demanded Karavise. He rippled his fingers in assent, and her eyes took on a dangerous glitter as if, despite the obvious futility of such an attempt, she contemplated physical assault—murder—anything in the world to forestall that order. "How are you called? I should like to know my enemy's name."

The Vardrul's eyes rested upon her, black as Cognitive shadow. "Grizhni," he replied.

The two prisoners traded astonished glances, and Devras ventured at last, "That is a human name. There was a famous family of that name in Lanthi Ume."

"Here long ago from Lanthi Ume came the fugitive Grizhni Matriarch to give birth to her son, founder of the clan."

Another amazed flutter of recognition.

"Then you own much that is human," said Devras. "And you

234

cannot be altogether our enemy. Our purpose in coming to these caves was not destructive. We hope to save ourselves, but not necessarily at the expense of your people. The philosophers tell us that peace alone develops the habits of mind and heart conducive to lasting contentment. Dalyon is wide. There is room for two races Surface. May we not have peace?"

"Five hundred Great Vens ago, perhaps," said The Grizhni. "It is too late now." His flesh dimmed cadaverously.

A low hum arose in the corridor. A guard entered, conferred briefly with his Patriarch, and withdrew. The Grizhni turned to the prisoners. "Another human has been taken. He is thought to be a savant of Lanthi Ume, and for that reason his mouth has been stopped, his wrists bound, and he is under constant surveillance."

The prisoners displayed no emotion.

"If there are others, we shall find them quickly," continued the general. "And perhaps this new one will prove communicative, as you have not. I leave you now, and we will not meet again. From this place, you will proceed to the Invisible Falls. I regret that necessity, but there is no choice."

Neither prisoner chose to inquire into the nature of the Invisible Falls.

"I am convinced there is little to gain in questioning you. Therefore I promise that no unnecessary pain or indignity will be inflicted upon you. If you have any request possible to grant, now is the time to speak it."

"There is one," said Devras, after a moment's thought. "When we were searched for weapons, the guard took from me a silver bracelet. It is an old keepsake of my family, the only memento I own, and it would please me to have it back again."

"Granted." Stepping to the exit, The Grizhni addressed a command to the guards. There was a brief glint of rock-light on metal as a silvery object changed hands. The general turned back, extending the Fennahar Bracelet.

Devras took it, and his fingers touched the other's open palm. He was not prepared for the sudden brilliance flaring from the Vardrul's flesh. He could not know the powerful current of warmth and oneness that surged only at the touch of a kinsman; a warmth The Grizhni had thought lost forever with the death of Grizhni Inrl. Taken aback by the light in the Vardrul's flesh and the fire in the great black eyes, Devras took a step backward, breaking the contact.

The warmth vanished in an instant, leaving The Grizhni once more cold and solitary. He wondered if he had dreamed it. Taking a step forward he grasped the prisoner's wrist firmly, and his hiir leaped even before his mind recognized sensation. He did not stop to think, and the words sang forth strongly, "You are my kinsman."

The prisoner appeared uncomprehending, and The Grizhni added, "Your touch is the touch of a kinsman. Surely you recognize it?"

Devras was silent, staring down at the hand still imprisoned in the general's luminous clasp. Certainly he felt something faint and unfamiliar thrilling along his nerves, something nameless whose significance he could not begin to guess. Inner confirmation rose to battle reason. Confused, he replied, "I don't understand. There's a mistake."

"No. There is no mistaking the touch of a kinsman."

"Impossible. We are of different races. I am not of your people." Devras's objections were halfhearted, curiously devoid of conviction.

"There is, as you perceived, something of the human in me," said The Grizhni, black eyes fixed upon the other's face. "There are men numbered among our clan's Ancestors. They were humans of Lanthi Ume."

Devras could hardly sustain the midnight stare, and could not look away. Deeply and instinctively he believed in the truth of the general's words. Something in his blood and bones responded, some ancient recollection struggled in the depths of his mind like a mute ghost fighting for a voice. Still he resisted. "You call yourself Grizhni, and that's the name of a once-great House of Lanthi Ume. But it is not my House. I've seen the genealogical charts of my family, and I'd remember if the name of Fal Grizhni appeared there. It does not, and there's no evidence of any connection."

"The connection exists. I would trust *this*"—the long glowing fingers tightened upon the human wrist— "above all else. There can be no mistake; you are of Clan Grizhni."

"Fennahar," said Devras, slowly as if dazed. "Har Fennahar."

The Grizhni's flesh flickered at the sound of the name. "Repeat quickly," he requested, and Devras complied. The Vardrul's ocular ridges contracted. "There is the answer, my kinsman, and there is the connection. Your clan-name has come down to us in our spoken history as a distorted echo. For us, it is H'rf'nnahrzh —altered, but surely the same name."

"One of my ancestors came to this place," Devras remembered, "a very long time ago, many generations ago. He is still remembered—Rillif Har Fennahar?"

"H'rf'nnahrzh R'l, Patriarch of his clan. In the time of war he came to our caverns and lived among the Ancestors through the Small Vens, although a human. And when he departed, with him as his consort went the Grizhni Matriarch, never to return. But her son remained to take a Vardrul consort and thus found Clan Grizhni."

"The Grizhni Matriarch? Great-Grandfather Rillif was said to have married a woman named Verran. 'A fair Lanthian widow, who loved the sunlight.'" Devras quoted the old family chronicle.

"Verran, widow to the Fal Grizhni Patriarch, greatest savant of Lahnzium. Here she fled in fear of her consort's enemies, and here she remained for many Great Vens. I have never known her, though her consort I have sometimes known. But she is Ancestor to us both. It is through her we both trace our descent, it is through her that our blood connection is established, and it is through her that I discover a brother/kinsman, when I had thought myself the last of all the clan."

Light blazed from The Grizhni's flesh and eyes. Despite his amazement, Devras warmed with inner certainty. He believed it. He believed—no, he knew—that it was true. And he, who had also thought himself the last of his clan, perfectly comprehended the mind and heart of the inhuman kinsman, for in that instant they were twin to his own. Motionless, separated yet unbreakably joined, the two of them stood wondering. They might have embraced then, had not a dispassionate voice broken in upon them.

"A brother/kinsman that you will send to the Invisible Falls?" inquired Karavise dryly.

Her voice recalled them to unhappy reality. After a pause The Grizhni replied, "No harm shall befall him by my agency. No hand shall be raised against him."

"Then what are your intentions regarding us?" asked Karavise.

A measure of brilliancy fled The Grizhni's skin. The question admitted of no easy answer.

"Will you release us?" she persisted. "Or will you imprison your kinsman?"

The Grizhni lapsed into flickering silence. Impossible, almost inconceivable to inflict damage of any sort upon a kinsman—his *last* kinsman. On the other hand, the new Grizhni/H'rf'nnahrzh was wholly human, a hereditary enemy whose motives in seeking the caverns were suspect. The two attributes—kinsman and enemy—were overwhelmingly contradictory, utterly irreconcilable, their conjunction a ghastly paradox. No acceptable course of action was possible, and The Grizhni was confounded. He needed time, time to think. "It is too soon to judge," he answered at last. "And now is not the moment to deliberate. The clans await Surface and I must join them. We will meet again upon my return and there will be much to speak of. Until that time you will remain here under guard, and no harm will come to you, provided you do not attempt to leave this chamber. Farewell for now, brother/kinsman." Loosing his kinsman's wrist, The Grizhni exited the cell; paused to issue orders to the guards at the entrance, then continued along the corridor toward the Chamber of White Tunnels.

Devras stood gazing after him until the cool, deliberate voice of Karavise intruded on his thoughts and broke the spell.

"Devras. He must be stopped. I'd have attacked him with my bare hands if I'd thought it would do any good."

"No good," Devras murmured absently, eyes still fastened on the gap through which The Grizhni had departed. "The clans have already reached Lanthi Ume, he told us."

"They may be defeated yet if Raith Wate Basef turns back the darkness that poisons us. Raith is a prisoner, we don't know where, but perhaps we can liberate him without knowing. Remember what he said about that machine, the Cognitive heating device? Devras, are you listening?" she snapped.

"Yes, I remember," he replied, jolted from his reverie. "He said the device maintains the warmth of the tunnels. Without it, much of this space would be uninhabitable, since Vardruls can't stand the cold. Ah, I see what you're thinking." Abstraction fled and his attention focused sharply. "Destroy the device, and we'll see what Raith spoke of—Nature's self-assertion, and a sudden, intense chill to stupefy the Vardruls."

"All of them struck senseless at once," she nodded. "And Raith, wherever he is, may evade his unconscious guards and go on to complete his mission."

"Perhaps he could, if someone destroyed the machine. But you and I aren't likely to do it. How should we get past the three armed guards out there? Have you any ideas?"

Karavise silently considered and rejected a succession of possibilities. She shook her head.

"As far as we know, Grono is still free," Devras reminded her. "We must hope that he'll think as we do. If anyone is to reach that device, it's Grono."

Grono, however, had other ideas.

Not very much time elapsed. Devras sat on the floor as he had sat prior to The Grizhni's entrance—back to the wall, hands clasped around bent knees. Beside him rested Karavise, her posture identical, her narrowed eyes fixed on the exit through which the guards were visible, the tenor of her thoughts easy to guess. Devras's own thoughts raged in confusion; plots, plans and stratagems warring with astonished preoccupation. He must devise some means of delivering himself and his companions; but he could not think of it, could not concentrate, could not govern the mind that *would* fly back to The Grizhni's revelation, heedless of all restraint. And then his dilemma was resolved as uproar broke out in the corridor, where furious human shouts mingled with alien melody and steel clashed on steel. His head jerked up and he jumped to his feet. Karavise did likewise. Grono's warlike tones were unmistakable.

"Your Lordship, you are saved! A rescue, Master Devras, a rescue!"

Devras and Karavise ran to the exit and looked out to behold the valet, King Pusstis's cavalry saber in hand, engaged in combat with three radiant guards. It was hopeless, absurd. Grono was an old man, already weakened by exposure to Cognitive darkness, and he knew nothing of swordplay. His thrusts and slashes were passionately inept. Even as they looked on, a Vardrul blade whipped the air a hairsbreadth short of the valet's face. Grono's eyes widened behind his spectacles. He gasped and stumbled backward, sword flapping. The Vardruls pressed in, and Devras sprang forward to grasp an uplifted luminous arm from behind. Whirling, the Vardrul wrenched itself free, fluted, and raised its blade. Devras fell back as the blade descended. Steel just barely kissed his forearm, and a trace of red appeared.

"Master Devras!" Grono's scream echoed shrilly. Saber waving wildly, the valet charged and the guards converged to meet him. Blade struck blade, steel rang, and a skillful twist sent Grono's saber flying. The sword hit the wall, ricocheted and fell, but never struck the ground. The descent was neatly arrested in midair as a skeletal claw closed around the hilt. Instantly the blade leveled and flashed through the rock-lit air to pierce the breast of a Vardrul guard. The guard fell without a sound, and the dripping blade slid free. Almost without pause, a second lightning thrust and lunge dispatched a second guard. The others watched in disbelief as the wasted, corpselike figure with the ruined right arm and the eyes of sulfurous flame butchered the third and final guard. And then, before they could think or react, the feverish, lethal thing with the sword turned on them to demand hoarsely, "Where is he?"

They gaped at her in silence.

"Wate Basef," said Mistress Snarp, aspect calm and barely human. "I am taking him back to Lanthi Ume. You will hand him over to me."

They did not answer, and the saber twitched. The yellow gaze fixed on Karavise. "Speak or I will kill your woman."

She was not prepared for Grono's sudden onslaught. Without a word the valet jumped to grapple for the sword. Snarp fell back momentarily, recovered, wrenched her arm free and launched a kick that sent her opponent staggering. A second kick drove him backward into the wall. He grunted and fell to his knees. She struck his face and he went over backward, head knocking against stone. Collapsing full length, he lay still.

"Grono!" The shocked cry was wrung from Devras, and Snarp's eyes shot to his face.

The corridor was momentarily clear.

"The machine," said Karavise coolly, quietly.

Devras did not look at her. He was staring at Grono, who lay ominously quiet.

She tugged his arm. "The machine—now."

Snarp turned from the prostrate servant, who was unconscious or dead, and in either case useless. She addressed his companions without emotion. "Where is Raith Wate Basef? You will lead me to him." Saber in hand, she started for them.

Devras and Karavise turned and ran. Snarp made no move to hinder their flight. Expressionless, she stood watching them go. The fugitives displayed a stubborn reluctance to surrender the criminal Wate Basef. Forcible extraction of the information she required would involve a long and arduous effort. Far better, and infinitely more efficient, simply to let them lead her to her quarry. She would quietly follow wherever they led, and at the end of that road waited Raith Wate Basef. A minute or so would give them a good lead, but not too good. Snarp silently counted the seconds. When the allotted time was up, she tossed the clumsy saber aside and moved forward at a moderate trot.

The fugitives' pace was far more taxing, and they could not maintain it long. Frequent glances back along the tunnel revealed no sign of Mistress Snarp. It would seem they had managed to distance the Enforcer.

Or perhaps she chose to remain with Grono? What will she do to him? How could I have left him lying there helpless, not knowing if he's alive or dead? How could I have done that? The wretched, guilty self-recriminations burned in Devras's mind. With all his heart he regretted each step that carried him from his

240

fallen retainer's side. He glanced at Karavise, pale and intent beside him. *Would she doubt or hesitate? No, for she thinks only of Lanthi Ume, nothing but Lanthi Ume.*

Insensibly their footsteps slowed. They were tired, lost, confused. The passages split and twisted, forked and converged bewilderingly. In their alarm they had not noted the route by which they came, hours earlier. The pathways were numberless. Which of them led back to the chamber of the heating device? At the next divergence they paused, struggling for breath. Still no sign of pursuit, and their eyes met in mutual inquiry. Then Devras felt the first faint warming of the Har Fennahar bracelet at his wrist. He took a step into the right branch of the fork, returned and tried the left. The silver band heated perceptibly. "This way," he announced, and Karavise followed without question.

Through the rock-lit corridors, to the right, left, again left. Devras leading now, with a cautious certainty that increased along with the temperature of the Fennahar Bracelet. Karavise right behind him, trusting in the power of a long-dead savant's invention. Back and forth along a series of sharp zigzags that seemed familiar, out into a tunnel and on, the silver band burning now, almost blistering his flesh. Pace quickening hopefully, success nearly in sight, and then sudden disaster in the form of two Vardrul sentries.

The creatures came gliding from a tributary passage. At sight of the humans their flesh darkened, and trilling calls escaped them. An expert flick of a steel-tipped staff backed Karavise against the wall, needle-point inches from her breast. Devras drew back as the second sentry advanced with leveled staff. His eyes scoured the tunnel for a loose rock, a stick, a weapon of any kind. There was none. The sentry was moving in on him. What chance of closing with the Vardrul and wresting the staff from its grasp?

Karavise read his thoughts upon his face. "Devras—go," she commanded dispassionately. "Run." He hesitated and she added, "The machine—destroy it."

"I left Grono. I won't do the same to you."

"Smash the machine. Do it, or we've come here for nothing. Do it. Go."

She was right, of course. Sick at heart, hating her implacable logic and himself, Devras fled.

The Vardrul sentry followed a few paces, then halted, arrested by the warbling call of his companion. The female prisoner was dodging, feinting, shouting in her cacophonous human voice. Her tiny, repulsively blue eyes darted this way and that in obvious prelude to a break for freedom. The invaders were to be taken alive if possible, and it would require at least a pair of kinsmen to control this one. The other human, her companion, would escape for the moment, but they would find him again soon enough. In the meantime, the guard returned and together the Vardruls managed to subdue the human, trapping her against the wall and jabbing her with their staves as her resistance warranted.

Karavise shot a quick glance down the corridor. Devras had vanished. Her struggles ceased, and her captors led her away. No one noticed the scrutiny of the solitary figure crouched in the shelter of a nearby niche in the wall. Snarp had observed the entire scene from her hiding place, awaiting with interest the outcome of the conflict, witnessing the capture of the Duke's daughter and the flight of her accomplice. As Devras Har Fennahar rounded a bend in the tunnel and disappeared from sight, the Enforcer half rose to follow. But the two Vardrul sentries and their prisoner still blocked her path. Briefly she deliberated, knotted muscles aquiver with impatience, left hand clenched upon the hilt of her knife. The swift removal of all three obstacles would free her to continue the hunt. Quick and deadly though she was, however, a triple execution could scarcely be accomplished without strife and outcry certain to attract unwelcome attention. Therefore Snarp sank back on her haunches and waited, frustration gnawing her vitals. When it was over—the prisoner removed and the corridor clear again—only then did she emerge to seek the lost trail.

Unaware of human pursuit, oblivious to all save the overriding compulsion to perform his appointed task, Devras hastened along the corridor without effort at concealment. The Fennahar Bracelet, hotter by the moment, burning hot, was scorching his wrist red, but he scarcely felt the pain. As the bracelet heated, his stride lengthened. Excitement and determination banished exhaustion, and he sped along at a pace approaching a run. Around a bend he hastened, past the etched stalagmites and shadow-sculpture friezes; and then, heart slamming his ribs, under an archway and into the great chamber beyond to confront the remembered Cognitive device with its foursquare construction and hemispherical domes.

He paused in the doorway, panting for breath. In that moment he heard musical voices humming along the corridor behind him, heard them drawing near. His eyes raked the chamber, lighted upon the border of polished smooth stones ringing the dais that supported the machine. He ran to the border, stooped and tugged at a stone. The smallest of them was almost too heavy to lift.

Straining and tottering, he managed to raise the rock above his head; paused to fight and overcome a quite palpable reluctance. Then, the vulnerable point in the doomed construction obvious, he brought the stone down on a glinting dome.

The dome, far stronger than it appeared, did not shatter as he expected. But a great crack marred its surface and white light leapt within the murky depths. A curious odor reached his nostrils, a corrosive unsettling smell, a lightning smell. He lifted the rock and struck again, this time breaking a hole through the hemisphere. White light flared again, far brighter now, and the odor intensified. The charged air crackled just below the level of audibility, and tiny white bolts bled from the hole.

Devras froze, and that curious reluctance took hold of him again, burgeoned and swelled to swamp his will; an effect so pronounced that he wondered if Terrs Fal Grizhni's creation was equipped with a Cognitive self-defense. But the regret that gnawed at his resolve was natural, spontaneous and resistible. Jaw set, he smashed the stone down on a second dome, breaking it open with a single blow. The miniature lightnings blazed their way to freedom. Wisps of black vapor drifted from the machine and he heard or felt a rumbling, the sound of a distant storm, something born in pain at the heart of the device, near-inaudible but darkly vibrant.

Quickly now, before remorse returned to sap his courage, Devras lifted the rock high and struck with all his strength, smashing the two last domes in quick succession. He dropped the rock. Chest heaving, he stared down at his handiwork.

Nothing of the hemispheres remained but a heap of shapeless, glinting fragments. Bolts of radiant force played amidst the bright wreckage. The bolts were waxing in size and strength, arcing high and wide. The lightning smell singed his nostrils and Devras withdrew. Stepping down from the dais, he retreated as far as the exit, where he stood tense and poised to flee. The rumbling increased. The woeful thunder filled the chamber, overspilled into the tunnels beyond, boomed for miles through the caves. Vibrations shook the air, the walls, the floor. The machine itself shuddered visibly. A final growl of thunder rose in pitch, higher and higher, thinning to a scream. Devras shrank back, instinctively throwing an arm across his eyes. As he did so a shrieking blast rocked the caverns, and Terrs Fal Grizhni's gift of friendship to the Vardrul clans exploded in a violent burst of blue-white flame.

Chapter Eighteen

When cannon fire boomed from the great fortress guarding the landward approach to human Lahnzium, the clanmembers massed before the wall were not unduly alarmed. The army, under the temporary command of the F'tryll'jnr Lesser Matriarch, parted like a silent sea; black-swathed kinsmen flowing invisibly under cover of utter darkness. A wide chasm opened between the halves of the sundered force, and into this gap the blindly aimed artillery blasted harmlessly. The Vardruls watched with interest as fire bloomed atop the human ramparts, each blossom succeeded seconds later by a dull, deep-mouthed report. Jets of muted red-orange streaked the black air. Cannonballs ploughed the empty expanse of soil, and the kinsmen wondered what would follow.

They did not have to wonder long.

The useless barrage ended. The gates swung wide and from them issued a motley crowd of citizens. Their blazing torches barely served to lighten the Cognitive darkness, and they moved in a dirty-gold cloud. They were no soldiers, that was clear even to the alien Vardruls. The feeble light played upon ax-welding tradesmen and their wives, pike-bearing craftsmen, peasants armed with staffs, picks, and even rocks; women brandishing sendillis oars, a scattering of sword-bearing aristocrats, and a discrete contingent of well-equipped Ducal Guards surrounding his Grace Bofus Dil Shonnet, titular commander-in-chief. It played upon the host of refugees who, thwarted once and for all in their efforts to escape, had been forced to turn and fight at last. It played upon sweating, grim-jawed faces, both human and near-human; for the Zonianders, Denders, Vemi, Feeniads and even a few ethereal Children of the Lost Illusions had elected to fight alongside native Lanthians. The defenders were slipshod, ill-armed, and ill-organized. Moreover, most were feeble and feverish. Sickened by exposure to the darkness, their clumsy movements revealed weakness. For all of that, they flung themselves forward with a fervor born of hatred and despair.

Shouting wildly, they surged across the plain, and the Vardruls hummed in wonder at the sight. The kinsmen had never expected the hitherto defensive enemy to take the initiative, never expected so bold and desperate a stroke. Ill fortune indeed that this unlikely attack should be launched in the absence of the Grizhni Greater Patriarch, but the commanding F'tryll'jnr Lesser Matriarch was entirely competent to deal with the matter. Coolly the Matriarch held back her black-swathed, nearly invisible followers, allowing the Lanthians to advance unhindered, far into the gap that stretched between the divided halves of the Vardrul army. And then, when the sick and disorganized human mob—for it was little more than that—began to sense the enemy presence all around them, the jaws of the trap sprang shut and the Vardrul forces swept down upon them from both sides. The torches were extinguished in an instant and the clanmembers doffed their midnight wrappings to fight as they were accustomed by the light of their own luminous bodies. All disrobed save the columns of F'tryll'jnr and Lbavbsch kinsmen that the Matriarch, crafty and scientific, sent circling through the dark to block the humans neatly front and rear. When the lethal ring was complete, the defenders enclosed within, the battle began in earnest. The humans, though unexpectedly fierce and resolute, were no match for the vigorous, confident, battle-hardened Vardrul troops. Many were the kinsmen who fell beneath the flailing blades and cudgels of the defenders, and many the time that human impetuosity nearly succeeded in breaking a vital gap in the Vardrul ranks. The circle held, however. The Lanthians and their allies were clearly doomed. Zeal alone could not sustain them for long, and gradually the initial hysterical force of the attack began to dissipate. The superior health and discipline of the clanmembers manifested themselves then, and the humans were driven in upon themselves, hemmed in more securely, blocked and trapped. They were falling now, falling beneath the Vardrul blades, their rank red blood dirtying the soil. And the fluting, trilling calls of the clans arose and sang in triumph through the dark to the walls of Lanthi Ume, as steel clashed and sank in flesh, resistance weakened and men died screaming.

The force of the explosion flung Devras backward through the exit, clear out of the room. For a moment he lay where he had fallen, then rose bruised but unharmed to view with reluctance the devastation he had wrought. The smoking ruins of Fal Grizhni's heating device lay scattered throughout the chamber. Atop the dais rested the largest chunks of fused, distorted metal;

and over these the tongues of white flame crackled. Dense black clouds of smoke drifted across the floor, while a faint dying sizzle faded into silence, absolute silence.

Devras stared, a little dazed.

And now what happens?

"Well?" he whispered aloud, and the whisper seemed loud as a shout in the empty quiet room.

No response. No result. Nothing.

In the midst of his uncertainty, he was conscious of disappointment, a sense of intolerable anticlimax, and even a curious sense of shame. The deed of violence on which he had thought so much depended had proven itself irrelevant. An act of senseless, wanton destruction, pointlessly pernicious. A useless betrayal of his newfound kinsman. And it had all been for nothing.

Nothing.

The word rang in his mind. He shook his head to clear his brain of echoes.

Well, where shall I go? After Grono? He'll need my help if he's alive.

Karavise?

No—Raith. If I can set him free, then perhaps some good may come of this even yet. How shall I find him in this place?

Then he remembered the savant's cherished satchel, filled with Cognitive articles.

The bracelet will lead me to him.

He glanced down at his red and blistering wrist. The Fennahar Bracelet was cool now, flesh-cool as it had not been since the day he entered Raith Wate Basef's lodgings in the Mauranyza Dome. He hadn't noticed when the telltale heat went out of it; probably at the moment of the machine's destruction.

If I find him, there'll be guards about.

Weapons? One of the sharp-edged fragments of the ruined heating device? Too hot to touch. A rock? Too large to carry. There was nothing, and he would have to do without, for now.

Now—where to go? Where would they have taken Raith? The bracelet gave him no clue. Choosing a direction at random, he hurried along a passage richly clothed in azure slime. The silver band remained cool.

Cool. The air seemed to have lost something of its tropical warmth, if not its humidity. Heavy and still as ever, but marginally less oppressive. Imagination? Devras hurried on. A fork in the tunnel. Left passage—right passage—he tried each, without result. The bracelet did not alter. But the atmosphere *was* changing; there could be no doubt. Not imagination, no. An unmistakable chill, refreshing and invigorating—at first. Devras took a deep breath of the first temperate air to reach his lungs since the night he had fled into Fal Grizhni's shadow—how long ago? The sensation was pleasurable, a faint reminder of times—they seemed distant—spent out-of-doors in the sunlight, where the fresh winds swept the world clean.

Down the tunnel, cool bracelet, double back and try another route. And now the coldness was surely intensifying and a slight breeze stirred the air to chill the sweat that bathed him head to foot. How could a breeze blow below ground? He shivered, less with cold than with tension, for the draft in this deep place seemed an impossibility, and the air itself was charged with a palpably threatening force he could not identify.

Farther along the corridor, taking note now of his path, for he meant to remember the way back. The warmth still bled from the rock-lit air, the impossible breeze whooshed through the tunnels, and the bracelet continued flesh-cool. The electric air trembled, subtly malign, shivering in his lungs and upon his eyes. He sensed the imminence of cataclysm as Nature, flouted and thwarted throughout the generations, prepared to wreak vengeance at last. The intimation of power building and gathering itself mounted like the atmospheric tension preceding a thunderstorm. His nerves tingled in sympathetic response. There was an endless split second's silence, and then the storm broke with a roar. Its force beat him to the floor, where he crouched hugging himself in a vain effort to ward off the brutal onslaught of the cold.

The breeze swelled to a shrieking, bitter gale that lashed through the tunnels, savaging all in its path. Screaming for vengeance, the huge wind blasted the realm of the Vardruls, sparing nothing and no one. The cold dammed by Cognition for centuries came rushing back in a furious tide that sent the temperature plunging within moments to wintry depths never known in that place before. Water condensing out of the sodden air crystallized to coat floors, walls and ceilings with icy glitter. The fungi gardens darkened and died, succumbing to frostbite within seconds. Ice filmed the standing pools. The slime upon the walls expired, and the rock-light glowing through layers of frozen, blackened vegetation, shone dim and gray and deathly.

As for the inhabitants—those few not fighting Surface with their kin, for the most part the very young and the very old—the dreadful chill smote them like a weapon. Taken wholly unaware and unprepared, they had no time to fortify themselves—no time to build fires, to wrap their vulnerable flesh in protective coverings, or to seek those chambers and tunnels warmed by hot springs; the ancient caverns first sought by the fleeing Ancestors and proof now against Nature's vengeance, for their warmth was never lent by Man's Cognition. There was only time to embrace the kinsmen swiftly before the cold overpowered them, smashing its way along their veins, dimming their light and freezing their blood, their senses and their minds. There was no defense against Cold Stupor. The awful paralysis froze them all within minutes, all save those lucky few standing within the vicinity of natural hot springs when the cold wind struck. Young and old, weak and strong, they fell. When the howling ceased and the gale's force was spent, the discolored rock-light illumined a desolate scene; a wilderness of coldly silent tunnels and chambers; a population of bodies prostrate, senseless, still, and all but lightless.

Raith Wate Basef—bound hand and foot, gagged, and doubly guarded—understood the significance of the icy blast when it came, knew its cause and could predict its effect. Neither the precipitous drop in temperature nor the sudden death of the purple slime upon the walls surprised him. Likewise he could anticipate the onset of Cold Stupor in his two guards. Brown eyes intent above the gag, he watched the Vardruls closely. Soon the light faded from their flesh, their ocular ridges expanded, and soft warbling cries escaped them. Beyond doubt they recognized their own danger, for their great eyes were cloudy with terror. Wate Basef himself was shivering violently, and only the gag held his teeth from chattering. If he—hardy human and fully clothed —felt the cold so intensely, what must it be, he wondered, for the bare-skinned, supersensitive Vardruls?

Clinging tightly to one another, the two brother/kinsmen made their halting way toward the exit. A few paces short of the fissure, Cold Stupor conquered them both. Still entwined, they slumped to their knees and thence to the floor. The light faded from their flesh and they lay pathetically still.

Wate Basef was not inclined to pity. Assured of his guards' unconsciousness, he set about freeing himself. By dint of vigorous rubbing of cheek against stone wall, he managed to dislodge the gag. Restored power of speech simultaneously restored his power of Cognition. Reluctant though he was to sacrifice one iota of precious Cognitive energy, the present emergency demanded expenditure. He spoke, and the binding cords fell from his body. He rose and left the prison-chamber.

He remembered the way back to the chamber of the heating

device, from which he and his companions had been chased what seemed like eons ago. He had noted the route, and now he made his way back through the frosted corridors with minimal uncertainty.

He had half expected to find his three companions awaiting him beside the remains of the device they'd managed to destroy, but the chamber was empty. Fused wreckage, still smoking in the cold air, was scattered across the floor. An explosion had obviously taken place, but its perpetrators were nowhere to be seen. Where had they gone, and why? Perhaps they were off searching for *him*? There was no time to ponder the question.

Wate Basef still retained the image revealed by Cognition, knew exactly the location of the treasure they had been so near when surprised by the Vardrul guards. Through the fissure on the far side of the room, and just beyond. There lay Terrs Fal Grizhni's writings. They had been that close. But now there was nobody left to stop him, nobody to interfere, for the Vardruls were stupefied and helpless. If he failed now, the blame would be his alone. And the possibility of failure was very real. Did he, Raith Wate Basef, possess the power to break the Cognition of the greatest savant of all time? No question but that he possessed considerable ability of his own, though somehow that power had never been truly focused, never perfectly mastered or controlled. There was much he could do, and more yet that he possessed potential to do. But talented though he was, he had always fallen short of true greatness—the sort of greatness possessed by Nes the Eyes, by mad Nulliad, and above all by Terrs Fal Grizhni. There seemed to be a gateway of heart and mind that he must pass in order to reach the highest Cognitive level; a narrow crack of an opening through which he must somehow herd a cloud of moths—his thoughts. He had never altogether succeeded, never forced all of the winged creatures through, and he wasn't certain that he could do so now. Grono's various taunts and gibes were ringing in his mind. The valet's challenges had hitherto gone unanswered; but they would be answered now, one way or another.

Wate Basef walked across the room, through the fissure and into a tiny passage fanged with ice-glittering stalactites. At the end of the passage lay the chamber of his vision, the vault known to the Vardruls as the New Stronghold, wherein lay the greatest treasures of the clans; a place devoid, even in these strife-filled Small Vens, of a locked portal.

There wasn't a great deal to see. The Vardrul simplicity of taste was manifest here. He took it in at a glance—a small, plain, functional room of irregular shape; rows of niches of varying size carved into the stone walls from floor to ceiling; a light, movable platform, obviously for use in reaching the topmost cavities; a single slant; assorted bundles, sacks and packages wrapped in rough-woven fabric occupying the niches. He didn't know precisely what he was looking for. Grizhni's writings might take the form of a book, a set of scrolls, an unbound sheaf of notes, even a Cognitive Cube. They might or might not include Cognitive aids. Of human, Lanthian, Selectic manufacture, they would be easily recognizable. They might be anywhere in the room, for no immediately obvious principle of order governed the arrangement of these articles. One possible clue, however; Grizhni's possessions were ancient. Perhaps the fabric covering them would show signs of age. Accordingly Wate Basef scanned the niches for wrappings worn and frayed. Three threadbare bundles he opened, to discover in turn a beautifully carven two-handled drinking vessel; a set of plain stone tablets whose function was not apparent; and an entire bagful of individually wrapped and padded Lightcrystals of J'frnial, whose splendor would ordinarily have astonished him. Now he barely glanced at them.

Mounting the movable platform, Wate Basef surveyed the upper niches, and what he saw in one of them caused him to curse himself for a fool. There rested a package bound in linen brown with age. Not the coarse woven fiber of Vardrul make, but linen—the unmistakable product of human hands and there before him all the time, had he but the eyes to see it. Anticipatory tremors shook his fingers as he drew the package from its resting place, descended and loosened the wrappings. He knew, knew with absolute certainty without needing to look, that he had found what he sought. Then the fabric fell away to expose a crumbling folio volume; a roll of parchment; a leather binder dry and cracked with age; and a thin plaque of gold incised with words and shapes. Wate Basef's heart beat fast. For one moment only, he allowed himself the luxury of wonder. For a single moment he paused to marvel. Then, very gently, he opened the binder. The page before him was filled with bold, decisive handwriting, only a little faded, and still legible as it had been upon the long-ago day that Terrs Fal Grizhni penned it.

The notes were written in Lanthian which, despite its archaic form, was perfectly understandable—in fact, the writer had possessed a style of admirable clarity, as well as a mind of extraordinary power. Passages of unusual significance were entered in the old Selectic Code, which afforded Raith Wate Basef little difficulty. The savant skimmed the contents urgently, yet turned the brittle pages with extreme care, for they crumbled almost at a touch. Alone in the ice-rimed stronghold of the Vardruls, he read by rock-light. As the genius of Terrs Fal Grizhni revealed itself to him, his admiration gave way to awe.

In the Chamber of White Tunnels, the Grizhni Greater Patriarch stood with F'tryll'jnr Drzh, the Zmadrc Lesser Matriarch, and Dfjnr'l Gallr. The Patriarch was swathed in a great black hooded cloak, for the conference's conclusion marked the moment of his return to the clans massed on the plain before the wall of Lahn-zium. In the shadow of the hood his face shone with faint but unmistakable light, and his companions rejoiced at the sight. They knew nothing of the newly discovered Grizhni brother/kins-man; yet it was clear that something had affected the Patriarch's hiir for the better. In all probability, Knowledge of Ancestors had soothed his spirits.

Conference completed, orders and instructions duly issued, The Grizhni stepped to the hexagonal slab that was mate to the Wandering Flat. Before he had uttered the simple activating sylla-bles that would hurl him into wild white space, the caverns shook and the icy gale rushed screaming upon them. The force of the wind flung The Grizhni to the floor, and the cold smote him like a sword. For an indeterminate period—hours, surely; an eternity —he was helpless, paralyzed, deafened by the howling, battered by the wind and the merciless cold, and in pain, terrible pain. It went on forever while he, Greater Patriarch of all the clans, gro-veled helpless and agonized. Instinctively he drew the black folds of his cloak about him, wrapped himself tight, hands clenching spasmodically, twisting to bury themselves beneath the fabric; arms up to shield the face, knees drawn to chest level, long white body contracting.

Perhaps the black cloak saved him from Cold Stupor. Or per-haps it was more than the artificial insulation—maybe the human qualities that had plagued him all his life served him at last, lending him resistance to the cold far beyond the power of other Vardruls. Possibly it was a matter of will. Whatever the reason, The Grizhni managed to retain control of his own mind and body. He felt the lassitude, the fabled torpor pressing upon his con-sciousness, weighting his eyelids, dragging at his lungs and heart. Lying there pressed to the floor, he fought it back and drove it off. And when the wind died, the howling ceased, and silence descended upon the frosted chamber, he rose; unsteady and lightless, but aware.

His companions enjoyed no such good fortune. The

F'tryll'jnr, Gallr and Zmadrc kinsmen lay white and nearly life-less, plunged in deep Cold Stupor. For a moment The Grizhni regarded them—without assistance, and a fire, there was little he could do for them. Then all thought of the plight of those three was driven from his mind by his sudden, unerring insight into the nature of the catastrophe. In one instant of revelation, he knew the cause of the cold wind's onslaught, inferred the destruction of the heating device at the hands of invading humans, and divined the purpose behind the vandalism. The voice of a highly Cognitive Ancestor tolled in his mind, and he knew what the humans wanted, and why.

He left the Chamber of White Tunnels at a run. The swift beat of his heart and the rush of colorless blood through his veins helped to fortify him temporarily; but even as he ran, he felt the cold like an iron weight pressing upon his mind and will, held off for a little while by determination alone.

The distance from the Chamber of White Tunnels to the chamber of the heating system was not great, but seemed so to The Grizhni. The journey through the deathly tunnels stretched interminably, and all the while, silence reigned in that ice-bound place. The only sound to be heard was the thud of his own hurry-ing footsteps. Here and there along the corridors lay the motion-less bodies of the children and the old ones, alive but not alive. If they survived Cold Stupor, their minds might well be ruined—another atrocity inflicted by Men, always by Men. The merest suggestion of luminescence brightened The Grizhni's flesh, and rage quickened his footsteps, driving the cold from his mind for a time. Presently he passed beneath the archway and into the chamber of the heating unit. For one brief instant he paused to survey the wreckage, shocked despite his expectations; and he felt the sheerly human rage blaze uncontrollably, the alien fires engulf his mind as they never had before, not even in the midst of battle. His black gaze jumped to the fissure on the far side of the room. He did not doubt what he should find beyond it. Hiir rising, he hastened toward the New Stronghold.

The shrieking wind passed on at last, and Devras arose from the floor. He was hugging himself and shivering. Acclimatized to near-infernal heat, he now could scarcely bear the sudden chill. Crystals of ice flecked his hair and clothing. He shook them off and they glittered unmelted to the floor. For a moment he stood there, adjusting to this latest form of wretchedness; then his mind began to work again and he hurried forward along the corridor.

As he went, the cold from the floor worked its way through the thin soles of his cheap shoes to numb his feet in seconds. Farther along, on feet that felt like blocks of wood, and then he felt a flush of warmth at his wrist, very welcome for its own physical sake as well as for its significance. Only one more turn into a branching passage, and he came upon a chamber containing a pair of dull-fleshed armed Vardruls who lay with limbs entwined, sunk in deep Cold Stupor. Beside the guards lay a familiar leather satchel. In a corner of the room a tangle of fibrous cord and a damp rag suggested the recent escape of a captive. Wate Basef had gotten away, and now he would head directly for Fal Grizhni's records, wherever in this maze they might be. There was no way to track him, no way to find him, but one thing was sure. The savant would know, for obvious reasons, that at least one of his human companions had managed to reach the chamber of the heating device. To that chamber he would inevitably turn, once his task was complete; and there was the place to await him.

Pausing only long enough to collect the satchel and both the Vardrul blades, Devras began to retrace his steps.

For Raith Wate Basef, it was a revelation. He was a savant, a senior member of the Select and very well versed in the arts of high Cognition. He had read widely and studied deeply, but nothing encountered in a lifetime of dedicated application had prepared him for what he now discovered in Terrs Fal Grizhni's writings. No wonder, no wonder this man was a legend, known even yet as the greatest of all savants. His knowledge had been vast as eternity, the scope of his mind immense and awesome; but it was not in these things alone that Fal Grizhni's true genius lay. Rather it had to do with a certain inborn insight, a singular ability to identify connections between apparently disparate Cognitive elements, to perceive patterns all but undetectable and from those patterns to derive inspired conclusions; in short, for a remarkable, never-to-be-duplicated personal vision.

Fal Grizhni's force and individuality were not to be absorbed by way of a notebook, however revealing; but a great deal else was. Here the savant had scrupulously recorded each procedural detail of his greatest Cognitive accomplishments, including the Death of Light. The workings of his powerful mind, his methods and technique, if not his source of inspiration, were made beautifully clear. In reading, Raith Wate Basef saw the means by which the Death of Light had been conceived, refined, and executed. In seeing these things, he was able to see, as the toiling savants of Lanthi Ume had not, the means by which Grizhni's Cognition might be broken once and for all. It would be a fairly straightforward if by no means easy procedure; the apparent simplicity offset by the prolonged focus of concentration, will and effort required. But the very means by which the Death of Light had been effected suggested a method of achieving such focus—a startlingly unconventional method, to be sure, but huge in its potential. The concept, complete and daring, exploded into his mind to rattle and shake loose a shower of fresh observations and ideas. For a time the new excitement of it held him rapt. Fal Grizhni's works were nothing if not inspiring. It was as if some measure of the writer's brilliance had fired the reader.

Absorbed, fascinated, Raith Wate Basef failed to note the new arrival. He did not hear the light footsteps on stone, and it was without warning that a pair of long white hands closed on his throat. Wate Basef was jerked to his feet. The notebook fell to the floor. Its spine broke and the fragile yellow sheets spilled in all directions. The savant found himself staring up into a blazingly white, near-fleshless countenance whose great black eyes were impossible to forget. In that astonished instant, he recognized the Vardrul general last glimpsed leading his troops along the bank of the River Yl. No time now to ponder the general's inexplicable presence. He couldn't think, he couldn't breathe. A sharp, wrenching heave sent him staggering sideways to crash against the wall. Half-stunned, he slipped to his knees. He saw the towering, black-draped figure start toward him, and he could not move. The powerful hands descended, forced him to his feet, slung him where they chose. Wate Basef literally flew, struck the wall again and dropped to the floor. Something of his confusion must have communicated itself, for his attacker answered the unspoken question in musical Lanthian:

"You have killed the warmth, damaged our home, injured the helpless and defiled the Ancestors' treasures. Your death drains poison from our wound."

No time, no time to argue, plead or temporize. The hands were upon him again, and in that grip he was helpless.

"Not here. Your blood will not sully this chamber." Without effort, The Grizhni hurled his victim into the short passage that led to the large outer room.

The savant scrambled to his knees. Before he could rise, he was forcibly hauled erect and propelled from the passage. Through the fissure he reeled, into the chamber of the ruined heating device, where he performed a desperate shuffling dance and so maintained his footing. But not for long. Three long strides and the general caught up with him. A long white hand clamped down on his shoulder to spin him around. The same hand lifted, withdrew and whipped forward to smash against his cheek and jaw. His head snapped sideways and he fell full length amidst the chunks of warm wreckage. For a moment he lay where he had fallen, ears ringing and eyes dim. Then, lifting himself on knees and elbows, he feebly attempted to stand. A ruthless kick flipped him over on his back. Through the mists that clouded his vision he discerned a black-clad, flame-eyed figure looming above him, seeming to tower to the ceiling. The figure bore one of the oddly sized Vardrul knife/swords. The blade was rising, flashing in the cold rock-light, poised on the verge of descent. Helpless, Wate Basef lay staring up at it. Then a flat familiar voice cut through the fog blanketing his mind:

"You will hand that man over to me. In the name of the Select of Lanthi Ume, I claim him."

Eyes both human and Vardrul turned. Framed in the entrance stood a skeletal, battered figure—yellow-pale, worn with illness, wounded and festering, yet almost visibly charged with energy. Snarp's face was expressionless as always. The dagger in her left hand quivered with eagerness to fly.

"He is mine," said Snarp.

Wate Basef's mind and vision cleared. He cast a quick glance up at The Grizhni, who stood motionless, probably astounded by the human female's effrontery.

Snarp did not propose to repeat her commands. Hesitating no longer, she let fly the knife. Quick though she was, The Grizhni was her equal. He spun, black cape flaring, and the blade tore harmlessly through the heavy fabric without touching flesh. A moment later the steel clinked to the floor.

Before the dagger hit stone, Mistress Snarp was leaping forward, Living Wire coiled and ready.

"Mine," she muttered. "In a sack."

The Grizhni swirled to meet her, and she threw. The Wire hissed through the rock-lit air to settle about the Vardrul's neck. It tightened, but its efforts were impeded by the bulky fabric of the victim's hood. Rather than pausing to fight the Wire, The Grizhni sprang straight for its mistress. Perhaps prolonged travail had impaired her a little, for the unorthodox move took her by surprise. There was only just time to draw another knife before he was upon her. They came together with a clash of steel on steel. Hissing, Snarp leapt, slashed, leapt. The Grizhni's blade whistled in response, and Snarp sprang out of reach, only to see her adversary tear the Living Wire from his throat without apparent difficulty. Her face changed then. Teeth bared in fury, she ducked

255

in low under his guard and rose to drive straight for the great black eyes.

Raith Wate Basef did not stay to watch. Dragging himself to his feet, he lurched unsteadily across the room, back through the fissure and into the tiny passage that led to the New Stronghold. Within the passage, he paused to catch his breath and clear his head. He was bruised, shaken and alarmed, but unhurt. Still alive and whole, with all faculties intact. He looked back at his battling enemies, and his mind resumed activity. Whatever the outcome of the conflict, the victor would kill him. He could, as a savant, destroy or incapacitate both combatants by means of Cognition. But Cognition directed against sentient beings demanded inordinate expenditure of energy, and he could not afford it now, not if he was to have enough strength left to accomplish his purpose. For that, he needed every shred of Cognitive force he possessed.

Wate Basef glanced up at the great stalactites lining the short passage, and saw in them his answer. With his enemies' steel clashing behind him, he drew back into the New Stronghold, and there he used the ancient, simple Cognition known as the Falling Stones to bring the stalactites crashing down, dozens of big stone spars to block the passage floor to ceiling. Having thus immured himself, the savant paused a moment to gather courage and determination before turning once again to Terrs Fal Grizhni's priceless notes, which lay scattered across the floor like dead leaves.

As the stalactites fell, both Snarp and The Grizhni froze for an astonished instant. Then Snarp, with a snarl of vicious frustration, turned and struck for the other's throat. Back and forth the conflict raged from one side of the room to the other, The Grizhni inwardly amazed to find this small, scrawny female the most ferocious human he had ever encountered. He assumed she wished to rescue the Lanthian savant. Probably she was the savant's consort, or at the very least his sister/kinsman. Only the most intense affection could account for the abandoned, almost lunatic zeal of her efforts in his defense. It was beautiful in its way, this fiercely blazing loyalty of hers. He had not reckoned human beings capable of such oneness, such love. Cruel indeed to quench her gallant light.

Snarp leaped, spun, slashed and lunged. Her breath was coming in short quick gasps, her much-abused body tiring at last, so close to the goal, and still her ghastly, alien adversary held her from her rightful prey. She had seen him, blade poised above the breast of the supine Raith Wate Basef. The creature wanted Wate Basef for itself, and should not have him. Never.

"Mine," Snarp panted. "Mine."

Slash, jump, dodge, spin. The White Demon was still unwounded and she was tiring, tiring as never before. And for the first time in all her days as Enforcer of the Select, the thought of defeat entered her mind, and it was not a prospect possible to contemplate—it was intolerable, unbearable, it burned. There would be no defeat. She would take that bald head at last, and carry it back to Lanthi Ume as she had promised. In a sack. But she was flagging, feral speed slackening.

Desperate fury made her reckless. She saw an opening, thrust and lunged. Her blade whipped across the back of his hand, drawing colorless blood. His weapon dropped to the floor, and triumph glared hot in her eyes. But she had miscalculated, lunged too far, off balance. In a movement too quick to follow, he caught her flying wrist, twisted the dagger from her grasp, and swung her light body against the wall, where he pinned it with the weight of his own. His grip jumped to her jaw, just below the ears. He held her head tightly between his two hands. She struggled, hissing, teeth bared, striving in vain to reach one of her concealed blades, any one of them. Her yellow eyes, savage and unconquered, burned into his from a distance of inches.

"You shall not be parted from him long, brave one," said The Grizhni, almost gently, in Lanthian. He twisted and jerked abruptly. A sharp cracking sound followed. He released her and Mistress Snarp dropped to the ground, her neck broken. The Grizhni looked down at her, and his flesh was all but lightless. Slowly his gaze traveled from the corpse to the fallen stalactites barring his way to the New Stronghold. He walked forward, grasped the nearest stone spar, pulled it from the pile and tossed it aside. Took another, removed and discarded it. And another. The fourth was stuck, one end buried, the other wedged securely against the wall. He wrestled with the spar for a few moments, then gave it up and paused to rest. He was unwontedly tired, his listlessness more than the recent exertion could explain or justify. His limbs seemed leaden, his hiir was down, and oppression weighed upon his heart. It took a moment to recognize the telltale signs of Cold Stupor. The icy air was exerting its effect. Violent exercise, willpower, the insulation of the cloak, his own human tendencies—these things might preserve him for a time, but not forever. Sooner or later the cold would conquer and the Stupor would take him. The Grizhni thought then of the Chamber of White Tunnels, which lay not far distant. A quick escape via the White Tunnels, and he would find himself Surface with the clans, before the wall of Lahnzium, in the warm and delicious dark. They awaited him there, needed him to lead the final attack. He stood, black eyes fixed upon the exit. He actually took a step in that direction. And then, filtering through the chinks and crannies that riddled the stalactite barrier, he heard the human savant's voice rising and falling in rhythmic, chanting cadences, and knew beyond doubt what it meant. The spirit of some distant Ancestor spoke to him, and he recognized the workings of Cognition. Unless the savant could be stopped, the warm shadow above would fade, and disaster would overtake the clans.

Fervor renewed, The Grizhni attacked the stone barrier, working swiftly with hands already numbed and bloodied.

Kneeling on the stone floor, Fal Grizhni's notes spread out before him, golden plaque held lightly in one hand while the other traced its incised figures, Raith Wate Basef was well on his way. Already he had performed the preliminaries. Having prepared himself within, he was now gathering the power and momentum needed to send his mind flying along the lucent, rising curve whose zenith was marked by the brilliant inner explosion of Cognition. His mental speed was increasing; he experienced the familiar floating sensation, but more precarious and unstable than any he had ever known, as this Cognition transcended anything he had ever before attempted. There was a wildness to it, an uncontrollable thrilling element, and he was traveling faster and faster—

And then in one moment it was gone, snuffed, and he was slapped out of flight to find himself kneeling solitary and disoriented in a little stone chamber. For he had heard the scrape of stone on stone, the grumble of rock shifting and weight resettling. He knew what they portended, and it broke his concentration in one stroke. The Vardrul general outside was tearing the barrier down stalactite by stalactite. It might take a little time, but not too long before he succeeded in clearing a hole large enough to admit his passage. So much then for Raith Wate Basef's Cognition, so much for Lanthi Ume and Dalyon.

He couldn't afford it, couldn't permit himself defeat, not now. His temples throbbed and his palms were wet, even in that cold air. He paused a motionless moment to collect himself, and then began again. Again the rushing approach that preceded mental flight, the gathering momentum, awareness of barely governable power—

A thud of falling stone outside, and a vibrating shock ran through the pile of stalactites. A hail of tiny fragments rattled down, and Wate Basef's eyes sought the barrier. A small stone icicle slid from the top of the pile to land at his feet, and his jaw clenched, and Cognition receded. He made a mental grab and missed; he had lost it again. It took an extraordinary degree of self-control to stop short, to wait, to relax every knotted muscle as the enemy without worked inexorably through the barrier. It took every ounce of willpower he possessed, but he did it. When he was calm, when he was certain, the chanting utterance resumed.

The Grizhni could no longer feel the stones beneath his hands. His fingers and palms had lost all sensation. His arms were heavy, and it took an effort to lift them. He was horribly cold, chilled to the blood, to the very heart. Worst of all was the torpor pressing upon his mind, dulling his senses and slowing his thoughts. Beyond all things he longed to stop, rest, surrender to the overwhelming weariness. He couldn't afford it, couldn't permit himself defeat, not now. The clans relied upon their Greater Patriarch, trusted him. He had already failed them once. Disaster had struck the caverns, and the damage was immense; but that cold devastation was as nothing compared to the danger now threatening the army Surface. The clans might well be annihilated, unless their leader succeeded this time; unless he forestalled the savant.

The Grizhni redoubled his efforts, forcing the sluggish arms to work faster; and now he was making visible progress. The pile of discarded stalactites beside the fissure was growing as the barrier shrank. He had advanced well into the passageway. The human voice was louder, clearer; chanting its way through the tangle of sharp-pointed spars and into the chamber beyond. The sound spurred him on. His hands flew and now at last there was an opening, a chink through which he could spy the savant kneeling on the floor of the New Stronghold. So close—almost close enough to touch. The human's face was pale, blank, eyes wide open but blind. If he perceived his foe, he showed no sign of it.

The Grizhni tore at the edges of the hole, ripping the stones out and hurling them aside. The aperture was growing. He had torn his hands on the jagged, broken rocks; they were covered with colorless blood. No matter. Larger now. Larger yet. Clear the way. And yes, that would serve, he could pass through, it was done. Done.

The Grizhni halted. He was unarmed. His steel blade lay on the floor in the outer chamber. Turning, he swept from the passage, and found himself face to face with Devras Har Fennahar.

Devras stood before the dais strewn with still-smoking fragments. He carried a leather satchel and two Vardrul knife/swords. Attracted by Wate Basef's voice as well as the clatter of falling stones, he had made straight for the fissure, his progress halted by The Grizhni's unexpected emergence.

For a moment the two stood staring. Then The Grizhni advanced, passing the corpse of Mistress Snarp without a glance, and with the Vardrul fluid grace of movement stooped to reclaim his blade. Devras's gaze jumped from the dead woman, to the armed Vardrul, to the fissure from which Wate Basef's voice issued. Comprehension was swift on both sides.

"Do not think to interfere, brother/kinsman," said The Grizhni.

"You'd kill him because he's human? You cannot kill us all. Spare him, he's done you no harm."

"No harm?" Sudden light glowed beneath the black hood. The Grizhni's gesture encompassed the ruined device. "He has dealt us a wound that will be a long time healing."

"Not he. I destroyed the machine and I did it alone." The Grizhni's ocular ridges jerked and Devras added, "Raith was still under restraint at the time. If you doubt, then ask his guards when they wake." He could almost feel the other's shock. That sense of connection, of mutual knowledge he had sensed upon the first meeting, was stronger than ever.

"It is not certain they will wake," The Grizhni answered after a pause. "The kinsmen have sunk in Cold Stupor, from which many proceed to the embrace of the Ancestors."

"They die?" It was Devras's turn to be shocked. He had not begun to guess the consequences of his deed. "I did not know. But I am the one to blame. If you would punish the guilty, I submit willingly. Raith has done nothing."

"Even now he strives to break the Cognition of the First Grizhni Patriarch."

"He seeks only to banish the darkness poisonous to humans—only that. There is no harm to the Vardruls in that. He would save the lives of his own kind, and that is no crime. Spare him. Brother/kinsman."

The flesh of The Grizhni flickered as if the other's words struck a chord of response. The flickering was brief, and soon his light steadied. "He would do more harm than you can know. He must be prevented, but so much I promise—he shall die cleanly, swiftly, without anguish. It is necessary." He glided toward the fissure.

Desperate, Devras cast aside his burdens, save for a single weapon. Interposing himself between Patriarch and prey, he stood before the fissure, knife/sword in hand. "No," he said.

260

The Grizhni halted, staring at the blade in disbelief. "It is impossible. We are kinsmen."

"As you said—necessary." Devras spoke with apparent calmness. In reality his emotions rioted. Not the least of them was grief.

"You would threaten a kinsman. That is humanity, its essence expressed in a single action. I have always fought the human taint within myself, but I will let it rule me now. Stand aside, brother/kinsman, or I will kill you. The savant dies in either case."

"Not while I live."

The Grizhni undulated the fingers of his empty left hand. The next instant he shot forward in a lunge that came within an ace of finishing the matter then and there. Devras jumped hurriedly aside, parried clumsily. The Grizhni whirled, black cloak billowing, dropped his arm, thrust in low with the grace of a dancer. His movements were expert and certain. Only the sickly, continual flickering of his skin gave evidence of his horror. He sought to kill a kinsman, his only living kinsman. It was the stuff of nightmares.

Devras stumbled backward, awkward and alarmed as if he'd loosed a panther. He had never been drawn to combat or violence, never acquired more than the rudiments of swordplay essential to any gentleman's education. The weapons with which he had practiced were long and light, altogether different in feel and handling from the Vardrul blade now in his hand. Moreover he was exhausted, debilitated through long exposure to the darkness, and above all slowed and half-paralyzed by profound reluctance to shed the blood of his newfound relative. The Grizhni was taller, far stronger, and infinitely more skillful with the sword than he. There was virtually no hope of overcoming the Vardrul general. He could only hope to hold the other off for a little while, just long enough, perhaps, for Raith Wate Basef to achieve Cognition. Behind him he could hear the savant's voice rising, falling, rising again at a steady, even pace.

Faster, Raith.

But there was no hurrying Cognition.

The Grizhni feinted, pivoted, slid lithely under the other's guard, and his blade ploughed a gash along Devras's ribs. There was a moment's shock, an odd sensation of cold pressure upon exposed tissue, followed by fiery pain and blood.

Devras and The Grizhni recoiled simultaneously, as if identically wounded. Again the inexplicable current of mutual understanding surged, and Devras sensed his adversary's inner turmoil, his warring impulses, his misery. And he sensed something more;

261

the stroke that tore a shallow gash along his side could have pierced his heart had The Grizhni chosen.

"You are not a warrior, brother/kinsman," said The Grizhni. "Be wise. You cannot stand against me long." His voice was musical as ever. There was nothing in his face or manner to suggest the heaviness that burdened his limbs, slowing movement, freezing heart and mind. There was nothing to suggest the terrible effect of the merciless cold. And nothing at all to reveal his increasing sense of urgency. The human brother/kinsman must surrender within moments, or there would truly be no choice but to kill him.

"Long enough," said Devras.

Behind him, Raith Wate Basef's voice.

Another quick slash, a clumsy parry, a thrust, and Devras was forced back step by step, steadily back until he stood within the fissure itself; shielded by stone on three sides, the savant's voice rising and falling behind him, the tall and deadly adversary before him. The steel sang, his defenses were beaten aside, and The Grizhni's blade licked in to drink his blood. A line of red appeared upon his chest. Again the suspicion, no, the quick certainty, that the thrust was not what it might have been, and that by The Grizhni's choice. The blade withdrew and Devras's own steel followed, lancing miraculously through his opponent's guard, which seemed for a moment unaccountably weak. The Vardrul sprang back, sustaining nothing more than the merest touch upon the forearm. Devras, semi-paralyzed by nameless instinct, had not thrust at the body so briefly exposed.

Raith's voice, still rising and falling. Not finished yet.

A little more time, hold him off just a little longer.

The respite was brief. The Grizhni was back in a moment, but it seemed his attack was slowing, fierce momentum slackening, movements losing their swift precision. The light of his flesh dimmed perceptibly, and his great black eyes were losing their brilliance. Devras, breath rasping and wounds aflame, felt his own strength wane. The Vardrul blade seemed weighted with lead, and his arm ached with lifting it. The Grizhni was pressing him close, driving him back.

Raith's voice louder, nearer. The Grizhni advancing—

No.

Devras took the offensive then with an inexpert stroke that The Grizhni deflected with ease. And then the Vardrul's left hand closed like a vise upon his right wrist. Devras, unfamiliar with the eccentric style the Vardrul sword/knife demanded, was taken completely by surprise. He was powerless in that grip, and his sword arm was immobilized.

Raith's voice, steady and sure, almost exultant. Cognition close, no doubt, but he would never reach it now. He would not live that long.

The Grizhni's hiir leapt, for in that moment of contact the familial warmth filled him and he knew the oneness that only the touch of a kinsman carried. His blade descended unblooded and he flung his young brother/kinsman unharmed from the passage. He was exhausted, drained. The brief warmth had already vanished, and the cold had spread itself all through him, conquering body and mind. He was swaying, tottering. Fog misted his eyes and the weariness was overwhelming. He could not fight it any longer. He must rest, if only for a little while.

But the clans, who relied upon him—one last task for them, then rest—

The Grizhni turned back to the gap in the barrier. He could barely see it now. Took a step toward it. And then the suicidal human brother/kinsman was back with him again, unarmed as far as he could tell, unbelievably fighting him with bare hands, dragging him back and away from the New Stronghold. He strove in vain to lift his blade, and it was pointless in any case, for he could not kill his own kinsman, could never kill him. The weapon dropped from his numb and useless hand. The Grizhni fell. Through the deepening mists he discerned a face bending over him. He could not read the alien human expression. But the other grasped his hand and he felt once more the warmth of a kinsman's touch. It was the last sensation he carried with him as he sank into darkness and Cold Stupor.

Devras looked down at the still, nearly lightless figure of the Grizhni Greater Patriarch. The faintest lingering touch of luminescence informed him that The Grizhni was still alive. Once assured of this, he raised his head and only then did he realize that the voice within the New Stronghold had ceased.

Chapter Nineteen

❧❧❧❧❧

Devras rose and stepped to the barrier. Through the gap he could see the body of Raith Wate Basef stretched prone and motionless on the floor of the New Stronghold. His heart lurched, and then he was crawling through the hole and into the Stronghold to kneel at the savant's side.

Unconscious? Dead?

Neither. The savant stirred. His eyes opened and he sat up slowly, shoulders sagging.

"Are you sick? Did he hurt you?"

"No. Just tired."

"Is that why you stopped?"

"No."

"Why, then?"

"Finished."

"Finished?" Devras cast a quick glance about the chamber. All was tranquil, silent and cold. Ancient, yellowing sheets of parchment lay scattered across the floor. "And—?"

"Done. Cognition. Success." He noted the younger man's bewilderment, and a ghost of the old sarcastic smile lightened his drawn face. "What did you expect, lad? Earthquakes? Lightning and fireworks?"

"Some sort of sign. After all, when the heating device was smashed—"

"Who did that?"

"I did."

"Good thing. They'd caught me, you know. Trussed me up with a gag in my mouth. It was only because of what you did that I was able to get away."

"That's why I did it. Only I wish there'd been some other way."

"There wasn't. You were clever to think of it."

"Karavise, actually."

"Ah. Where is she? And Grono?"

"I don't know. They captured Karavise, but she may have

been able to escape the same way you did. If so, she'll come straight here if she remembers the way. As for Grono—" Devras's voice faltered. "He tried to protect Karavise from the Snarp woman. She smashed his head against the wall and I don't know if he's alive or dead."

"Snarp reached this place. She attacked the Vardrul general, who would otherwise have killed me."

"And lost her own life in doing so. She's lying dead outside. You heard them?"

"I heard nothing, once I'd begun. So Snarp is gone, and she died to save me? That's pretty. And the general?"

"Alive, but stupefied by the cold." Devras hesitated, on the verge of saying more. He stopped himself. It was not the time. "And now? Shall we see to Grono and Karavise?"

"A couple of minutes, lad. A couple of minutes to catch my breath, that's all I need. You look as if you could use a rest yourself. Been cut up some, I see. Courtesy of the general?"

"Yes, but nothing serious." Minor though they were, the cuts throbbed painfully. Devras spent the next few minutes stanching the flow of blood. This done, he raised his eyes and gazed about him, still baffled by the silence, by the lack of any tangible manifestation of Raith Wate Basef's Cognitive activity. Turning to the visibly tired savant, he inquired, "Are you really certain you got it, Raith? Are you sure it worked?"

Wate Basef smiled faintly. "Quite sure," he said.

It was less a battle than a massacre. The field was strewn with bodies, the majority human. Their initial burst of energy fading, the sick and disorganized Lanthian defenders were scarcely formidable opponents. Most of them fell with pitiable ease. The Children of the Lost Illusions were particularly ineffectual, and the Denders downright pathetic. Not that the Vardruls drew much distinction among victims. The defenders were to be slaughtered without exception. Only the complete purification of Dalyon's Surface assured the future safety of the clans, righting the wrongs and fulfilling the desires of the abused Ancestors. Thus the kinsmen killed scientifically and with mechanical efficiency, as Men had murdered the Ancestors in Great Vens past. Most merciless were the Vardruls of Clan Zmadrc, whose Ancestors still whispered to them of the great slaughter once inflicted by Lanthians upon the clan, within the sacred confines of the Zmadrc deathpool chamber itself. Now the human debt would be paid in full. The Zmadrc kinsmen shown fire-bright in the darkness. Their reddened weapons slaked the thirst of generations, and their song of triumph mingled with the screams of hapless victims. Where the Zmadrcs fought, the ground ran dark with blood, and the kinsmen savored the hitherto exotic taste of true vengeance.

Sick and feverish though they were, some of the humans offered considerable resistance. Pockets of explosive ferocity riddled the mass of defenders. Here and there the swordplay was swift and expert, an ax swung vigorously, a barrage of rocks flew straight and true. Here and there the kinsmen fell in clusters beneath the strokes of a well-directed blade. Some of the laborers were skillful with their staffs and clubs; and a number of the women armed with sendillis oars were surprisingly dangerous.

Nowhere was resistance fiercer than in the vicinity of the Duke of Lanthi Ume. The kinsmen, though ignorant of the Duke's identity, could not fail to recognize his significance. His Grace was the only human upon the field surrounded by a group of disciplined, uniformed fighters. Commander Frayner and the last remnant of the Ducal Guardsmen had accompanied their ruler. Now a band of well-armed, competent and loyal soldiers ringed the Duke, their bodies and bayonets shielding him from harm, their occasional musket fire blasting the kinsmen at close range. Clearly the short, pudgy man peeping out from behind his human ramparts must be a Patriarch of note, and therefore a worthy target. Wave after wave of Vardruls broke upon the wall of Guardsmen. The wall stood firm and the kinsmen were repeatedly repulsed. Opposition roused the determination of the Vardruls, who converged upon the spot by the score.

The threat to their Duke infused new life into the veins of the failing humans. Vigor briefly restored, they launched a fiery counterattack, driving the kinsmen back and building piles of Vardrul corpses about the perimeter of the Guardsmen's circle. Fluting death cries rode the hot black air.

It could not last long. The Vardruls, focusing their power upon a single point, began systematically to rip the human defenses. The Guardsmen went down one after another, and Bofus took note. He saw the men about him fall and die. He saw the gaping wounds and smelled the blood. He recognized at last the hopelessness of the Lanthian position and the imminence of death—his own, and that of all his fellow humans. Finally he thought of his vanished daughter, almost certainly murdered by these unnatural aliens, and the thought of his Karavise in their glowing hands exerted a peculiar effect. Bofus's mouth was working, his sweaty hands clenching and unclenching. After a moment he knelt and wrested a musket from the grasp of a dead Guardsman. Stepping to Commander Frayner's side, he jabbed and thrust with all his strength, felt the bayonet sink into the vitals of a White Demon. The creature fluted and fell, its light swiftly fading.

Frayner glanced in surprise at the man beside him. "Stand back, your Grace," he advised.

Bofus shook his head. He thrust again at the nearest Demon, and this time his stroke was parried and returned. A Vardrul blade hissed down upon him, and the Duke froze helplessly.

A blow from the butt of Frayner's musket deflected the steel and sent the Demon staggering. "Back, sir," the Commander repeated.

The Duke shook his head again. Taking a firmer grip upon his weapon, he resumed his efforts and his inexperienced thrusts were unexpectedly effective. Two more Demons he killed, and his blue eyes filled with horror to see them fall and die, but his efforts did not slacken.

The Duke's activity drew the attention of the Vardruls, who warbled in wonder at sight of the human Patriarch's self-exposure. Their wonder soon gave way to eagerness, and they pressed their attack with redoubled enthusiasm. The F'tryll'jnr Lesser Matriarch herself glided forward to battle the opposing leader, and Bofus read in her brilliant eyes. The Guardsmen closed once more about their threatened lord, and the F'tryll'jnr kinsmen rallied in support of their Matriarch. Shouts of human defiance arose, the Vardruls trilled in melodious response, and the two groups came together violently.

Duke Bofus, hemmed in by protectors against his will, stood fidgeting in deepest shadow. The broad backs of his tall Guardsmen blocked his view of the enemy, whose glowing bodies furnished the primary source of light. He could hear the sounds of battle all around him—the ring of steel, the thud of blows, the grunts, cries, screams and warblings. His nostrils were filled with the stench of blood, gunpowder, fear and Cognitive darkness. But he could see nothing.

Or could he? It seemed to Bofus, and at first he wondered if he imagined it, that the quality of the darkness was changing. The shadow seemed to have lost something of its oppressive intensity. No longer did it press upon his flesh with an almost tangible weight. Somehow the air seemed less foul, less purely repugnant to human lungs. Was it truly changing, or was he simply growing accustomed to the ghastly atmosphere? The stench —was he getting used to that too, or was it fading? He took a deep breath. The air was hot, heavy and malodorous; and yet— and yet—

The battle raged on, and he noted that the Guardsmen fought

267

with unusual vigor, as if their failing strength had been renewed. And there was a subtle stirring in the air, not a breeze—nothing as clean and natural as that, but some suspicion of motion, of life, of—what?

Change.

Bofus wondered if anyone else perceived it. He was probably the only being upon that field not actively engaged in combat. Perhaps the others were too preoccupied with war and death to notice. But the air *was* shifting and, it would seem, cleansing itself. It was not his imagination, definitely not.

Then it struck Bofus that the outlines of his Guardsmen were sharpening. He could surely see them better now, see their broad backs in silhouette, the movement of their arms and shoulders, even catch an occasional faint flash of weaponry. And the bodies beyond, the host of luminous enemies—their flesh shone clear and bright, as if the surrounding shadow had lost something of its supernatural hunger. Yes, he could see them better now.

And better yet. For the darkness was fading and it was perceptible, quite unmistakable now. Black was giving way to deep charcoal gray, and nobody upon that field could miss it. In that moment of realization, the Lanthian defenders knew a surge of such hope and spirit as they had not experienced since the day their sky had been blotted out. Shouts arose from human throats, the music of the Vardruls changed, and the Lanthians rallied strongly.

Currents stirred the cooling atmosphere, the darkness faded and now the gray forms, struggling like violent ghosts amidst the heavy mists, were discernible. Heartened, the Lanthians forgot their sickness and despair; turned and for a while longer, almost miraculously, held the attacking army off. As they fought, the surrounding shadow faded, faded magically all across the battle-field, until it was no darker than the thickest of twilight fogs. Men, women, Vardruls, and a patch of the surrounding ground were visible; and the humans, wild with elation and burgeoning hope, fought titanically. The Vardruls were temporarily thwarted. Many of them were falling. Nevertheless, the kinsmen still possessed every advantage of numbers, health, strength and experience; and the F'tryll'jnr Lesser Matriarch did not for a moment doubt the ultimate triumph of her followers.

But the Matriarch did not know—could not know without possessing wings to carry her high over Dalyon—that the shadow was contracting as it faded. Quickly it was shrinking, pulling in upon itself with a speed far exceeding its initial rate of growth. She could not know that the Cognition of Raith Wate

Basef had destroyed the protective atmospheric cloak once and for all. Nothing told her that the darkness was pulling back from the coastline of Dalyon; or that Jherova, outermost of Lanthi Ume's Nine Isles, already lay beneath a sky bright and clear. The Matriarch could only observe that the air lightened, that the delightful fragrance faded, while the human enemy fought on with troublesome determination. Had the Grizhni Greater Patriarch been present, no doubt he would have devised some means of bringing the battle to a swift triumphant conclusion. The F'tryll'jnr, possessing no such genius, placed her confidence in the clear superiority of her forces.

None of them present upon that field, neither humans nor Vardruls, were prepared for the great rush of Cognitive wind that swept the remains of the darkness before it, ripping the last grey veil from the heavens. It was noon. The sun blazed in a cloudless blue sky. The hard, brilliant light lanced down, straight into the unprotected eyes of the Vardruls.

Even the humans, creatures of sunlight, were not immune. The sudden unaccustomed glare startled and dazzled them. Their eyes watered and their vision swam momentarily. This was as nothing, however, compared to the effect of the cruel rays on the Vardruls. The kinsmen's screams were shrill with fear and anguish; such dissonances had rarely been known to issue from Vardrul throats. The great, sensitive eyes were pierced and ravaged by the light, which struck upon their nerves like a sword of fire. The pain was dreadful, the demoralization complete. Dropping their weapons, the kinsmen reeled and staggered in tortured confusion. Utterly sightless, they were for the moment utterly defenseless as well.

The humans recovered quickly. Pupils contracting, they lifted their eyes to the sunlight that was their birthright; beheld their enemies blind and in agony. Jubilant screams escaped the Lanthians. A roar of human triumph arose to greet the sun. Sickness and weakness were truly forgotten now; they vanished. Commander Frayner of the Ducal Guards sent his steel plunging into the breast of the F'tryll'jnr Lesser Matriarch. The Matriarch fell and the Guardsmen cheered savagely. All across the field, similar scenes were enacted. Confidence mounting by the second, the trapped Lanthians smashed through the wavering line of Vardruls, then turned to rain bloody ruin upon their enemies. The helpless Vardruls fell by the score, by the hundred. Unable to defend themselves, they fled; shielding their streaming eyes against the merciless light, they stumbled in blind retreat. Their flesh was deadly dull, their cries discordant. The Lanthians pursued them as they went, striking from behind and cutting them down in droves. Soon the ground was littered far and wide with chalk-white corpses. As the ruined, panicky creatures staggered from the scene of disaster, most of the humans were willing to let them go. Not all, however. A contingent of Lanthians, deaf to the pleas of their horrified Duke, pursued the routed army from the field, systematically slaughtering all sightless laggards. Presently the pursued and pursuers disappeared into the distance, blocked from view by the granite rise known as the Crags. A trail of still, white bodies remained to mark their passing.

Devras and Wate Basef emerged from the passage to find the Grizhni Greater Patriarch stretched unconscious on the floor at their feet. The Grizhni's flesh was lightless, his breathing imperceptible. Devras looked down at him with compunction and something like guilt. "He'll recover?"

"Quite likely," Wate Basef replied.

"He told me," Devras continued with an effort, "that Cold Stupor may be fatal, and sometimes it destroys minds. Did you know that?"

"The first, yes. Not the other."

"You did not tell us. Did you also know that the Vardruls have left their children and their very old ones here in these caverns?"

"No. But if I had, it would have made no difference. Listen to me. These Vardruls are our bitter enemies. There is much about them to respect, even admire, but that doesn't change the fact that they'd kill us all if they could. I don't relish abuse of the helpless any more than you do, but the alternative—destruction of our own kind—is even less palatable. Perhaps the Vardruls have good reason to hate us, perhaps they're even justified in reclaiming their stolen land—but those are questions I'm not prepared to address. When all is said and done, our loyalties must lie with our own people, our own blood."

Devras stared down into the face of his unconscious kinsman and said nothing.

"As for this creature before us, don't forget what he has done. Remember the massacred human settlements, the innocent blood on his hands. He's a merciless killer."

"No. He could have killed me, you know," Devras answered in a low voice. "Then he could have reached you, and there would have been no Cognition. He chose to let me live."

"You're mistaken there. If he had any notion what I was about, there's nothing in the world he wouldn't have done to stop me."

270

"One thing he wouldn't, it seems."

"I don't pretend to understand you. But come, don't reproach yourself. You had no choice, and in any case, the Stupor isn't necessarily fatal. There are many of the Vardruls, safe in naturally heated chambers, who will have escaped the worst effects of the cold. They'll give aid to the less fortunate, keep them warm, and if that's done promptly, the chances of survival and recovery are good."

"I want this one to survive. Keep them warm, you say?" Removing his coat, Devras covered the still, black-caped body.

"You are unaccountably sentimental." Wate Basef's smile was sour. "Have you any idea what you're doing? This is the Patriarch of the Vardruls. He's a dangerously effective general, a threat to humanity, and if he survives, there's no reason to suppose he might not rally his people to lead them again against Lanthi Ume one day. All things considered, self-defense almost demands the elimination of such a—"

"Stop there," Devras requested, and Wate Basef broke off, startled by the note of emotion in the younger man's voice. "No more. We've done more than enough to them already."

"If you'll stop and think what they've been doing to us—"

"Hardly without provocation, from their point of view."

"What would you know about their point of view?"

"I'll tell you some day, Raith. Right now, let's find Grono and Karavise, if they're still alive. And then let's see about going home, if there's still a home to go to, and if we have the strength to walk there, both of which I doubt."

"Which of the old philosophers taught you such pessimism?"

"None. It's all my own."

"Lad, we've done what we came to this place to do—what we had to do for the sake of our homes and our lives. You don't regret that?"

"I regret the necessity."

"Regrets are pointless. You pity the Vardruls now. Would you rather they succeeded?"

"Of course not. But what we've done, however necessary, makes me feel ashamed."

"Both sides, human and Vardrul, have shamed themselves."

Together they left the chamber of the demolished heating device to wander the ice-clad corridors in search of their lost companions. Devras had a clear recollection of the route that would take them back to the site of Grono's last battle. He followed it with reluctance, terrified of what he might discover. A terrible image burned in his mind—a prostrate white-haired figure, mo-

271

tionless, pallid as any Vardrul, grandiose loquacity silenced forever. And all because his loyalty had driven him to follow his master unwillingly into darkness.

They were nearing the spot now. Coatless and chilled, Devras was shivering slightly. And then the warm blood rushed through his veins as a white-haired figure—neither prostrate nor motionless—came stumbling wearily around a bend and into view. Grono halted at sight of them, and his tired face lit up.

"Master Devras! Master Devras!"

"Grono, oh it's good to see you! Are you all right?"

"Right enough, your Lordship, considering. The Snarp person has bruised my body, my skull and my pride, but I shall endure misfortune in meek patience, as always. What has become of the Snarp person?"

"Dead."

"Excellent. There is justice in the universe. And Master Wate Basef—" Grono addressed the savant civilly but without warmth. "You are well?"

"Quite well, Grono."

"And her Ladyship? Where is her Ladyship?"

"Captured," Devras told him.

"The Duke's daughter in the hands of the White Demons? Oh, monstrous, monstrous! We must rescue her at once!"

"Perhaps we already have," said Devras. "Notice how cold it's become?"

"Indeed, uncomfortably so. And your Lordship is coatless, which cannot be healthy, not in your Lordship's wounded state!"

"The cold stupefies the Vardruls," Devras continued patiently. "Including Karavise's guards, we hope. If so, she's probably escaped, in which case she'll try to return to the chamber of the heating device."

"Ah, rare fortune! Then let us not keep her Ladyship waiting. And when we have found her, what then? Does Master Wate Basef resume his ill-advised endeavors?"

"Master Wate Basef has concluded them," the savant replied with the merest reflexive hint of a cackle.

"What, you admit defeat at last, sir?"

"Quite the contrary, I claim victory. It's done, Grono. We've accomplished what we came here to do."

"You discovered those mythical writings?"

"Discovered and used them."

"But nothing happened, I take it."

"Wrong, my friend. Aboveground, the darkness recedes even now. Fal Grizhni's Cognition is broken at last."

272

"So you say, Master Wate Basef. So you say."

"You doubt my veracity, Grono?"

"It is at least equal to your Cognitive ability. As for the conquest of the dark, permit me to observe, sir, that I'll believe it when I see it."

"Fair enough. Then let us find Karavise, and then think of leaving these caves before the Vardruls begin to recover."

"Leaving? We're going home now?" For the second time within moments Grono's face lighted, then quickly darkened again. "But how shall we ever find our way out of this dreadful place? And even if by chance we should reach the surface, we'll be back in the midst of the ghastly darkness." Wate Basef opened his mouth, but the valet hurried on. "And if the darkness has indeed vanished, which frankly I find difficult to believe, we are still a long, long way from home. We are sick and exhausted and we have no food. Where shall we find strength for such a journey?"

"We'll find it if we must," said Devras. "After all, 'Human strength is akin to human vanity. Rarely is either altogether exhausted.' "

"Heselicus, sir?"

"Lapivoe."

"Very good," Wate Basef broke in, "but perhaps there's an easier way. You'll remember seeing the Vardrul general marching at the head of his army. Then suddenly the general was here in the caves. So swift a transition suggests the existence of a Vardrul ophelu, similar to the device that carried the four of us from my lodgings in Lanthi Ume to the workroom in Castle Io Wesha. If we could locate such a device, we might use it to transport ourselves."

"Transport ourselves where?" asked Devras.

"To the site of the second half of the ophelu, wherever that may be. Probably somewhere along the bank of the Yl, since that's where we first saw the general."

"What if we should pop up in the midst of the Vardrul army?"

"Then our embarrassment will be short-lived. But it's not likely. The Vardruls were marching swiftly upon the coast. By now they must have left the ophelu far behind them."

"Even so, we don't know where to find the thing we want. Can your Cognition direct us, Raith?"

"Perhaps, but not yet. It's going to be another little while before I'm capable of achieving Cognition again. In the meantime, we hunt for a polished polygonal slab set into the floor. The two of you should recognize it when you see it."

"A polished slab set into the floor, Master Wate Basef? Not long ago, I passed an entire roomful of them," said Grono.

"What, that many? Where?" demanded the savant.

"Not far from here. Shall I show you?"

"By all means. At once."

"No. Karavise first. She may need help," Devras said.

His companions nodded. Together they set off in search of Karavise.

When the bitter wind came howling through to chill the tunnels, Lady Karavise watched with interest as her Vardrul captors faltered, tottered and fell. Their light faded and they lay still, sunk in Cold Stupor. Karavise herself was shiveringly miserable. Physical discomfort, however, did not for one moment slow her mind. She knew at once that Devras had succeeded in his mission. She knew too where to find him. Ridding herself of restraint—for her wrists and ankles had been bound—was an infuriatingly prolonged procedure. The knots were tight and well placed; at times she almost despaired of loosening them, but eventually the cords gave way. Free at last, she stepped over the bodies of her erstwhile guards and hurried to rejoin her ally in the chamber of the heating device.

Remembering the route imperfectly, she committed errors and many times was forced to retrace her steps. The distance was not great, but the journey seemed endless. Finally she reached the chamber she sought, to find it quiet and empty save for a pair of recumbent figures. One of them, female and human, sprawled motionless amidst the scattered remnants of the ruined machine. Karavise approached with caution. One glance at the unnatural angle of the neck told her that Mistress Snarp was dead. A few paces distant lay the Grizhni Greater Patriarch.

Karavise crossed to his side and stood looking down at him. She stared for some time and eventually her face, at first expressionless, began to change. He was unconscious and utterly at her mercy. She could afford to admire his strength, intelligence, and even his odd, alien beauty. But when he awoke—what then? Would he return to the surface to lead his army in triumph through the darkened streets of Lanthi Ume—*her* Lanthi Ume, destroyed and despoiled? How many had he killed already and how many more would he kill before he was done—this lethal creature of Lanthian descent? In him lived all the vengeful malice of Terrs Fal Grizhni, and she hated him as she hated his ancestor, who had cursed the city. Now was the time to destroy the menace, now while he was helpless. One stroke of a steel blade—

and such a blade lay on the floor close at hand—and Lanthi Ume, if not saved, was at least to some degree avenged. Fal Grizhni, the author of destruction, murdered by proxy.

Karavise knelt to take up the Vardrul blade, and remained kneeling, steel poised above her enemy's throat. Her hand, usually so steady and capable, was trembling. One stroke would do it.

But no. Too cruel. No.

The Grizhni's body was partially covered by a coat that she recognized. It belonged to Devras, and she knew why he had placed it there. He had wished to protect his only kinsman from the worst effects of the cold, and he himself must now be suffering as a result. She thought of the exchange in the prison-chamber, the moment of mutual recognition, and in remembering that was forced to recall as well the Vardrul general's gentleness with his new relative, his immediate acceptance of a human kinsman, the loneliness perceptible even to her, the presence in him of something akin to a human sense of decency. She thought too of his intelligence—his devotion to the interests of his people, his burden of command—things with which she herself was already too familiar. She comprehended his responsibilities and choices perfectly—had she been placed in his position, her decisions would have been identical, and so she had admitted. In understanding so well, it became impossible to regard him as a faceless enemy, a criminal, monster or mindless force of destruction. He was a sentient, complex being; a leader, and a great one at that, seeking to ensure the welfare of his people.

If she harmed him as he lay helpless here, it was no execution, but murder, plain and simple. No matter what her motivation, no matter what justification she might devise, she would be stained with crime. Her conscience would be blackened, and she would live with the guilt for the rest of her days. And Karavise felt a slow cold horror creep along her veins as she knelt contemplating the helpless general and his offered throat. Her temples throbbed, the pressure was building behind her eyes, and the tension must surely find outlet soon, in action or else in a storm of tears. A ridiculous notion—tears at such a moment—and she had never cried from childhood, having learned long ago to control such outbursts. Nonetheless, there was a tightness in her throat that she remembered from long ago. Was it grief, or remorse—or dread? Sorrow for The Grizhni—or for herself? She drew back sharply, and her arm dropped to her side. Almost she made as if to rise. Then she did what she always did in moments of crisis;

turned to the one unvarying source of strength, courage and purpose. She thought of Lanthi Ume.

She thought of the city buried beneath a poisoned shadow and prey to alien conquerors, led by the one before her. She thought of the citizens sickened and slaughtered, the towers fallen, the palaces razed, the canals fouled. She imagined Lanthi Ume, fairest of all cities, broken and utterly destroyed forever.

Her spine stiffened. She lifted the Vardrul blade, positioned it carefully above The Grizhni's throat; paused a moment to steady her shaking hand; then stabbed straight down with all the strength she owned.

Before they reached the chamber they sought, they saw Lady Karavise emerge. Her back was straight and her aspect calm, but something in her too-still face caused them to fear. Following an instant's hesitation, they hurried toward her.

Karavise advanced to meet them. "Well done, Devras," she approved. "And Grono, I am delighted to see you safe."

"I thank you, Madam," Grono replied. "But what of your Ladyship? If you will permit me to observe, your Ladyship appears somewhat—"

"The heating device has been destroyed," Karavise interrupted expressionlessly, "and the Vardruls have been stupefied by the cold. Now, Raith, you'll continue the search for Grizhni's records?"

"No need," Raith told her. Her brows arched, and he explained, "I found them and it's done. It's done."

"Indeed." She was clearly skeptical.

"I assure you, the darkness aboveground recedes even as we speak. By now, Lanthi Ume is clear." She appeared unconvinced, and he added, "You'll see for yourself as soon as we get back."

"That will be a long journey," said Karavise indifferently. "Provided we find our way from the caves to begin it."

"We're hoping for better things," Devras told her. "Grono believes he can lead us to the ophelu that the Patriarch used to transport himself here."

"So I will attempt, provided your Ladyship is fit to undertake the search."

"Why should I not?" Karavise inquired levelly.

"You seem—not quite yourself," Devras told her.

"No? I am well, and more than ready to leave this place." Her voice was low and well modulated as always, but somehow her companions fancied they heard the ring of steel. "There is nothing to stay for, unless Raith wishes to collect Fal Grizhni's writings and carry them away."

"I thought of it." Wate Basef smiled wanly. "For a time I was tempted. But I'm a savant of the Select, and no thief. The great Terrs Fal Grizhni wouldn't have wanted me to take his writings, and that's one ghost I don't want haunting my nightmares. I won't cross the old King of Demons."

"In that case, let us go." Without another word, Karavise turned and moved swiftly down the corridor, as if fleeing the chamber of the heating device. Somewhat taken aback, her companions followed.

Grono soon took the lead. True to his word, the valet had a good if not precise notion where to conduct them. Through the chilly corridors they marched at a steady pace; past the silent excavations dotted here and there with the still, white forms of stupefied Vardruls, along the luminous galleries, around the bends and twists and jogs. A couple of times their guide led them astray, and they found themselves in regions unfamiliar. Each time they retraced their footsteps, doubling back to the last recognizable landmark and proceeding from that point—a tedious, frustrating process, but one that eventually brought them to the Chamber of White Tunnels.

It was as Grono had described—a small, plain room, whose only adornment lay in the many polished hexagonal slabs set into the natural stone floor. Near the center of the room rested three motionless Vardruls—F'tryll'jnr Drzh, the Zmadrc Lesser Matriarch, and Dfjnr'l Gallr, all of them cold and dull-skinned. Devras spoke quickly, too quickly, in the hope of deflecting the stab of conscience. "Why are there so many, Raith? Are they all functional, or is this designed as camouflage—or decoration?"

"Let me take a look." Wate Basef inspected the slabs with care, paying particular attention to the symbols inscribed upon the raised stone border of each. Stepping over the prostrate Vardruls, he knelt beside the smallest hexagon, running his fingers lightly over its surrounding bands of variegated stone. Marginally satisfied, he stood to disclose his findings. "As far as I can determine, each and every one of these slabs will carry us—somewhere. The inscriptions are in a simplified version of the old Selectic Code. According to the evidence they present, the slabs were Cognitively created, but designed to be used without Cognition, which makes sense in light of the circumstances. Apparently, mere repetition of the very simple litany carved into the stone will activate each ophelu. It's crudely executed—the creator must have been a savant of considerable native ability, but

277

lacking finesse. It's effective, and it couldn't be simpler to use. What I cannot tell you, however, is where it might send us. Each slab bears a symbol that must disclose the location of its sundered half. Such symbols will be intelligible to the Vardruls, but I can't read them. So there you are. If we travel, we travel blind."

"We should be used to it by now," muttered Grono.

"We travel blind, or else we start walking," said Devras. "We're not likely to come up in the middle of a lake, or inside a volcano, are we?"

"No, but we might find ourselves lost in the midst of the inland wilderness, far from home and help," the savant warned. "To my mind, it's worth the gamble. My Cognition is exhausted for the moment, and the rest of you are tired to death. There are Vardruls conscious and active still walking these caverns. If we should meet them now, we're not fit to defend ourselves."

"The ophelu, then," said Devras.

Grono acquiesced without argument. Karavise seemed apathetic, a condition her companions ascribed to exhaustion.

"Which one, Raith?" asked Devras. "If any among us has an instinct for such things, it's you."

Wate Basef chose one, perhaps entirely at random, perhaps not. The others joined him upon the gleaming block. The savant read the inscription aloud, repeating it over and over. And then without warning they were caught once more in the wild white wind, flung through whirling icy space, spun and buffeted, overwhelmed and overpowered, and moments later set down in a different place.

White into black, like life into death.

It was black all around them again, black as the shadow of Terrs Fal Grizhni; but somehow they knew it was not the Cognitive darkness, for something of the intensity was missing. A certain indefinable malignancy was absent. The air was close, still and very stale—the atmosphere of a small, confined place. Very small and perfectly silent.

Devras reached out blindly. Directly before him, inches from his face, he felt flat, vertical, rough-hewn stone. Up, down, to the sides, the stone continued. A wall. He reached to the left, encountered another wall. He stood in a corner, his right shoulder touching Wate Basef's left. Behind him Grono's breath rasped in distress, and that was the only sound to be heard. There was no conversation for a time, as the four of them slid their hands in mounting alarm over the stone walls that hemmed them in on all sides. They stood pressed together in a cubicle some three and a half feet square—a place of unutterable solidity; somehow that was evident even in total darkness. A minute cavity in the living rock.

A tomb.

"Buried alive," whispered Grono, voicing collective suspicion.

Devras felt the sickening rush of instinctive fear then—his own and his companions' terror boiling fiercely to raise the pressure in that confined space to crushing levels. His heart throbbed and he gasped for breath. The air in the cubicle was already stuffy. With the four of them there, how long before it was exhausted? How long before—

The even voice of Wate Basef broke in upon his horrors.

"This slab was surely placed here for a reason. Now, let us be diligent and find the way out."

The cool voice in the close darkness somehow checked the rising tide of panic. Devras managed to calm himself. Courage partially restored, he began running his hands over the walls, back and forth, slowly and methodically covering the entire surface. Moments later he discovered a small, circular protrusion that captivated his fingers. Intrigued, he pushed, pulled, twisted and worried the protrusion, eventually dislodging a tapering spike of stone. The spike slid easily from its socket, and a beam of light came shooting into the cubicle. The light seemed hard and bright compared to the soft, dim luminosity of the caverns. He blinked, then applied his eye to the hole.

"What do you see, your Lordship?"

"Nothing much," Devras answered. "Grass and hills, that's all. I don't recognize them. But it's daylight, Grono, daylight! Wherever we are, there's light out there!"

"Then stand aside and let a little of it into this place, lad," Wate Basef suggested.

Devras obeyed, and the thin beam entered to lighten the miniature dungeon. He could just discern his companions in faint outline. He saw patches of the rough-textured wall, caught the gleam of the ophelu underfoot. And there, down low and in the corner, the faint light glanced off a smooth convexity, polished and rubbed to a dull luster over the ages by the touch of innumerable hands. He pushed at the bulge and, having stumbled upon the appropriate pressure point, tripped a hidden mechanism. With a very soft rumble, a stone door swung aside and sunlight streamed into the compartment, temporarily blinding the occupants.

279

Moments later, watering eyes shielded against the glare, they stumbled forth from the belly of the Master, largest monolith of the Granite Sages, out onto Gravula Wasteland, where the wind blew cool, magnificently clean and fresh. The four of them drank the clear air. Behind them rose the Sages, harboring ancient secrets; before them, the rolling, barren terrain, stretching north to the hills of the Nazara Sin. To the south, Lanthi Ume, hidden by the rise of the Crags. And off to the southwest, in plain sight and no more than a few hours distant—Morlin Hill, crowned by Raith Wate Basef's Castle Io Wesha.

"Home." Wate Basef expelled his breath in a sigh.

"Light," said Devras. "Raith has done it. The darkness is gone."

"What makes you think it was ever here?" asked Grono. The others stared at him, nonplussed, and the valet added, "Well, why should we think so?"

"The general told us that his army had reached the gates of Lanthi Ume," said Devras. "The Vardrul army would have traveled with the darkness."

"And you believe *him*," sneered the valet. "For all I can see, everything is just as it was when last we were here."

"Not quite. Look up in the sky," Devras advised.

"Sir?"

"The red star is gone, Grono. You recall the star that shone by day? Gone."

"Well, what if it is, your Lordship?" Grono shrugged dismissively. "What is that to us?"

"Perhaps a great deal, but never mind. Soon we'll hear from those left in Lanthi Ume—"

"Father," murmured Karavise. It was the first time she had spoken aloud since they had reached the Chamber of White Tunnels.

"—and then we'll know what went on while we were gone."

As it happened, they did not have to wait that long. The journey back to Io Wesha took many hours. Exhausted as they were, they were forced to stop often for rest. The sun was lowering redly upon the horizon when they paused halfway up Morlin Hill to survey the surrounding countryside. Off in the distance rose the towers and domes of Lanthi Ume, bright in the late, warm light. Amidst the dusty clouds of recent battle, tiny figures were struggling across the plain, away from the city. It was the stricken remnant of the dazzled Vardrul army, fleeing as best they could for the shelter of the Nazara Sin. Behind them ravened the furious Lanthians, intent on butchery.

The four on Morlin Hill watched in the silence of fascinated horror, until at length Grono observed, "Master Raith, of course you realize I never truly doubted you."

Chapter Twenty

The night following the recession of the darkness and the defeat
of the White Demons, all of Lanthi Ume rejoiced. Crowds
danced and sang in the streets beneath a clear sky full of stars.
Impromptu fireworks blossomed, their colored reflections span-
gling the canals. Wine flowed, old enemies made their peace,
future generations were conceived. A host of lighted dombuli
dotted the waters, citizens thronged the lamplit walkways, golden
lights glowed from the palace windows, and the ghostly blue
lights atop Ka Nebbinon Bell Tower glimmered through the gentle, natural darkness. The breezes that swept the city were fresh,
cool, and sea-scented. A glorious moon shone overhead, and joy
reigned over all.

Joy's reign was soon contested.

The blessed sun rose the next morning upon a scene of carnage. The plain beyond the city wall was layered with corpses—
human, near-human, and pallid-demonic. The first order of
business, demanded by self-preservation, was clearly the disposition of the bodies—burial and obsequies for the Lanthian defenders, and mass burning for the White Demons, among whom
no prisoners had been taken. The magnitude of this task was
daunting, and organization among the survivors inadequate. The
Duke Bofus, who had emerged from the battle unscathed, might
ordinarily have been expected to take charge of the matter, but
his Grace's leadership, though benevolent, was wavering at best.
It was therefore necessary to turn to the Select for assistance; but
the citizens, distrustful as always of the Order, hesitated to do so.
At length a band of the boldest approached the Victory of Nes, to
be met on the Victory Pier by a group of disheveled, exhausted
black-robed men. Drained by their own unremitting toil, by heat,
poisoned air and illness, the savants were incapable of overcoming the problem at a single stroke. What they accomplished by
Cognition was the temporary preservation of the bodies against
decay. So much they could do, thus eliminating the immediate
danger of pestilence; and the Lanthians were forced to content

themselves with this. No citizen presumed to question the Selectic role in the conquest of the darkness, but speculation was lively. It was thought by many to be the work of Preeminence Vaxalt Gless Vallage. Who else, after all, could have accomplished such a feat? But no one was certain. Gless Vallage—through modesty, perhaps—maintained silence, and the Select, as always, revealed nothing.

Within the city itself, all was chaos. The day wore on, and the tenements and public edifices were converted into makeshift hospitals to house the hosts of the wounded and darkness-sickened. There the surgeons and Selectic savants labored without rest. The streets were filled with the homeless, the hungry, the dazed and the horror-stricken. Aimlessly these unfortunates wandered the littered wynds and alleys, past the deserted altars of Ert, past the charred and blackened patches where the great bonfires had blazed. Here and there lay the bodies of Bexae, Zonianders, and Denders murdered for their possessions or in some cases for their supposed lack of humanity. And among some of the surviving humans, a sense of shame began to darken the glow of victory.

Hunger was endemic. The grocers' booths, the butchers' and poulterers' stalls were largely closed. The farmers' market had disappeared long ago, many of the bakeries had shut their doors to the public, and cookshops were a thing of the past. In the better inns and taverns, meals were sold at inflated prices. The flight of the outlying farmers, together with the total collapse of the shipping industry, had cut off the flow of foodstuffs into the city. The wealthy still ate luxuriously, but the poor were beginning to starve. The days passed and Duke Bofus, kindly and concerned, attempted a distribution of bread to the deprived. Unfortunately his Grace's efforts, though well intentioned, were distinctly ineffectual. Equally ineffectual were the Duke's attempts to house the homeless, bury the dead, or impose any kind of order upon an increasingly confused, alarmed and resentful populace. Among the most agitated and frustrated were the numerous refugees, eager to return to their inland homes, but unable to undertake the journey without provisions. It was apparent even to the most loyal Ducal adherents that his Grace's administrative abilities were less than mediocre.

In the midst of the widespread unrest and confusion, the unheralded return of Lady Karavise Dil Shonnet and her three companions went almost unnoticed by all save the enraptured Duke. Bofus, to be sure, wondered at his daughter's transformation. Pallor and a sickly aspect were to be expected in the aftermath of her sojourn in darkness; her air of brooding, melancholy introspection was harder to explain.

The return of Karavise attracted little attention at that time. Her public announcement of the Cognizant Raith Wate Basef's role in the conquest of the darkness caused surprisingly little stir. It was still believed by many that Preeminence Gless Vallage was the civic savior—he was, after all, handsome and magnetic, while Cognizance Wate Basef was smirky and bald and paunchy —but the citizens rarely concerned themselves with the arcane activities of the Select. It was assumed that the savants would sort matters out for themselves. Many resolved to withhold judgment until his Preeminence had spoken; in the meantime, it did not signify greatly which of those alien creatures known as "savants" had been at work. The results were all that mattered.

Similarly insignificant was Karavise's acknowledgment of her young Szarish companion as the Lord Devras Har Fennahar, master of great Fennahar House. At any other time, the news would have caused a sensation; just now, nobody cared. Of infinitely greater concern was the announcement that the Duke, tired and overburdened, had chosen to abdicate in favor of his energetic young daughter. Popular though Bofus was, his retirement was greeted with relief no less than regret. Ceremonious transfer of power completed, the startled, curious and hopeful eyes of Lanthi Ume focused upon the Duke's successor. Karavise took her new responsibilities to heart, throwing herself into her work with such intensity that her father lost all sight of her for the space of a week. At the end of that time, fearing for her health, he sought her out.

Bofus knocked on the closed door, then entered the plain, well-ordered office at his daughter's invitation. He found her sitting at her desk, quill in hand and documents spread before her. She was pale and there were circles under her eyes.

"Kara, dear," he clucked his concern, "you are not looking well."

"I'm perfectly well, Father. Just a little tired, that's all."

"My child, you must eat, you must sleep, or you will make yourself ill and break your father's heart."

"I'll rest later. Right now, there's too much to do."

"Oh, Kara, there's more to life than work, surely. You've been away so long, and I've scarcely seen you since your return. I long for my darling girl's company. Set the work aside for now, come have a bite to eat, and chat with me. There is a delightful lunch set up in the window alcove of the Peacock Room. We'll eat sweet fruit, sip cool wine, and watch the sunlight sparkle on the Lureis. Come, child."

"It sounds lovely, Father." She smiled rather wistfully. "But I can't now. Another time, I promise. Soon."

"Oh my Kara, I fear for you. What are these matters that keep my daughter from her father's side?"

"There are so many, so very many, I can't name them all. There's so much to do, I don't know when I'll ever get through it. And it's all been allowed to slide for so very long—" Noticing his hurt expression, she caught herself up. "That is, the darkness has done us great harm. The city is filled with hungry, homeless people who need help badly. But there's very little food coming in right now, so I'm working on a program to redistribute existing supplies on a more equitable basis. I'm also providing temporary shelter for the destitute in some of the largest of the public buildings—the Vayno Fortification, for example."

"Kara darling, you are good and generous, but those Lammish fellows garrisoned in the Vayno will never agree to your plan."

"They don't need to agree." Karavise smiled grimly. "I've already sent them packing. They're gone, and they'll never be back. Foreign soldiers will never set foot on our soil again, that I promise."

"My child, my child!" Bofus's blue eyes widened in distress. "What have you done? You make me fear. The Keldhar of Gard Lammis will be greatly offended, deeply grieved."

"He'll survive."

"My dear, the Lammish soldiers were present in the Vayno because Lanthi Ume is in debt to Gard Lammis. Those were the terms we accepted, and we must keep our bargains. That is only right."

"Father, the Lammish have exploited us for generations. They've charged us usurious rates of interest on our loans. We have paid our debt many times over! If you'll just take a look at our account ledgers—"

"I do not need to look at account ledgers to know that we must deal fairly and honestly with our friends."

"Friends! Ha!" Noting his look of worry, she softened her tone. "Father, we *are* dealing fairly with them. Remember the riot upon the day you visited the statue of Jun? You told me about it, and I've had the matter investigated as best I can. That day Lammish soldiers attacked and slaughtered a number of Lanthian citizens—our own people, Father. Well, I've already sent word to the Keldhar that the indemnification I set upon the lives of our citizens more than clears the balance of the Lammish debt. In fact, according to my calculations, he owes us; but in exchange for unconditional return to us of the Vayno Fortification and the Fortress of Wythe, I am willing to let the matter rest. Now what could be fairer than that?"

"I don't know." Bofus shook his head. "I just don't know. I am not at all certain the Keldhar will agree."

"He doesn't have much choice." The grim smile reappeared. "The city of Gard Lammis was damaged by the darkness as we were. I've been informed that all there is in disarray. The Keldhar has many domestic problems to deal with at the moment. He's in no position to deal with Lanthi Ume as well. That's where we've got him—and about time, too."

"And after the Keldhar has solved his problems? What then?"

"By that time we shall have fortified ourselves to such an extent that we'll have nothing to fear from Gard Lammis. To that end I intend to renew and revitalize the old Lanthian militia. The structure already exists, but it has fallen into disuse. I'll change that. Moreover, I shall engage the assistance of the Select. Too long have the savants and the citizens regarded one another with mistrust. The abilities of the Select might easily be employed in the interests of Lanthi Ume, to the benefit of all."

"But Kara—nobody wishes to meddle with those Cognizant fellows. Oh, I grant you, some of them are human enough, but on the whole—"

"They can do much for us if properly approached, and we need them now. We need them for Lanthi Ume, to make her strong and well again."

"Upon my word, you've admirable ambitions, my dear!"

"You haven't heard all of them, Father. There's much more. For example, I intend to commission construction of new ships. We need to build our navy. What's more, the harbor is empty, and we may need vessels to bring us food. There's no telling what harm the darkness has done to the crops. Until the farmers have returned home to tend to their land, we've no idea how much can be salvaged. If the damage is great, we'll face famine next year, and we'll be dependent upon foreign imports."

"Oh, I hope that doesn't happen! I do hope that doesn't happen!"

"So do I, but we must be prepared. Of course, many of our own people will return with their ships as soon as the news of our deliverance is noised abroad, but I don't plan to depend on them. We'll have new vessels."

"But—but—I mean—it's all very splendid, but how shall we pay for all this, dear?"

"Oh, there are various possibilities. I won't bore you with a list. One method involves heavier taxation of the nobility, who haven't pulled their fair weight in centuries."

"I do hope you will be careful, Kara." Bofus tugged at his goatee. "You don't wish to make powerful enemies, now do you?"

"A certain measure of resentment is inevitable, but it will be more than offset by the gratitude of the Commons. I shall make myself very popular *there*, I can tell you, and their support will strengthen my position enormously. As for the nobles, don't worry, Father—I'll take care not to milk them too ruthlessly. As I once told Devras Har Fennahar, excessive greed is self-defeating."

"Devras Har Fennahar? The Devras who went *out there* with you was the same fellow who wrote all those letters a time ago? The young pretender to the Fennahar title?"

"He's not a pretender, Father. I've very good reason to accept him as the genuine article, and I have officially recognized him as such."

"Then I'm sure you must be right, my clever girl."

"And there's another thing I'm right about, although I'm afraid you're not going to like it much." She met his eyes with a hint of defensive defiance. "I have already dispatched emissaries to Hurba to discuss the possibilities of betrothal with the Duke."

"Oh, Kara, *Kara*—"

"Please understand, Father. The interests of Lanthi Ume demand this. The military and economic assistance of Hurba would prove invaluable now, and we shall obtain them upon most favorable terms if the Hurbanese negotiate in expectation of an alliance by marriage."

"My child, I beg you to reconsider. You will never be happy as the Duke's wife!"

"I have no intention whatever of becoming his wife."

"I do not understand this." Bofus shook his head in sad bewilderment. "It cannot be right, it cannot be good. I do not understand."

"Then don't try, Father. It will be all right, I promise. Only trust me. I hope," she added with a trace of a smile, "you're not still determined to marry me off to Vaxalt Gless Vallage?"

"Oh no, dear. I see now I was wrong about that," Bofus admitted. "Not that Vaxalt isn't a dear, good soul—a fine man and a great friend. But he is not quite what I thought. I'm sure he means well, but during the time of darkness, his leadership of the Select wasn't all it might have been, in my opinion. He did not

287

seem to accomplish a great deal. Perhaps no one could have done better, but somehow he seemed, well—lacking, somehow. I am sorry if I sound unkind."

"Of course you don't. What you're saying doesn't surprise me at all. I'm only sorry that I'll have to deal with him as Preeminent of the Select. I wish it could be someone else. The savants ought to elect Raith Wate Basef their Preeminence. He's the one who banished the darkness. No one else could have done it, and he should receive the recognition he deserves. I'll reward him publicly myself, as soon as I figure out what to confer upon a savant."

"You know, I still find it hard to believe. Wate Basef is such an odd, uncomfortable sort of person. Are you sure he did what he says?"

"Entirely sure, Father."

"Then you must be right. I only hope that whatever he did is permanent. I heard rumors that the king of the White Demons is a very formidable general, quite a terrifying creature. He led his army to the very gates of the city before he was stopped. What will become of us all should he return?"

"He will never return."

"Why, Kara—Kara my darling girl—what's the matter? You're crying!"

"No I'm not. A speck of dust in my eye, that's all." She wiped her eyes brusquely, and the tears were gone. "See? I'm fine. And now I must get back to work, Father. There's so much to do."

"Very well." Bofus surveyed her anxiously. "Very well, my dear. I'll hope to see you later on, then. In the meantime, is there anything I can bring you? Something to eat, perhaps? A posset? Cushions for your chair?"

"No thank you, Father. I have everything I want," said the Duchess of Lanthi Ume.

While Karavise and her father conferred, another interview took place not far away.

Gless Vallage and Wate Basef sat in the exquisite receiving chamber of Vallage House. Here all was luxury and artistry. One entire wall of the room consisted of a single gigantic, perfectly transparent piece of glass, which could never have been manufactured without Cognitive assistance. Through the glass the silver sweep of the Lureis Canal was visible, together with an array of miraculous palaces. The curving walls of the room had been cunningly painted by foreign artisans and displayed a perfect continuation of the actual cityscape, thus creating an illusion

288

that was one of the time-honored wonders of Lanthi Ume. Raith Wate Basef did not find the images confusing, and thus they failed to fulfill their owner's intent.

Gless Vallage was arrayed in topaz velvet, for he planned to dine with the former Duke later in the day. His appearance was effortlessly elegant, as always. Raith Wate Basef, in his rumpled black robe, with his haggard, tired expression, appeared particularly wretched by contrast.

"Raith, I am honored to receive you," murmured Vallage, flashing his practiced smile. "You have become something of a celebrity among my savants, you know. There are extraordinary rumors concerning your recent activities, and I assure you I long to fathom the mystery. All of us wonder which, if any, of the stories are true. Enlighten us, my friend, and receive the recognition due you. But stay, I will call for wine."

"Don't trouble yourself, Preeminence." Wate Basef's smile was far less agreeable and less attractive than that of his host. "My visit is neither social nor convivial, and it will be as brief as humanly possible."

Vallage's brows rose in polite inquiry.

"I've been away from the city for some time," Wate Basef continued. "I've seen much, learned much, thought a great deal, and perhaps accomplished something of importance."

"And what is the 'something' you've accomplished, Raith? The speculation, as I've mentioned, has been intense. There is wild talk that your absence in some manner accounts for or is connected to the abatement of the recent atmospheric disturbance."

"Atmospheric disturbance?" Wate Basef's sarcastic smile made its reappearance. "Come, surely his Preeminence of the Select cannot fail to recognize High Cognition?"

"I do not think that is really the point in question," Vallage replied with an air of patience.

"What is, then?"

"The need to issue a formal Selectic statement disclosing the nature of the recent phenomenon—its inception, progress and eventual conclusion. It is, I would say—and I hope you agree—the duty of responsible, knowledgeable men to regulate the information reaching the populace, thus providing reassurance and unobtrusive guidance. This must be done as quickly as possible if the Select are to maintain public credibility."

"Oh, I'm in full agreement about issuing a statement, Preeminence, and more than willing to lend my assistance. Here is the gist of our statement, then. Long ago, the Cognition of Preeminence Terrs Fal Grizhni created a vast potential menace. He ordered circumstances in such a manner that a certain confluence of natural occurrences would trigger the action of the Death of Light. He could not know exactly when this would happen, but he recognized its inevitability. Through chance, the ax fell during our lifetime. Poisonous darkness arose at the heart of Dalyon, and spread outward toward the sea. The darkness so lethal to humans was highly hospitable to the Vardruls of the caverns, who—perceiving the phenomenon as a fulfillment of their own ancestral prophecies—emerged to reclaim the surface land they believed to be rightfully theirs. Owing to my research in the Selectic Archives, I knew what was happening and why. I did not, however, know how to prevent it—nobody did. Such knowledge could only be gleaned from the records of Terrs Fal Grizhni himself. There was reason to believe that those records might be found in the caves. Therefore I traveled to the caverns in the company of the present Duchess Karavise, Lord Devras Har Fennahar, and Fennahar's valet Grono. Together we discovered the old writings, through which I gained enough understanding of Fal Grizhni's methods to break the Death of Light Cognition, banishing the darkness and thereby contributing to the swift destruction of the Vardrul army."

"That is a rather startling claim, Raith. Quite extraordinary, in fact." Vallage steepled his fingers meditatively. "Naturally I do not impugn the veracity of a fellow savant, although the accuracy of your interpretation is perhaps subject to debate. What concerns me greatly is the effect of your—er, colorful assertions upon the public. It ill becomes us as savants to arouse and inflame public sentiment. In doing so without justification, we debase and discredit our own Order. I urge you to remember that, and reflect. Before you speak, think of the Select, and also of yourself—and it is for you, Raith, that frankly I am most concerned. I should not like to see you suffer public humiliation, and therefore I must stress the danger of extravagantly self-aggrandizing claims altogether unsupported by proof."

"Not altogether unsupported, Preeminence. My companions —including the Duchess—will confirm my statements."

"Your companions—even the Duchess—are not remotely competent to judge Cognition. Alas that the evidence they provide carries little if any weight."

"The Lanthian people might perhaps disagree, Preeminence. We shall see. In any case, I did not complete our Selectic statement. Shall I go on with it?"

Vallage inclined his head.

"Prior to my departure," Wate Basef continued, "I made every effort to warn the public and the Select of the approaching danger. I also sought popular and above all Selectic assistance. In these endeavors I was deliberately opposed by my Selectic Preeminence, who not only attempted with considerable success to suppress all information I might provide, but eventually went so far as to place me under arrest—an act far exceeding his legal authority."

"I acted according to my lights in the best interests of Lanthi Ume." Vallage spoke with grave sincerity. "Whether I exceeded my authority is unclear, in view of the circumstances that appeared to exist at that time. There are many who will feel I was justified, if it comes to that. But there is little point in dwelling upon the hostilities and mutual misunderstandings of the past. I trust we are both of us larger than that."

"Following my escape from Lanthi Ume," Wate Basef resumed as if he had not heard, "the Selectic Preeminence dispatched a professional assassin upon my trail."

"That is absurd."

"Snarp is dead, by the way. In case you didn't know."

Vallage was silent.

"Upon my return to the city," Wate Basef continued, "I made certain inquiries into the activities of the Selectic Preeminence during my absence, and the answers were fairly enlightening. I didn't need to be told, naturally, of the many who died due to his Preeminence's refusal to permit them early warning of their danger. The ranks of new graves tell me all I need to know of that. No, please don't say anything, Vallage—not quite yet. What I hadn't known, until I came back here, was anything of your solitary unsuccessful attempt to turn back the darkness. Nor did I know the nature of your research in the archives of the Nessiva. Nor, finally, did I know of your refusal to lift a hand to assist the other savants of the Order in their desperate efforts to break Fal Grizhni's Cognition. When I learned these things, they did not surprise me, for they supported the conclusions I had already drawn."

"Conclusions?" Vallage's smile was indulgent.

"I told you I had thought deeply while I was away. You'll be flattered to know that much of my cogitation centered upon you. Why, I wondered, would a Lanthian savant and peer work against the city wherein his interests so clearly lay? For no one, Preeminence, not even I, could doubt your ties to Lanthi Ume. What then could be the motive? Your own fears? Or honest ignorance, perhaps? No. To give you your due, you are neither fearful nor ignorant."

"What am I then, my dear Raith?" Vallage's faintly amused composure remained intact.

"Inordinately vain and shallow. Callous, unscrupulous and intensely acquisitive. Contemplation of that happy combination, I felt, would surely yield me my answer. And I believe it has."

"I will not resent your personal attack, which only reflects the bitterness of your own failure to rise within the Select. If maligning your Preeminence affords you some consolation, I would not deprive one less fortunate than myself. As for the answer you seek, it is not difficult. I freely admit my failure to turn back the darkness. In that there is sadness but no shame, for every savant of the Select failed equally. We failed and yet Fortune smiled upon us, for the Cognition with which we could not deal broke spontaneously, of its own weight as it were, or perhaps as a result of some vital flaw in its author's technique, long ago."

"'Broke spontaneously, of its own weight'! Hypocrite! You know better than that, and so does every member of the Select."

"I cannot say that I do. My dear Raith, there appears to be very little evidence to the contrary, beyond your word. I feel it is my duty to give you fair warning that I do not intend to support your claims before the Council of the Select. Our opinions differ on this point, and I must follow my conscience—as the savants, no doubt, will follow theirs."

"You'll never convince them, Vallage. They'll never believe you. They know your hostility toward me."

"There is no hostility. That is your great error." Vallage's mellifluous voice was kind. "Always you must blame your own personal failures upon the imaginary prejudices of your superiors. You hurt no one but yourself, Raith. I can only hope some day you will understand, and change. In the meantime, our fellow savants recognize the unfortunate bias of your viewpoint, and they will form their opinions accordingly."

It took Raith Wate Basef a few moments to master his anger. His bearded face was pale with wrath, but his voice was under perfect control when he replied, "Preeminence, I will have tangible evidence to present to the Council."

Vallage's expression changed minutely. "You have not brought Terrs Fal Grizhni's writings from the caverns?"

"I did not so presume. No, if I'm correct in my surmise, the evidence I seek is here in Vallage House. Which brings me back to the question yet to be answered—that is, what was your Preeminence's motive in suppressing all news of the approaching darkness? Why deny the danger, why conceal it, why risk Lanthian lives? In my opinion, you were arrogant enough to believe that you could deal with the darkness single-handed. Your spectacular public attempt to do so argues as much. You would not have exposed yourself thus had you not possessed good reason to believe in your own success. Probably you'd practiced in secret. When you stood before the people, up there on the city wall, you expected triumph and acclaim."

"I very nearly had them."

"I doubt that you even came close. But would you risk so very much for glory alone, Preeminence? I think not. I believe there was greater inducement than that. And what form might that inducement take? What might the Vardruls of the caverns offer the Selectic Preeminence to betray Lanthi Ume? Certainly not money, titles or land. You already have those things, to excess. What then would tempt his Preeminence? A prize of extraordinary artistic beauty or rarity might do it. So too would any object possessing power to augment the force of the Vallage Cognition. The first thing I thought of was Grizhni's records. But I know you don't have those, and I doubt you would have acted without payment in advance. What, then? Since my return, I've researched the Vardruls, gathered all information available, and concluded that the Lightcrystals of J'frnial might well have proved irresistible."

"Raith, I have tried to maintain the forbearance that your limitations warrant, but my patience is wearing thin."

"Then I will finish quickly. I believe you were bribed by the Vardruls. If I'm right, the evidence probably lies in Vallage House, most likely in your workroom. Third floor, to the right of the staircase, isn't it, Preeminence?" Rising from his chair, Wate Basef made for the door.

"Stay where you are, Basef." Gless Vallage sprang to his feet. "How dare you?"

Without troubling to answer, Wate Basef strode from the receiving chamber. Gless Vallage caught up with him at the foot of the stairway. The silver-haired savant was shaking with fury. "Where do you think you're going?"

"To your workroom, Preeminence. Did I fail to make myself clear?"

"I forbid it."

Wate Basef sped up the stairs.

"Did you hear me, Basef? I forbid it! You will leave this house at once, or I will have the servants eject you forcibly."

Wate Basef appeared deaf. Gless Vallage ran up the stairs after him. On the third floor Wate Basef turned to the right, making straight for the workroom door. His host intercepted him.

"Leave at once, Basef," Gless Vallage commanded. "I will not tell you again."

"Why so determined to bar me from your workroom, Preeminence?" inquired Wate Basef pleasantly.

"Because it is private, and your intrusion is more than offensive. It is not your place to roam Vallage House at your own pleasure."

"Oh, surely a tour of your workroom is a minor courtesy to extend to a fellow savant." Smile fixed securely in place, Wate Basef reached for the knob.

Vallage closed his eyes; spoke quickly, surely.

A hiss, a sizzle, a crackling of force. An exclamation escaped Wate Basef and he snatched his hand back from the door. The fingers were reddened and blistered. For a moment he stared at them, then lifted his eyes to his host.

"There is an end to the matter," observed Vallage, composure restored. "You may leave now. Rest assured I will not forget this incident."

"That is true," said Wate Basef slowly. "You will not forget it." Bowing his head, he too spoke softly, gestured fluidly, and once again reached for the doorknob.

Vaxalt Gless Vallage stiffened as if his face had been slapped. For a moment he stared, visibly startled to encounter a Cognitive opposition far greater than anything he would have expected of such an adversary. His hesitation was minimal. Drawing a deep breath, he marshalled his forces and held firm.

Raith Wate Basef's hand was arrested several inches from the door. Crackling, hissing noises accompanied his efforts to break through the invisible barrier.

A perceptibly malignant smile twisted Gless Vallage's lips as he watched. "Give it up, Raith," he advised, good-humored again. "If you could overcome my Cognition, you and not I would be Preeminent. Spare yourself further embarrassment, and leave while you can."

"A study of Terrs Fal Grizhni's writings affords many insights," Wate Basef observed mildly. "Things are not quite as they were." He spoke again in a low voice and as he spoke, pushed forward. The crackling sounds increased in volume, and blue light played upon his flesh as his hand approached the doorknob.

Vaxalt Gless Vallage swayed on his feet. Fine eyes narrowed, he clenched his fists and braced himself, exerting his utmost Cognitive force.

Raith Wate Basef found he could not move. His right hand, his entire right arm, were paralyzed. A deep hot pain was raging along his nerves, lapping his arm in invisible fire, rising higher, spreading swiftly, licking at his heart and brain—

He focused his mind and his will. He spoke and gestured. He drove forward with all his strength, with everything that he was or could be concentrated in a perfectly controlled thrust that carried him straight through the barrier. His hand closed on the knob. A tremendous flare of light illuminated the corridor, a shower of sparks flew and a dying fizzle signaled the violent wreck of Cognition. A mental detonation slammed Vaxalt Gless Vallage to the floor, where he lay still, eyes wide and unseeing.

Raith Wate Basef walked into the workroom. A quick survey of the contents sufficed. Little dreaming that his sanctum would ever be violated, Gless Vallage had made no effort at concealment. An ornate casket in an unlocked cabinet contained half a dozen flawless Lightcrystals of J'frnial, whose glory astounded and bedazzled. Wate Basef could not help staring, for a time. Now he could understand, almost sympathize with the temptation that had overcome Vaxalt Gless Vallage. He closed the lid upon the crystals with reluctance, tucked the casket under his arm and exited.

Gless Vallage sat on the floor, back to the wall and head bowed upon his breast. He raised his head slowly as his enemy emerged from the workroom. He noted the casket in the other's grasp, and his eyes closed briefly. Raith Wate Basef paused at his side.

"Vallage." Wate Basef's tone was neutral, almost matter-of-fact. "I've something to say. Look at me."

Gless Vallage met his eyes unwillingly.

"At the next Congress of the Select, I will challenge you for Preeminence. In view of what has happened here today, we both know that I will win. There's more. I intend to bring charges against you. Your actions have been more than despicable, worse than treacherous—you are a traitor to the Select, to Lanthi Ume and to humanity. You have wrought untold destruction, and you are indirectly a murderer. These Lightcrystals obtained from the Vardruls furnish all the evidence I'll need to convict you. Assuming you escape criminal prosecution, you will at the very least be dismissed from the Select, to live out your life as an Expulsion. All this is of course exactly what you deserve. Yet there is a way to avoid it."

Gless Vallage waited in bleak silence.

"The public humiliation of the Selectic Preeminence besmirches the entire Order. I do not wish to see my colleagues touched by your disgrace, and for that reason alone, I offer you a way out. Resign, Vallage. Relinquish your Preeminency before I take it from you. Withdraw voluntarily from the Select, and preferably from Lanthi Ume. Live as best you can, and do not attempt to meddle in affairs of the Select again. If, by the way, you think to fight the charges or to convince the public of your innocence, let me assure you that you won't succeed. You'll lose your reputation, your liberty, and possibly your life in the attempt. Be wise, Vallage. Resign."

Raith Wate Basef departed.

For a long time Vaxalt Gless Vallage sat motionless on the floor outside the workroom. His eyes were blank and staring; he had the look of a man broken by forces too powerful to withstand. For many hours he sat there alone. Eventually, however, his Preeminence's very pronounced quality of resilience asserted itself, and he began to rally. Collecting the remnants of his shattered pride, he examined the debris and concluded that the damage might not be altogether irreparable. In fact, all things considered, matters might have gone a lot worse.

Disaster had befallen. Yet Vaxalt Gless Vallage, resourceful and creative as always, would surely manage to turn the situation to some advantage.

There was a world elsewhere.

With this thought in mind, his Preeminence rose and entered his workroom, locking himself within. One of the binders lying on the table contained his notes on the subject of Whorlo's Winged Conveyance, Cognition suited to the transportation of extra-large objects. He studied the notes with care.

The savant worked through the rest of the day, and far into the night. When the sun rose the next morning, the dawn light shone upon a wide expanse of newly empty ground bordering the Lureis Canal. At the center of the property yawned a huge pit wherein the foundations of a great mansion had rested for centuries.

Vallage House was gone.

The abrupt loss of their nearest neighbor intrigued but did not distress the residents of Fennahar House. Devras and Grono had matters of far greater significance to occupy their minds.

"When," inquired Grono, "does your Lordship intend to commence entertaining?"

"Entertaining? Are you serious? I haven't given it the slightest thought," said Devras.

Master and servant stood in the great banqueting hall of their new home. The ice-storm splendor of the crystal chandeliers was muffled in canvas wrappings. The interminable polished table and its scores of matching chairs were likewise obscured—and yet the room was superb, as indeed was all of Fennahar House. It was only the second day of the newly invested Lord Har Fennahar's residence. Devras and Grono were attired in second-hand garments of decent quality. The ravaged rags that had carried them through the caverns had been discarded, and the tailor engaged by Devras had not yet completed his first commission. They had barely begun to acquaint themselves with the wonders of the family mansion. There was so much to do—everything from exploration, to perusal of the lists of Fennahar holdings, to the hiring of a complete household staff, and beyond—before they would even begin to feel at home. And Grono was dreaming of parties.

"Your Lordship must think of it," Grono insisted. "Your Lordship's new position carries many social obligations."

"It's an alien concept. There's never been any money."

"That circumstance has altered drastically. Your Lordship possesses one of the great fortunes of Lanthi Ume. Permit me to remind you, sir, that all concern with mundane financial matters is now beneath your Lordship's dignity."

"I will try to keep that in mind. As for entertaining, it will have to wait—"

"It cannot wait. It shall not wait," proclaimed the valet.

"Why not?"

"It behooves your Lordship to establish prompt and close connection with the great Houses of the city. Only in this manner may your Lordship obtain introduction to maidens of appropriate age, rank, beauty and fortune, from whom the future Lady Fennahar may be selected."

"Lady Fennahar!"

"To be sure, sir. You are the Lord Har Fennahar. It is your Lordship's solemn duty—nay, a moral imperative—to provide yourself with an heir."

"Grono, I am eighteen years old. There's all the time in the world to think of heirs!"

"Ah, there you mistake the matter, sir. There is never as much time as one thinks. You are young and strong and healthy. Fortune grant that you continue so! No doubt to you life seems eternal. But what of me, sir? I am ancient, feeble, broken in health—"

"You're healthy as an ox, and you know it."

"—weak, doddering and pitiable. I could go like *that*, sir, at any time. And if I should fall into the blind cave of eternal night —if I should be called to that longest, darkest journey—how do you think I would feel, knowing that I leave behind me a lord devoid of issue, unmarried and all alone? How do you think I would feel about that, Master Devras?"

"Grono, what an unconscionable fraud you are!"

"Not so, sir! And even if I were, wasn't it Heselicus who said, 'A noble deception diverts the gods, who yawn at honest mediocrity'?"

"I don't remember Heselicus saying that."

"Well, if he didn't, he should have."

"Look here, Grono, I'm anything but reluctant to meet the ladies—"

"That is excellent, sir, excellent! As it happens, I have already drawn up a list of suitable candidates." From his breast pocket, the valet withdrew a long strip of paper covered with handwriting. "You will note that the names of the most promising of the delectable damsels are starred in red. My own particular choice inclines in favor of the delightful Lalliana Cru Beffel. While it is true that she is somewhat dwarfish, snaggle-toothed and inclined to flatulence, yet her House is one of the greatest of Lanthi Ume. She possesses a vast fortune and a vast family, which last augurs well for her fertility—"

"Wait. Stop there. As I was saying, I'm ready—eager, in fact—to meet the ladies as soon as possible. But for the rest—marriage and heirs—they're going to have to wait a few years."

"Reflect, Master Devras, reflect! If you should die without an heir, all our suffering has been in vain. The weary trek, the risk of our lives in the caverns, all for nothing—"

"My dear friend, we didn't undergo that trial to secure a title and fortune for me. There was a great deal more to it than that, both for others and ourselves."

"There wasn't for me," Grono muttered.

"Come now, I believe there was. Think of everything we saw and did and learned. The world contains so much more beyond my books and philosophers—"

"I've been telling you that for years, Master Devras."

"And now I believe it. I want to see more, do more, experience more at first hand. That's one of the reasons why the marriage and heirs must wait a bit."

"Not the worst reason, I suppose." The valet still looked unsatisfied.

"Grono, it's not time yet. There's too much that's new, too much unsettling. If I tell you something I learned in the cave, perhaps you'll understand. I haven't told you before, because it's not easy to speak of." The valet's expression was avid, and Devras continued, "The Vardrul general—you saw for yourself what he is—we spoke in the caverns, and we learned that we share a human ancestor. He is my kinsman."

"Truly, sir? That *must* be upsetting."

"There's more. He could have killed me, down there in the caves. Had I died, Raith would have fallen as well, and the darkness would never have faded. The general chose not to kill me, because, I think, the idea of kinship was more important to him than anything else. Somewhere out there I have a kinsman to whom his family, however distant, meant that much—and somehow that changes the world for me. I'll probably never see him again, but I'll know that he exists. Wherever he is now, I hope ne is well and content; I hope he is happy and at peace."

In the caves far below the surface of Dalyon, the shattered remnants of the Vardrul clans gathered upon the shore of the Grizhni death-pool. The kinsmen were swathed in heavy cloaks, for the air in the unheated chamber was cold, a condition well suited to the melancholy occasion. Beside the pool lay the still, lightless body of the Grizhni Greater Patriarch. In one chill hand the Patriarch clasped a parcel containing an ancient folio volume, a roll of parchment and a leather binder filled with notes. Upon his breast rested a thin plaque of gold incised with words and shapes.

The obsequies were performed. Vardrul harmonies rose to celebrate the final Ancestral joining of the Patriarch. The death-pool received the body, which sank to take its place among its kinsmen; and the waters closed over the last descendant of the House of Grizhni.